T0088993

SO BRIGHT A DARKNESS

FICTION

Kraftgriots

Also in the series (FICTION)

SO BRIGHT A DARKNESS
FICTION

Chidubem Iweka

Published by
Kraft Books Limited
6A Polytechnic Road, Sango, Ibadan
Box 22084, University of Ibadan Post Office
Ibadan, Oyo State, Nigeria
+234 803 348 2474, +234 805 129 1191
E-mail: kraftbooks@yahoo.com
www.kraftbookslimited.com

First published 2014

ISBN 978–978–918–155–1

= KRAFTGRIOTS =
(A literary imprint of Kraft Books Limited)

First printing, September 2014

 Dedication

For Dada Iweka

❦‖ Prologue ‖❦

Okafor ran wildly through the jungle, the phantom captain and his ghoulish platoon in hot pursuit. The faster he ran the more they gained on him. The earth suddenly became marshy and slippery under his feet, impeding speed and balance. He came to an intersection where the jungle paths crossed and saw a mound of earth about four feet high. Just beyond the mound stood a giant iroko tree. Intuitively, he knew that if he jumped over the mound and quickly climbed up the tree, the ghostly captain and his soldiers would lose him. Much as he tried to leap over the little mound it became as difficult as scaling a prison wall. Suddenly, a large dark object like a scattered mass of hair came down from the sky spinning like a cyclone. It enveloped Okafor's upper body, forming a cocoon around his head. Okafor struggled to pull the hair off his face as he felt a physical uplift. He was airborne. When he succeeded in getting rid of the stifling mass of hair, he found himself at the pinnacle of the iroko.

The ghostly group had ceased chasing him and turned into normal human beings. They stood at the foot of the iroko tree hailing and cheering Okafor till he woke up from the dream, the nightmare.

He got out of the bunker where he had spent the night and rushed out to get ready for his trip to the camp.

⟨꒰ One ꒱⟩

Sergeant Major Okelue Okafor swaggered out of the Quarter master's office in his usual pompous manner– the godfather of seventh battalion. He had been in the army very long, long before any member of the seventh infantry.

On this hot and humid afternoon, he strode leisurely through the jungle camp; chin up in the air, his massive chest bulged viciously under his sweat-soaked khaki. His carriage always made him seem larger than his six feet, four inches and two hundred pounds.

Okafor was tough, mean and arrogant. He had a natural knack for making other people, especially his subordinates, feel uneasy in his presence. As he passed a group of noisy recruits in their spotless green uniforms, a plague of silence swept through them. Their shiny black boots came together in honorary attention.

Okafor responded. "You lousy bunch of tenderfoots lounging around with silly smiles on your faces. Don't you know there's a war going on? Hey you!" pointing at a tall lanky recruit of about nineteen. "What's your name and number, boy?"

"Private Kosime, 2001 NA/ 1431, Sir," he replied.

"Ok, Private, I hold you responsible for you and your friends here. Report to the C-tent in ten minutes and sign up with Corporal Ngefa. We'll be leaving for the front in an hour."

"But, sir," protested Kosime, "we have been assigned on home guard in the village."

Okafor's eyes flashed red. An instant frown seemed to bind his face into a cold angry mask. "Attention!" he barked. "Are you disobeying my order? Now move it! He-e-a-a! Hup! Hy! Hup! Hy! Hup! Hup!"

The men scuttled off in different directions, marching to the military beat of his 'hups' and 'hys.'

Okafor smiled with satisfaction as he watched them go. Having been a bully all his life he enjoyed such privilege which the army provided and he, too often, exploited.

Okafor's parents were banished from their homeland when

he was a teenager, for an atrocity his father committed. When he joined the army, the soldiers became his tribesmen and the Seventh Battalion his tribe; a tribe in which he accumulated much power and influence over the years. It was long ago that the rumour circulated through the seventh infantry that Okafor had no home. Some said he was an outcast banished for life while others rightly rumoured that it was his father that was. In spite of his hostility and arrogance, Okafor was held in high esteem for his bravery. His reputation had been set when he destroyed two enemy tanks in one day.

When the democratic government of President Charles Aguiyi was seriously threatened by militants, General Idris had moved swiftly, sending Captain Chuka and the Seventh Infantry Battalion to the rescue. The ensuing skirmish had at first seemed to be all there was to the conflict. But shortly, the Third Amoured Division had to be called in to combat the superior firepower of their militant allies from across the border. The small-scale skirmish soon escalated into a full battle of attrition, taking fatal tolls on both sides.

Sergeant Major Okafor took the war as if it were his own personal battle. He hated how ruthlessly the militants used women and children to shield themselves from the federal troops.

He was obsessed with winning the war. It was his war and though he wanted to win it alive and unhurt like everyone else, he was prepared to take the maximum risk.

He came to the jungle camp once a week to sign for supplies, enjoy a half decent meal and a cool bath at the paramedic quarters. On this particular day, he was assigned by Captain Chuka to pick up reinforcements of men and ammunition. He took a short walk through a row of palm trees to the paramedic station—two large green tarpaulin tents skilfully nestled under a group of umbrella trees.

In the tent, Okafor was greeted by his girl, Miss Chiadi Okolo, who worked with the paramedic team of the seventh battalion. She was a gigantic big-boned woman with a short neck and puffy cheeks. She wrapped her sturdy arms around Okafor who swept her off the ground with ease.

As he carried her in his arms and stared into her eyes, Okafor felt an overwhelming surge of emotion through his body. His love for her was intense and childlike. Before her, he had not loved another woman and now, wished for no other but her. The feeling that sparked off between them was mutual and spontaneous the day they met. Little did they know that they had one binding factor in common; they were from the same town. After they were introduced by Okafor's friend who came from army HQ a diligent friendship evolved that same day. Finding out later that Chiadi was also from Obodo Ogwari intensified Okafor's love for the homely woman.

Okafor's yearning to return to his homeland one day, had become an obsession. Meeting Chiadi and falling in love with her yielded a missing link in his life, a link to his kinsmen. He felt like one who had won a trophy.

The strict traditions of Obodo Ogwari from the ancient days discouraged intermarriage even with their close neighbours. With the coming of the Europeans, civilization forged deeper into the hinterland and surrounding towns but never entered their small ancient community. In time, they became socially estranged from their neighbours, interacting with outsiders only in trade and services.

Obodo Ogwari women were rarely found abroad. Therefore it was a special omen of good luck for Okafor to find Chiadi Okolo, not only in the army but in the same batallion as he. At first he had wondered if she or her parents were likewise victims of banishment but later found the contrary. Her father had been a chauffeur to an expatriate agriculturist, a whiteman who lived in Jos. Chiadi and her siblings were born and raised there. It was in her adulthood, owing to their father's death, that pilgrimage and acquaintance with the homeland began. Chiadi never forgot a certain trip she made to Obodo Ogwari wearing her military fatigues, how the villagers made an embarrassing spectacle of her for wearing trousers. Had it not been their dread of the army, the Okoti Age Grade who were the youngest constituted grade at the time would have been ordered to chase her out of town with whipping, slapping and dousing of sand. However, the disdain in their eyes was enough to send the message across: You are not welcome in trousers. It had upset but amused Chiadi when she later found out that her wearing trousers was a stiff indictment on her moral values, with a strong suspicion that she would corrupt their young girls to the waywardness of city folk. Nevertheless, Chiadi felt drawn to some of their conservative virtues, surrounded by a world rife with corruption and unbridled evil. Chiadi and Okafor often argued over fractional versus total change in Obodo Ogwari. Chiadi believed that change should be partial and gradual starting with minor traditional anomalies. Okafor in his usual blunderbuss approach to life believed in turning Obodo Ogwari into an ultra-modern city overnight.

Afterall, all the towns around them had become modernized. Only Obodo ogwari rejected the fruits of conventional civilization. Sometimes Chiadi thought that Okafor's approach might really be the right one. Could the hard-set ancient ways of the Obodo Ogwarians be changed by a mellow approach; could that big omelette be made without breaking many eggs? In the end, she agreed with Okafor that if there was to be any change at all, it had to be big and drastic.

She beamed with delight when Okafor set her down. "How's my old soldier doing now?"

"Just great and I see you're doing fine yourself," Okafor bellowed. They held each other lovingly for a few moments, swaying from side to side.

She broke loose. "Come on to the back you old leopard. I've got your bath water ready. And when you're through we can go to my quarters. I fixed you a delicious monkey hips and rice dinner."

I've been looking forward to your cooking." Okafor smiled broadly and swallowed hard.

This was a treat that could have brought him to the jungle camp every day rather than once a week that regulations allowed. Two paramedics watched them with hushed amusement. They found it awkward and impractical to see Okafor's fierce and war-like nature transformed into tender love at the sight of the very homely Chiadi Okolo. Must be true love.

They passed through the wide tent passage, flanked on both sides by miscellaneous hospital equipment and computers on school-type desks. To the right were two large cubicles also made of tarpaulin but fortified on the sides with wooden slats. These were used as emergency operating rooms. Several paramedics sat on the chairs and desks, arguing about the latest war report.

The jungle camp paramedical unit was not a very busy place. The few doctors and nurses only worked hard when the local hospital had an overflow of casualties. Seldomly, this broke the monotony of issuing malaria pills and paracetamol to villagers. At times they treated self-inflicted bullet injuries of new recruits, by which some rookies tried to exempt themselves from being sent to the war fronts. The point-blank blasts, splattering the wounds with gunpowder always gave them away. The enemy usually didn't come so close to shoot their foe.

Outside the long tent, Chiadi turned right and stopped in front of a small adjoining tent. She stood beside the V-shaped entrance while Okafor stooped and entered. He flipped the tarpaulin-covering shut behind him. Chiadi waited patiently while he undressed and handed her his boots and dirty fatigues.

Inside the main tent, a young corporal was asking the paramedics of Okafor's whereabouts when he saw Chiadi with a gigantic pair of boots and dirty uniform to match. She told him where to find the 'old soldier.'

"What do you want?" Okafor growled, after he heard his name the third time.

"The new battalion commander just arrived and wants you to report to the C-tent immediately, Sir," the corporal answered.

Okafor was furious. "Can't you see I'm taking my bath? Hey! Go tell him you couldn't find me, tell him something."

"He seemed very angry and he knows you're around. Sir, it's probably best you come with me."

Okafor took a quick bath and put his clothes on. There was no time to eat the dinner Chiadi fixed for him. Accompanied by the corporal, he marched off angrily towards the C-tent. Okafor was disturbed. For many years he had enjoyed almost the full privileges of an officer. This was merely because both Captain Chuka and the previous battalion commander had been his boys in training camp. They both gave him more privileges than any other N.C.O. in the entire federal army. Approaching the C-tent, a large tarpaulin sanctuary, Okafor was shocked to see the recruits he had selected earlier filing into several army trucks and jeeps. A tall robust officer who could be no other than the new captain was supervising the loading. Two soldiers with automatic rifles poised at hip level stuck closely to him like gangster bodyguards. The captain pranced from one vehicle to another, issuing orders in a loud hoarse voice. The air was suddenly filled with the sound of rugged motors as the jeeps cranked to life.

Okafor marched up behind the captain and alerted him with a loud stamp of his boots and a salute.

"Sergeant Major Okafor reporting for duty, Sir."

"So you are Sergeant Major Okafor, eh?" the captain asked. "I am Captain Achebe, your new commander. I arrived at the war front two hours after you left to pick up this reinforcement. Sergeant! You've been gone for three hours and you know what shape your unit is in without this reinforcement. I am placing you under open arrest. You are to move on to the front with these men immediately, under the supervision of my lieutenant of course and not ..."

"Sir, I have an explanation," Okafor interrupted.

"I don't want to hear it!" the captain yelled. "I've been asking a few questions around here and it seems I may have to give you a crash course on how to be a good sergeant," he added sarcastically.

"I am a Sergeant Major," Okafor said coldly.

"What difference does that make to me?" Achebe rattled on. "I've also looked at the past supply orders and I see you come out here once a week to sign for supplies. From now on, you will remain at the front and my lieutenant will take care of the orders ... And another thing, don't ever let me catch you not wearing your rank. Staff sergeant or sergeant major, wear it!"

Achebe turned around to respond to a nurse who was holding up a paper for him to sign.

Okafor felt a giant claw ripping through his empty stomach. A splitting headache panned across his temples as he shuffled towards his jeep. His mind raced confusedly with thoughts about his future with the battalion. He could visualize the impact of his 'demotion.' No more striding through the jungle camp like a monarch inspecting his kingdom ... Chiadi's delicious dishes and affection.

The jeeps and buses started to roll out slowly forming a convoy along the narrow dusty road that led to the war zone.

The sun was still burning hot but the trenches were cool and refreshing, shadowed by an ocean of trees and tall bushes. Except for an occasional burst of machine-gun fire in the distance, the front was silent, very silent. No sounds of chattering monkeys or even squirrels skipping through the shrubs. These jungle inhabitants seemed to have also fled from the perils of the war zone.

*   *   *

At the war front, Okafor darted behind a stack of sandbags where Corporal Audu was kneeling with several privates, eyes fixed on the enemy location.

"What is going on here, corporal, why all the alert?" Okafor asked.

Audu answered without taking his eyes off the enemy. "We don't know yet, Sir, they've been drilling and rejoicing all afternoon. It's like they received a secret weapon or something."

⊘‖ Two ‖⊘

Philip Carter stepped out of the classroom feeling quite light-hearted as usual. Two of his students, Chuka and Amechi, shadowed him closely. Chuka was carrying Carter's briefcase and Amechi, his textbooks. Carter loved teaching and the entire students and staff of Obodo Ogwari Boys High School made him feel the most needed and useful he had ever felt as a teacher. 3C was his favourite class. He loved the infectious spread of silence that swept through the room whenever he entered; the way they scrambled up behind their crude desks and uttered in unison, "Good afternoon, Mr Cata." What thrilled Carter most was their attentiveness and eagerness to learn. It gave him pleasure to see their little scrubbed and oiled black faces looking up at him with an undivided attention he never knew existed amongst high school students. Well, not after teaching in two public schools in New York City.

After each Friday class with 3C, there was always a mad rush for Carter's books and briefcase. Chuka and Amechi were the lucky ones who got to walk him home that weekend.

"Mister Cata," Chuka called. "When you go back to America, can I come and visit you?"

Carter smiled broadly. "Of course you can come and visit me, Chuka, and you too, Amechi."

The boys grinned their satisfaction.

The only problem was that Carter might never go back to America. After all, there was nothing and nobody to go back to.

Carter was a natural teacher if ever there was such a thing. Better yet, if professions were tailored for humans from the womb, Philip Carter would have emerged at the maternity ward, pen in hand, ready to start marking exam papers.

Due to his humanitarian nature, Carter could have been a social worker or if he had been a wealthy man, a philanthropist.

Since there were no millions to give away to starving children in Africa, teaching in the ghetto schools of New York had been his natural choice; schools where he would educate the young ignorant and underprivileged blacks and Puerto Rican toughs.

14

'*Give them the home training they never got at home.*' Carter's pet motto.

All that was behind him now together with the fast life, freeways, police sirens and everything about that carnivorous Big Apple. He was glad. Two unsightly scars on his back were unwanted souvenirs from knife wounds inflicted by two of his students, both in their early teens, on separate occasions.

Some of the teachers used to laugh at Carter's fruitless determination to correct and morally educate. He had lapsed into periods of self-pity and failure-struck moods whenever an impromptu search by school authorities turned up drugs or weapons on one of his supposedly reformed students.

A fellow teacher who had been with the Peace Corps told Carter about village schools in Africa and Carter thought it was too good to be true – a teacher's paradise. He was on a Nigeria Airways flight to Lagos the same month he received an invitation to teach at Obodo Ogwari High School.

*   *   *

Obodo Ogwari High School had been a mission school from the early colonial days. After the missionaries left, the school continued to run on the same modus operandi but under the supervision of educated natives who still respected its Christian foundation.

There was a chapel for Sunday services and a Bible knowledge session once a week for every class. Carter was often amused by their haphazard dedication to Christianity while still holding their traditional deity, the Ideamala, in the highest religious plateau.

It was hard for Carter to continue his social work since the cultural gap left him absolutely no clues where to begin. Moreover, the school was run by the respective pecking order of principal, teachers, prefects, and class monitors who, collectively, handled law and order with the strictest and most impeccable discipline. Religion was the last frontier open to Carter in his personal quest for humanitarian fulfilment. He knew he could accomplish a lot if he picked up where the missionaries left off. Onward, Christian soldier! This could lead to something big; a report from some obscure New York newspaper, a feature story in *Time* magazine and then … Good Morning, America! And before you know it, movie rights!

15

Carter did not bother to educate himself with the doctrines of Ideamala but he knew there was a sacred eagle or kite or something … and maybe sacrifices. Nothing ever went on in the school in relation to the Ideamala – one of the missionary rules, passed down over the decades. The pioneer students of the school had been sons of local Christian converts. But, after the missionaries were all gone, non-Christians infiltrated and later flooded the small populace. They accepted Christianity and the Bible knowledge class as they would physics and chemistry.

As Chuka and Amechi followed him closely, Carter's mind sauntered over the incident that led to his first folly at Obodo Ogwari High School.

Six months after he came to Obodo Ogwari, three senior students came to his house to discuss the prospects of continuing their education in America.

Carter offered them soft drinks and they chattered on excitedly while thumbing through the catalogue of American universities. When Carter managed to bring up religion, the boys' faces grew keen and intent with hope of picking up Bible class pointers from their kind teacher. Was there an end to this man's kindness? This large balding white man with bushy red hair, a meaty sun-parched face and gentle childlike eyes who, already to them, represented a peculiar father image. Carter continued eagerly when he saw their interest but as soon as he voiced his opinion on the superiority of Christianity over the Ideamala, their faces drew into odd blank expressions like statues of badly carved ebony.

Carter panicked. Knowing how much the boys respected him, those blank expressions masked their true feelings. He sought for a way to put them back at ease but they left almost immediately with flimsy excuses. Carter took a seat close to his front window watching the boys as they walked slowly towards their dormitories.

A million golden arrows jabbed a continuous flow through the mesh of beads that draped his open window – a message from the falling sun. Darkness came fast that evening and found Carter still sitting in the same chair, staging re-runs of the incident in his mind. Finally, he dismissed the entire subject, ate some cold yams and jollof rice and went to bed. That night Carter could not sleep. He was experiencing a presentiment of impending doom. Even the mosquito net that encased his double bed seemed like a ghostly shroud that would soon carry him to the depths of hell. The air was cool outside but the house was still warm from the afternoon's infernal heat, which kept Carter under a constant film of sweat. The jungle music, which had bothered his first few nights at Obodo Ogwari but later became a lullaby, came back in frightening bursts. Owls hooted, frogs croaked, canines howled in the distance and crickets screeched with a dozen other nocturnal jungle inhabitants, performing happily in a symphony whose conductor had long gone berserk. Somewhere in the distance the bird howled ....

*   *   *

Carter stumbled into a laboured sleep without really associating his weird feeling with the evening's encounter with the boys. He dreamed of many places and events of happier times in New York, Miami ... beaches and miles of bikinis and tanned skin ... California ... beautiful parks ... swimming pools ... beauty pageants ... he was the judge ... And all of a sudden, out of nowhere, came this gigantic bird about the size of a full-grown elephant. It chased Carter through those same parks and beaches, which now became slums and ghettoes and robbers' dens. The whores and pimps and drug addicts jeered at him while some slashed at him with switchblades as he ran from the giant bird. The bird pursued Carter clear across the Atlantic Ocean to the west coast of Africa.

Carter woke up sweating like a gravedigger in the tropics. He sensed that someone was in his room but heard nothing. The jungle symphony had stopped and all was silent. Something stirred. Carter froze stiff. His fleshy face quivered in an attempt to ask who it was. His teeth rattled like pebbles thrown across a concrete floor. He heard a grunt that seemed to come from the centre of the room, then came slow deliberate steps towards the bed. With each step came a faint jingle of metals.

"Stay away from me," Carter whispered. "Stay away." He covered his face with the sheets but a compelling force that he could not resist made him look up and he saw it standing on the window ledge.

It could have been a hawk except hawks did not grow that big. It must have been over five feet tall, filling up most of the long colonial window. The moonlight shone on its baldhead and neck, its large eyes throwing occasional sparks of red. It grunted and moaned – human sounds but definitely not an invitation to a cocoyam harvest. Somehow, Carter understood every moan – every grunt ... Suddenly, it howled. It was a nerve-shattering high-strung cry of a soprano in deep torment. Carter threw the sheets over his head and froze. A loud clap of wings informed him that the bird had taken to the dark skies. Carter lay under the sheets shivering till a loud knock on his front door interrupted his rhythm.

"Philip, Philip, are you there?" It was the voice of Emeka Emodi, the mathematics teacher, Carter's best friend and next-door neighbour. Carter was far too terrified to recognize the voice. He grabbed a box of matches from under his pillow, raised the net and scrambled out of bed. He dashed to the open window and closed it, then struck a match to light his palm oil lantern. A very foul rotten odour filled the entire room. As soon as Carter looked up, ears peeled to the knocking on his door, he saw it – the head of a white ram that seemed to be floating in mid-air. The blackened tongue was sticking out, its mouth wide open and teeth set in a menacing snarl. Fresh blood dripped from its severed neck, its black eyes staring blankly at Carter. Its coiled horns held two cracked rotten eggs that dripped their foul contents over the white mane. Carter lowered his head and vomited, throwing churned yams and jollof rice on himself.

The head drifted towards Carter. The lantern dropped out of his hand and he screamed.

Emeka Emodi kicked Carter's door open and found him in the bedroom curled up on the floor and whimpering like a lost cub. It took Emodi some time to calm him down after several cups of cocoa in the sitting room. Carter slept at Emodi's house for the rest of the night.

The next day, Emodi arranged for two priests of the Ideamala to perform "neutralizing" rituals in Carter's house. They were both old and clad in loincloths and both carried large satchels made from rawhide. There was a solemn deathly presence about them. They spent about an hour in Carter's bedroom while Emodi waited with Carter at the front porch. Occasionally, the teachers heard what sounded like chants or smelled smoke. The two old men left with the same funereal atmosphere they brought with them after having a few words with Emodi. Their message was short and simple: Carter must never interfere with any native traditions or else ....

⊛‖ Three ‖⊛

The militants opened their attack with a barrage of artillery fire which continued for twenty minutes before the infantry assault. They came out in hundreds, automatic rifles firing persistently while their mortar crew maintained a steady bombardment on Captain Achebe's troops.

Sergent Major Okafor poised his AK47 and opened fire only to realize, not to any surprise, that a few of the new men were huddled together in the trenches. Okafor kicked the closest man in the rear.

"Get up and fight, you cowards!"

The men scrambled for their guns. Okafor returned to his position. It was then that he noticed a very strange phenomenon. The militants had all taken cover on the ground except one. He was leading the attack, walking upright while firing short bursts from a heavy machine-gun. Okafor had seen the tall warlike Masai tribesmen and the lanky nomadic Buzus but never anyone so huge. The man must have been a little over eight feet tall. He had no clothes on but a short coil of cloth wrapped around his waist and passed between his legs to cover his manhood. His jet-black skin sweated and glistened in the sunlight, exaggerating his huge bulging muscles. Okafor could not believe his eyes. The HMG similar to the one the giant was carrying was a weighty stationary gun, not usually portable yet the man handled it with ease, firing and advancing steadily. Okafor was not exactly scared but he shifted uneasily and ceased shooting when he realized that their weapons were useless against the giant. From his point of view, their bullets were either passing through the man's body or making detours around him. But surely, they were not stopping him. Okafor was quick to identify the giant as one fortified with the legendary Odeshi talisman. He had heard so much about it but had never witnessed it first-hand. A witch doctor's powerful combination of ingredients, worn on the body, or drunk as a potion, would establish a spiritual force field that would prevent high velocity, metal projectiles especially bullets from reaching the subject. Many who had claimed to have acquired the Odeshi had been shot and killed instantly without a chance to tell the native doctor that he failed. Okafor picked up a telescopic sniper rifle, took aim, bringing the giant's mid section into the cross hairs of the scope. He pressed the trigger. He was certain that he had scored a bull's eye on the giant's chest yet the huge man kept coming and firing, unhurt. A rush of panic swept through Okafor's body. His hands felt weak and partially paralyzed as though unable to carry the weight of the rifle. This was usually his initial emotion before he waded into grave danger. Like a seasoned stage actor who uses his first bout of nervousness to deliver a superb performance, Okafor had a way of turning this momentary terror into boundless bravery. So many fantastic stories had been told about the Odeshi charm. From the tales he remembered, Okafor decided to try one of the fetish options that was rumoured to be effective against it. He quickly scooped up a little sand with the open nozzle of his rifle and taking a steady aim at the giant he fired. The bullet did not enter. Okafor was now certain that this terrible giant who fired bursts from a heavy machine gun was wearing a supernatural bulletproof cloak.

At times like this every soldier in the unit who is a traditionalist reconsidered the effeciveness of his protective charm or the deity that he worshipped. As a traditionalist from Obodo Ogwari, Okafor was not particularly scared of sorcery and bewitchment. Though he left Obodo Ogwari as a boy, his father never let him forget their rich cultural and spiritual heritage. Okafor had fully inherited from his father, faith in the all encompassing power of the Ideamala. Okafor was fearless as long as he was in his right. One with Ofor–the state of being right–had the greatest natural protection, courtesy of the supreme God Almighty, lesser deities notwithstanding. As an Ogwarian, Okafor believed that wherever he was, the Ideamala would protect him. His father taught him that the water from the Ideamala caves which was given to every newborn child in Obodo Ogwari ran in his veins and registered him in the guidance and protective services of the Ideamala which it rendered to all natives. He told him that the water was a product of three underground streams with rapid currents that met in a confluence, a chamber in the cave where the three mysterious streams simmered and steamed like boiling water yet when scooped up with a special chalice it was cold to the taste as ice water. Okafor's father said that the frequent drinking of this uncanny water was the answer to the longevity of the keepers one of whom was known to have reached the age of seven hundred and twelve years before his disappearance.

Faced with the problem of this apparently indestructible giant, Okafor's mind flashed through his spiritual heritage and instantly felt rejuvenated in inner strength. Thoughts of the protection of the Ideamala was always a gratifying elixir for him.

*   *   *

Captain Achebe had also come to this alarming realization that the giant may be indestructible. He radioed his mortar crews and relayed the guerillas' coordinates. Achebe's first set of shells completely devastated the rebel attack. Many were hit and the rest fled towards their base. Achebe and his men maintained steady firing, mowing them down as they ran. Alone, the giant kept shooting and advancing.

Captain Achebe gave a ceasefire order and called a bazooka crew to his side. There was a shocked silence throughout the entire seventh infantry as they watched the giant in awe. The cracking sound of his HMG chattered over the still atmosphere. Less than fifty yards to the trenches he stopped and ceased firing. Time seemed to stand still. The giant swung his large head from side to side. He must have been about fifty years old, maybe older, suggested only by the long creases around his eyes and cheeks. The rest of his body looked like that of a twenty-five-year-old body builder. His hair was like a mass of thick ropes hanging down his back and chest. Through time, the ropes had interlocked and matted together, forming thicker sponge-like strands. He just stood there for what seemed like hours to the scared men.

"Who is your commander?" he questioned, in a surprisingly high-pitched strident voice. The men were a bit relieved to hear him speak. It somehow reassured them that the man was human, maybe.

"I am Captain Achebe." After a slight hesitation, "What do you want?"

The man came a little closer. "You must put down your arms and surrender or you will all be wiped out!"

The tension was unbearable. The young recruit in a helmet climbed out of the trench and ran. Two others followed. The giant casually leveled his gun and fired, killing all of them.

22

"Surrender! Now!" he yelled.

Okafor watched the scene anxiously. He had already decided that the only way to gain respect from the new captain was to pull a heroic stunt that would be worthy of merit to the entire battalion. But, this situation was far beyond the scope of his plan.

At the Captain's orders, two bazookas were fired. Both shells exploded around the giant but he was unharmed. A third shell made a direct hit on his heavy machine gun and shattered it. He fell over backwards then sat up with a flabbergasted mien. Apparently he had tripped and fallen when the gun scattered in his hand, but definitely not from the impact. For a moment, he sat on the ground looking very confused.

Okafor saw his chance and yelled, "Catch him!"

Nobody moved. He scrambled out of the trench and ran towards the giant. The big man was straightening up when Okafor threw his first punch, connecting the giant's stomach with a loud thud. He rewarded Okafor with a left hook that sent the sergeant major tumbling over the dusty earth.

Captain Achebe was out of the trench with seven of his biggest men and took cover behind the sandbags. He ordered Okafor to stop as he got ready to attack the giant again.

"We shall all rush him together. Now!" Achebe yelled.

The giant, realizing what lay in store for him, turned and fled. Okafor pursued and dove into the man's legs, bringing him down amidst a cloud of dust. The Captain and his men were all over the giant before he could gather himself together. They pulled his hands behind him and were tying him up when the militants opened fire killing a lieutenant and three others. The giant broke loose and tried to get up but Okafor dealt him a heavy blow behind the head with a rock. He passed out. They all lay flat on the ground while bullets whistled past. The captain radioed his mortar crew to resume bombardment of the militant base. The rest of the soldiers in the trenches opened fire covering them as they crawled back to their position. Okafor requested for some rope with which he bound the giant's hands and legs. He threw the loose end of the rope, which he had tied to a piece of rock, back to the men. Captain Achebe and his men pulled the giant while Okafor crawled abreast.

With the help of Corporal Audu, Okafor made the man sit up

with his back against a stack of sandbags in the rear of the trenches.

Captain Achebe watched Okafor's movements with an occasional glance at the militant base. He was amazed by the sergeant major's courage. Achebe felt like going over to the sandbags to congratulate Okafor but the captain's pride stood in the way.

He yelled out to Okafor, "Next time you want to catch a militant by hand, ask for my permission first and I'll surely give it to you, Sergeant Major." Sarcasm still rang clearly in his voice.

The gunfire exchange had stopped when the giant regained consciousness. The captain and his men tried in vain to make him talk. He merely stared at them with a contemptuous scowl. Several officers took close shots at him with their automatic rifles. It seemed as though they were shooting blanks. The captain ordered the men to go back to their trenches when a scrawny old sergeant secretly approached Okafor and claimed that he knew something about the giant.

"Well, don't just stand there," Okafor growled. "Tell us what you know."

"I'd rather whisper it to you in private, Sir," replied the sergeant. "If I'm wrong, I don't want the boys laughing at me."

Okafor took him aside and stooped to hear what the little sergeant had to say. After a short discussion with him, Okafor rushed into the closest bunker and came out with a pot of water. The men watched curiously from their trenches as Okafor emptied the clay pot over the man's head. The water trickled down slowly soaking the giant's jungle of matted dread locks. The giant did not seem disturbed, instead he regarded Okafor as one would a lunatic. But, when Okafor started to poke and search through his hair, the man became nervous. He shook his head furiously from side to side. Okafor looked under his chin and armpits. When he dipped his hand into the giant's loincloth, the men laughed. They thought he was verifying his manhood but they all froze when Okafor's hand came out holding a gourd. It was a small container with a curved narrow neck, closed off at the top with a piece of cork. He pulled off the cork and a foul pungent odour filled the air. He held the gourd away from his face, undecided what to do with it, then he tilted it and a viscous green liquid flowed out. He smashed the gourd on a rock.

Okafor was walking away from the rock when the corporal shouted, "Sarge Major, look!"

Okafor whirled around and saw a tiny crab and a beetle, both drenched in the smelly green liquid crawling away from the shattered bits of gourd. The sergeant who had whispered to Okafor came forward and said that the crawlers should be burned.

"Get me a lamp from the bunker," Okafor called out to the men in the trenches. Okafor poured kerosene on the crab and beetle and burned them as the men watched in silence. The sergeant looked at Okafor and nodded. Okafor picked up a Mark IV bolt-action rifle that was leaning against the sandbags. He cocked it and placed the muzzle on the man's forehead. The giant recoiled with fear and his eyes pleaded with Okafor but neither said a word. Okafor pulled the trigger.

The man's head split open like a giant clamshell, splattering blood and white brain matter on the sandbags.

Okafor knelt down beside the dead man and pulled out his knife. The captain and others watched, speechless, as Okafor rolled the man over on his face and flipped his long hair over his head. He made an incision behind his head from ear to ear, tearing off the scalp with his left hand. Captain Achebe was an old soldier and had killed many men but had never been so close to a scalping. His stomach churned with a sudden attack of nausea. He entered his bunker feeling sick.

Okafor made a few more cuts around the man's head then pulled the scalp and hair from his head. He held up the hair for everyone to see, both hands in a bloody mess. Several men applauded and the rest watched in absolute disgust.

The men brought water in clay pots with which Okafor washed the blood off the giant's hair before he hung it to dry in the sun.

For the next few days, there was no fighting between the seventh infantry and the militants. The giant was dead and buried but his long tangled hair dangled from a tree beside the sandbags. It was a constant reminder of the hideous incident to the men and a stimulating topic of conversation.

The scalp was completely dry and the hair looked just as lifeless as when the owner was wearing it. Okafor woke up one early morning and cut it down from the tree. He spent about an hour in his bunker sewing it onto the handle of a leather hand fan. Before the sun came up, he was already out, fanning himself despite the coolness of the morning air.

The giant's hair dangled from the handle. Some of the men came close to admire his 'artistic' design. The more superstitious ones maintained a safe distance.

Captain Achebe came out of his bunker, took one look at Okafor and went back in. He had a few ideas on how to deal with the sergeant major but he did not want to lose face with the men for turning against their hero. Moreover, he was then convinced that it would be unwise to have a man like Okafor for a personal enemy.

Okafor paced around for a while fanning himself vigorously. He was actually waiting for the captain to come back out. Finally he got bored and decided to go for a walk towards the depot. He entered the jungle in high spirits leaving the trenches behind. He ran into a mortar crew who surrounded him, asking numerous questions about the giant. He finally broke loose from the excited mortar men feeling like a celebrity and made a left turn off the path.

He found a soft mattress of dried leaves under an umbrella tree and sat down. He smoked a cigarette, leaned his back on the narrow tree trunk and fell asleep with the fan lying on his lap.

The men in their trenches were still discussing Okafor's use of the giant's hair to decorate his hand fan when they heard a loud, piercing scream that resounded through the jungle. The mortar crew that was closer to the source raced in the direction of the sound.

*   *   *

Okafor tried to get up but the hair strapped him by the neck onto the tree trunk. His tongue stuck out and he attempted a second scream but strands of the giant's rope-like hair crawled into his mouth and nostrils, choking him.

When the mortar crew found him, Okafor was still seated with his back against the tree. His eyes, dilated in an attitude of frozen terror, peered through the mass of scattered hair as he fought to pull the hair off his face. When they got close to him, Okafor was struggling with an entangled mass of the giant's lifeless hair.

They stood perplexed as Okafor flung the hair away from him. It landed on a cassava mound several feet away.

Terror-stricken, Okafor still had his hands shielded protectively over his head when he became aware of the men standing before him. Gradually, he came to a realization that he was still alive and well, free from the giant's hair. Okafor looked at the heap of matted dreadlocks lying on the cassava mound, its lighter strands stirring harmlessly in the gentle morning breeze. Slowly, he turned to the men and grinned sheepishly.

"I wa ... wa ... was asleep and ... eh ... I could have sworn that this thing ..." Okafor ended his stuttering speech midstream realizing how ridiculous he would sound if he told them that the hair was trying to kill him. He broke into a strange bout of laughter and the mortar crew joined. None would have dared laugh at Okafor for having a fight with a lifeless mass of hair, a wig. But now that he was the one that first found it funny, the men enjoyed a hearty laughter with him.

"You must have had a bad dream, Sir," said a short stout lance corporal who stood closest to Okafor.

"Yes, a nightmare," Okafor replied absently.

As he got to his feet, Okafor could feel a severe tenseness and discomfort on the frontal part of his throat. He pulled out some strands of hair from his mouth and spat to get rid of the foul musty taste of the dirty dreadlocks. He led the way towards the front line bunkers, shuffling listlessly.

The lance corporal picked up the giant's hair by the fan handle. "Sarge major," he called, "you forgot your fan."

Okafor ignored him and kept moving, stumbling on the rough terrain of dried cassava sticks and scattered mounds of earth.

It didn't take long for Okafor to regain his confidence and composure. The mortar crew that had come to the scene of his uncanny experience had passed it off as a simple mid-morning nightmare. Even Okafor himself was still uncertain of its reality. His neck still hurt and his mouth tasted foul. There was still a stinging in both his eardrums from when the hair crawled into his ears ... or when he hallucinated that it did. He made a mental note to break a kola nut and pour libation of gin to the Ideamala in gratitude for saving him.

〈♦‖ Four ‖♦〉

During the weeks following Carter's bizarre experience he grew quite contented to be just a respected teacher in the school and with that came a mounting interest in Native Medicine which he preferred to refer to as 'voodoo.'

It was exactly two months since Carter's encounter with the bird that Chuka and Amechi walked briskly behind his long strides.

"Mista Cata," Chuka called, "are you not going home?"

Carter glanced around, startled. They had passed his house and were approaching Emodi's hibiscus hedge.

"Eh ... no ... I eh ... I thought I'd say hello to Mr Emodi," he lied. "Here, boys," handing Chuka his keys, "put my stuff in the house for me and have some soft drinks while you're there."

They both thanked him and trotted back towards the house.

Carter walked beside the hedge towards the entrance of Emodi's driveway. Straight ahead on the dirt road beyond the school gates, he could see some women on their way from the market. He lingered for a while to admire their rhythmic hips that swayed under colourful waist wraps. Some had wide metal pans or baskets skilfully balanced on their heads. The one who caught Carter's attention had a plastic bag in one hand and led a little boy with the other. She was tall, well-built and beautiful. Her nicely-formed hips strained against a tight-fitting skirt, her large breasts quivering with each step, under a loose shirt – Carter's shirt. She had the urge to wave but did not. He did too but remembered Emodi's warning about the town's saintly expectations of their teachers. Her name was Ngozi. She was a teacher at the local primary school.

Their first meeting had been an event of speechless but mutual fondness on Ogwari High School grounds. After Emodi introduced them the following day, Ngozi took an immediate liking to Carter's sense of humour and from that day a secret affair began. It was a joyous event for Carter who was sick of his clumsy trysts with the local women. Most could not speak English and would grin sheepishly at his amorous advances. However, sex still reigned a most universal language.

Ngozi was different. She was not only educated but also intelligent and in love with Carter. He was crazy about her. Carter had already proposed marriage and she accepted. Presently, she was in the process of breaking it subtly to her extended family, her intentions of marrying a white man with bright red hair. Meanwhile, Emodi advised them both to maintain a 'midget profile.'

Carter found Emodi on his front porch relaxing on an easy chair, legs outstretched and rested on an ebony stool. He was stripped down to a pair of brown shorts.

"Good to see you, Philip." He beamed, displaying a row of white teeth that made a conspicuous contrast with his jet-black skin. Emeka Emodi was a little man with a long bony face, big eyes and a large meaty nose that provided an ample resting place for his tiny bifocals.

A gourd of palm wine and some calabash cups were set beside his chair while three flies buzzed noisily over the sponge cork.

"I was just waiting for the first lucky chaps to pass by and share this good stuff with me," Emodi said.

Carter pulled up an upright chair and sat down while Emodi poured the sweet-smelling white liquid.

"Real good," Carter confirmed as he set his cup down. "Emeka, there's something that's been bothering me and I'd like to ask you a few questions if you wouldn't mind. It's about that bird."

Emodi chuckled. "I was wondering when you'd get around to it."

Since Carter's new interest in the supernatural, Emodi had taught and showed him a lot. He took Carter to ancient shrines and sacrificial rocks and even to the famous witch doctors' market at Ose-okwodu where one could purchase every uncanny ingredient from ground leopard teeth to shrunken human heads. But, Carter had never asked questions about the Ideamala bird and Emodi understood.

"Well, what do you want to know, Philip?"

"First, among many others, how did you come to be at my door as soon as the bird left? If I remember correctly, you were already knocking before I ... eh screamed."

"Simple, Philip, I saw the boys leave your house that evening, one of them being the adopted son of the fifth keeper of the

Ideamala. I sensed a certain mood in their movement that evening and started asking questions. So when I heard the howl of the Ideamala later that night I sort of, like you Americans say, put two and two together."

Emodi took a sip of his wine. "Consider yourself lucky, my friend. The bird has never visited anyone in over ten years and left without leaving a corpse or serious bodily damage to the transgressor, as a warning."

"And why did I deserve such a special visit just for preaching Christianity?"

"Philip, you have to know that this town is rather primitive compared to our neighbours who are all gone with civilization and technology. Visitors are welcome in Obodo Ogwari but there is an unwritten law that nobody should rent or sell land to non-natives. Resident teachers are allowed to settle here only because they live inside the institutions and usually don't interfere with the tradition. Even now, we don't have native doctors anymore. The Ideamala priests are enough for our spiritual needs."

"Why do you have such a law?" Carter asked.

"Well, despite the resistance made by the priests of the Ideamala in the early days, Christianity still took a stronghold but the so-called heathens still have the upper hand. Both factions have reached a unique compromise and the elders of Obodo Ogwari decided a long time ago that only strangers moving in with new ideas can break this religious stability that also ensures good moral standards in the town." Emodi smiled, shaking his head. "And along you came, preaching Christianity to that boy. You knew he was the keeper's specially chosen, adopted son. Did you not?" he asked Carter.

Carter looked away feeling guilty. "Yes ... I did."

"And the day before, you gave him a pocket Bible and a crucifix."

"Yes," Carter answered. "But the boy has plans of going to school in America; he's going to get more than a Bible and a cross. Over there they've got evangelists and Jesus freaks on the streets."

"That boy is never going to leave this town. I talked to a few elders and one of them told me in confidence; not only is that boy the keeper's son, he was chosen for priesthood when he was three years old."

"What?" Carter was shocked.

"That is the truth, Philip. The boy doesn't know it yet but they are allowing him to get some of our type of education before they move him up to the caves to be initiated. So you see what your transgression was with the Ideamala? You hit it in its home ground."

Carter nodded absently. His mind was back to the night of the bird's visit.

"Now you see why the bird paid you a special visit," Emodi added.

"Why do you always say 'the bird' as if it's the same one that's been hanging around for centuries?" Carter asked.

Emodi sipped his wine slowly, his big eyes peering at Carter over the old-fashioned eyeglasses. "I thought I told you."

"Told me what?" Carter queried.

"The old men that cleaned up your room, how old would you say they are?" Emodi asked.

"Eighty-five, ninety, tops." Carter guessed.

Emodi chuckled, then slowly, a serious frown crawled over his face, creasing his shiny black forehead. "My dear Philip, we have six keepers of the Ideamala. Each of these men possesses specialized skills like the power to heal, tell the future, bring or drive away rain and help villagers with their crops which includes irrigation and enriching the soil and many other skills that meet the town's needs. These priests have been keepers of the Ideamala for centuries but nobody knows the origin of the bird."

"And it's the same bird?" Carter quipped

"One and only," Emodi answered. He stood up and walked into the house with a motion of the hand that told Carter he would be right back. Carter sat there alone on the porch feeling lonely all of a sudden. Emodi emerged from the house with some sheets of paper stapled together at the top left corner and gave them to Carter. The prints were faded or smeared with carbon in many places.

"This is a photocopy of a portion of Obodo Ogwari history that might interest you," said Emodi.

Carter ran his large forefinger impatiently over the first page, setting his speed reading skills into motion. He read the second page more slowly often pausing to decipher the smeared print while his face flushed from red to sickly white.

In a nutshell, the three pages of history recorded the coming and going of the British missionaries. There were three of them, Morgan, Patterson and Cook who built the school with the help of villagers. They started on an elementary level, teaching geography, arithmetic, Bible knowledge and most important of all, English language – the medium of communication.

The villagers accepted Christianity without any suspicion of it being a rival to the Ideamala. Apparently, Morgan had discovered how dedicated the natives were to their deity and prevented his peers from presenting Jesus Christ as a direct opponent of the Ideamala. Morgan knew that the full introduction of Christianity to such dedicated worshippers had to be done with tact and cunning.

The people of Obodo Ogwari took the Bible like an entertaining storybook after Cook and some smart village men translated it. Even the herbal keeper of the Ideamala came by to compare medical skills and techniques with the missionaries. All went well until Cook and Patterson accused Morgan of bending the rules of Christianity. They both accused Morgan of encouraging the villagers to serve "God and Mammon" at the same time. Patterson and Cook launched a big revival, denouncing the Ideamala and placing Jesus on the highest pedestal. They lost ninety percent of their congregation that day. The few villagers that came back were merely thirsty for education.

The following morning after the revival, Cook was found hanging from a tree. It had rained that night and the only footprints they found around the tree were Cook's and those of a giant bird.

Patterson passed off Cook's death as suicide due to lack of faith, the bird's footprints as staged or coincidental.

The night after their second revival, terrifying screams awakened Morgan who found Patterson close to a point of insanity. He was yelling that it was only a dream and that the bird was after him but he'd soon wake up. There were two large holes where his eyes had been. Blood flowed freely from the sockets. Unable to cope with blindness, Patterson drowned himself in a well soon afterwards.

Morgan, who had remained passive during the revivals, was the only survivor. He continued with his own style of Christianity, offering the good book as a guideline for good moral practices to which everyone agreed. A sneak approach, but it suited the villagers fine. Morgan lived in Obodo Ogwari until he was eighty-six and died of natural causes. In his lifetime at Ogwariland he had subtly converted many natives to Christianity.

By the time Carter finished reading the papers, he felt a coat of goose pimples on his body like droplets of cold dew. The thought of a close encounter with such an aged evil bird made him shudder.

"And it's the same bird," Carter stated absently, staring blankly at Emodi without seeing him at all. His mind was rolling. "It just doesn't make sense; an ancient bird hanging and drowning people, opening locked doors without keys and slaughtering people like animals and you guys worship it?"

"We don't worship the bird itself," Emodi said, defensively, "but what it represents."

"What does it represent; tit for tat, annihilation of helpless competitors, cold-blooded murder?" His voice quivered emotionally. He was almost crying.

"Take it easy now, man," Emodi snapped. "Let's not expose our dirty loincloths in the market-place. I have never confronted you with the slave trade and the millions of my people who were dumped overboard into the mouths of fat-bellied sharks have I?

Carter looked embarrassed, "I'm sorry ... I guess I got a little excited there." He straightened up.

"Think nothing of it, Phillip, I know how you feel," Emodi replied. "Sometimes I wonder where I stand, myself."

"What I don't understand is how a bird manages to do all those things," Carter said, pouring more palm wine in his glass.

Emodi sank deeper into his easy chair. "Where do we go when we die? And is there really an invisible entity that inhabits the human body? These are some of the inexplicable phenomena of life. Nuts that even the most brilliant scientists and occultists have not been able to crack." Emodi sat up and took a big gulp of wine then continued.

"Science makes it seem like everything has an explanation but that is only if we can learn how it functions, which in itself explains nothing except that which is physical ... mechanical ...

But what about the abstract, the supernatural? How does the Ideamala bird keep its priests alive for so long? How does it move objects, induce sleep on its victims and project itself into your dream? Nobody knows. Morgan, the last of the missionaries left a lot of writings when he died. His theories based on the Ideamala include some of the earliest genuine works on hypnosis and telekinesis, which was obviously ignored out of prejudice and ignorance. Who is there to blame? Try connecting those qualities to a bird and the Westerners would put you in a lunatic asylum and throw the key away. Since most humans never learn to utilize their brains to the fullest extent, the sixth sense and super intelligence of the keepers can only be attributed to the teachings of the bird, which if you asked me, is not really a bird. But don't ask me what it is because I don't know."

Carter absorbed every word with a lump in his throat. He knew Emodi was being frank with him. After all, Carter had understood every message the bird gave him that night ... every grunt, every moan, every single warning – telepathy!

"You talk about hypnosis, Emeka, but for all I know the hypnotist has to get the attention of his subject before he can hypnotize. How do you explain that?" Carter demanded.

"I don't know and wouldn't go trying to find out. And by the way, Philip, the students of Okoro dormitory are going to the Itah tomorrow and I thought you might want to come along."

"What's the Itah?" Carter slid forward to the edge of his seat.

"It's a sort of ... primitive lie detector test."

"You mean with some sort of a voodoo machinery run by a witch doctor?"

"It's native science performed by a native priest," Emodi corrected.

"Sure I'd like to come along," Carter beamed, but on second thought, "though if it has anything to do with the Ideamala bird, maybe I shouldn't," he added flatly.

Emodi laughed at Carter's sudden withdrawal. "Philip you have to understand that the Ideamala is everyone's friend as long as you are living here without interfering with its work, thereby inhibiting its service to the people."

"Does the principal know about this trip to the Itah?" Carter asked.

"Well, let's say he reserves a deaf ear for such occasions because he has a few influential Christian parents to answer to also. But on the other hand, most Christians don't interfere since it's generally believed that only guilty ones refuse to go to the Itah."

"So what is it you're trying to find out?"

"I'm sure you must have heard about the thefts in Okoro House. Since this school term started, students in that particular dormitory have been losing a lot of valuables.

Whoever that's responsible has eluded every trap set so far. So, the only alternative is the Itah."

"This, I've got to see ... sure I'd love to come, Emeka, if you think it's alright."

"I'm sure it's alright. Be ready at nine o'clock and wear your worst clothes. And Philip ..."

"Yes?"

"Whatever you do, don't interfere. All right?"

"You can count on me," Carter answered.

Carter lay in bed that night thinking about the trip. There were mixed feelings but sleep came easy after he convinced himself that he could conform and deal with the town's customs. The message had been clear with every grunt, every moan. Conform or die!

*   *   *

Daylight crept out of its hiding place like a bashful bride while songbirds chattered their encouragement. This was Emodi's favourite time of the day when the air was not so hot to breathe in large volumes of exhaustion. It was his jogging hour.

Trotting around the soccer field, Emodi thought about Carter, wondering what his motive was for coming to Obodo Ogwari. Didn't every white man that came to the Third World have an ulterior motive that would achieve his personal ends? Ends that would be achieved through exploitation of the unsuspecting, ever-vulnerable and uninformed tribesmen. From the slave-driver to the last missionary, all came to achieve a selfish end. As for the great doctors and scientists who came down to Africa to discover vaccines for tropical diseases, didn't their names go down in history, weren't the drugs patented and sold in their names? Didn't the missionaries who brought Christianity to save the 'cannibalistic natives,' hope to retire to paradise, passing through large golden doors labeled "Whites Only" while their cannibal converts would pass through the small wooden back door labeled 'Negroes', not niggers. Of course the Negroes would leave their bows and arrows behind but bring along their bongo drums strictly for entertaining the superior angels … And the Bible told us all men were created equal.

Emeka Emodi had thought he had all white men figured out until he met Carter.

Emodi was an academic genius, a 'curse' which had helped pass him through five years of pure hell in an elite private college in England. He had received a double promotion while still in his third year at Obodo Ogwari High. It was the only logical thing for the school authorities to do since Emodi was already helping the finalists and even teachers with academic work. The maths and science teachers were not ashamed to seek his advice on certain problems since his ingenuity was an established fact – an academic freak.

When the federal scholarships came up, Emodi got the cream of the crop which landed him in Keaton College, England, class of 1968.

The board of directors showcased Emodi as their first and only negro student. They hoisted him like a big black flag in every school catalogue and brochure which was to remind the world of their readiness to racially integrate … with one very black negro. For poor Emodi, it was hell on earth. The rich white students treated him with utter disdain. His academic brilliance did not help but worsen his subhuman status, bringing rivalry and jealousy to that one negro who stayed on top of almost every class.

No matter how much the authorities tried to make him accepted, the final decision was up to the students. In the bathrooms, they forced Emodi to use the same toilet and shower cubicle which only few liberal students used after him.

The seed of racism was planted in Emodi, festering like an incurable sore on a human foot that would gradually spread and gnaw away the vital organs for survival. By the time he returned to Obodo Ogwari, the seed had sprouted laying a taproot deep into his tortured mind. After his return to Obodo Ogwari he never desired a part of city life anymore. The village gave him a feeling of security and warmth, which he never valued or noticed before he went to England. Emodi never discussed his ordeal in England with anyone because he knew no one would understand. Racial prejudice to the villagers wasn't really practical but a myth. After all why would anyone dislike you because you have a different colour of skin?

When Carter came to Obodo Ogwari, Emodi simply hated his guts. He couldn't understand why everybody liked him so much.

... Just look at them ... those ignorant class 3c bastards. The way they warm up to the redhead, trying to please him and do favours for him. The way he rubs their little "wooly" heads like pet dogs ... monkeys ... those little fools ... if they could only see through that reddish smiling face, his ulterior motive ... Oh! Yes ... didn't they all have a selfish ulterior motive ... camouflaged by a smile ... oh! Yes, down here they have to smile because they're outnumbered like I was in England, only I couldn't smile my way out ... those little 3c fools ... one day they will learn ... maybe you will learn that an epileptic white man who lets a dog lick the spit off his lips may not condescend low enough to shake your little black paws ... oh! Never mind the redheaded devil, he has an ulterior motive ... just see him when he's crossed the ocean, he'll be just as mean as the next white ... those little fools ... maybe one day they'll learn that they're just too black to be human ... too human to be so black ... just too black for comfort. ... I threw my slippers away because the African stepped on it ... he is nothing but an intelligent ape ... we should mark every plate he uses ... my father is on the board and promised the African must go ... good thing we assigned him a special toilet and shower, who knows what new diseases he brings from the jungle ... why don't they send the nigger back to Africa ... and God created all men equal ...

During Carter's first week in Obodo Ogwari High, he sat in all the classes, familiarizing himself with their styles and teaching techniques. Visiting Emodi's class hadn't been easy for him due to Emodi's repulsive attitude. After that day they avoided each other.

Five

Captain Achebe was sitting on the roof of a bunker, smoking a cigarette when Okafor came up and saluted him.

"Sir, I wish to have a discussion with you."

"My ears are open," the captain replied gruffly. "Speak."

"The militants are chanting war songs which means they're planning to strike. As we all know, Sir, this sector is the last stronghold of the militants and if we crush them here, the war will surely come to an end in no time."

"Tell me something I don't know," the captain replied and drew fiercely on the cigarette.

"What I'm suggesting, Sir, is that we strike first, now that their secret weapon is no more. Their morale is low. They're just bluffing and chanting war songs."

Achebe looked at Okafor with indignation. "Since when did you start making decisions for me, Sergeant Major? Didn't I tell you that things have changed around here? You can no longer exercise the ..."

"I am not trying to exercise anything, Sir. All I'm saying is that the enemy must be living in fear since we captured the giant and it's time to strike before they do."

"Enough!" the captain yelled. "I make the decisions around here and I say no!"

"Maybe Okafor is right, Captain," the lieutenant interjected. He was sitting with his back resting on a stack of sandbags.

"I don't want to hear it!" Achebe retorted. "My decision is the law."

More soldiers were becoming interested in the argument. Gradually they gathered around the bunker whispering and making snide but hardly audible remarks against the new captain. Okafor was their hero; there was no contest on the issue.

The lieutenant's support and comments by the rank and file was an elixir for Okafor. "I'm not trying to run your battalion for you, Captain," he said with a sardonic grin. "But, I'm still of the opinion that there can't be a better time to strike if we want an easy victory in this war."

"We may even be late, Captain," said the lieutenant. "We should have struck immediately after we killed the giant. I should have thought of it."

The Captain thought Okafor's insistence was utterly disrespectful and even bordered on punishable insubordination. Okafor was fired with his zeal and all conditions seemed to concede to his high-flying ambition.

Above the din of the rank and file, the captain's key words that mattered to Okafor and those who stood closest to him were, 'rebellion and sabotage.' Though these words struck the lieutenant with alarm, Seargeant Major Okafor was too far down ego lane to give a care in the world. Already, news of his heroic capture of the giant had spread through the nation and beyond. The chants of his name by some soldiers only served to add an unnecessary booster to a morale that was already bursting at the seams.

In that very rare strike of providence that brings about the cause and effect of peculiar events, a sniper's bullet came suddenly and ended Captain Achebe's life. The lieutenant was seriously wounded and while Okafor and the medics attended to the lieutenant, machine gunfire erupted from the enemy lines. Achebe's men ran for cover. The medics removed the corpse of Captain Achebe and secured him in a close cluster of mango trees. Taking advantage of the high morale of the men, Okafor took immediate charge and deployed them in readiness for war. In jest, one of the soldiers brought down the giant's hair from where it was hanging and clowned around with it. Since Okafor's strange encounter with the dreadlocks, he had carefully avoided further contact with it. He had told the lance corporal who brought it back from the cassava farm to hang it on a tree for all to see and appreciate. It was, after all, a trophy for the entire command and not his alone, Okafor had conveniently stated.

"Let us make ourselves a secret weapon," the soldier said putting the dreadlocks on his head. The fan handle stood upright on his head like a horn. Some of the soldiers laughed and cheered him on while others watched with mixed feelings.

Okafor glanced at him disinterestedly. Though he was filled with an uncanny premonition, he didn't speak but shrugged and went on with his preparation for the attack.

"You're not tall enough to act the giant," Corporal Ngefa

teased. "Give it to Private Ekedi and make him strip down to his underwear."

"Yeah!" another voice called from the trenches. "Put Ekedi in the giant's loincloth and let's scare those militants to death."

Ekedi was only six feet nine inches tall, dark but nearly as muscular as the dead giant. Dressed in the giant's loincloth and dreadlocks, his dark muscles rippling and musty from the mild heat of the morning sun, did give the private a peculiar impression of the late giant. He grinned and flexed his muscles at the men and patted the horn down to the back.

*   *   *

Okafor opened his assault on the rebels with heavy mortar and artillery bombardment before the soldiers moved in. It was as though the militants were already resolved to give up the fight before it began. They put up a mild resistance for just ten minutes and when they started to retreat their defenses broke down completely.

Private Ekedi turned out to be a foolhardy actor in his role of playing the giant. He tried his possible best to imitate the dead giant's attitude of indestructibility, exposing himself as he advanced steadily firing short bursts from hip level, with a sub-machine gun.

Years later many members of the Seventh Battalion, historians and others who acquired war tales from oral tradition attributed the victory of that war not only to Sergeant Major Okafor but also to Private Ekedi and his costume.

The militant guerillas were completely devastated by the government forces who routed them completely. Many laid down their arms and surrendered while others absconded.

Okafor was quick to call the divisional headquarters to report their victory, requesting for an occupation army and reinforcement to take over the rebel base and to infiltrate the interior and suppress any remnants of resistance. This action was a follow-up to his speedy deployment of the men and sharing of extra ammo before the final offensive began.

*   *   *

It was after the fighting ended, when the paramedics moved in to collect the dead and wounded that Private Ekedi was found.

Okafor was interrogating a dark bearded man among the captives when Corporal Ngefa rushed up to him and whispered into his ears.

"I told them not to take him away with the rest until you come," Ngefa said as Okafor followed him back toward their own base.

"Ngefa, you know I don't like suspense, so tell me what happened to Private Ekedi. Did a shell make a direct hit on him or what?" Okafor asked impatiently.

"I can't say what happened to him because I don't know. Just wait till you see this," Ngefa replied, walking briskly.

Okafor pushed aside a few soldiers and paramedics who were gathered around the strecher on which Private Ekedi lay. Much as he tried to control his emotions Okafor felt giddy, goose pimples spreading from his head down his entire body as he set eyes on the dead private. He moved his right foot slightly backwards to have a better balance on the ground as his mind flashed back to the morning of his weird encounter with the giant's dreadlocks. Now, he was quite certain that it hadn't been a dream but an uncanny reality.

The giant's long matted hair had formed a cocoon around Ekedi's head, strapping so tightly that it was obvious the skull had been crushed, the head compressed to a pulp half its former size.

Crusts of dried blood covered the hair on the surface while a little fresh blood still seeped out through the strands.

"Cut him loose before you move him," Okafor said, turning to leave.

"It's not that simple," Ngefa replied. "None of these men would dare touch that cursed thing and you can't blame them."

"What about you, Ngefa, why don't you do it?"

"Who, m-m-me?" Ngefa stammered. "I sprained my fingers during the attack, I can't."

"Cowards!" Okafor muttered under his breath and turned to the medics. "Get me a pair of scissors and a knife and I'll do it myself. We can't let this man be buried with this thing on his head. The man was a hero, you know."

Okafor cut the dreadlocks off Ekedi's head while a steadily increasing crowd of soldiers, medics and nurses watched, mostly in disgust. A young private in torn trousers turned away from the crowd and vomited. When Okafor was done with the messy job, he called for kerosene with which he burned the pieces of the giant's fragmented locks.

Private Ekedi was buried along with his dead colleagues and Okafor ordered a twenty-one-gun salute in his honour.

⟨ᴅ‖ Six ‖ᴄ⟩

Emodi was having a chat with a junior student one day and gathered that Carter was opposed to the way their history teacher treated slavery and bigotry as if a fairy tale and the victims, merely figments of some creative storyteller's imagination. Carter had gone to the principal to tell him that the students, some of who sought admission to universities abroad, were not well prepared to handle a racially prejudiced society.

Emodi laughed. Why didn't he think of that himself? He knew how naïve East and West Africans were in the old days when it came to matters of racial discrimination; lack of adequate communication systems. After all did he have to go to England to become suddenly conscious of his blackness while just down here in South Africa, blacks lived in just as much or greater oppression than southern plantation blacks did in old America?

After speaking with the boy, Emodi went out of his way to strike up a conversation with Carter. The two men became friends after that and for the first time, Emodi was seeing Carter not as a white foe, but as a man ... his first good white man ... ulterior motive?

Emodi's morning jog ended in a sprint to his front porch. He sat down on the staircase breathing heavily, chin rested on one knee.

Two large frogs eyed him suspiciously for a moment then leaped off the porch into the bushes beside the house. He looked across the fields and saw signs of life in one of the dormitories – Okoro House. The students were up early and excited about the trip to the Itah.

Carter appeared in the driveway, carrying a gourd of palm wine as Emodi got up to enter the house. Carter was wearing a pair of faded jeans and a bright red shirt which surprisingly clashed with his red hair.

"Morning, Philip," Emodi called tiredly, entering the house. "Come on in."

"You think we can polish this off before we go?" Carter asked.

Emodi looked back. "Where did you find that this early?"

"My student's father, a palm wine tapper ... woke me up this morning while making his early rounds. It's very fresh."

"You're getting too popular in this town, Philip, if you keep this up, you'll soon be running for office of resident witch doctor," Emodi teased.

"I'd rather run for Ngozi's bridegroom instead," Carter retorted, quite serious.

Emodi knew that Carter's reply was more of a question so he answered. "I know how anxious you are, Philip. Ngozi is a nice girl and well beyond the age of consent but the way our tradition goes, she still has to get consent from the elders in her family line and as soon as she gives me the word I'll start arranging for the nuptials."

"Great man! I'm really counting on you."

The sun had already risen and was intimately soothing like a lover's breath when the two teachers stepped outside to join their anxious students. They were both tipsy but composed. The students were gathered in front of Emodi's house looking sporty in their navy-blue shirts and khaki shorts. The senior prefect stepped up and told Emodi that a problem had developed. Two new students said they would not go to the Itah. One was a pastor's son and the other had stepped on broken glass the previous day and couldn't walk.

The preacher's son was about thirteen. He was a chubby boy whose large shifty eyes were almost pleading each time they settled on Carter or Emodi.

His name was Joseph. "My father will kill me if he finds out I got involved with juju."

"You're not getting involved with juju, Joseph, we're only trying to carry out a simple test," Emodi explained.

"My father will kill me," Joseph cried.

It took a while to straighten out the preacher's son before they set out on their trip. The boy with a bad foot was provided with a bicycle that had a rear carriage on which he sat while his mates took turns to wheel him through the winding jungle paths. He seemed nervous but grinned broadly each time the bicycle bounced or wavered precariously in the hands of a smaller boy.

The path was narrow and lined with very low shrubs and trees that grew evenly bigger into thick dense vegetation on both sides of the path.

There were thirty students on the trip with the bicycle couple in the lead, Carter and Emodi in the rear. Occasionally they would run into a woman with a clay pot of water on her head or a palm wine tapper with his gourds and climbing gear. They had been walking for half an hour before being joined by a pack of monkeys. The monkeys kept their distance swinging from tree to tree in the same direction as the boys, chattering and making faces. They seemed to be protesting about something. From the way the boys were giggling Emodi knew that something was wrong.

Looking carefully among the students, he saw the problem. An infant monkey was clinging lovingly to the arms of a boy.

"Chuka! drop him quick," Emodi yelled.

Chuka set the little monkey down. It ran into the bushes and up the trees to join its kinfolk and they all chattered away into the depths of the jungle.

"A-w-w, should have let the boys have their fun," Carter protested.

"No, Philip, these packs can be dangerous when they sum up enough courage," Emodi replied.

"Poor little monkeys," Carter added, smiling.

... *Monkeys? ... monkeys ... what* monkeys? – Emodi thought – *oh! the monkeys on the trees of course.* Emodi glanced at Carter ... ulterior motives ...?

Carter had poured the rest of the wine into his war surplus water bottle which he had picked up at a Manhattan pawnshop.

Emodi accepted the bottle when Carter offered, swallowed a mouthful and handed it back to him.

"Philip, I would like to ask you a question but I don't want you to misunderstand my angle because it's something that just crossed my mind," he lied, "and I was wondering what made you come here."

"You mean to Africa or particularly to Obodo Ogwari?"

"Both."

Carter went on to explain about his love for teaching and social work and how it was so difficult and discouraging for him in the New York schools; about the scars on his back and finally, the Peace Corps connection that brought him to teachers' paradise.

He ended with how glad he was, now living in Obodo Ogwari, even though the salary was so much lower and living conditions drastically less luxurious.

Emodi was convinced of Carter's sincerity and was even sorry about his scars but found himself pressing harder. "But, Philip, what made you want to help all those poor underprivileged blacks and Puerto Ricans?"

"You know something, Emeka? I could just say that I love helping people and then you'll ask why not poor whites because I think I know what your angle is."

He took a long pause as if undecided on whether to continue talking or not, then a long drink from the army bottle.

Emodi was silent, waiting and walking. From a nearby tree, a grey parrot squawked as it kept a watchful eye on the procession of intruders.

"You know, I'm not really from New York," Carter said, like a casual confession. "My ancestors came originally from the state of Mississippi. My great great-grandpappy, Abraham Billy-Joe Carter, was one of the biggest and most ruthless plantation owners in his time. He was noted as the man who knew how to get the most work out of slaves and you know what that means. When he died, his son, Abe junior, took over and turned out to be a far more wicked soul in trying to beat his father's reputation."

Carter paused to drain the last few drops out of the bottle. In spite of the wine's potency which made it a little easier for him, it was evidently a subject he would have rather left alone.

"One day, Abe Junior found one of his slaves who was supposed to be at work, sleeping in the barn. He had him dragged out to the fields. The man's five-year-old son was brought forth and hanged right there on a tree before his eyes and the rest of the plantation slaves. Though the little boy was cut down from the tree and was saved from choking to death, it was still a most heinous act that is hardly believable ..."

"I believe it," Emodi interjected flatly.

Carter stared at him inquiringly then continued. "The little black kid was a playmate of my great-grandfather's who was only six years old then. He saw everything from the mansion. When he grew up, he helped a lot of slaves escape to the north. When his father died, my great-grandfather set all the slaves on the plantation free, issuing them Bills of Sale for their freedom, free of charge.

My own father died after I was born and I was rasied by my old grandpappy whose involvement with blacks was not taken lightly by the whites but he continued with his work knowing they were out to get him. One rainy day, he was killed trying to save a black family whose house was set on fire by the Ku Klux Klan. My mother sold the farm and we moved to New York.

"If I had followed my grandfather's footsteps, I would have been with the protestors in the march on Washington ... but I never could find enough guts ... social work was one field I really considered and I mean real social work and not like all those job hawks out there who treat it like it was all about papers and numbers. Anyway, I love teaching and in certain New York schools, I could do a little bit of my own style of social work as well. I was unlucky to always assign myself the arduous task of reforming some incorrigible ghetto kid whose mind was probably too far gone to ever make a meaningful contribution to the cause of mankind. But, who was I to pass judgement? I worked with several black organizations, but for some reason there was always a difference in opinions and I felt rejected. I soon found myself an aging meddling white man who never achieved his father's dream or any dream."

For the first time since Carter started his story, he smiled. "When I came to Obodo Ogwari I was thrilled to be, for the first time, in a society where racial tension is non-existent. They never even heard of it." He laughed, then his forehead wrinkled instantly into a frown.

"But you, Emeka Emodi, you're different, I never could understand what was bugging you but I knew you hated me the moment we laid eyes on each other. We're friends now sure, best of friends ... but I know it's still there, lying, waiting ..."

"Mr Emodi," the prefect called. "We have reached the Uzo-Mkpi and the boys in front are getting a little scared. They would like you to lead us from here."

"The boys eh? What about you, are you not afraid?" Emodi asked.

"No-o," lied the senior boy shaking his head with panic-dilated eyes. "I'm not afraid but the boys will prefer you in front since

47

the keeper here knows you."

The Uzo-Mkpi was a point where the path forked into two different tracks, forming a v-shape. The path to the right sloped down through a cluster of palm trees to a river below. Carter paused for a moment at the v-junction looking down through the ragged barks of the swamp palms at the water below. The sun bounced merrily on the fast currents, reflecting on a few torsos and hands and heads of people swimming and washing in the river.

The path to the left was not cleaned and trimmed as the one to the river since it wasn't used as often. Although villagers took turns to clean the path for the keeper, it still bore signs of neglect which contributed to the eerie atmosphere. It was not so easy for the bicycle crew to move through the carpet of twigs and dried leaves. The passenger had now stopped grinning and was clearly paranoid.

A few hundred yards from the Uzo-Mkpi brought them to the cave's entrance.

Emodi had the boys form a single line linking hands till they formed a long tight chain. He stepped between two large boulders that marked the cave entrance, beaming a powerful flashlight before him. The cave was cool and refreshing after they had trekked in the hot sun.

Carter was a little disappointed. Making the trip in broad daylight had almost assured him there would be no hanky-panky involved in detecting the criminal. But, the darkness of the cave would make foul play a cinch. He could picture one of those aged keepers leaping out of a dark corner of the cave and submitting one of the boys into confession with a rusty ancient knife in his back. He thought about the Ideamala bird and shivered. He could almost feel its presence in the cold entrails of the cave.

Emodi thought about his conversation with Carter as he led the boys deeper into the dark cave. The air was getting colder and so were his thoughts. Of course Philip Carter had something to prove to himself, driven by the wishes of his father. Maybe his motive was not like the other whitemen – the slave traders and treasure hunters, fame seekers and the rest who were after material things. But, Philip Carter had a conscience to satisfy and the expectation of his dear dead grandfather to live up to …

He had a dream to achieve, Emodi thought, a little spitefully ... And when he was rejected in America, he came down here where he could find more obedient blacks ... the great white saviour. Doesn't every man have a price which isn't always money or promise of fame and beautiful women? Emodi mused. For some, it's respect, pride and abstract things of that nature. Just let them maintain their pride and you may have just bought their favour for less than a halfpenny or a billion naira ... priceless. Give Philip a chance to successfully reform a couple of black ghetto kids and his entire year is made. Down here, there are no ghetto kids so he turned missionary.

Emodi felt a revolving feeling of spite for Carter and then for himself for resenting his friend who had strived so hard to integrate. But now Carter seemed to him to be torn between natural goodness and self-righteousness because he had something to prove.

Emodi was startled by a little boy dressed in a green veined material with holes cut out for the head and arms. His face was set in a serene expressionless countenance.

In his hand was a flaming torch, the mid-rib of a dried palm leaf soaked in palm oil. It illuminated the large chamber into which he led them to wash their hands and feet in fountains that sprung from the cave walls. Obeying the boy's instruction, they left their shoes and sandals in the fountain chamber. He then led them through a wide passage into a fairly large hall where the keeper received his guests.

The hall had a high ceiling and to Carter's relief, brightly illuminated by sunlight that shone through many cracks and crevices in the cave roof. Flaming torches were extinguished and flashlights turned off as Carter turned in circles, marveling at the ancient images that were carved into the stone walls. The floor was covered with animal skins. Huge wooden statues, depicting warriors in action, stood at three corners of the room. At the fourth corner of the large chamber was a small shed about three feet high built with four wooden poles and a thatch roof. Under the hut was a large wooden black mask in the background and in front were seven bronze idols placed around a bronze statue of the bird. A large python lay coiled amongst the statues apparently asleep. Hanging from the roof of the shed were animal and human skulls of various sizes. Next to the shed was a large cubicle partitioned off with strings of crude bells and shells and long strips of hides and skins. The little boy disappeared through the entrance and emerged minutes later with the keeper amidst a chaotic sound of bells. The boy was beating a small drum with a curved stick.

The keeper was carrying a small weaved basket that was blackened as if it had been smoked. He was the 4th keeper of the Ideamala. His name was Uli. A single piece of dyed white cloth draped his body, leaving one shoulder bare. On his head was a bright red cap with large black and white feathers stuck all over it in their ceremonial style. From his shoulder hung a rugged satchel made of rawhide. Uli looked much older than the two keepers that had come to Carter's house. His face was not very wrinkled and his movement was firm but his scaly legs and clawed toes that had nails like chips off a turtle shell, were subtle signs of his uncanny age. Emodi guessed six maybe seven hundred years old, going by the uncharted but relatively accurate records of oral tradition.

The old man walked to the middle of the room and tied the black basket to the long string that hung from the ceiling. He motioned the students to come closer.

Nobody moved.

The little boy stopped beating the drum. Still without uttering a word he organized the students in a circle around the keeper and made them hold hands. Carter stood next to Emodi in the circle whispering questions faster than Emodi could answer.

The keeper chanted and muttered under his breath for a few minutes with his eyes closed while the students watched in silence. He opened his eyes and from the bag withdrew a looped piece of rope about three feet long. It was like a hangman's noose except the knot was simpler. The rope, like the basket, was black with age and handling. The keeper removed the lid, stuck the loose end of the noose in the basket and replaced the lid. It was then that signs of life emanated from the basket with faint screeching and squeaking sounds that sounded like rats and again like chicks.

The keeper spoke. "Welcome to the house of Ideamala." He flashed a friendly but amused glance at Carter who stood out like a large Rhode Island red cock in a cage full of blackbirds.

Around the middle of the cave wall was a large boulder with a flat top. The keeper climbed up the boulder stepping on the roughly chiseled stairs. He sat down cross-legged on the top and addressed the black teacher.

"Son of Emodi, you the teacher will go first to show the boys what to do." Then he resumed his low-pitched guttural chanting.

The little boy, seemingly out of his serene character, was now sitting cross-legged behind the keeper, twiddling his thumbs.

Emodi walked slowly to the middle of the room where the basket swayed gently at the end of the string, the black noose dangling harmlessly from under the lid. Bending slightly he put the noose around his neck, looked up at the keeper and declared. "I am not responsible for the stolen goods that belong to these people assembled in the figure of the full moon and if I am, I lay my life down to the Ideamala." Emodi paused for a moment then removed the noose from his neck and went back to his place in the circle. The prefect was next.

Carter whispered, "I don't know what is supposed to happen, Emeka, but I can tell you which one of the students stole the stuff, it's only logical ..."

Emodi hushed him up as the prefect was putting the noose around his neck.

Carter's eyes wandered around the room searching for more items of interest than that 'dumb' rope and basket. He wished he had brought his camera but wondered if Emeka would have let him take pictures.

As for the lie detector test, he was convinced who the itchy-fingered boy was and would just wait till the pilferer got to the noose and see what happens. Carter was so absorbed wondering if the human skulls under the shrine were those of missionaries or slave drivers that he did not see him approach the noose.

The boy had his hand a few inches from the noose then whimpered with fear. He swirled around and with one hop and a leap, his hands were around Emodi. He was crying. "Please don't let the Ideamala get me, Mr Emodi, I've been stealing food from the prefect's locker. Please don't let him get me; I was only hungry ... please!"

His arms were clasped tightly around Emodi's waist, his bandaged foot pointed upwards, heel grinding into the leopard-skin carpet.

"Nobody is going to hurt you ... now stop crying and be calm."

The other boys looked on in wide-eyed surprise. Somebody giggled and stopped. The keeper opened his eyes and watched silently with a look of wise understanding.

"So, this is how it works," Carter stated. "The guilty guy gets scared out of his wits by looking at that black rope. I could have told you who it was before we got here. This boy stepped on broken glass so as to be exempted from coming here. Didn't you see how nervous he was when ..."

"The prefect and I thought as much, Philip, but I'm trying to find out ..."

"Mr Emodi," the prefect intervened. "I never noticed any food stolen from my locker and that is not why we're here." He turned to the boy. "Okoli, did you steal the gold pendant Obidi got for his birthday or the new shirts Nkana's mother brought him last week or the ...?"

"No, n-o-o ..." the boy cried. "I swear to the Ideamala; all I took was some cans of baked beans. I was hungry ... please forgive me, prefect."

The prefect turned to Emodi. "I believe him. Can we continue?"

The test was resumed. The preacher's son, Carter's second suspect, put the noose around his neck. His eyes were dancing nervously while he declared his innocence. Nothing happened.

Carter sighed with disappointment. He could have bet money on the boy's guilt. Now, he was convinced the test had backfired so his eyes continued their tour of the ancient hall. The place was a museum, Carter thought, except it was practically still in use, functioning naturally and heaven knows for how much longer.

The sun had taken refuge behind the clouds giving the keeper's den a weird eerie aura. Carter's renewed interest in the skulls was suddenly broken by a mass sharp intake of breath by the boys when they gasped with shock. Carter's eyes flashed to the rope. It was such a quick unsteady glance that at first he thought his eyes were deceiving him. He gazed, and sure enough the noose was tightening around the boy's neck. The loose end of the rope that disappeared into the basket was not moving at all so Carter was sure that nothing was pulling it tight from within the basket. It was the knot itself that was slowly closing in as if an invisible finger was drawing it shut.

The boy stood petrified to a trance. Either he could not believe what was happening or was too scared to make his confession. By the time he stammered out a few throttled words the rope was too tight around his neck. His tongue stuck out, his eyes bulged. Then Carter came to a sudden realization ... Chuka! The boy with the monkey, the boy who carried Carter's briefcase from class. Chuka's tongue had only been sticking out for several seconds, but seemed like minutes to Carter.

Carter looked at Emodi inquiringly and found his face calm, as if nothing was happening. The other students had relaxed after the initial surprise. The keeper kept chanting. Carter was so alarmed and confused that he didn't see the rope slackening from the boy's neck. He lurched forward towards Chuka who now had his hand around his neck. Emodi reached out to hold Carter back but could not bring himself to grab on to Carter's shirt like he intended to. Instead he let him slip by towards the deathly rope and basket. Emodi's hand was still in mid-air when Carter reached for the noose.

"Philip, don't!" Emodi managed to shout.

Several boys cried their warning but Carter was reaching out for Chuka's neck. In a flash, his hand diverted and gave a vicious tug at the basket end of the rope, apparently to yank it loose from the basket. At the first contact with the rope Carter's body shook and quivered violently as if a high voltage of electricity had passed through it. He fell back clutching at his head. His teeth bared in a deathly grin, his eyes flashing wildly. When Carter staggered towards the entrance, the boys broke the chain to let him pass. The howl of the Ideamala bird resounded through the chamber seemingly coming out of the cave walls.

Carter fell on his knees still holding his head then crashed to the floor, face down. He lay still and unconscious. It all happened so fast. Emodi and the boys stood rigidly in their places, looking like the rest of the ebony carvings.

The keeper, consequently responding to the emergency, rushed out of his cubicle carrying a small clay pot with a miniature broom sticking out of it. He stirred the contents of the pot with the broom and brushed the brown liquid across Carter's lips, forehead and hair. He then withdrew a tiny gourd from his satchel and blew two pinches of its powdery contents up Carter's nostrils, using a reed pipe.

Carter opened his eyes. He stared distantly at the faces around him as if he had never seen them before and laughed; a careless chilling laughter of insane degeneracy. The boys drew backwards. The keeper rushed back into the cubicle and came out with a wooden box.

"Philip … Philip, are you all right?" Emodi was kneeling down, feeling a little foolish at the absurdity of his own question.

Carter leapt to his feet when he saw the keeper approaching. The old man had taken off the dyed wrap and was clad only in loincloth, and a hat of bright red feathers, a necklace of bones and little shrunken skulls hanging down to his stomach.

The keeper's operating attire must have scared Carter in his distorted state of mind. Eyes wide open, he held out his hands as if a shield against the keeper and slowly backed towards the exit.

The keeper shouted at Emodi not to let Carter go. Emodi made a move but Carter spun around and disappeared into the dark passage before Emodi could get to him.

Emodi gathered the terrified students and led them back to the school. He then went into the village and reported the incident to the king and elders.

* * *

A search party of twenty-five men was formed in less than an hour. They set out towards the cave, combing the pregnable parts of the jungle around the main path as they went. The party was at the fork in the path when a woman coming from the river told them that there was a mad white man dancing by the river. Emodi was happy to know that Carter had made it out of the caves but the way the woman had said 'mad' made his heart sink. Emodi knew she meant 'insane.'

They found Carter stark naked and foaming at the mouth. He was sampling a line of American popular dances to a few boys who cheered him on. Apparently, all the women had left out of sheer embarrassment. Emodi tried to force back painful tears when he saw Carter. He was certain his friend had gone mad. Emodi remembered that Carter had told him earlier how shy he was when it came to dancing, even in dimly lit nightclubs. But there he was by the river in broad daylight strutting to an unheard beat with no style at all – his manhood dangling before him. As Carter himself would have said, letting it all hang out. The men held him down while Emodi forced the little gourd of liquid sedative the keeper had given him down his throat. While they waited for Carter to fall asleep four of the men fashioned a stretcher from tree stems and leaves.

* * *

Carter's betrothed, Ngozi, was sitting on his front porch crying when the men brought him home. Evidently his condition had outweighed her fear of local gossip.

She wore a gown made out of tie and dye material of blue circles in white motif. A bold belt of the same cloth strapped her waist, not so tightly but enough to give accent to her curvaceous stature. Ngozi had the looks that would have been deemed fit for an African princess. She was lithe and dark with proud, luscious lips, high cheek bones, a radiant smile that all gave her quite a regal demeanour. Yet, in her eyes lay an expression of warmth and tenderness. Ngozi Okechiukwu came from a family that was considered privileged in Obodo Ogwari due to their early, almost genetic association with the keepers. One of her ancestors Igboneme Okechiukwu had worked as an apprentice of the second keeper, acquiring a vast knowledge in the very unconventional and successful brand of alternative medicine. From then on the Okechiukwu kindred became the official helpers of the second keeper, hence they became the link between the keepers and the outside world.

Carter cherished fond memories of his first meeting with Ngozi. Though it had seemed like love at first sight for Phillip, it hadn't been so for her. It was during the Obodo Ogwari Boys Secondary School inter-house sports competition. She was cheering her younger brother, Ugo, in the hundred-metre race when Carter saw her. As she hopped and waved amid the cheering crowds, the end of the race was totally lost to Carter. All he could see was a dark enchanting goddess that skipped and danced in a world existing only for him and for her. It was only when Emeka Emodi tapped him on the shoulder that his consciousness returned to the field of Ogwari High School. A little later after the race, when Ngozi was still laughing and rejoicing with her friends, her eyes met with Carter's longing stare. She became instantly self-conscious and shy. When she was leaving with her sister, Carter's eyes trailed her every graceful step. At the school gate, just before they veered off beyond the school fence, Ngozi turned and their eyes met in one last consenting moment. The cupid had struck and the feeling was mutual. Carter consulted Emodi later to arrange an introduction between him and the girl. He was disappointed to hear that courtship in the Western sense which pervaded most of Igboland was non-existent in Obodo Ogwari. Here one had to make the most in-depth enquires in any sense or form regarding the woman he desired and thereafter request for her hand in marriage. Officially there would be no prior holding of hands, no hugging and kissing and definitely no pre-dowry coitus.

Carter was strongly confident that the girl he saw at the field was made for him. In fact he intuitively felt that meeting and marrying her was one of the prominent reasons that moved fate to bring him to Africa. What he felt in his heart could not be infatuation but true love. He asked Emodi to express his interest to the girl and if she felt the same way, to arrange for enquiries the Ogwari way.

⟨ೞ⟩‖ Seven ‖⟨ೞ⟩

Emodi and the men took Carter to his bedroom and strapped him down on the bed. Ngozi picked up a broom and started sweeping the leaves from the floor with no verbal apologies or excuses to the people in the room. By Igbo custom it was a silent and simple way of asking guests to leave.

The men got the message and filed out of the house in silence. Ngozi fetched a bucket of soapy water and started to clean up Carter's bruised and dirty body.

The principal of Obodo Ogwari Boys High School, the Honourable Walter Mbikosi, MA English Language, University of Nigeria who had acquired a partial British accent, arrived shortly. He was a mousy little man who was almost always wearing a suit and bowler hat, all in his endeavour to affect the ways of the cultured Briton. He was also part Christian which did not help place him on top of Emodi's list for village man of the year.

In his bottle-neck diction, Mbikosi condemned Emodi's idea of taking Carter back to the keeper for treatment the next day. Before he left, he gave Emodi two choices. He could first submit his resignation in the morning before going to the keeper or retain his teaching position and drive Carter to the American embassy where he would be provided with a 'specialized psychiatrist.'

How stupid could a man get? Emodi thought.

Would I stake a mere teaching job against my friend's sanity if I were sure which treatment would be more effective? The American embassy would surely send him to a little padded room with bolted down furniture and a dim barred light on top, followed by a series of slow therapy over weeks ... even years. But the keeper's treatment ... more basic ... final ... probably like the quick lowering of an axe that will either cut the chains that shackle your ankles or miss and sever your legs ... But it's all my fault. Did I say friend? Talk about staking a friend's sanity against my job. What was I staking when I let him slip by me towards the rope and basket ... Maybe it's not my fault because I'm sick ... those five dreadful years of sickness. Even my subconscious is plagued with a chronic case of racial sickness. Just like Philip's forefathers and the white bigots of South

Africa ... should Philip be accountable for the evil deeds of his ancestors against the helpess innocent black folks ... women ... children.

As much as I had wanted to avenge my five years of sickness which never left me since, I will not allow my children to be consumed by the plague of racial hatred but will teach them to beware of not the downright bigots whom you can't miss but the smiling rednecks with masks to cover their ulterior motives ... ulterior motives? ... What about Philip's ... To hell with it. After all he wants to live and die here, to make an honest woman of Ngozi ... to blend with us ... in a way he has overachieved the goal that his grandfather set for him ...

Emodi was so absorbed in his thoughts he did not see Uli the fourth keeper and the little boy come in. The boy was carrying the old wooden box on his head.

"I have come to make your friend well," said the keeper.

Excited, Emodi bounced up and hugged the keeper and held him tightly. "You think you can, Uli? You think you can?"

"Let go of me, young man," the keeper growled. "I said, I have come to make the white man well."

The keeper spent about an hour alone with Carter before he left with the little boy, giving instruction to Emodi that Carter should be allowed to rest. "Don't wake him up to eat or drink or for anything. Just let him sleep, and no loud noise."

Emodi tried to present Uli with a live cock, kolanuts and a keg of palm wine but the keeper declined.

"The whiteman has come here to help us," the old man said. "I will accept nothing for his treatment."

*   *   *

Phillip Carter woke up dazed. A euphoric feeling enveloped him as he viewed the scene before him as though he were encapsulated in a big soapy bubble. He had never been on hard drugs but the strange distant mood made him ponder what he had injested or smoked to put him in such a state. His speculation was right. The combination of potions and inhalants the fourth keeper forced on him in his semi-conscious state had caused the hallucinatory feelings. Carter stared blankly at a grossly distorted image of Ngozi who sat at the foot of his bed looking anxiously at him. He turned his head laboriously to the left and saw Emeka Emodi seated on an upright wooden chair smiling at him, his face seemingly enlarged and grotesque.

"Hi, Phillip," Emodi greeted in a thunderous voice that made Carter cover his ears with his hands.

"Speak softly," Ngozi advised Emodi. "The keeper said that he won't be able to withstand any loud sounds for the next two days or so."

"How're you feeling, Phillip?" Emodi asked softly this time.

"Don't try to talk, just nod or shake your head," Ngozi advised.

Carter nodded, childlike and obedient. The look in his eyes was enough to inform Ngozi and Emodi that the mental state had returned to normalcy, despite his flustered countenance.

Carter's mind, though hazy and confused, was beginning to recollect the ordeal he had been through since he touched the rope of the Itah. The few hours he suffered insanity were very vivid in his mind. Even when he danced naked before the villagers in the stream, his conscious mind had shunned and abhorred it yet a stronger entity within him had dominated his actions. He was conscious of his madness but could not do anything about it. Carter was like a passenger sitting in the back seat of a crowded bus with failed brakes, aware but helpless. Even in his partial consciousness, he was terror-stricken. The mischievous spirit that enveloped him had come with an aura of severe threat and malevolence that kept him completely docile.

Carter fell into another laboured slumber and woke up six hours later feeling tired but refreshed. Ngozi had gone home. Emodi assisted him in bathing and changing into fresh clean clothes.

After he ate some fruits and drank a large mug of water, Emodi took him on a walk around the school premises. Some students came close in solemn-face to say "sorry" which made Carter pleased in a very special kind of way. In his own culture back home no one said sorry in such manner for a tragedy they did not cause.

The keeper's potion had put Carter to sleep for twelve hours. He woke up dazed. His few hours under the spell of madness now felt like a nightmare. He returned to his teaching job three days later after a serious session of interrogation by the principal.

It was five months since Carter recovered from the crazy spell of the Itah. Emeka Emodi was just rounding up a mathematics session with class 4b when the school bell rang. The ringing was rapid and lengthy, to usher in the break hour. The class was virtually deserted when Phillip Carter walked in, wiping his chalky palms with a big brown bandana.

"Hey, Phillip," Emodi greeted.

"What's happening, Meks?" Carter responded using the nickname he had coined for Emeka.

"The students are going for an excursion," Emodi said. "My 3C session is cancelled. I'm going home."

"Me, too," Carter replied. "I'll fetch my books so we can walk home together," he added and hurried out of the classroom.

The road to the teachers' quarters was hemmed on both sides by cherry hedges, interspersed on both sides by an alternate arrangement of mango and amarelle trees. They lined the leaf-littered road, offering a shaded coolness from the hot but mild winds that blew across the sun-parched football field.

"Whenever I see that gleam in your eyes, Phillip, I know that something is amiss," Emodi said. Streaks of sunlight shone through the branches and danced on their bodies as they walked.

"I've always admired your sensitivity and intuition," Carter said earnestly. "As a matter of fact I have an urgent matter to discuss with you."

"I hope it's not about the Ideamala Bird again..."

"Oh! not at all," Carter interjected and remained silent.

Emodi walked and waited. Carter wasn't a man to be pushed. He was one that took quick and impulsive decisions and stormed through the enactment with pomp and zeal. There were no half measures for Phillip Carter in anything he set his heart to do. It was this same gung-ho attitude towards life that made him leave New York and relocate to this remote village without electricity and pipe-borne water, to start off where the missionaries stopped.

"I want to naturalize and settle here for good," Carter said as he walked beside Emodi.

Emodi looked startled. "I beg your pardon," he replied. He had heard Carter well but wasn't sure he drew the entire meaning from his words.

"I know you're going to tell me to think about it seriously but that won't be necessary; believe me, Emeka, I've been pondering over it for months," Carter stressed defensively as if expecting some opposition from Emodi.

"I've been thinking about my roots for a long time and wondering how I can ever go back to New York or is it to Mississippi after witnessing the caring, organized, and close-knit families you run here. I want to be part of it if you'll have me," he ended his speech abruptly and waited for Emodi's reply.

Emodi who had been silent through Carter's monologue suddenly stopped and turned to face his friend.

Carter was pensive. He stopped.

Emodi held out his hand to Carter who immediately seized it in a firm handshake.

"Welcome home, my brother," Emodi said beaming with smiles.

Carter was pleased but also surprised. "Just like that?" he asked.

"Just like that," Emodi replied and drew Carter close to him. They embraced, slapping each other on the back. When they separated, they shook hands again pumping vigorously.

"I thank you so much for accepting me without question or hesitation, Meks, but I know there may be more difficult hurdles ahead. How do we start?"

"Well, I can't think of any other Umunna, that is the combined family unit, for you to join than mine. However since you're bent on marrying Ngozi, who is my relative, I think I'll have to find another Umunna for you. It would be tantamount to incest, in fact an abomination, for you to marry from your own kindred," Emodi said in a laughter-filled voice.

Carter laughed happily. "I was really looking forward to becoming your brother, Meks, but if that would make me lose Ngozi, I think I'll pass."

"Never mind, Phillip, I'll buy some palm wine tomorrow and visit Ichie Ezeaputa who is the head, the Diokpa of my mother's Umunna. I'm sure they'll be glad to accept you as their son."

"What exactly is the Umunna?" Carter asked.

"It's the extended family unit which consists of several groups of families within. The Umunna for instance in my family system has seven extended families. These groups of families each called Imenne belong to a larger unit called Umunna which encompasses several Imennes or batches of families that trace their roots for centuries back to one man or a couple of brothers."

"That is awesome!" Carter said, surprised. "There must be hundreds of you in an Umunna, and you don't intermarry?"

"No we don't."

"How can you keep track of who and who's your relation, especially in distant lands?" Carter asked.

Emodi scratched his head in thought. "Well, in most towns, the mere mention of a girl's village of origin reveals her ancestry. But, here in Obodo Ogwari our ancestors greatly abhorred the abomination of incest therefore women from every Umunna have a title like, Onowu, Asilugo, Abadagu and so on."

"You, mean that the title of a woman you meet in Lagos or say in London, for instance, tells you can or can't have an affair with her?"

"Exactly."

"Wow! That is purely unique." Carter beamed excitedly. "Now, I've got to be part of this order; my children after me and so on. When do we start?"

"Right away," Emodi answered. "Let's go into my house and sit down. We've got to draft your citizenship application to the immigration department."

❂❘❘ Eight ❘❂

The Seventh Infantry Battalion marched in the proverbial pomp and pageantry, led by Sergeant Major Okafor. Amid sporadic bursts of jubilant gunfire, a brass band and cheering crowds of soldiers and civilians alike, they marched into the national stadium.

Hordes of local and international journalists swarmed the venue competing for vantage points for their numerous cameras and equipment.

President Aguiyi flanked by General Idris and a host of other top dignitaries sat on the stage with their entourage to receive the victorious soldiers. Every one of them was promoted a rank higher and decorated with a medal except Okafor who was made a captain. The past inadvertent omissions in his promotion were taken into consideration.

As Okafor was being decorated with medals of honour, a racous noise erupted from the left flank where the security men were holding back an agitating crowd. Before he was called to the podium to be decorated, he wondered why the crowds in that section were so excited. Upon closer observation, Okafor noticed Chiadi with some elderly men behind her. They were trying to get through the security men to come closer to the stage.

"What is the problem over there?" General Idris asked his aide-de-camp who moved off simultaneously towards Chiadi.

"They are my people, Sir," Okafor said to the general, his eyes shifting respectfully away from the general's gaze.

"Your people eh?"

"Yes, Sir," Okafor replied.

The general turned to a military police officer who stood guard behind him. "Tell my aide to let them through; just Okafor's people."

*   *   *

When the event ended, the president and all his men zoomed off, sirens blaring, leaving a motley crowd of service men and civilians straggling about the stadium.

Chiadi and the elders sat in a small restaurant that was annexed to the stadium gate. When Okafor entered, they all stood up.

The leader wore a red cap with a white eagle feather stuck to the side to flaunt his chieftaincy status. He was very lean and dark. His leathery black skin clung so fast to his bony face, as though he had been dried and smoked over an open fire for many years. He was over ninety years of age but still possessed the nimbleness and agility of a much younger man. He introduced himself as Ichie Onowu, Prime Minister to the king of Obodo Ogwari.

"I am here on behalf of Igwe Ezeobi Ajulufo the fifteenth, king of Obodo Ogwari and your own kindred who have bothered us for many years to bring you and your brothers and sisters back home." The old man cleared his throat and paused tactically, allowing the bit he had said to be absorbed.

"Oh yes! My son, we have come to inform you that in spite of the twelve good years left to complete the period of your father's banishment, the Igwe and the entire people of Obodo Ogwari have met in the town square and agreed that we grant an unconditional pardon to your father."

"Yes! That is our decision," an aged fair-skinned man in a blue caftan concurred.

"Yes, we all agreed," another bearded elderly man affirmed.

The rest of the group pledged their acquiescence with nods and grins.

"Your courage and heroism," the old man continued, "has earned great fame and recognition not only to you but to Obodo Ogwari. My son, you have put our town on the map of the world. Therefore, we have set the upcoming yam festival day to honour you in the town square. It shall be a day of reconciliation and joy when you and your brothers and sisters shall be reunited with your kinsmen. That day, we shall eat from the same plate and drink from the same cup with joy. My fellow brothers of Obodo Ogwari, I salute you." The old man finished his speech with an air of pride and magnanimity, as if he had just granted Okafor an award greater than those bestowed upon him half an hour ago by the army general and the president himself. They searched for the expected joy and elation in Okafor's face but didn't find it.

Throughout the old man's speech, Okafor maintained a vague countenance that shielded the deep emotional turmoil he was going through. On one part he felt like bursting into a jubilant song that his kinsmen had finally come to apologize. They had defied the traditional decorum and came with an unsolicited pardon rather than let him crawl to them when the period of banishment was up. His favourite native proverb, agbalusia ngene, ekulu ngene nua, that those who polluted the stream shall later drink from the same stream, had come to pass. On the other hand Okafor felt like ordering his boys to give them the 'VIP' treatment he normally gave to rogues and rebels. He would strip them down to their underwears, cover them with tarpaulin and leave them in the hot sun for their skins to soften well for his rawhide whips. The arrogant manner with which the old man spoke incensed Okafor but he was still aware of the customary respect given to elders especially the Ndi Ichie-titled chiefs of the king's cabinet. He had to restrain himself since the reunion with his kindred was his ultimate wish. Without the pardon, he would never eat and drink officially with his townsmen for twelve more years. The food Chiadi cooked and ate with him was even wrong. He would not be able to marry Chiadi or any other native of Obodo Ogwari until the ban was lifted. Okafor cleared his throat and stood up.

Chiadi noticed the fearsome gleam in his eyes and made a surreptitious plea with her hands, bending an imploring head to the side. Their eyes met and he paused. His eyes softened a bit and he began to speak.

"Ichie Onowu, my fellow people of Obodo Ogwari, I greet you and thank you very much for granting my father this special pardon. I am most grateful for your kindness and thoughtfulness." Okafor cleared his throat again and paused to watch their smiling faces and nods of acceptance.

"But then I wonder," Okafor continued, "would you have given us this pardon if I hadn't succeeded so well in my career as a soldier? Would you have granted this pardon if I hadn't, as you said, put Obodo Ogwari on the world map, would you have remembered me? Oh! I'm sure there are others before me who have not been pardoned. Some have even died lonely shameful deaths in distant lands and no one cared. Ask yourselves, is it fair?"

"But, son," the old man cut in, "life is not always fair; these things are done by merit. Those ones did not merit …"

"Well I don't appreciate that kind of merit, Sir," Okafor snapped. "For many years, my father took us from place to place, while he searched for work. As a farmer he had no other work experience and soon after my mother died in an uncompleted building while giving birth to a set of stillborn twins, my father resorted to alcohol. After we were forcibly ejected by the building contractor, we had to disperse. Staying together as a family was not doing us any good. I found work with a trailer driver who traveled long distances across the border and stayed with him until I was old enough to join the army …"

"You don't have to recount all these experiences to us, Okafor," the man in blue caftan advised. "Every family banished from their homeland has their own sad stories. It is the price you pay…"

"Let me finish!" Okafor said coldly. The fearsome gleam had returned some to his eyes.

"Allow him to get it all out," Ichie Onowu stated.

Okafor scowled in indignation and resumed his monologue. "Do you know how I've felt for years wondering what happened to my father and my brothers? My father, I heard, worked in a factory and fell into some type of machinery that hacked him to pieces. Of course we know he most probably committed sucide. My sister, out of desperation, became the fourth wife of an old dibia who turned her into a mindless slave."

"How about your two brothers?" the old man asked compassionately, a mischievous tinge in his gaze.

"I haven't been able to trace them. I don't even know if they're dead or alive," Okafor replied sadly. "Now tell me, what am I coming home for? With whom am I coming? Alone with all the bad memories and the shame that has followed me around all these years?"

"Are you trying to say that you reject our pardon, that you're not coming back?"

"Well … not exactly. Do I wish to remain a single tree standing in the wasteland? No, I shall come back but only on one condition."

"And what may that be?" the old man asked.

"That the laws of banishment in Obodo Ogwari be reviewed and all natives banished for whatever offences, pardoned."

66

"Abomination!" shouted the man in blue caftan. "The laws have been with us for centuries and even when others were changing, we kept our ancient laws and that is why we are admired today as the only town in these parts without crime and moral decadence. We cannot change."

Okafor laughed dryly and shook his head. "We blame the white man for all our social and moral woes yet it was when the missionaries came that our neighbours stopped throwing away their twins and infants that cut the upper tooth first. It was when the missionaries came that we stopped eating our fellow humans or offering them as sacrifice to the gods and many other atrocities. Banishing our fellow brothers from our homeland for half a century for stealing a cow or a goat seems to me an atrocity itself and I think it's time we opened up to change. Our neighbours in the seven sister towns have all changed."

The man in caftan and some others in the group started to protest but Ichie Onowu held up his hand for silence.

"Let's not be too hasty, my brothers. Captain Okafor may have just expressed the opinion of half the cabinet chiefs including myself. Before we leave, Captain, we have some presents for you from the king." He turned and nodded at Chiadi Okolo.

Chiadi bounced up from her chair and gave Okafor a mischievous wink before she rushed out. Five minutes later she came back with two men who were both carrying travel bags.

Okafor's attention went to the bags wondering what kind of presents the king would send him in bags. Customarily, he would have expected a goat and yams or in the least, some bottles of imported hard liquor. It was the broad smiles on the young men's faces that shifted his attention from the bags. One of the men called Okafor 'Boboh', the pet name their father used to call him. Immediately, Okafor recognized them. He rushed to his brothers, Ibe and Kenechi, and hugged them one after the other without saying a word. He was dumbfounded with joy. He did not try to hide the tears that started to flow down his cheeks.

Nine

Emodi stood on Carter's front porch, hollering at him to come outside. His extra lively and boisterous disposition came from the anxiety to surprise Carter with a piece of news and to share the sweet palm wine he had stumbled on. Emodi had gone to a neigbouring village to convince an old tapper to send his children to school and received a fairly large gourd of fresh wine as a gift. He set the gourd on the patio table and called out to Carter to come with cups.

Carter emerged smiling broadly. He had two large glass mugs in his hands. "The moment I heard that tinge of excitement in your voice, I knew you must have come up with something good," Carter said as he sat down on one of his locally made patio chairs.

Emodi filled the two mugs to the brim. "You ain't heard the best of it yet," he replied, borrowing Carter's American manner of speaking. He took a sip from his mug and smacked his lips in savour of the strong but sweet and sour nkwu enu. "As I was coming back from Ugagwo, the village where I got this wine, I received word that my uncle, Ezeaputa, wanted to see me so I went straight there."

"And what did he say?" Carter asked anxiously.

"Relax, my man, as we say to a child, don't suck a lump on the skin, the breast is coming" Emodi teased.

"Oh! Come on, Meks, quit all that suspense and tell me what it is," Carter pressed on.

"Guess what, the king and all his chiefs held their normal meeting to deliberate on this year's upcoming Yam Festival and after the meeting your matter was brought up by Ichie Ezeaputa. Guess what again ..."

"I've run out of guesses. Emeka Emodi, just shoot."

"Well ..." Emodi adjusted the collar of his shirt and inspected his nails perfunctorily.

Carter rolled his eyes and looked up to the bright blue skies in feigned boredom.

"Well ... can you beat this?" Emodi asked, his entire face lit up with excitement. "Unanimously, and I mean totally, the king, Igwe Ajulufo and all his chiefs have decided to confer us with chieftancy titles, Ugoabata and Okwuluora and it shall be done on the Yam Festival day. Take it from me, only very few people have been graced with such honour."

Carter leaped inwardly at the news of his upcoming conferment of an ozo title but there was no physical reaction except for a strained smile that danced momentarily on his lips.

"What's the matter? Aren't you pleased with the news I brought you?"

"I am greatly honoured," Carter said earnestly. "But ... I just wonder ... why us? We're just high school teachers in Ogwari, who would have been okay with a normal quiet occasion. What have I personally done to deserve this special honour?"

Emodi shifted uneasily on his chair. "I know I shouldn't tell you what I'm about to tell you now but what the hell!" Emodi bit on his upper lip and reflected for a moment. "I heard that in the meeting of the king and council, they decided that since the white man came into Africa many centuries ago all our people have been doing is borrowing and borrowing. First we borrowed their religion and then their language; we took their names and some have even forgotten theirs completely. We have even gone as far as borrowing their culture and mannerisms, even their food." Emodi paused and took a sip of wine.

"But in your own case it's the reverse. You have not only defied but disproved the negative status quo and stigma that the Western world has branded on us for centuries."

Emodi paused again and rotated the mug of wine on his opened palm, then his voice took on a raspy and emotional quality.

"Phillip, you have shown true love for our people and I speak with every conviction that the people of Obodo Ogwari bear the same brotherly love and affection for you."

Carter bowed his head slightly, looking downwards. He was obviously moved by Emodi's words. His ample cheeks blushed as a flurry of wind blew his long red hair across his face, as though to hide his mild embarrassment. He flicked his hair to the side before he spoke.

"When I came here, I wasn't coming to settle down for good. I wasn't even sure what I was going to meet. But, when I arrived I saw that I could be a little useful to the kids and maybe a couple of villagers as well. However, it's basically all about number one, me! Where I can get fulfilment, job satisfaction and all that." He took a sip of wine and licked his lips. "Well, if the Igwe and his chiefs decide that I deserve an honour for doing my thing then so be it. But, mind you, I don't have money to fete the entire guests of the yam festival. How about you?"

Emodi broke into laughter. "Now I know why you've been nervous about the whole thing. Stop hiding you miserly old rascal." He laughed some more. "You have very loyal relations now. The entire town sponsors the Yam Festival through the age grades and just wait and see what the people will do before that day."

For a while the two friends drank in silence each reflecting on his own inner thoughts.

Carter held the gourd by the neck and shook vigorously to mix the potent dregs with the little liquid that was left.

"The dregs of the wine is usually left for a man that has a task at hand in the home. One who's wife is eager to conceive." Emodi smiled slyly, a mischievous glint in his eyes.

"I know and that's why I'm going to consume most of it," Carter replied. "Ngozi and I are gearing up for that desirable task ahead." He poured a fair share into his mug and then in Emodi's.

As he watched the white sediments swimming in the liquid, Carter felt the warmth and flighty solace that wine always provided. The mild concern and apprehension he was experiencing over his yam festival conferment subsided. This, he felt also, was a good time to ask his friend certain sensitive questions about the town. There were many strange things that puzzled him about Obodo Ogwari and its people but he never bothered to pry. Though the natives were kind, peaceful and friendly, Obodo Ogwari was an ancient town, full of rules, secrets and spiritual intrigue. Carter knew he had to tread softly in order to fully adapt and be accepted. Despite Emodi's friendliness Carter knew he was clannish and sincerely bound to his ancient culture and its preservation. Nothing was more important to this traditional man who practically shelved his London degrees to settle down in his primitive village.

The two teachers were down to a quarter of the gourd before Carter appeared to have become a little restless. Emodi noticed.

"I know something is itching you, Phillip, so, let it out; the Yam festival I suppose."

"No-o- No!" Carter replied. "It's about certain things concerning the town."

"Like?"

"Well, em ... I noticed, for starters, that villagers apparently practise some kind of birth control. You don't have too many kids like other Africans. Then there's this issue of longevity. There're hardly any youth and infant deaths here. I've always wondered whether it's just coincidence or sheer luck but now I'm sure it has a reason. Almost all the young corpses are brought back from the cities. In fact I haven't witnessed the burial of any resident of Obodo Ogwari who died before the age of eighty five. I don't even want to go into the ages of the keepers of Ideamala, the Gundu priests. That one is for the book of dinosaurs and the ice age. Frankly speaking, Meks, these are things among others that have been bothering and puzzling me."

"You are very observant, Phillip," Emodi said passively. "When the time comes the unknown will be made known. The leaves that cover your eyes shall drop and you will begin to see the light."

Carter looked expectantly at Emodi hoping to get a little more information. But, the decisive ending of his statement clarified that nothing more was forthcoming. Carter would just have to wait for the right moment if it would ever come. He picked up his glass and drank the last dregs of the wine.

Carter's desire to settle down in Obodo Ogwari had not come as a surprise, even to Ezeaputa and the Igwe. After his encounter with the Ideamala Bird, the villagers had expected him to abscond from the town as most visitors had done. His second encounter with the ancient bird which rendered him temporarily insane should have been his final reason to pack his luggages and head back to New York City. But, not only had he stayed, the man Carter became more involved in the social life of Obodo Ogwari. He attended funerals, marriages, wrestling contests and other functions in the village and began to learn the native language.

While Emodi remained his bosom friend and cultural guide, Carter made numerous friends throughout the town. When he started to attend social functions without Emodi, the villagers began to see him differently. Carter was no longer a visitor who came to village ceremonies like a curious tourist, guided by the native, Emodi, but one who came, like any other villager, to pay his respects or social obligations to the celebrants or mourners. Phillip Carter had become one of them. The only area where he felt lacking was in the family structure. Carter found out that the extended family network with its complexities of marital and maternal relations was his only deficiency in connections. In this close-knit web, everyone was related in a round about way either by marriage, maternal or paternal kinship. As soon as he married Ngozi, Carter would be hooked up to her family as an in-law. He was very pleased with the knowledge that his marriage to Ngozi would not only make him an in-law, an Ogoh, but immediately weave him into the fabrics of Ngozi's extended family systems. As an Ogoh, he would be entitled to so many rights and privileges and also commitments and responsibilities. With his ever-growing knowledge of the customs and traditions Carter already knew among other facts, that he would be officially notified of every event in his Ogoh's family and that he would be responsible for providing a cow and the burial mats, bamboo barks, the coffin for the burial of Ngozi's father whenever he passed on. This was by virtue of Ngozi being the first daughter of her father. Furthermore, Carter's assimilation into the Ifeadigo clan would, on a much larger scale, weld him onto the ancient structure of the family extensions as if by paternal birth. Once he was accepted, there would be no discriminations or prejudices. Carter would get his share of meat for every goat or cow slaughtered on behalf of the Ifeadigo and would also contribute his own share in decision-making and for the burial rites of every married male that died in the Ifeadigo clan among other customary functions.

⟨⟩‖ Ten ‖⟨⟩

The Igwe of Obodo Ogwari sat in his ancient throne musing over the wind of change that was brewing in the spiritual realm of his kingdom. It had been revealed to him in a dream four market days ago before Igo, sixth keeper of the Ideamala, came to report his own revelation.

With fabulous tales of the ancient sixth keeper's supernatural abilities, Igo was rated a legend in his time. He studied the Bible and the Koran and researched other religions of the Far East and India in a quest to compare and improve his own skills. From Emodi he procured books and old newspapers and read with ardour.

When Igo came into the king's compound, he was greeted by the young men who kept watch over the palace. In the ancient days they dressed in warriors' regalia complete with amulets and talismans and armed with spears, bows and arrows, crude daggers strapped to their arms. Now, the young men were physically unarmed and wore shorts and T-shirts. However, they had easy access to a cache of double barrel shotguns, two sub-machine guns and plenty of live ammunition. The guns had been brought by a visiting miner called Jake Sanders who had armed his personal guards with the weapons after an attack by night marauders while prospecting for precious stones. Jake Sanders came and asked the king for a temporary place to reside, from where he would take off to the sites, a village two miles away. He told the king that he had heard about the sanctity and honesty of his people and wanted to use his town as a base. The king, Igwe Ajulufo xv, took an immediate liking to the loud and boisterous American who ate kola nuts and alligator peppers and drank up two gourds of palm wine that were set before him. Jake Sanders was given a wing of the palace that was originally built for visiting emissaries, and the like, who came to the remote area for one purpose or another. When Sanders moved in, he came with his guards and his guns. But, he was soon to find out that the bodyguards and arms were only necessary when he crossed the boundaries of Obodo Ogwari and entered the neighbouring lands. The king had told him, the day they met, that no self-respecting thief or bandit in the area would venture into Obodo Ogwari to steal. The Igwe let him know, as a matter of fact, that nothing had been stolen in the town for over fifty years. Slave traders who strayed beyond their boundaries and kidnapped two boys working on the farm over two centuries ago were found roaming aimlessly within the farm for days till they were arrested. By the time the first keeper's assistant was sent to deal with them three days later, they were already dying of hunger and exhaustion. Meanwhile the boys had been rescued and sent home.

Jake Sanders became a regular companion of the Igwe in the evenings when he came back from his prospecting trips with his motorcycle convoy. Obodo Ogwari was almost surrounded by high rocky hills and deep wide gullies, leaving only one adequate approach, a table land with a narrow jungle path for bikes and pedestrians as the only entrance into the town. This was deliberate, to prevent cars and larger vehicles from entering the town to bring undesirable social and cultural changes. Igwe and Jake Sanders would eat roast yams and smoked venison and drink palm wine, chatting well into the night. At times Sanders would stroll alone toward the caves. The Igwe's halting English improved tremendously in the year that Jake spent with him. Jake was a thrilling diversion to the aging king who was confined to his palace. By tradition, certain ancient Igbo kings never left their palace except during the yam festival, Ofala, when the king appeared publicly and gave his subjects a chance to see him once, annually. The Ofala was a highly festive and colourful celebration in Obodo Ogwari that villagers looked forward to each year. The occasion had a set, customary procedure that was strictly followed each year when the new yam was ushered in. Cannon shots introduced the festive day at the break of dawn. From morning the king's palace came alive with the playing of the uffio musical instrument, like the ekwe, but a bigger hollowed tree trunk also played with two sticks. It was played by a skilled uffio player in the special way.

Large quantities of roast yams were brought before the king which he dipped in salted peppered palm oil and shared to the children in the crowd. There was a mad rush among the children who all wanted to receive a piece of yam each from the king's hand. In Ogwariland and environs, this exercise was called Ikpo Onunu. The age grades appeared before King Ajulufo playing their various brands of music, singing and dancing while presenting their gifts. The next stage, then came Jake Sanders' best part in all the programs of the Ofala, the Owuwa. In contrast to the king's first appearance in his flowing colourful robes and a dazzling crown when he danced majestically through the Ofala grounds smiling and waving at the cheering crowds, his appearance in the Owuwa was a lot different. The Ofala being a day that visitors even from other towns attended, it was believed that even enemies who planned evil for the king also would attend. Over the centuries it had become customary for the king to retire to his palace after the first appearance and change into a warlike regalia decked with charms around his waist, arms and neck and carrying a big flat golden sword.

Upon his re-emergence, Igwe Ajulufo's attitude and demeanour became mean and hostile. His musicians changed to an up-tempo percussive song with ancient war chants. The king danced through the same cheering crowds now surging at clusters of people with his sword, ready as if for a kill. This part of the ceremony called Owuwa, was a message to visitors with evil intent to leave or face whatever consequence, physical or spiritual, that may ensue.

At Jake's first Ofala experience, when Igwe Ajulufo emerged in his battle-ready attire, his demeanour mean and aggressive, Jake was curious. A court clerk from the city who was attending the celebration explained the significance of the Igwe's act to him. The American quickly organized his bodyguards. While the king charged at the teeming crowds with his cabinet chiefs, warriors and musicians close behind him, Jake Sanders followed firing into the air with his automatic shotgun and shouting: 'Let's get dem evil suckers out of this show for good.' Simultenously, his bodyguards blasted away with their double-barrel shotguns. Some celebrants who took to their heels and didn't come back were deemed clandestine enemies of the king and elders. Some were innocent visitors simply scared of firearms. Nevertheless the reaction caused by Jake's participation gave more relevance to the advent of Owuwa in the Ofala celebration. It was to be the most memorable celebration in recent times. Jake repeated the same act in the following year's yam festival and thereafter discharge of firearms during Owuwa became tradition in Obodo Ogwari. When he was 'transferred to Monrovia' by the mining company, Jake Sanders left the guns and plenty of live rounds of ammunition for Igwe Ajulufo who was sad to see him go. All subsequent Ofalas were graced with gunshots during the Owuwa and soon other kingdoms began to adopt the new custom.

*   *   *

Igwe Ezeobi Ajulufo sat on his ancient throne reminiscing on the memorable period the American spent in his kingdom when Igo stepped into the large mud hall. The Igwe's court where he presided over cases was an expansive red-mud structure that could seat over a hundred people on polished mud benches that jutted out of the walls with colourful yellow and blue designs of abstract motif. In this same court his forefathers had tried cases of murder, violations of official infanticide and other atrocities.

Two aged midgets of the Nri clan sat on small stools intricately carved from ebony wood. In other kingdoms they were usually medicine men who gave the king spiritual guidance and protection. In Obodo Ogwari, dwarfed by the Ideamala, they were simply symbolic figureheads of culture; ones whose presence was necessary in every notable dynasty, who stood in readiness to cleanse the land of any possible abomination.

"Eze ga adi ndu lue mgbe ebighi ebi, may the king live forever," Igo greeted Igwe Ajulufo

"Ichie Igo, you are welcome." Ajulufo addressed Igo as an Ichie simply as a mark of respect.

After they had eaten kola nuts and drank some shots of home-made gin, the Igwe spoke. "Whenever Igo visits me very early or very late I know he bears very good or very bad tidings. Which shall it be this time?"

"Igwe, I wish I knew what it is but I know it is good and it is bad ..."

Igo's words were broken by the king's laughter. "Good and bad, indeed," the king commented in a tone of amusement. "What puzzling manner you speak, sixth keeper. What on earth can be good and bad all at once?"

Igo did not share the Igwe's high spirits and humour. His face remained grave and focused.

"Igwe ka ala," he addressed the king with a special mark of respect to convey the seriousness of his visit. "A great catastrophe is about to befall us. Everything we hold and stand for as a people is about to be destroyed."

The Igwe's face tightened instantly into a frown. All traces of humour disappeared in the twinkle of an eye. The sixth keeper was the custodian and guardian of security and culture in Obodo Ogwari. He was the Commander-in-Chief of the Obodo Ogwari armed forces yet there was no army. Single-handedly the sixth keeper many generations before had defeated a troop of British soldiers who came to arrest Igwe Emenanjo Ajulufo of Obodo Ogwari for ordering the killing of six slave traders. The sixth keeper had dipped an old tattered broom in a clay pot of dark potions and waved it at the soldiers setting sergeant against corporal and officer against rank and file, in fierce quarreling. It was later reported in Obodo Ogwari that the officer who led the operation went home and reported that Igwe Emenanjo Ajulufo whom they were ordered to arrest was dead. The decision was said to be unanimous among the soldiers after they came out of their trance-like fisticuffs.

Since the protection of the town rested solely on the sixth keeper it was serious for Igo to make the pronouncement he just did to Igwe Ajulufo.

"Don't spare my feelings," said the king, "don't oil your words. Give it to me straight."

Igo twirled the ivory bangle around his wrist in thoughtful fidgeting. "Igwe, a great change, one that we have not known before, is coming our way. The government is going to build an express highway through Obodo Ogwari ... not only is it coming through our town, its course is right by the caves ...."

"The cave of Ideamala? The sanctuary of the Gundu?" the Igwe asked, sliding sharply forward to the edge of his throne.

The sixth keeper nodded sadly. "Yes, my king, but we must fight. Let it go down in the history of this country that the people of Obodo Ogwari put up a great fight to protect that one special thing they have strived to protect over the centuries."

"You sound as if all is lost already," the king said.

"I'm afraid ... I don't quite understand the revelations. It's as if … I don't quite understand, yet."

The king frowned in a moment of recollection. "Then this must have something to do with a dream I had four market days ago … A great wind blew from the direction of the city. The great bird of Ideamala stood at the crest of a high hill, its wings spread wide as though to protect its eggs from the powerful wind. At first, the bird's body and wing feathers served as a shield, preventing the wind from getting past it. Then, all of a sudden, the body feathers started to molt and then the wings, then bits and pieces of the goose-pimpled body parts until the entire bird disintegrated into nothingness. The hill crumbled into dust and dispersed in the wind."

The sixth keeper shook his head, pessimistic. "The hill in your dream represents the caves and of course the bird you saw needs no introduction. Your dream confirms my message."

"When you came, Ichie Igo, you told me your message was good and bad. Is there a good part in all this?"

The sixth keeper smiled. "Igwe ka ala. The catastrophe that is to befall us seems horrible even to think about but signs of the aftermath seem bright and good."

"What do you mean by that, Igo?" the Igwe demanded gruffly, wondering how evil can suddenly turn good.

"I kept pushing the waves … searching to know our fate," Igo answered urgently. It was clear from the urgency in his voice that this was the climax of his visit to the Igwe; the culmination of his shocking revelations. "After the express road rapes and violates our people then what … What becomes of us?" Igo asked a rhetorical question.

"Shame and humiliation," the Igwe interjected, "death and disaster, no doubt."

"I don't think so, Igwe. What kept coming up was a strange brightness, like the glow of a distant star in a dark, cloudy night." Igo's face became flushed, his greenish eyes keen but remote, as if he was seeing the vision just then.

"There were always pockets of darkness but that strange aura of shining brightness was mostly there. Each time it appeared I was seized by uncontrollable happiness."

"I don't know what you're talking about," the Igwe protested, shaking his head impatiently. "Come back to my language, Igo."

"Igwe, this is why I said that the future appears to be good even after the road goes through …"

"Abomination!" Igwe screamed.

"Who are we to say?"

"But the Ideamala …" Igwe started to argue.

"Don't we have Chiukwu, the universal God?"

"Is there a doubt?" Igwe asked.

"Who stands over all gods," said Igo.

"It is unthinkable, the Ideamala works. Osebuluwa, God, installed it."

The Igwe was visibly shaken by this conversation that seemed nothing short of blasphemy against their deity, blasphemy that may attract punishment, repercussion. It seemed apparent that the sixth keeper had been tainted by his ardent interaction with other religions and cultures through the numerous books that he read. There was a strained silence between them while the two old men searched their minds and souls for that deep-seated intuition that often led one to right decisions at such crucial moments. For Igo, his decision needed less mind search. After the numerous hours spent in searching the spiritual realms in his cave dwelling, there was very little doubt in his mind as to his final judgment on the issue.

"Igwe ka ala," Igo began. "I know you're not so happy with this news I have come with. In fact you now doubt my genuineness. Even the other five keepers will surely isolate and abandon me on this issue if I was to go to them but I didn't. Don't forget, I am the sixth keeper, the keeper of the oracle and divination. I hold the mystery of the ages, yet I hold no power to change anything, just to report my findings and that, I have done to the best of my ability. Igwe, may I take my leave?"

"Wait," the king said in a pleading tone. "I believe you, Igo, but my question is if the road must come through here, why fight it?"

"It is the fight that would lead to the light," Igo replied and their eyes locked in a moment of mutual understanding.

◟‖ Eleven ‖◞

In the early hours of the morning, the giant drums at Ogwari hills began to speak. They pounded and rumbled pausing with emphatic intervals in the esoteric language of the drums. The sound filtered through the dew-spangled forests into distant quarters of Obodo Ogwari and to some neighbouring towns. The dull hammering roused man, beast and birds alike from the depths of their pre-dawn slumber, informing those who could interpret the sounds, of the oncoming event. Four market days earlier, a town crier had gone round, a metal gong in hand, and announced to the villagers the oncoming ceremony of Phillip Carter's integration with the Ifeadigo umunna. Now, the invitation by the giant drums was only a reminder. Those who could interpret the drum language told others that the day had arrived for the American to join the ancient lineage of the Ifeadigo.

The man, Ogbuefi Akunne Ezeako, who played the speaking drums had inherited the skill from his father. In spite of the coldness of the early morning breeze, beads of perspiration sprouted on Akunne's upper lip, his neck and arms as he pounded deftly on the high-strung leather.

A winding hunting track had led Akunne and his grown son up the Ogwari Hills, Ugwu Ogwari, the highest vantage point in the land where the two giant ancient drums were mounted. It had spent over a century in the Ibenagu family until they were unable to produce a suitable successor to take custody of the drums. This brought about a search and final selection of a musician from the Ezeako clan. The selected custodian was usually one who exhibited certain rhythmic traits and other creative talents especially in puns and coining of proverbs, a poetic man.

When the aged Ogbuefi Akunne climbed up the sturdy ladder to the platform that would give him access to the colossal twin drums, his forty-year-old son, Ntupuanya, who was taking over from his father, applied palm oil to the flames of the banana bark torch. The torch had given them light as they trekked through the forest to the base of the hill. It had also deterred wild animals from attacking them as they went up the cold lonely trail. But, when Ogbuefi began to play the threat of wild animals ended. No animal would attack them then with or without the torch. The rythms enchanted both man and beast.

Ntupuanya had practically taken over operation of the speaking drums from his father but on special occasions, Ogbuefi Akunne insisted on playing out the codes himself. In this same magnanimous spirit Ogbuefi decided on making Carter's announcement himself, he had rejected the yams and live cock Emodi and Carter brought to pay him homage for the drum announcement, sharing only the palm wine and kola nuts with the two friends and few visitors that were in his house. The old man was very fond of Carter. Sometimes when he passed by the school he stopped to visit and chat with the whiteman. Emodi used to be quite amused listening to their awkward but diligent conversation. Somewhere between Ogbuefi's halting English, Carter's faltering Igbo and lots of hand signals, they were able to churn out a conversation. Ogbuefi admired Carter's outgoing behaviour and humility. Most of all, he was fascinated by Carter's red hair. Ogbuefi had seen many a whiteman in his day but they were mostly clean cut blonds and brunettes. The blonds did not thrill him so much since his village albinos had yellowish hair. He never deemed it possible for a human being to have such long red hair as Carter's. In his mind, he often likened Carter to a big white cock with a shining prominent red comb. Since it would be rude to coin a name for him using the Igbo name for cock, he decided that Carter was more of a white eagle, Ugo, than a rooster and named him, Ugoabata, meaning: an eagle has come which also connoted Ugo as an eagle feather being the official symbol of an ozo title. Finding out that Carter desired to naturalize in Obodo Ogwari was very thrilling for Ogbuefi Akunne. He loved Carter as though he were one of his sons. Other white men he had known did not behave like Phillip Carter who often came into his Iba, the large round hut that served as his sitting room, and ate roasted yams with a mixture of palm oil, peppers and oil-bean seeds with him from the same wooden mortar. Gradually, the name Akunne coined for him began to take hold until Carter became known to the entire town as Ugoabata. Titles were very important to them especially for men above middle age. It was disrespectful for youths to address elders by their first names, especially for old bachelors like Carter who had no children so as to be called Nna Chika, the father of Chika, or the like.

When Ogbuefi picked up the twin clubs he used for the drum message, he started with a sharp monotonous pounding that bore no message at all. It was simply a sound to rouse and catch the attention of those who were still in bed. Many villagers who had distant farms were up at that time in preparation for their trip to the farm or long treks to distant markets. Following the sharp pounding, Ogbuefi began to greet the king, Igwe Ezeobi Ajulufo, calling him the mighty king above all kings in the region. The drums wished the Igwe everlasting life before it began to salute the villagers.

"Obodo Ogwari ekenee mu unu. Obodo Ogwari mma mma nu ..."

All of a sudden, he stopped, dropped the drumsticks and rubbed his perspiring palms together. It was a tactical pause that primed the attentiveness of the villagers who were now eager to know what announcement the drums had to make. Whenever the ancient twin drums spoke, the people of Obodo Ogwari listened and responded.

In Ogbuefi Akunne's own poetic coinage the drums told the people that Ugoabata was about to join the Ifeadigo and that food and drinks would be so plentiful even the sons of Anayam could not finish it all. Anayam was a legendary king who had hundreds of wives and thousands of children. In truth, the food to be consumed at Ama Osinachi would be so plenteous that Carter alone could not have afforded it. After he brought the token food and drinks that Ezeaputa asked for, the Ifeadigo extended clan contributed mounds of yams and cocoyams, chickens, goats, venison, palm oil and other food items for the occasion. Unmarried teenage girls had gathered huge heaps of firewood for the women of the extended family who would come out *en masse* to cook in huge cast iron pots.

Right after Ogbuefi relayed the vital message, he developed a complex rhythm from the last message and kept playing it for a while, building a song out of it. Faster and faster he drummed till it peaked in a rumbling crescendo and petered out in dull echoes that were instantly absorbed by the damp ominous jungle.

The king, Igwe Ezeobi Ajulufo was a light sleeper, especially in the wee hours of the morning that was usually dark as a moonless night. When the speaking drums roused him from his shallow slumber, the Igwe sat up on his feather-quilted mud bed and listened. The information that the day had come for Ugoabata to join the Ifeadigo brought a smile to his face. It would be a sight to see, a special occasion to be enjoyed. At times like this he almost wished he could disguise himself and attend the event incognito. As the drum message was relayed, the Igwe was certain that the old man Ogbuefi Akunne who had practically retired from service was at the helm of the drums himself and not his son, Ntupuanya. Igwe Ajulufo wished, for the sake of posterity, that Ntupuanya would one day acquire the full skill of his father, his musical and poetic talents. As the tempo of the speaking drums progressed towards a crescendo, Igwe Ajulufo got up from his bed and began to dance, a slow regal gyration that seemed to make mockery of the extremely fast beat. Ugoabata I was most appropriate for Phillip Carter. The man was white like an eagle and had come from afar. Once again, the Igwe marveled at Ogbuefi Akunne's ability to coin new adages, proverbs and titles. It was not a coincidence that the name had been suggested by the same man who had been the guardian of the twin drums for sixty years. Ugoabata I was to be Phillip Carter's ozo title, specially dubbed by the king himself; Ugoabata the first, of Obodo Ogwari. It was to mark an epoch of Ugoabatas in the Ifeadigo family dynasty.

*   *   *

The Ama Osinachi was suddenly filled with the voices of many excited village men, women and children. They had been holding a respectful silence in observation of the speeches made by various men of prominence in the village. At the head of the gathering was Ichie Ezeaputa, a member of the king's cabinet and the oldest male of Umu-Ifeadigo family line. Ezeaputa had invited members of the cabinet and ozo-titled lower chiefs to receive Phillip Carter, who was to be inducted into his immediate family. It was not an unusual practice. Many families in villages across Igboland had come as visitors, settlers who later attached themselves to an umunna after being officially integrated. The only extraordinary factor in this case was that Carter was a Caucasian. So far in the history of the region, no whiteman had ever made such a request. Some had come and settled as visitors, lived their lives in various villages, died and were buried. Some had kept mistresses and fathered children out of wedlock but none had officially wanted to blend traditionally, genetically.

When Emodi went to see Ichie Ezeaputa to discuss the issue with him, he had been pensive, worried about how the old chief would respond to it. The Ichie was a man given to impulsive temperaments. He was a kind but complex man whose principles were diverse and unpredictable. When Emodi presented Carter's intention of joining his umunna, Ezeaputa's face took on a puzzled expression before he broke into an uncontrolled laughter. Emodi was embarrassed. He stood staring at the Ichie, a sheepish grimace crossing his dark countenance. He waited anxiously for the old man to complete his laughter to find out what was so funny. Ichie Ezeaputa laughed till tears seeped out of the corners of his eyes. When he spoke, his shoulders still shook with titters.

"Didn't they always tease us, your mother's people, your Ikwunne, for being the smallest umunna in the town?" Ezeaputa spoke, his eyes gleaming excitedly. "Now we're going to be the only umunna that has a whiteman as our clansman."

Emodi laughed. Now he could see the Ichie's humour though not so vividly. The old chief had a better knowledge of how Carter's induction into his family system would counter some minor problems in his umunna.

"Yes, I agree," the Ichie said seriously. "Go back and tell your friend that we shall be glad to accept him as our brother in Umu-Ifeadigo family. I have personally watched that man over the years and I know he's a good man."

"What must I do next?" Emodi asked.

"I shall hold a meeting with my people and then we shall give you a date and let you know how many gourds of palm wine, kola nuts, goats and foodstuff to present as his own contribution for the occasion and we shall make our own effort. Meanwhile I shall see the king and discuss it with him. I'm sure he'll have no objection."

"I'm sure," Emodi agreed. "Our Igwe is a liberal man."

*   *   *

When Ichie Ezeaputa presented Carter's request to Igwe Ajulufo, the aged king sat in thought for a few minutes then turned to Ezeaputa.

"I think it is alright," the Igwe said. "Somehow, I wish Jake Sanders had done the same. Phillip Carter is a good man. I give him my blessing."

Ezeaputa thanked him and stood up to leave. When he got under the arc of the wide doorless entrance the king hailed him. "Ichie Ezeaputa!"

"The Igwe shall live forever," Ezeaputa replied.

*   *   *

Emodi and Carter were invited to a cabinet meeting at Igwe Ajulufo's palace. After extensive deliberations, it was unanimously agreed, among the chiefs, that the two teachers would write to the Minister of Works in Abuja to ask him to divert the express road from Obodo Ogwari.

꧁‖Twelve‖꧂

The Federal Minister of works and Housing had given a standing order to his aides and office staff to submit every letter, no matter how trivial or inadequate, for his perusal. This order was his own humanitarian ploy to prevent his assistants from excluding the layman's letter from reaching him. The Honourable Minister, Alhaji Isa Jibril, was a fair and humble man who sought after justice and equity. In his days as a lowly civil servant, he always expressed his dissatisfaction with the seclusion of senators and representatives from the people they were supposed to be serving. What use was a public servant who didn't have an ear to the ground, who wasn't in touch with the grassroots? he had often asked his colleagues.

When the letter of Igwe of Obodo Ogwari came to the Minister's office, Alhaji Jibril read the strongly worded letter which Emeka Emodi and Phillip Carter had drafted for the Igwe. He was intrigued. Though the letter had been type-set on computer with a comely letter-heading of a red crown flanked by a curious setting of elephant tusks and cowrie shells, the signing of the letter had been a smeared thumb-print. The aura of the letter fascinated the Honourable Minister, but the content rather incensed him. At first he doubted its genuineness. It had to be fake. Detractors were probably at work in an attempt to prevent this apparently backward village from development. Why else would anyone in his right mind try to prevent an express road from passing through or near his village? When Alhaji Jibril read the strange letter a second time, he changed his mind. The letter had to be real. It was decisively not a fake. He intuitively discerned the earnest plea of the king in his noble quest to protect the ancient heritage of his people. In spite of this new understanding, Alhaji Jibril could not begin to see the need for anyone to keep his community shrouded in primitivity, these modern times. Whatever rich cultural heritage they had would flourish best, garnished by the amenities of civilization, Jibril reasoned. Unless there were other hidden agenda that prompted the king and his council to keep civilization out. What if there were traces of precious stones in small

86

quantities, kept secret by a select few, he wondered, or were they involved in some illicit trade, maybe a major marijuana cultivation? There had to be a hidden reason why the king didn't want the construction of a road that other towns were begging for. Alhaji Jibril called his personal assistant and gave a date for the delegates of Obodo Ogwari to meet with him personally as was requested in the letter.

*   *   *

The Ama-Oliora was a big circular clearing surrounded by tall and imposing trees that stood like monolithic guards protecting the large arena. The ground was flat and partly sandy making it quite adequate for children to play.

Men were seated on long tiered benches, built from Iroko planks, once rough but now browned and smoothened from ages of use. The women folk sat separately and were clothed more colourfully than the men while boys and girls loitered in scanty dresses.

Eight costumed girls in their teens accompanied by musicians danced and sang, performing a routine they had learned for the last yam festival.

The rowdy atmosphere was suddenly broken by several large bells that clanged unmetered, introducing a spread of silence among the people. The king and his cabinet chiefs were entering the arena. The king did not come himself and was not expected to attend. But, the symbol of his office was present, a big flat golden sword that was held by his ten-year-old son. The boy was lean and dark and had a serene look on his face. He was clad in a long immaculate-white robe with a red cap that clung snugly to his head. His red cap was to express his elevated status as the king's heir. The boy was an ozo-titled person and so was privileged to wear a red cap. The king's symbol was his entitlement as he was meant to lead the Ndi Ichie, senior chiefs of his father's council, to the Ama-Oliora.

The Onowu who was the traditional prime minister followed the boy closely whispering advice when necessary, while the other Ndi Ichie followed in a single line procession. The Onowu and his fellow Ndi Ichie wore longer red caps that distinguished them from the snug red cap of ozo title. Their young wards, boys, carried their leather satchels, stools and large bells that rang randomly as they walked in attendance beside the chiefs.

After the chiefs were settled at the centre of the ama, kolanuts and garden eggs were served in a large, wooden platter for the rightful person to use in prayer to bless the occasion and the guests before commencement of the ceremony. Without much deliberation on who was the privileged one, the Onowu acknowledged the presense of the king, and taking a brief formal permission from the ten-year-old heir who smiled and nodded, Onowu allotted nuts to elders from different quarters of the town before he began to pray. Seated on his stool with a kolanut between his thumb and forefinger he asked God to bless the kola and all the drinks and food to be consumed in the arena. He prayed for a successful union of Carter and the Ifeadigo clan asking God to chase away the bad spirits that may try to forge quarrels and disaffection between them.

"I seh!" the people answered.

Onowu prayed for the lives and progress of the guests and participants and asked that whatever blessing bestowed upon them should also embrace him. Finally, he prayed that the kola when eaten should bless and nourish everyone present.

"I seh!!" everyone responded loudly in acquiescence of Onowu's prayer.

Phillip Carter was summoned. He came down from where he sat with Emeka Emodi and other men. Carter was dressed in a blue flowered shirt and black trousers, his hair tied to the back with a string off a bamboo stem. He was asked to kneel before Ichie Ezeaputa and some aged members of the Ifeadigo clan. When Ezeaputa began to speak there was instant silence. Those who attempted to carry on quiet conversations were hushed by the young men who shouted reminders that an Ichie was speaking. Ezeaputa greeted the king and Ichies thanking them for the great honour accorded to him by their attendance.

"Umu-Ifeadigo, kwenu!" Ezeaputa hailed the Ifeadigo.

"Yaa!" they answered in unison.

"Kwenu!"

"Yaa!"

"Obodo Ogwari, kwenu!" he hailed the natives.

"Yaa!"

"Kwezue-nu!" he hailed all.

"Yaa!" they all answered, including the chiefs.

It was a kind of greeting that sparked off immediate enthusiasm and keen attention to the speech that was on hand.

"Today, we assemble because of a man who was once a stranger in our midst but who not only wants to become one of us but has already done so and we have accepted him."

There was a general hum of support for the Ichie's words.

"Therefore, whatever we shall do today to make him our own is only to fulfil the law."

Ichie Ezeaputa held out his hand and helped Carter up from his kneeling position and made him stand before the Ifeadigo elders.

Using Nze Ogugua, who was the second oldest Ifeadigo as a symbol, a fresh palm frond was used to join Carter's left wrist and his. Kola was broken, blessed by Ezeaputa and given to both men and they ate amidst a general applause. A bowl of yams and spiced palm oil was presented and they both ate from the same bowl. Again a spread of cheers. The two men, left wrists linked by palm frond, shared a cup of palm wine before Ichie Ezeaputa approached them with a crude knife.

Carter's heart leaped in alarm. He immediately suspected that the Ichie was coming to perform a blood covenant between him and Nze Ogugua. He almost started to put up a protest, while wondering in panic what part of their bodies would be cut to let out blood to be injested as a blood bond.

Ichie Ezeaputa raised the knife. "Today Ugoabata, Phillip Udeoyibo, you have become a free and full-fledged son of the Ifeadigo clan and Obodo Ogwari. Ezeaputa cut the palm frond that linked the two men and a wild applause rent the air. Nze Ogugua was the first to hug Carter, then Ichie Ezeaputa, then everybody else. Carter hugged and shook hands with hundreds of people. When it came to Ngozi's turn, he held her more tightly and for a longer period than others, which brought about another round of applause.

After congratulations, feasting and merriment began. Ntupuanya started to play.

It was long after the ceremony that Carter learnt that his fear when Ezeaputa approached him and Nze Ogugua with the crude knife had been intuitive. Such an induction ceremony in the old days would have been wrought with fetishism, blood covenants and oath taking before a shrine but, with the coming of the Gundus, the Ideamala, such practices had slowly disappeared without any direct instruction by the strange old men.

At the end of the ceremony Carter went home escorted by the youths and other well-wishers.

He had finally joined with the Ifeadigo and acquired a culture of strict moral discipline, communal commitment and responsibility. He had become a full-fledged village man.

Four market days after the family induction, one early morning, four aged men of the clan took Carter to the pinnacle of Ogwari Hills. They made a long trek through the valley, north of the caves before they could circle the land that was given to Carter and his descendants to come.

*   *   *

One of the Ifeadigo elders, as they walked, told Carter that members of their clan, though the smallest in Ogwariland, were the biggest land owners. Their forefather, a hunter of repute, many centuries ago, stumbled upon the Gundu in their final quest for the Ogwari cave. The hunter guided them to the caves and in return, they asked him to make a wish.

The hunter wished for a vast land inhabited then by a clan called Idama. According to oral tradition, the seven Gundu simply marched through the villages of the Idama unseen, upsetting cooking pots set on rock tripods, bumping into villagers and prominent village heads, confiscating their hats and staffs, creating a general impression of ghostly visitation. After the third day, the Idama elders decided that their land was haunted by powerful evil spirits and moved out, leaving the vast fertile land for the hunter whose name was Ifeadigo.

The vastness of the land awed and worried Carter. What would he do to put the land to use to compliment and justify the portion that was allotted to him? How would he raise money to cultivate the land? He was soon to find out that the clan that gave the land to him would help provide labour for its cultivation, for a portion of the proceeds. Natives worked for each other and no one ever went hungry for lack of food. The second keeper ensured that crops were well nourished with water and nutrients also for a token portion to meet the keepers' frugal needs of fruits, vegetables and nuts.

The Gundu had trekked thousands of miles, over a century, through many cultures of Africa before they found the Ogwari hills. Folklore sang that the priests only stumbled on the Ogwari caves by chance while a strong legend revealed that they had been searching for that particular cave for ages. After they found it, Obodo Ogwari was to be their last dwelling place forever or until they went back to where they came from. They would employ every skill and force to ensure that nothing, not even the federal government, disturbed their simple and primitive existence and most importantly the secret of the Gundu that lay hidden in the Ogwari caves.

*   *   *

After the bird's visit Carter despised himself for being such a lukewarm Christian. He had every knowledge and proof that good staunch Christians were immuned to the workings of dark powers. At an apartment where he once lived in Jamaica, New York, a Haitian voodoo practitioner chanted loudly and made a general nuisance of himself. Some of his co-tenants ganged up and petitioned to have him removed. The man was summoned by the estate manager who showed him the jointly signed petition, coaxing him to leave quietly without further event. Not only did he refuse to move but insisted that all nine of them who signed the petition should pack out within two weeks. In a fortnight eight of the tenants moved out, not without tales of spiritual harassment through dreams, strange and uncanny occurrences within their apartments and a general feeling of unprovoked terror whenever they drove through the gates of the apartment complex. Only the devout Christian from Ohio who led the crusade against the Haitian stayed undisturbed. He remained and eventually forced the voodoo man out with offensive and destructive prayers. The other eight who had fled from the complex were professed Christians also, some of whom never missed a Sunday service. But they were not firmly placed in the practice of their faith.

Carter's mind sauntered to the incident Emodi told him about the three missionaries, Morgan, Patterson and Cook. Carter presumed that the two who died in the claws of the Ideamala were not stable enough in their faith to have been so utterly devastated by the ancient force. Emodi had made it seem as if Morgan, after the death of his colleagues, had submitted to the Ideamala but Carter was not so convinced about that. The following Saturday, Carter mounted his rickety old Harley Davidson motorcycle, which he had purchased from a headmaster in the neighbouring village of Obodo Akata, and set out for the city library. It was a trip that took him through winding jungle paths, hilly woodlands with sparse vegetation and wide stretches of grasslands. The zone in which Obodo Ogwari was situated had one of the most divers landscapes in the state.

There were seven towns called Ebo-nasaa, meaning seven clans, who were supposed to have come from the same origin over eight centuries back. Obodo Ogwari, Obodo Akata and Obodo Ite being the first three in order of seniority. Their customs and traditions were the same even from the early days as they all originated from one source. Many centuries ago, seven strange settlers with peculiar magical powers came and settled in the caves of Obodo Ogwari. They avoided the rich fertile plains of Obodo Ite. They also shunned the waterlogged lands of Obodo Akata that was perfect for vital cultivation and desired only the dangerous and unexplored caves of Obodo Ogwari infested with wild and ferocious beasts. These weird but friendly visitors brought with them a new way of life, traditions and norms that would set Obodo Ogwari apart from their six counterparts. These new settlers introduced a deity, a giant bird, to the people of Obodo Ogwari as the ultimate physical and spiritual lawmaker, judge and executioner. The Ogwarians called the deity Ideamala. The newcomers referred to themselves as the Gundu. They had traveled from afar, crossed the River Niger and came into the Igbo country. Oral tradition has it that they spoke a strange language that was peculiar only to their small group. It did not take them long to learn the language of their hosts. They were said to have acquired the Igbo dialect of Obodo Ogwari with such zeal and speed that showed their intention of settling down permanently. However, after several centuries their own language which they used only for themselves remained exclusive with them. It was only in this aspect of language that these settlers differentiated themselves from their hosts. All other actions they exhibited were of service and integration with the Ogwarians.

Their eagerness to help the people of Obodo Ogwari using their special skills endeared them to their hosts instantly. The keepers were neither interested in the acquisition of land or property. As time wore on they imbibed various forms of control on the Ogwarians as was commensurate with their growth. Within half a century of the keepers' arrival, the people of Obodo Ogwari became noticeably more advanced in all aspects of life than their six sister clans. In trade, farming, medicine, animal husbandry and the general quality of life, the Ogwarians became a model people and rose far above their neighbouring towns. However, with this newfound culture came a gradual withdrawal from their neighbours. In a subtle and natural course of selection they isolated themselves not in pride and egotism; they had become very self-effacing.

*   *   *

When the Igwe ordered that Igo the sixth keeper would accompany the delegation to see the minister of works, it created fresh complications for Emodi and Carter who were handling the trip. Keepers were not allowed to spend the night away from the caves. The trip from Obodo Ogwari to Abuja, the federal capital, by car would take no less than six hours which meant that they had to depart a day prior to the appointment, sleep over and be in the minister's office the following day. When Emodi told the Igwe about this problem, the old monarch's response was that of polite nonchalance. The two teachers were both city men and should know what to do, he had stated. He reminded Emodi that high chiefs of his cabinet were not allowed to sleep abroad, how much more a Gundu priest. The only option now left to them was to fly to the capital in the morning, keep the minister's appointment and take an evening flight back.

The idea of flying did not alarm but thrilled the sixth keeper. Emodi and Carter could see it in his eyes. He neither declined nor agreed instantly but said would give them an answer the following day. He went back to the caves. The next day was a Saturday. Emodi and Carter were sitting on Carter's front porch when Igo approached them smiling broadly.

"What did your oracle say?" Emodi asked, smiling back at him.

"I am free to fly," the sixth keeper replied.

"What if we miss our flight or something, and can't make it back?" Carter asked.

The smile on the Igo's face vanished "Oh! that would be horrible. But, that would not happen. I'm sure," he said.

"But, what if it does happen that we get stranded somewhere outside Obodo Ogwari, just a hypothetical question?" Emodi asked.

The keeper was instantly thoughtful. Worry lines rumpled his black forehead as he settled down on the ebony stool that Emodi pulled up for him.

⟨୬‖ Thirteen ‖୬⟩

The honourable minister took a sip from a tall glass of mixed fruit juice and sat back comfortably in deep thought. Tufts of light brocade billowed down from the wide v-neck of his agbada robe, covering most of the leather armchair on which he sat. In consideration of the petition of the Igwe of Obodo Ogwari, he had decided to apply his intuition and inner judgment while interrogating the delegates of the Igwe who were waiting to see him. From their response the minister would seek to discover any hidden reasons that would cause a people to reject reaping one of the most basic fruits of civilization. He had also decided that he would later send spies to Obodo Ogwari to find out the hidden truths. There had to be some personal hidden factors that motivated the king and his confederates.

When Emeka Emodi, Igo and Phillip Carter were ushered into the minister's office, Hon. Jibril was slightly startled by the motley crew. Emodi was dressed in an immaculate white shirt, red tie and black trousers. He could have been a banker or a sales executive. Igo had that mark of the ancient titled chief. A single batik cloth draped his body, knotting off on the left shoulder, leaving both arms bare. A thick yellowing ivory amulet braced his left bicep, his feathered red cap topping off the archaic traditional mode. Phillip Carter wore a big orange jumper, his long bright-red hair glossy and combed.

The minister started to protest to his aide for bringing in two groups at a time but he pre-empted with a ready answer: "They're together, Sir."

During the introduction, Emodi made special emphasis on Carter's indigenous status; 'a bonafide resident and naturalized native of Obodo Ogwari whose official immigration documents of citizenship are in process.' Emodi did not want any further embarrassing questions about Carter's concern in the matter. They had been through all that with the minister's aides in the waiting room.

"I have your petition here before me," the minister said, "but I don't quite understand it. Can you please elaborate?"

Emodi cleared his throat and began. "Sir, with all due respect to the wonderful work you've been doing across the nation, making it possible for trade and development to reach the hinterland through your road projects, we are here not only to commend you but also to express that our town, Obodo Ogwari, is not an average town and will lose more in material and spiritual wealth if the stereotype civilization and development comes into it. An express road will surely bring about sudden undesirable change. This is why we're here."

"How does your view sit with the rest of the natives?" the minister asked.

"Well, there can never be a hundred percent support on every issue but I can assure you, Sir, the remoteness and conservativeness of Obodo Ogwari is the pride of most natives, home and abroad," Emodi replied.

"Which doesn't mean that when all factors are weighed on the scale that most would like to see their primitive village remain without modern roads, electricity and pipe-borne water. What do you say to that?" the minister asked.

"Sorry, but I'd like to say my bit if ya'll don't mind," Carter interrupted. "Now, I moved here from New York to teach for a while and go on back but it was what I saw in Obodo Ogwari that made me want to stay."

"And what did you see that is not in all these other villages who desire to be developed?" the minister asked.

"I came and I found in Obodo Ogwari," Carter began, "a people with a rich cultural heritage, abundant food and excellent medicine; I found a society with virtually no crime. In Obodo Ogwari there's no theft, no murder, no tribalism. They've never even heard of racism, Sir, we're talking about a town where nothing has been stolen in over sixty years. Yes, there's no electricity or pipe-borne water but one has to sacrifice one thing to gain another. Sir, if the forfeiture of express freeways, electricity and pipe-borne water is the price to pay for this bastion of peace, justice and security that we have in Ogwari, then so be it. To hell with the cars, the cellular phones and the stock market." Carter slid forward on his chair.

"Honourable Minister, pardon me if I'm coming out harsh but Obodo Ogwari may be one of the last places on earth where life is being lived the way the Creator wanted it. A model Garden of Eden. Re-route your road and let this perfect order in Ogwari last another few hundred years. Thank you, Sir."

All through Carter's speech, Jibril stared at him sometimes intently and other times distantly. His highly skeptical and suspicious mind was trying to size Carter up. What was his ulterior motive? Did he have any? A white man who lived in a very remote village without basic amenities; a New Yorker who wanted to keep civilization out. What was in it for him? Was he just a sentimental fanatic or cultural preservationist or was there a hidden agenda? Jibril decided to be a little provocative in a bid to draw them out.

"I'm sorry gentlemen but to be frank, I don't quite believe that there isn't a hidden motive in your quest," the Minister said. "I hear there's a drug racket going on in your town ... cultivation of illicit plants eh? Traces of rare gems, you know, precious stones and a very big cover-up by your king and his cabinet. What do you say to that?"

Emodi, Carter and Igo were shocked beyond words. They exchanged furtive glances at each other and then at the minister. Emodi was incensed but his respect for the office of the minister checked the annoyance that had quickly swelled in him. As he made to speak, the Sixth keeper cleared his throat loudly. He had not said anything since they entered but now wanted to break the silence.

"Honourable Minister," Igo addressed Jibril. "I am the keeper of the sixth shrine of the Ideamala ..."

"Oh! You're a native doctor," Jibril stated.

"He's not a native doctor," Carter corrected. "He's a Gundu priest."

"Thank you, Teacher Carter," Igo said and continued. "I respect your office but your office has not respected me, Minister Jibril. You have insulted my king and the rest of us by implying that we have something to hide in rejecting your express road. In that case we shall arise and go back to our king and tell him what you said. But before we leave I want to make a promise to you!"

"Go ahead," Jibril replied.

"I promise you that no express road is going to come close to Obodo Ogwari, now or ever. Let's go, boys." He stood up.

Emodi and Carter got up slowly and hesitantly. Igo had ended the meeting so abruptly. It was not how they wanted it but they had to go with the old man.

"Fine, you're free to go," said Jibril. "I still can't understand you people. Look, I can show you hundreds of applications in that file cabinet of various communities begging to have dual carriage roads run through their towns to enhance trade and communication, agriculture and social development. You three can never convince me that you truly speak the minds of the majority of your people."

"Sir," Igo addressed Jibril, "I want to ask you for the last time to change the route of your express road to avoid Obodo Ogwari. Our town is the last frontier, the final stronghold in the preservation of culture and our native heritage. Obodo Ogwari is a museum, a natural archive that is still functioning and growing in richness. Our medical department still succeeds where your modern medicine fails, our psychic section ..."

"Very good," the minister clapped his hands mockingly. "When our road comes through, you will have more patients and clients and the whole world would come and marvel at your preservation, ha! ha! You will become a tourist attraction." He became suddenly mean. "Please, leave my office before I have you thrown out."

"Come on, boys, let's get away from here," Igo said and moved to the door with Carter and Emodi close behind him. He opened the door, stood in the doorway and took a hard look at Jibril.

"We shall not allow that road to go through," Igo said to the minister. "In fact, no superpower, be it the Americans, can run that road through Obodo Ogwari." A low guttural tone.

The minister stood up from his chair. "Is that a threat?"

"No, but as I stand before you today before Olisa ebuluwa, God the Creator, I wash my hands in innocence from anything that would result from your obstinacy. You still have a chance to reconsider." Igo spoke coldly. There was no ranting or raving, only a stern pronouncement. His actions were delibrate and resolved.

"How dare you threaten me?" Jibril fumed. "Have this man arrested and detained until he can tell us how exactly he plans to stop a federal road from going through," Jibril ordered his aides and a uniformed policeman who had heard raised voices and were coming through the door.

Igo had to step back into the room to make way for their entry.

"Please, Sir, please," Emodi pleaded, "don't arrest him. He's a high priest, please."

The policeman that came in with the aides stood hesitantly. He was portly and had a good-natured face that was visibly disappointed when he found out that the old village man was the one to be arrested. He would have preferred to arrest Emodi. However, the huge young cop that followed had a mean scowl on his dark clean-cut face. He had clearly, that cocksure attitude of one with the full blast of authority behind him, who could get away with anything as long as it was order from above. When he came in and saw Igo and Emodi, he exhaled deeply and shook his head resignedly as if he was called in to squash a couple of ants.

Igo stood his ground, folding his arms across his chest in mild defiance.

"Sir, please ... we're very sorry, we're leaving ..." Emodi stuttered, many thoughts flashing through his mind. A keeper was forbidden to sleep abroad. Sleeping in police custody would be taboo and must surely be avoided.

When the policeman grabbed Igo's arm, Emodi was still facing the minister in earnest plea. At first contact with the sixth keeper's arm, the cop felt a slight tingling sensation in the middle of his palm but he ignored it and steered the old man around. When the tingle developed into an urgent itch, the policeman used the fingers of his other hand to scratch his palm. It was then that his problem became apparent. He scratched his arm and then his face, his thighs and his feet all in quick succession. In just a few minutes it was clear that a dozen pairs of hands working to combat the uncanny itching would not have sufficed. The policeman pulled off his shirt and trousers while scratching madly. His colleague and the honourable minister's assistants who touched him to help were immediately stricken with the highly contagious itch.

Jibril sat open-mouthed, gaping at his aides and cops as they scratched themselves violently, their clothing strewn about the maroon carpeting.

He picked up his intercom and pressed a button.

"Hello, there's an old man wearing a single dyed cloth across his shoulder and a red cap with feathers. Call some policemen to arrest him with guns. They must not touch him. I repeat, they must not touch him."

Igo laughed. "Do you think that is all I can do to protect myself? Call off that order or I will show you one greater than an itch ... Call off the order now! And give these men palm oil to drink and rub on their bodies. They will be fine."

The deadly gleam in the keeper's green eyes was enough to inform the minister that grave danger was lurking around the corner. He had only seen a sample.

"Hello," the minister spoke on the intercom. "Disregard my last instruction ... Yes, no policemen. And em ... Peter, do get me some bottles of palm oil ... Yes! I said palm oil! Are you deaf or what?" the minister barked and banged the mouth piece into the set.

"Remember what I told you," Igo said as he left, "I shall not be held responsible for anyone who attempts to put an express road through Obodo Ogwari. My hands are clean before God and man."

After Igo, Emodi and Carter left the minister's office, the two policemen and the minister's aide applied palm oil on their bodies and drank some quantities of it. By the time the itching subsided, the minister had second thoughts on letting Igo go scot-free after humiliating him and his staff. He thought it would bring much shame and scandal when word got out that an old village priest who was not even a proper boka, had so utterly harassed and intimidated him and his aides. The honourable minister picked up his mobile phone.

⟨⟩‖Fourteen‖⟨⟩

When Jibril put a call through to General Idris, the Chief of Defence Staff, he knew it was a jump in protocol. Neverthless, his deep-seated intuition coupled with the ease that Igo overwhelmed his policemen gave him the impetus to bypass the federal police for the army.

Jibril's very cordial relationship with the boisterous general also made him at ease in his breach of executive order. At worst, the general would insist that he passed through police first.

At the mention of Obodo Ogwari and a certain old priest General Idris became instantly interested in the matter and offered his assistance. A grave suspicion grew in the minister that there was more to it than met the eye. Obviously, there must have been a prior interest in high levels.

*   *   *

The three men of Obodo Ogwari left the minister's office and boarded a Peugeot 406 cab that was to take them to the airport. Soon as the cab pulled away from the kerb, a dark-blue Toyota Corolla followed, keeping two cars between yet hot on their trail. The passenger who sat next to the driver of the Corolla kept steady communication with the walkie talkie in his hand, relaying their location to Lieutenant Ifeajuna who sat in an office at the head-quarters of the Third Amoured Division.

Three traffic lights away from the ministry, a dark green Mercedes bus swung out of an adjacent lane, tore across the path of oncoming traffic and blocked the yellow Peugeot 406 that conveyed the three men of Obodo Ogwari.

The driver of the Peugeot screeched to a halt barely an arm's length from the bus.

Three soldiers had already leapt out of the bus before the vehicle came to a total stop. In seconds all nine soldiers surrounded the Peugeot and ordered the driver and all his passengers to come out slowly and place both their hands on the car.

The taxi driver was the first to alight and place his shivering hands on the hood of the cab. The soldiers yanked open the three passenger doors simultaneously and drew backwards to let the

Ogwarians come out, their assault rifles pointed at the occupants. The manner in which they kept a safe distance from the trio showed they had been briefed not to make bodily contact with them, especially the old man. Emodi stepped out of the front while Igo and Carter came from the rear, hands in the air.

"Teacher Emodi, with your permission may I show these boys the difference between a leopard and a pussy cat?" Igo said.

"No, no no!" Emodi replied urgently. "It's the one you showed them at the minister's office that brought about this. Let's just stay calm."

Igo shrugged. "Ok, but I'm not going to sleep in a strange land."

"Stand still! Don't move!" barked the lieutenant who led the team.

"Relax, Igo. Please, don't do anything out of the ordinary or Carter and I are dead."

"Let the white man step aside … step aside now!" the officer yelled.

Carter took a few steps away from the yellow taxi and stood, hands still in the air.

"The two of you, march to the Corolla and get in the back seat, now!"

Emodi and Igo obeyed and walked over to the blue Toyota and got in. Three soldiers hustled the taxi driver into the back of his cab and sat on both sides of him while another got behind the wheel and revved the engine. In just a few minutes the taxi led the way out from the scene of the arrest, followed by the car with Emodi and Igo. The bus with the rest of the soldiers came in the rear as they sped off leaving a flabbergasted Carter on the street of a city quite strange to him.

*   *   *

Captain Okafor lay alone in his posh hotel suite, flipping through the channels of the cable network. He pressed the down-scroll button with the tip of his right thumb; stations flicked by so quickly, never pausing long enough on one channel to make sense of the programme.

As he flipped through the channels, so did his mind skip through the events surrounding the advent of his new-found stardom.

Somehow he felt that this was time to exploit the wide publicity he was getting both within the country and across certain parts of the world. His story and pictures had appeared in some notable international magazines and TV stations but local journalists never seemed to tire of patronizing him. Even after the euphoria of his capture of the legendary giant and subsequent victory at the war front subsided, everything he did became news. It would be just a matter of time before he would become stale to the media if nothing new and exciting happened around him. He had to either pull another heroic stunt or keep doing notable things to stay in the news. The war was over and so was the opportunity of heroic stunts. A strong urge within him yearned to shed his army uniform and go into active politics. As a politician he would have more opportunities to put his influence and popularity to use. In the army he had enrolled in a school on-line and obtained a degree in education. Though the army had been like a home, a family to him all these years, it was not exactly like the real thing. There was no real sense of belonging like he would have had in Obodo Ogwari. Now that the banishment was poised to be lifted, Okafor felt a pang of guilt for his eagerness to leave the army. This feeling, he presumed, pronounced the old adage that when a young wife is brought into the house the aged one is driven out. The ban was practically lifted in his hometown and the army suddenly became undesirable. The only hitch he had was that the army was not a regular government ministry or private company where he could resign at will. Nevertheless in his own case, Okafor did not forsee much of a hindrance. He had sustained more than enough injuries to retire by reason of ill health. Moreover he had rendered a meritorious service to the nation and deserved it. Okafor was just making a mental note to get Nurse Chiadi to make a medical appointment for him when the intercom rang.

A crisp female voice from the reception desk announced that a Mr Ikeadi Ntukogu was there with another man to see him. At once, Okafor recognized the name of Ikeadi Ntukogu as his townsman. Though Okafor did not know the man in person, Ikeadi's name was almost legendary due to the event that led to his banishment some years before Okafor's father suffered his. Songs were composed in his name and the mysterious singing night masquerade exalted him. When Ntukogu left Obodo Ogwari over thirty years earlier he was branded a hero by some and a sadist and lunatic by others. Though he had killed a man in pure self-defence, by the strident laws of the land it bore the same punishment as murder.

Ikeadi Ntukogu's woes began the night he forgot his hunting knife. He returned to his house to retrieve it and found Okali Nwanna in an amourous posture with his wife in her bedroom. To the greatest chagrin of Ntukogu the man, Okali, was a rival hunter who often boasted of his trysts with other people's wives. When Ikeadi wanted to push and shove him out of the house, Okali became rude and abusive instead of running with his tail between his legs as Ntukogu had expected. Their minor tussle turned into a fierce fight. Okali Nwanna struck Ntukogu a vicious blow on the head with a machete. Ntukogu shot him at a point-blank range with his crude hunting gun and killed him. Ntukogu acted contrary to the law of the land which required him to take a few necessities if possible and run away to exile from there. Instead, he stood over the body of Okali Nwanna and wept. One guilty of murder had to escape as soon as he could before members of the last age grade assembled to do away with him. Once they arrested him within the boundaries of the town his life was theirs to do whatever they pleased. But, as soon as the culprit crossed the boundaries into a neighbouring town, even if he were still in their reach, they would not touch him for he had carried the abomination of bloodshed away from their land. No murderer arrested by the last age grade was ever seen again. But, if he crossed the border, he was free and would remain a freeman in exile for fifty years.

When Ntukogu killed Okali Nwanna, he stood beside Okali's corpse and wept bitterly. Crying, he picked up the dead man in his arms and headed for the king's palace. As he trudged on, hundreds of villagers came out from their homes and joined forming a long taciturn procession that swelled to over two hundred villagers. Their flaming torches lit up the dark night lending an eerie aura to the pitiful nocturnal scene. Blood flowed down Ntukogu's face from the machete cut on his head. By the time the procession arrived at the king's palace, a few young men from the last age grade had assembled in readiness for action.

But they hadn't reached six in number that formed the official quorum for an arrest.

The king did not appear for he was forbidden to see a dead body. Moreover, kings were not given to unceremonial appearances. Carrying the dead body of Okali Nwanna in his arms, Ntukogu addressed the villagers and the king's men who came out on his behalf. In a grief-stricken voice he told them how he had killed Okali in defence of his own life.

"I have killed a man who came into my home, violated my wife and almost killed me with a machete," Ntukogu cried as he spoke.

A streak of his own blood crossed his mouth, hanging crimson droplets on his upper lip as he spoke. The flames of a dozen torches that stood closest to him danced reflections on his rippling dark muscles awash with a mixture of sweat and blood.

"Yet I now stand to leave you, my people, to a distant land for fifty seasons. I say no! I will not run until I have asked you all this question. Is it fair? Is this a fair custom?"

He put the corpse of Okali Nwanna on the ground gently and straightened up. He was no longer crying.

"I shall now run to the lonely safety of life exile … if the last age grade have not already formed six to take me to the evil forest."

As Ntukogu turned around to run from the scene, Uzo-Onicha the king's scribe spoke.

"Ikeadi, son of Ntukogu," hailed the stringy dark elder whose pointed grey goatee bobbed strangely when he spoke. "You have killed a man in self-defence, yes, but you have killed a man. Our human sympathy reaches out to you but justice must be done for the blood of your victim to settle in the land."

"But what about my innocence?" Ntukogu asked.

"There is no innocence in bloodshed. Why you? Why must it be you that had to kill Okali Nwanna, self-defence or not, why? You must run for your life. That is all that is left for you, now."

A stir rose among the agitating villagers as two young men joined the crowd. The last age grade members had reached eight. The minimum of six members of the last grade that were required to arrest a murderer was a factor placed by the ancients to give a chance for the murderer to abscond to exile. His exile or his execution served the same penance of atonement. According to oral tradition, the execution by the last grade was introduced to check powerful warriors in the olden days who murdered recklessly and defied the punishment of exile thereby staying on to pollute the land.

The eight members surrounded Ntukogu and as they led him away, a voice rang out of the crowd urging Ntukogu to run for his life.

"Gbaa oso Ochu!" another voice goaded Ntukogu on. Soon another voice joined and so it went on till the crowds that followed them were chanting the same, urging him to run. Indirectly, the chanting was being directed to the last grade to let Ntukogu make his run. One by one, the hands that held Ntukogu left him. Ntukogu did not run. He marched on, his shoulders hunched with grief and humiliation. The members of the age grade followed. When Ntukogu branched off the path that led to the evil forest, the last few villagers who followed them dropped off. It was forbidden for anyone to follow. The arrest and execution of a murderer by the age grade was meant to be a quiet and esoteric exercise.

Ten years had passed before it was rumoured in Obodo Ogwari that Ikeadi Ntukogu was living in the capital city. The Ulaga children's masquerade sang of him as a hero whose ghost lived in a distant land while the mysterious night-singing mmuo, the Ayaka masquerade, immortalized the legendary Ntukogu, "who laid down his life to protect the sacredness of the family and marriage."

There appeared to be a diligent effort by the exiled Ntukogu to avoid contact with his kinsmen. But he kept abreast of the general events in Obodo Ogwari through a traveling merchant who peddled jewelry and household utensils on a rickety old bicycle. Okafor and Ntukogu knew about each other but had never met. Okafor was just a little boy when Ntukogu was led away by the village executioners to be put to death. Okafor's father was to follow in banishment many years later. Rumours abounded years later that the last age grade had broken the law and let Ntukogu escape. Others said that he had fought them and absconded in the rumpus.

Through his connections in the army, Okafor had found out that Ntukogu had lived and traded around some remote parts of

106

the north for a few years before he went to the Cameroun where he joined up with a wealthy merchant and later amassed a great fortune himself.

Though Ntukogu was over twenty years older than Okafor, he had developed a great respect for the younger man when Okafor's face started appearing in the media all over the world.

The army hierachy frowned at the publicity Okafor was receiving and ordered him not to grant interviews to the media. However, the die was cast. Okafor had become an instant public hero. The photographers caught zoom shots of him and journalists rode on bikes to Obodo Ogwari to trace his origin. After a newspaper features page revealed Okafor's state of banishment, the discourse of his modern day exile became a major topic for talk shows and tabloids. Ntukogu remembered all these past events with pride. Had Okafor been any free native of his hometown, Ntukogu would not have bothered to visit him. But, they shared the stigma of banishment which spontaneously forged a strong bond between them.

Okafor regarded the graceful elderly man that stood at his door with awe. He was tall and stood bolt-upright with a physique and disposition that suggested lots of exercise and outdoor activity. He was prominently grey at the temples and moustache but the rest of his hair was jet-black. At sixty-five, Ikeadi Ntukogu was healthy, wealthy and sturdy as an ox. With the strong homebound tradition spurring him, no amount of wealth would have made up for his living in a strange land. When his business colleagues talked of going home for Christmas he usually kept quiet. The woman he married had grown up in an orphanage and had no relatives except an aged matron. He had paid dowry to no one and had no in-laws. They had three sons and two daughters whom they raised with discipline and the fear of God. Despite his affluence and secluded life in a quiet Camerounian suburb, Ntukogu's troubled mind was ever homebound. An old adage that expressed one's desire to reincarnate seven times to Obodo Ogwari and never to any other town was especially true to Ntukogu. He often daydreamed of an event when he would ride into Obodo Ogwari amidst the cheering and hailing of his townsmen. However, with the fifty-year ban, he would be ninety years old before he'd be allowed to return. At ninety, if he lived that long, waving at the cheering crowds may be an exercise too strenuous for him to undertake. When he read of Okafor's call for the abolition of banishment his heart had leapt with joy. Okafor was the man to follow. After Ntukogu read his story in a magazine he decided to find Okafor and offer him all the support he could muster.

As they stared at each other, it was obvious that the respect and awe they felt was mutual.

"Captain Okafor," Ntukogu enthused rather rhetorically.

"Yes," Okafor answered. "Ikeadi Ntukogu!"

"Okafor Dike!" Ntukogu hailed in a loud voice.

"Ntukogu Odogwu!" Okafor shouted.

Ntukogu held out his hand. Okafor grabbed it in a firm handshake before they embraced slapping each other on the back.

The older man was the first to speak when they disengaged. "My son, you have made me proud. In fact you have wiped the many years of tears off my eyes."

"And you have done very well yourself," the soldier replied. "Please come in and sit down, Sir."

Ntukogu remained standing at the doorway. "Actually I just came to pay you a courtesy call and met a man at the reception, who is also looking for you, a white man, Mr Phillip Carter ..." He looked inquiringly at Okafor wondering if he knew Carter.

"Ugoabata of Obodo Ogwari. I've heard a lot about him but what's he doing here?" Okafor asked.

Ntukogu smiled. He now knew that Okafor was current with Ogwari news. "I'm not sure but he looked very worried," Ntukogu replied and beckoned on Ugoabata who was standing in the hallway, a short distance away.

* * *

The faces of the two exiled men of Obodo Ogwari took on grave expressions as Ugoabata finished his story about their ordeal, from the minister's office to the arrest of Igo and Emodi.

"I wish I knew you people were in town to see the minister," Okafor said. "I would have offered some help. I hear Jibril's a shrewd but honest person but I doubt if he has the wherewithal to change the course of that road construction. It must involve some serious alterations in logistics to change the decision."

"You're quite right about that," Ntukogu agreed. "But, it doesn't hurt to try."

"Well it's hurting now, my brothers," Ugoabata Carter retorted, "The issue of preventing the road construction is secondary at this point. Our primary concern now is to get Emodi and the Igo released ..."

"Oh! that wont be a problem," Okafor interjected. "Soon as I let the general know that they're my people I'm sure they'll be released. We'll go there tomorrow."

"That is the problem. We can't wait till tomorrow," Carter said. "Igo cannot spend the night outside the caves and survive. As the legend goes, after journeying across the earth for a hundred years they then found the perfect place, and vowed it would be their home forever or until they can go back to wherever they came from. Such a vow from the Gundu is not to be taken lightly. Whatever secret these priests have carried around with them for centuries lies in that cave. Get him out of that place and back to Ogwari, before the break of dawn tomorrow."

Okafor looked rather perplexed at this news.

"Now, I remember ..." Ntukogu spoke distantly staring blankly into the space between Ugoabata and Okafor. "The legend of the Ideamala ... The covenant of the Gundu which was made in the caves when they arrived many centuries ago forbids any one of these priests from sleeping away from the caves. My grandfather told us a fable-like story about a keeper, in the time of his forefathers, who suffered a mental breakdown and while he was wandering through the forest, he came upon and copulated with a woman who had gone to fetch firewood. The woman was found dead. She had bled from the pores all over her body including her ears, eyes and mouth. Her face was grotesque and bloated out of proportion, her tongue sticking out as if she had been strangled. Large chunks of flesh had been eaten out from various parts of her body, both her breasts totally devoured. The keeper himself was found a couple of days after, not only dead but rotted and dried, a gelatinous black mass."

"The way Igo kept harping on his need to get back home before dawn, I won't like to see what's going to happen," Ugoabata said.

"Well, in that case, I better get dressed," Okafor said. "We've got to move in immediately."

It was a cold dark cell. The floors were cracked and broken all over, exposing sand and crushed chalky plaster. Apparently, it was not a normal guardroom or holding cell but some decrepit storeroom that hadn't been used for years. It had no toilet facilities or proper ventilation. It was just a room.

Igo had been sitting on the floor for a better part of the few hours they had stayed in the cell. The wary look in his eyes worried Emodi. From what the old man had said, it was clear that he would have escaped even after the soldiers had them arrested. But, for the safety of Emodi who may have been shot in the process Igo had remained calm. Now that they were locked up in the cold dusty cell the opportunity of escape was reduced to naught as Emodi thought. He was torn between being thankful to Igo and the feeling of guilt for the old man's detention. If Igo slept in the cell till dawn his life would be endangered though Emodi didn't know exactly how. In his lifetime even in the generation of his great-grandparents, no priest of the Ideamala had ever had cause to sleep out of the caves. The only story they had to go by was that of the lunatic keeper who purpotedly raped and killed a woman in the forest. It had become a myth to the new generation. However, from the Igo's quiet wariness and fear, Emodi knew that all was not well.

"I'm sorry, Igo. I know it's all my fault ..."

"Not at all," the sixth keeper replied. "It was my choice to make."

"You're risking your life for me," Emodi said.

"One has to make sacrifices to attract good."

Emodi paused for a while, wondering how best to ask him about his condition. It was a vital question yet sensitive and awkward.

"I wonder how much time we have to get you out of here and back to the caves."

Igo looked at him and smiled. He pulled the batik cloth off his body and spread it on the rough floor, leaving on his immaculate white T-shirt, boxer shorts and his red cap. "I know what you're thinking, that I'll shrivel up and die by tomorrow morning. No. In actual fact, my condition won't become that bad in two days but the third day ..."

Igo's speech was interrupted by the rattling of the iron door.

Captain Okafor stood on the other side of the iron bars squinting to adjust his sight to the dark gloomy cell. Two soldiers armed with assault rifles stood behind him.

A fourth soldier who was unarmed called out the inmates' names from a sheet of paper in his hand. Emodi and Igo answered.

"Visitor to see you," the soldier announced.

"Ichie Igo, Emeka Emodi, good evening, I'm Captain Okafor."

Igo sprang to his feet and walked over to Okafor.

"Don't let him touch you, Sir," said the man with the sheet of paper, in a tight-lipped warning to Okafor.

Not heeding to the soldier's warning, Okafor bowed and took Igo's proffered hand into both of his, in a respectful handshake.

"Son of Okafor, you have grown into a big fine man just like your father," Igo said, holding Okafor's hands through the bars.

"Thank you, Igo, and you look just the same as when I saw you over twenty years ago," Okafor replied.

"We heard about your father's death. He was my good friend, ndo, sorry." Igo withdrew his hand and placed it on the iron bar.

"It's alright. You didn't make the banishment law," Okafor answered dropping his hands. It would have been disrespectful of him to withdraw first.

"Meet Emeka Emodi, school teacher, Ogwari Boys High school." Igo swept his hand towards Emodi in a slow and noble gesture.

"I remember Chukwuemeka Emodi. We were playmates in primary school." Okafor beamed a smile.

"Okafor, it has been a very long time. Listen, we don't have much time. We have to get Igo out of here, immediately."

"I know," Okafor answered. "Ugoabata and Ntukogu are here with me and I've been well briefed about the Igo's condition." He took his dark green beret off and scratched his head warily like a scholar in a tough examination.

"Well?" the Igo inquired, noting Okafor's unease.

"I'm working on it. I've gone to see General Idris." Okafor paused, turned around and addressed the three soldiers behind him. "Leave us."

"Yes, Sir!" the soldiers answered almost in unison and filed out hurriedly.

Okafor turned back to his kinsmen. "What worries me is that the General was very dodgy when I spoke to him about your release."

"What exactly was his reply?" Emodi asked.

"He was vague," Captain Okafor answered. "Couldn't give me a straight reply. Said something about waiting for orders from above."

"From above?" Emodi asked, surprised. "Could that be from the president? Just to release us? This is scary."

"Let's give it a few days," Okafor advised.

Igo looked intently at Captain Okafor as the soldier was about to leave. "Son of Okafor, go and tell them that I can't wait a few days."

Okafor shrugged and turned to leave.

Igo went back to his makeshift mat. Slowly and carefully, he smoothened out the rumples and creases in the cloth, stacking his sandals one atop the other. He folded his red cap and placed it on the sandals in completion of a rugged pillow.

Igo lay down and closed his eyes. He had warned Emodi not to try holding any form of conversation with him for another hour or two. When the old man's breathing became laboured with a faint wheezing sound, Emodi knew that he had either fallen asleep or slipped into some weird spiritual mode. One never knew what to expect with these ancient keepers, Emodi thought. He sat down on the floor in one corner of the cell from where he could keep an eye on the old man. The feeling of guilt was still heavy on Emodi. Nevertheless, he felt rather confident in Igo's company. The least he could do was to obey the old man's instruction. In a short while, Emodi fell asleep, his back leaning on the dark mosquito-splattered walls. All was silent.

⊙‖ Fifteen ‖⊙

The honourable minister's convoy snaked through the main gate of army headquarters, round the flower-hedged flagstaff and parked in front of the general's two-storey office block. Beacons on the pilot cars flashed red and blue lights as the minister stepped down from the back of his Lexus jeep. Aides, security staff and cops alighted from their various vehicles, slamming doors. Seemingly alert and agile, they positioned themselves around their boss in that sycophantic style that was to exaggerate the minister's net importance. By the time Minister Jibril got to the entrance of the building, only two of his close aides followed closely. They were greeted by armed soldiers guarding the lobby before the minister was led upstairs by the general's aide.

General Idris's office was outrageously large. It took up almost a third of the left wing of the second storey.

The General stood up behind his huge office table and came round to shake Jibril's hand. Together, they walked across a rectangular Persian rug that was spread in the centre of the room to the conference table.

Three men sat at one end of the long glossy black table. Jibril recognized Funsho Odutola, head of the secret service who disengaged from his opened laptop to shake the minister's hand. Odutola was clad in a light-blue suit. He looked worn and his tie was slack, Jibril noticed, as he exchanged pleasantries with the retired Brigadier General who was now head of the country's version of America's FBI. Next was the inspector general of police whom the minister had met on several occasions. General Idris introduced the third man as Professor Okediadi, a lecturer in philosophy and also the most notable authority in African customs and traditions. The gray-haired educationist bowed slightly as he shook the minister's hand.

"I must commend you, Sir, for the beautiful express inlets carved into remote areas, courtesy of the Works Ministry. Keep up the good work."

"Thank you, professor," Jibril answered.

"Shall we get down to business right away, I have to submit a report tomorrow morning," Idris said, settling down at the head of the conference table. "Let's begin by hearing the honourable minister's experience."

Jibril cleared his throat, seated opposite the secret service chief and the professor. "Gentlemen, truly I experienced a very strange and bizarre occurrence in my office but I didn't think it was that serious to have brought about this high-powered meeting. I had wanted simply to call the general or drop by and thank him for the quick response, but certainly not to discuss that old village man. I'm just curious why he so boldly challenges the authority of the government in building the express road through his village."

"That is just the question," said General Idris.

"But you don't worry about that old man. He's just one hopeless witch doctor who has a charm that makes people itch when they touch him," the minister replied with a frown. "What's the big deal?"

The professor chuckled. "Then, why didn't he itch himself? How come the white man and the teacher who made constant contact with him didn't itch?"

"Maybe they rubbed some antidote on their bodies or something and came to play out that little skit in my office to scare me into diverting the express highway." The minister spoke with conviction. "Well, I'm not scared. The road is going through."

General Idris put down the gold ink pen with which he was taking notes while the others spoke. He looked directly into Jibril's eyes before he started to speak. "Captain Okafor came to see me this afternoon. I noticed that he was very hyped up and unnaturally desperate in getting the old man released. I got suspicious and started pumping him for information. In the end he confessed that the man is his village man and that he belonged to some strange ancient sect or cult or something. Strangely he claimed that if the man is not released within twenty-four hours he would die in the guard room."

"Then it appears that he may commit suicide,'cause I know that twenty-four hours in the cell never killed anyone," the IG, said with a smile.

"I'm sorry, gentlemen, but I don't see how all this lecture is

114

important to …"Jibril started to say.

"Just exercise some patience and you'll see," General Idris said. He looked at the prof. and nodded.

Professor Okediadi looked a little irritated but didn't react. "The case of this old man we're talking about is more complex than you may expect," said the professor. "He may not be an ordinary being in the real sense of the word. This man in question is not only a priest of the Gundu cult but the sixth of the keepers which is the most peculiar section of the lot. There are certain speculations as to the origin of these priests who emigrated and settled in the caves of Obodo Ogwari many centuries ago. Arabic historians of the tenth and eleventh centuries AD wrote of a strange group of negroes highly skilled in magical arts that came down with Moroccan merchants and settled with the Tekrur people around River Senegal. These rather strange human beings were said to have come from the skies. It is not clear where else the Gundu resided after their short stay in Senegal but an Arab scholar named Elibekri, a century later, wrote of a very similar group that settled with the Soninke people in the ancient empire of Ghana."

Okediadi took a sip of cold water from the plastic bottle that was set before him. He withdrew a notebook from his briefcase, screened it and read:

"When these peculiar priests came to settle near the imperial city of Kumbi in the old Ghana empire, they found a twin city consisting of two separate centres six miles apart. Due to their religious and spiritual affiliations, they resided in Al-Ghaba, which was the administrative post of the Soninke empire. Often referred to as the prehistoric order of the Gundu, the strange priests upon their arrival, gained recognition, acceptance and favour by the ruler. They immediately became special guests and subsequently secret advisers of the Ghana of Ghana who accommodated them in an annex of his vast magnificent stone palace.

"According to archeological records excavated in recent times at a Kumbi-saleh site speculated to be the exact location of the Ghana's palace, these beings were not totally human in stature and physical characteristics when they first arrived from the Senegal. They had long spindly frames and their ears were thicker and rounder in shape, their heads a touch too curved at the forehead. Even the greenish tinge of their dull slant eyes was not altogether like descendants of the homo-habilis. Yet the Gundu were basically human in their looks and general disposition. In the course of their stay, they gradually changed to look like their hosts. Seemingly of their own conscious efforts they mutated slowly but surely in resemblance of their Soninke hosts. Even the light pigmentation of skin which they had, while in the company of the light-skinned Moroccans, darkened and became darker than the average black African." The professor paused and looked up to see if he had their full attention.

"After the Gundu priests arrived in old Ghana, they set up a temporary camp in the outskirts of the cities of Kumbi and Al-Ghaba. These were twin cities that cohabited side by side yet peculiar in culture and character. Kumbi was the home of North African traders, Muslims, who dominated the commerce of the region. They built solid stone houses and numerous mosques for worship and indoctrination of Islamic theology and law. Arabic scholars abounded who upheld the tenets of Islam and recorded historical events.

"On the other hand was Al-Ghaba, the more traditional and indigenous quarter, the governing body of the Soninke empire. Here, the Ghana of Ghana lived in absolute luxury in his grand palace furnished in style and affluence. He wore fine quality robes laced with gold and kept thorough-bred dogs in gold leashes and ran law courts where cases were tried and judgment meted out to offenders.

"Unlike the Muslims from the North, the Soninke people worshipped various gods and believed in the supremacy of ancestral spirits. They built shrines for each deity and everyone was free to solicit the help of the god of his choice. This factor offered the Gundu a more conducive habitat for spiritual innovations.

"Upon his coronation as the ruler, The Ghana of Ghana assumed a supernatural status with all the customary rituals that were part of his accession to the throne. He became the head of all the cults, the link between man and spirits, the living and the dead.

"Though the Gundu priests had traveled down with Muslim merchants from the North of Africa, it was certain that spiritually they shared little in common except in the exchange of magical and medical skills. However, when they arrived and set up camp near Kumbi and Al-Ghaba the Gundu were naturally drawn to the Soninke people whose religious diversity offered a more cordial and fertile ground for their own esoteric mode of spiritism.

"The Ghana himself was quick to discover the spiritual powers of the Gundu priests and soon after their arrival, invited them to reside in an annex of his great stone palace. The Gundus provided a tremendous amount of help and inspiration to the Ghana in his office as ruler and spiritual head."

The professor raised his head from the file. "Gentlemen, the Gundu priests may have settled briefly at a couple of places when they left Ghana but we believe that their home for the past few centuries has been in the eastern region of Nigeria. A remote and isolated town called Obodo Ogwari."

❧‖ Sixteen ‖☙

It was plain irony that Ismail Suraju would be scheming to leave the army just after one year in the force. In his primary school days, Ismail had boasted to his mates how he would become a soldier, come back to Birnin Bindiga with a big gun and they would go hunting. Even when he got into secondary school, the dream was still alive but with more mature intentions. His father, Malami Suraju, said it was the turbulence of Ismail's spiritual calling that made him drop out of secondary school in the middle of his third year, despite his brilliant performance and Malami Suraju's willingness to sponsor.

When Ismail left home the first time, he joined a truck driver as the driver's mate. When they traveled, they were gone for weeks transporting onions from the north to Lagos. Ismail did not miss home because his mind was set on success. He would come home one day, a wealthy man, and disprove his father's insinuations that his success lay only in spiritual work. One day without warning, the driver dismissed him with no explanation. It was from another driver's mate that Ismail found out that his employer, the driver, was afraid of him. He often saw Ismail in a dream torturing and tormenting him. The young Ismail went back to Birnin Bindiga when he could not find a job in Lagos. His paltry savings dried up very fast and he still could not find another job.

When he reached home, Ismail went to his father's day hut where Malami Suraju received his patients and clients. It was a big circular hut with a cone-shaped thatched roof. The Malami, as usual, wore a white robe that matched his white-turbaned head and pointed goatee. His holy Quaran, weather-beaten with age, lay beside him on the hand-crafted mat where the old man sat cross-legged. Malami Suraju, on seeing his son suddenly back from Lagos, bore a pensive but rather amused glint in his eyes. Among his children, only Ismail and his confused state of mind bothered the Malami who had spent most of his life helping and treating people yet he hadn't much to show for it. He did not mind. Suraju did not charge money for consultation or treatment, moral or spiritual assistance. He was grateful to Allah for providing abundantly for him through the generosity of people whom he assisted successfully. He did not have much in material possessions yet nothing of need was ever lacking in his household. There was perfect harmony between his four wives and numerous children. Malami Suraju was never doubtful that this was a special blessing from the most merciful Allah, a reward for his continual attempts at purity. Perfection could never be attained, he knew, but striving towards it was his life's devotion. The only problem he had was how to guide his first son successfully to his life's goal.

*   *   *

As he wiped off a tiny grease spot from the stock of his AK 47 assault rifle, Ismail considered once more the possibilities of his leaving the army. Halfway through training camp he was certain that he had made the wrong decision. It was too late to go back. The shame it would bring to his family, his father and grandfather, the extended family. Where would the scandal reach? That the first son of Malami Suraju was not man enough to go through the rigours of army training, a course that every Usman and Emeka went through with their eyes closed. Kai! Allah would not allow it, Ismail prayed. He persevered through training and was posted to the 82nd Division where he served for nine months before his sudden transfer to Headquarters. It was exactly twelve months after Ismail's posting that he sat in his guard post at HQ wondering how to get out. He had joined upon the insistence of his grandfather who retired from third infantry after a meritorious service: two exceptional promotions and a medal.

Malami Suraju wanted to stop Ismail from joining up but he didn't want to appear disrespectful to his own father. Moreover, he had to let the young Ismail explore, experience and make the final decision himself. If he was destined for spiritual work as was most obvious, not even the army could stop it. Ismail was just one more proof that one chosen for spiritual work was usually the one who least desired it. Of all the numerous sons and daughters of Malami Suraju, Ismail was the one who showed the strongest signs to succeed his father as an Islamic scholar and healer yet the young man did all he could to hide from the truth. Much as he wanted to let Ismail soar in freedom before the full realization of his life's vocation finally dawned on him, he had to let the boy know the truth: Total rejection of spiritual work for one who really had a true calling usually led to an untimely and disastrous end.

Malami Suraju had complete faith in Allah that if Ismail was to later take over from him, His perfect will shall be done. So, he only humoured his son at his many commercial escapades. Even when Ismail decided to head for Jos where he would take up a vocation as a professional driver, Malami Suraju had not tried to stop him.

Ismail completed his driver training in Jos and found work as an English man's chauffeur. The whiteman's maid, Jamila, was a beautiful brown-skinned girl who was suddenly possessed by the demon spirit, the Aljannu. The benevolent Briton, Mr Elkington, sought clinical help for the girl, despite Ismail's advice that she was stricken with the Aljannu and could not be treated effectively by a psychiatrist. After a Scottish doctor treated and issued a clean bill of health to Jamila she was brought home and that same day, she suffered a most violent demonic attack. That night, the male spirit within her spoke intimately to the English man mocking him about how he paraded himself in Africa as a big white boss while his wife cheated on him back in England. In a croaky jeering male voice, Jamila who was a shy, quiet and respectful girl, told her master that presently as she spoke, his wife was sleeping in a cheap motel with his best friend. Elky, as his friends called him, phoned London that afternoon and confirmed that the information was true. Immediately he sought advice from Ismail. At first, Ismail was tempted to bring his father to treat the girl but then he thought otherwise. After all he could "see" the Aljannu, the mean foul spirit that preyed on the young innocent girl like a vulture on dead meat.

Ismail could feel the power building up in him and before he could give further thought to the matter he found himself descending upon Jamila like a wrestler on his charging opponent. He clasped his palms around the back of the girl's head, his thumbs pressing down hard on her temple just as he had seen his father do countless times while casting out the Aljannu. Whispering holy words into her ears he pressed harder on the sides of her head, at times bending her finger backwards. He kept dealing with the demon with such intensity of spirit as would be in this very first spontaneous and highly emotional outing as a Malami until Jamila sneezed mildly. The Aljannu was gone. With further holy incantations he banned the unclean spirit from coming back into the girl. Afterwards, Ismail gave her spiritual directions and instructions on how to protect herself in future from the Aljannu. Ismail was chosen and had learned well from years of assisting Malami Suraju.

Few months after the exorcism that Ismail performed on Jamila it was obvious that the girl was completely cured. Thereabouts, the whiteman's amorous interest in his maidservant became apparent. In a month he paid off his gardener, stewards and other household staff. It was clear to Ismail that since Jamila's status in the house was going to change, she was no longer comfortable with the watchful eyes of those who once treated her as equals or even her superiors.

Ismail was the last to go. One day, soon after the others were dismissed, Mr Elkington called him into his sitting room and asked him to sit down. Jamila sat next to the boss, wearing red lipstick, her eyes layered with mascara. Clinging to her body was a blue frock that revealed her lithe contours. She looked as beautiful as ever. A fifteen-year-old girl she had recently acquired was already serving Jamila as she herself had done in that same house.

"Ismail ol' chap, I'm sorry I'll have to let you go also," Elkington said. "My plans and movement … going to be unsteady … you know."

"Yes, Sir," Ismail answered and feigned a little surprise and disappointment just to show some respect. Afterall he had been expecting the sack. Ismail's only anxiety was in puzzlement of what the man would give him as a parting gift. Elkington had settled his other household staff with gifts of home utensils, motorbike and money to start a small-scale business. Elky was rich, generous and wanted his entire staff to leave smiling, as long as they left him with his beloved Jamila to start on a clean slate. Ismail was not expecting much and having helped to deliver Jamila from the Aljannu, he felt a little guilty to be expectant of a special reward. Malami Suraju had taught him the virtue of serving without the expectation of material rewards. He had taught him the benefits of living a frugal life even in the midst of plenty. The spirit must be kept crisp and lively.

"You can see that I've given away all there is to give in the house," Elkington continued, "but I was thinking, it's better I do for you, something you would really appreciate. So... What is it that you desire? Something I can do."

The words of Elkington were clear to Ismail. It took him unawares and left him at a loss for words. Others had been given properties and huge cash gifts but he was being offered the gift of his choice, a blank cheque. However, Ismail's mind did not start revolving around money instead he thought of his life's dream to be like his grandfather.

"I would like to join the army, Sir," he blurted out.

"The army. Is that all?"

"Yes, Sir! If you can sponsor me, Sir."

"Splendid! We shouldn't have much of a problem there," Elkington said. "Incidentally, I have friends highly placed in the army. I'll ring one up tomorrow and see how we can get you started."

Ismail thanked his boss tremendously. He also thanked Jamila.

*   *   *

Elkington fulfilled his promise and facilitated Ismail's enlistment. When he was suddenly sent to HQ Ismail had no doubt that Elky had made the request for him to be adequately placed. All these factors contributed to Ismail's handicap in finding a way to leave the force in a hurry. Nevertheless, his reason for wanting to go home grossly outweighed all sentiments binding him to stay. The calling had grown immensely in him. He could naturally detect and effectively treat many health and spiritual problems brought before him by his fellow soldiers.

To the chagrin of Ismail's immediate boss, Sergeant Udoh, some had even tried to bring civillian patients secretly for Ismail to treat. Udoh had been a little harsh on this extracurricular activity of Ismail's until he also benefited from a successful treatment, a hormonal problem he had managed from boyhood. From then Ismail became his favourite private. Although he could have arranged to ply his spiritual vocation in the army, officially, Ismail did not want it that way.

He had battled to adhere to the strict doctrines of moral and spiritual purity that his father, Malami Suraju, tried to imbibe in him. However, it was in the army that he became a true Ustaz.

Were it to be in the Christian faith, Ismail would have professed to be born-again. From his perspective, a true Ustaz had no business in the army as a regular soldier. The message the Malami Suraju had subtly drummed into him over the years had finally sunk and settled. It was all very clear to him now, as though an intangible blindfold had been untied from his eyes. Now he saw that it was that same spiritual vocation which he shunned that finally earned him the blank cheque that brought him to the army, the last phase of his extracurricular training. He also 'saw' in the future that his final exit from the army was going to be dramatic and miraculous yet it had not been revealed to him exactly how it would happen. Not everything was revealed to a Malami, Ismail knew. There were things known only and only to the most merciful Allah.

Seventeen

Igo bounced up from his apparent slumber and stood like one roused from a terrible nightmare. He snatched up his batik cloth with both hands and snapped it in the air to shake off the sand and dust.

He slipped off his boxer shorts and singlet and folded them carefully. After folding the batik he sandwiched his cap and sandals, boxers and singlet in the last fold of the cloth.

The sixth keeper cleared his throat.

Emodi woke up, his back still leaning on the wall. He held out his hands and accepted the small bundle that the old man gave to him before he noticed that Igo was stark naked.

"Is anything wrong?" Emodi asked, startled.

"No," Igo answered. "I'm going home."

"How?" Emodi asked and got to his feet, Igo's bundle still in his hands. "Are you going to pretend to be mad or what?"

The old man was silent. He turned away from Emodi and faced the entrance of the cell. "Guards!" he called.

Emodi opened his mouth to speak, to urge Igo to put his clothes back on before the guards arrived, but no sound came. His mouth hung open as he thought better of the advice. His thoughts were distracted by the sound of approaching boots.

"After I leave, make sure you lie down on the floor and stay down," Igo said. The iron gate rattled. Emodi held his breath. Knowing that Igo was neither foolish nor shameless, his nakedness had to have a cogent reason.

Igo stood his ground staring fixedly at the entrance.

"Na wetin?" asked the unarmed guard who came in ahead of another two with AK-47 rifles slung on their shoulders.

"I want to use your toilet," said Igo.

Upon noticing the old man's nakedness, they looked at each other with rather amused smiles on their faces.

An old man in detention wanting to ease himself would not have posed much of a problem. However, this old man was not run-of-the-mill. A red alert had been placed on his detention status. They had wondered why the alert on the man came hours after the arrest. One of the soldiers had jokingly said they ran some tests on the old man and found something more horrible than AIDS.

"No problem," said the tall dark one, unslinging his rifle, "but you have to put your clothes on first, and don't try anything stupid. Our orders are, shoot-to-kill."

The second armed soldier, tall and slim, with that peculiar light-brownness of the Fulani stock also slipped his rifle from his shoulder and kept it handy in his right hand. Working on orders, they felt a little absurd to be excercising so much caution on this wizened old man whom they thought that anyone of them could have defeated unarmed.

As the Fulani soldier was apparently losing interest in the naked old man, Igo saw that he no longer had their attention.

"Hai!" Igo shouted at the top of his voice.

All three soldiers looked sharply at him, wondering why he shouted. He had their undivided attention.

From where Emodi stood, he could not see the old man's face. He missed that weird moment of extraterrestrial contact, that split second signal of spiritual enslavement that passed from Igo to his captives. To Emodi's greatest surprise, the unarmed soldier opened the cell and they all came in and lay down on the floor after placing their guns against the walls.

"Abdul! Abdul!" called a voice from beyond the entrance. A chubby dark soldier came in calling the Fulani who was too far gone to answer. He took in the scene in a flash and moved sharply backward to raise alarm then rested his eyes on the naked old man. He too came into the cell and lay down beside the Fulani.

Igo closed his eyes. His body shook and squirmed rigorously. His body temperature dropped rapidly to sub-zero. One who touched him then would feel as though it were a sheet of ice. All thought emissions and circumventions were consciously blocked, leaving a high-vibrational focus on his material transformation to the frequency of his spirit being. The meeting point was actualized. Still staring at the old man from behind, Emodi noticed Igo's body shake and vibrate as a definite alteration began in the colour of his skin. It changed from jet black to silvery white, a cloudy gas similar to smoke eddying on the surface of his entire body. In a flash, Igo vanished.

"Igo ... Igo ..." Emodi whispered in shock. He looked about the room in search of the old man. His only visible companions were the four soldiers who lay on the cracked dusty floor seemingly asleep. He remembered the instruction that Igo had given him and quickly lay down on the floor with the soldiers. The reason was now obvious to Emodi. When the sleeping soldiers would be discovered he would not be held responsible for their condition or for the old man's disappearance.

*   *   *

Igo moved into a long tiled corridor. He stepped lightly on his bare feet to avoid making much sound. Halfway down the hall, a colonel came out of an office and started towards him. Igo flattened himself against the wall to avoid physical contact with the colonel and his aide who tagged behind him like a boy after his father. When they passed, Igo followed them into a large open courtyard with a fountain. Water sprung from a bronze-like model of an artillery gun and poured into a huge black bowl from where thin spurts rose in wide looming arcs. He had considered in meditation how best to release himself from the guardroom without endangering Emodi. Igo knew he had the skills to take Emodi with him in his cell break but he rejected the idea. He had to leave him as a hostage for the government. If both were to vanish from the cell, it would definitely cause a serious security inquiry that would surely lead them to Obodo Ogwari. It was a tradition for the keepers of the Ideamala, the Gundu priests to squash any factor that would cause external attention to the town of Obodo Ogwari. If not for his desperate bid to survive, Igo would have yielded to be arrested in the minister's office, spent the duration of his detention in silence and probably gone home in a day or two. Now, he was certain that there was a special interest in him. Captain Okafor had said that General Idris was waiting for orders from above to release him. It was an alarming statement for Igo.

*   *   *

On that fateful day, he sat buffing his rifle, Ismail was exceptionally fired with such intensity of spirit that he could hardly contain. He was engaged in a strange outlandish euphoria, like an out-of-body experience. Ismail felt so light as if he would become air-borne with the gentle breeze that wheezed through the courtyard of Army HQ. Suddenly, he became spaced-out as he interwove from one dimension of psychic presence to another. What he saw filled him with awe. Strange fires burned around him without threatening him. Huge clusters of fire, molten and hissing stretched as far as the horizon yet soothing and refreshing to Ismail. Gradually he was adapting to these awesome and sometimes scary natural phantasmagoria. Ismail could now understand how his father was able to identify the spirits that their dog, Dansanda, often barked at. Such sights were locked in other dimensions of reality.

When Ismail 'saw' Igo moving across the courtyard, he was inclined to take it as one of the bizarre sights that filtered into his visions. But then, he realized that the image bore a close likeness of the old village man who was presently locked up in the make-shift guardroom. But, why did the old man's image appear so vivid yet so alien? Ismail wondered. Why was he naked? One final sign made Ismail certain that it was no apparition. The old man, conscious of his illegal escape, moved with stealth and caution, despite his invisibility. Quickly, Ismail assessed the situation and remembered that this was the same old man that was said to have performed some mysterious tricks in the honourable minister's office; the same man whose detention status was placed on red alert. Ismail looked around wondering if other soldiers in the courtyard could see the naked old man. It was obvious that no one else saw him.

"Hey! You," Ismail hollered at Igo. "Paapa! Stop there!"

Igo turned sharply to face Ismail.

Ismail's heart skipped and danced. He felt a sudden horrifying weakness. It was like he was looking at a ghost. Other soldiers who were with him, even the colonel who had stopped to chat with another officer, were all startled by Ismail's shout at an apparently imaginary person.

Igo was momentarily disoriented, confused. He had been sure that no one could see him. The colonel and his orderly, the soldiers? in the courtyard, all did not notice him. Why this particular soldier? Must be some kind of a spiritual guru. The quickest option for Igo was to overwhelm the soldier who accosted him, neutralize him and put him out of order as he had done to the ones who presently slept on the cell floor. He sought for Ismail's eye contact.

Ismail was struck by the force of the old man's gaze. Their eyes met in a clash that was transformed into a silent but thundereous bang like the onset of sonic booms. It was like the top of Ismail's head would blow open as he absorbed and accommodated the high frequency waves that emanated from the old man's still greenish eyes. Ismail staggered backwards and shook his head vigorously to shake off the impact. When he looked up again the old man was gone, vanished. He had lost the vision.

"Ismail, what is it?" Private Ojo asked. "Wetin dey happen?"

"E be like say Ismail don see devil," Corporal Essien joked.

Ismail ignored the joking Essien and answered Ojo. "It's that old man in the guardroom. I think he has escaped."

"But, there's no one there," Corporal Essien laughed.

"Ojo!" Ismail yelled. "Rush to the guardroom and see what is happening. I will stay here and watch for him. Take your walkie-talkie with you."

Ojo, who had witnessed more than enough of Ismail's spiritual powers to doubt him, sprinted away immediately towards the guardroom while Essien and another soldier, Austin, stood there laughing at them as if they were suffering from sudden lunatic delusions.

Ismail leaned his gun against the metal railings near his post and quickly spread his small praying mat. He sat cross-legged on the floor beside him. Picking up his charbi-prayer beads began to mutter inaudibly.

Bissimillahi rahmanir raliim. A'azu billahi minash shaidanir raliim, Inna lillahi wa Inna illaihir rajiun Laillalia illallali, muliammadur rasullilah, sala llahu alai, hi wa salam.

Igo stood transfixed in the courtyard undecided what to do next. Though he was still bent on escaping, he felt that he had to take a few minutes to revamp his line of action. The soldier who penetrated his shield of invisibility had certainly ruined the initial plan to be far gone before the discovery of his escape. Now that he was discovered everything seemed to have changed for the worse. What manner of human being was this that did not succumb to his gaze even when he released such powerful vibes at him. Igo was a little relieved after the impact to know that the soldier had lost vision of him. As he watched Ismail sitting cross-legged, muttering and rolling the string of beads between his fingers Igo made the conclusion that the soldier was some kind of spiritual freak and was getting back in spirit for further enagement with him. As Igo made to continue toward the main gate he overheard the soldier asking his friend to hurry and check the guardroom. His heart sank. He hesitated for a while pondering whether to go back to the guardroom and see what would happen but decided to move on.

Still sitting with legs crossed, eyes partly closed, Ismail kept muttering ... ascending in spirit, this time not for the vision of the old man to come spontenously as it did before but for him to search for it ... and to find it. His spirit was the base of his foundation from where he locked on to his mind and lurched into diverse realms ... A faint whistling sound came inside Ismail, shrill and angry as the burning intensity of his soul in motion ... vivid visions rushed to him in sight and sound ... Desert storms in high velocity blowing from opposite directions came crashing in tumultuous collisions ... Rainstorm ... Bold and fiery bolts of lightning splitting and tearing through the firmament amid deafening blasts of thunder ... Peace ... A clear still glistering lake ... quiet and profound in nature. Ismail opened his eyes wider and beheld the courtyard in a glaring but misty vision. He looked across to the right and saw the naked old man moving briskly toward the main gate. The soldiers at the gate lounged about in haphazard vigilance that was so typical of peace-time army.

Ismail's walkie-talkie cackled raucously with Ojo's excited voice. "Calling sentry two, calling sentry two, sentry two come in, over."

Ismail snatched up the walkie talkie. "Sentry two here, over."

"Sentry two, there's a problem here, in the guardroom. The old man has escaped. All our men are asleep inside the cell, over."

With the walkie-talkie in his hand, his rifle hanging on his shoulder, Ismail broke into a run towards the front gate.

"What about the second inmate? Over," Ismail yelled into the mouthpiece.

"Second inmate present, over."

"Bring him to the front gate, on the double, over."

"To the front gate? Over."

"On the double," Ismail shouted.

*   *   *

Igo reached the front gate, and found a fresh problem. A situation had developed. When he and Emodi were arrested and brought to Army HQ the huge black main gate had been open. Only a white bar that crossed the full breadth of the entrance was raised for vehicles to enter after clearance. There was a smaller gate with a guardhouse through which pedestrians were let in. Now, both gates were firmly locked to check the aggression of the mob outside. Over five thousand people stood beyond the gates in peaceful but rowdy protest. When he got closer, he read their placards and understood that these were retired soldiers who were protesting the lengthy delay in the payment of their pension benefits. They ranged from the very aged to teenagers who were apparently representing their old or sick parents.

Igo looked behind and saw the soldier running towards Ismail approaching fast. Igo had to move quickly and cross over to the crowd and mingle with them. Opening the main gate would have taken longer but going through the small guard hut crowded with soldiers would entail shoving people out of the way. Igo ran inside the guard hut and collided with a sergeant who fell against another soldier beside him. Igo pushed a man in a green caftan who fell against the small office table and jammed heads with the soldier that sat behind the table. Igo unbolted the outer door and stepped outside.

Ismail ran into the guard hut as Igo stepped outside into the crowds of retired soldiers. They milled around in their hundreds, a majority sitting tiredly on the side walks. Others patrolled with placards, chanting slogans.

"A prisoner has escaped and he came through here, Sir," Ismail reported to the most superior soldier in the room.

"What strange thing is happening here?" asked the sergeant as he helped the corporal whom he had knocked down when Igo ran into him.

"What kind of man was it that passed through here without our seeing him?" the corporal asked Ismail.

The sergeant had seen the door unbolt itself. "Ismail, what is happening here?"

Ismail did not answer. He dashed through the room and came out on the other side. A section of the crowd that faced the main gate were startled and apprehensive when Ismail ran out of the small gate in a confrontational attitude.

* * *

Ojo had gone past their post with Emodi whom he hustled out of the guardroom.

"Move! Move!" Ojo ordered Emodi pushing him into a trot. "Move! Move!"

* * *

Ismail stood staring at the crowd and they at him. Igo had crossed beyond two inorderly rows of people when Ismail called out to him.

"Hey, You! Old man, stop! I can see you. Come back here," he shouted loudly. The crowds fell silent wondering what pronouncement the army had sent this soldier to make to them.

Igo heard the voice. It was a familiar voice, the same voice that had challenged him in the courtyard. He stopped but did not turn around immediately. The soldier's persistence in accosting him had become a challenge. The soldier had proved to be some kind of spiritualist. Igo's pride as keeper of the Ideamala, a Gundu priest, did not accord him the liberty of running away from the soldier. When he turned to Ismail it was with force and intangible venom.

Ismail averted his eyes from Igo's jolting stare. He had learned his lesson from the first encounter. The other soldiers in the guard house all came outside uncertain how to respond to the baffling situation. Even the civilian in green caftan came out with them, an astonished look on his face.

Ojo pushed Emodi into the empty guard house and they exited to the other side where Ismail was addressing an invisible man.

"Ismail!" Ojo called excitedly. "I have brought the other man."

"Bring him here."

Ojo pushed Emodi past the soldiers and grabbed him by the shoulder to place him beside Ismail.

"Soldier-priest, allow us to go," Igo's voice boomed, seeming from nothingness. It was the first time he spoke.

The pensioners who stood around him were startled and drew backwards, looking around them to see where the voice came from.

"We have done nothing wrong, soldier-priest," Igo continued. "All we asked the Minister of Works was to keep his express road away from our peaceful village. Is that too much to ask? He said I was disrespectful and wanted to arrest me, a man young enough to be my great-great-grandson. I had to protect myself. I did not hurt anyone."

Before Igo got through the middle of his speech all the pensioners in the vicinity from where his voice emanated had backed off leaving a big arc hemmed with old people. Though only Ismail could see Igo, it was obvious to all the onlookers that the owner of the voice was apparently standing in that wide empty arc.

Corporal Essien and Austin who had mocked Ismail earlier now stood with the soldiers, all in utter puzzlement.

Ismail was moved by the old man's words. He could imagine with disgust, an express road of disgusting black tar stretching annoyingly through his quiet peaceful village of Birnin Bindiga. The trailers and the lorries, the rowdy settlers that it would bring. His sympathy went out to the old man. But, he had to do his duty as a soldier, to protect the interest of his unit as a priority.

"I sympathize with you but your escape will not solve the problem," Ismail advised, "instead it will make it worse."

"Must we all bend to their own brand of civilization?" Igo asked. "Must everyone desire express roads and railway lines?" We have practised our own culture and civilization for many centuries and we do not need another. Allow us to go back to our home."

"Sorry, I can't let you go," answered Ismail.

"And if I disobey?"

"Your son here will bear the consequences," Ismail said. He cocked his rifle, and leveled it on Emodi to bluff the old man. He hoped that the man would not call his bluff. Their eyes met. This time Ismail did not worry about the old man's enchanting gaze. The soft gentle look in Igo's eyes was enough to tell Ismail that the old man had surrendered, not out of acceptance of defeat but to save Emodi. The strong divine intuition that had grown in

Ismail over the years gave him insight on the man's character as he looked into Igo's eyes. Here was a man full of kindness and compassion yet extremely dangerous. Ismail wondered what would have happened in this final encounter if he hadn't brought Emodi as a hostage. Intuitively Ismail shuddered inwards to try to imagine how it would have been … He was certain that full confrontation with this phlegmatic old man would be in the least like walking into a cage full of hungry lions.

Igo kept looking into Ismail's eyes trying to read his thoughts as would have been so easy with other people. A cloudy blob blocked his feelers unto the soldier. He wanted to know whether Ismail would really shoot Emodi if he disobeyed the order to return to the guardroom. Now there was no way to be sure. The only choice left was to capitulate. Igo would not risk the young man's life. Not even to save his own.

An army officer stood adjacent to Ismail. He held a short wooden staff with a brassy knob. Igo trained his eyes on the buffed shining orb. It was to be his object of concentration. Now that his escape was nullified, the pressure of staying invisible struck him like a highly debilitating fever and hunger. He felt weak as his knees began to shake and shiver. He started to let go of his stoic intensity … long-suffering coldness and pain … He had to let go immediately, to release the load that was no longer valuable … Not minding his nakedness, he dimmed his eyes and rushed for the point of release as the image of the officer's brass knob faded from his view. A dull heat, soothing and rejuvenating crept into his body, susurating … caressing … No care, no worries … a point of life, in dark shadows of non-existence … Igo lost consciousness.

From Ismail's view, he knew the old man was going through strange changes seemingly from some kind of primordial imports, alien invocations and sorcery. He felt dizzy just watching the old man as he disintegrated slowly and finally disappeared.

The crowds had been quiet from the onset of Ismail's conversation with the unseen man. A contagion of silence rippled to the rear, even to those who had no clear view of the patch from where the voice of the invisible man came.

Slowly like a huge block of ice exposed to sudden heat, a misty apparition began to form in the image of a man. Little tongues of vapour leaping like cold fires, rose from the manly image till the texture of Igo's skin began to surface. All mist disssolved and the old man stood before the soldiers and the crowds stark naked, his jet black skin glistening a hue of blue in the glare of midday sun.

Silence ... Not a single soul moved, none uttered a word until the Igo stepped forward toward Ismail. Pandemonium struck; placards flew in the air as pensioners closest to Igo took off in quick flashes defying the constraint of age or bulk. Even most of the soldiers who stood behind Ismail drew backwards. But, on seeing him standing firmly to receive the naked man, the soldiers stood their ground. Before Igo reached Ismail, almost all the pensioners stood over a hundred yards away from the gates watching suspiciously to know if this strange display was some new aggression to be directed against them. Soon afterwards the organizers decided to end the demonstration for the day. Many were bruised and chaffed. They had fallen as they ran and some had been trampled on.

Ismail, trailed by Essien, Ojo and other soldiers escorted Igo and Emodi back to the guardroom. Despite the congratulatory words and friendly slaps on the back by his colleagues Ismail felt cold and unfulfilled. He had done his duty by arresting the old man yet he had no job satisfaction. The system was cold-blooded and wicked to have kept these two men in the guardroom for no good reason. All they wanted was to keep the rumpus of city life away from their peaceful village.

*   *   *

Igo touched each of the four soldiers that slept on the cell floor whispering short inaudible phrases into their ears. One after the other, they bounced up from the floor as if stung by a bee. They looked befuddled with sleep and remembered nothing about what had happened to them.

They were led away by military policemen for interrogation. By the end of the day, it became obvious that the four soldiers had been placed on some sort of detention themselves. Half a dozen new soldiers were deployed outside the room where the two men of Obodo Ogwari were held. They were all huge young men, mean and combat-ready, as if brawn and physical might were the necessary factors to keep the old man in the cell.

When Ismail was summoned to General Idris' office he knew that the top brass probably wanted to commend him for foiling the old man's escape. But again, he had doubts whether he would be blamed for some kind of interference or trespass into a matter that was too clandestine in nature. He quickly smoothed his flaying nerves with the self-assurance that he had done his job as a guard at HQ and no one could officially blame him.

General Idris sat bolt upright in his soldierly grandeur, his chest bedecked with colourful medals. A lovely light-skinned female lieutenant sat on a black leather arm chair staring into the computer on her laps. Though the posh and expansive office with its huge mahogany conference table, chilled air-conditioned atmosphere all impressed Ismail, he was not awestruck as the average private would have been. This new-found harmony with his life's spiritual work had given him a tremendous confidence. He was filled with great reverence and awe for his Creator, love and respect for his fellow man beyond any boundaries of race and status.

"Good work, Private Ismail Suraju," General Idris said, smiling broadly.

"Thank you, Sir," Ismail answered also smiling.

"Now, I want you to tell me how it all happened. Don't talk too fast so that Lieutenant Constance, here, can record; commence!"

Ismail told the general how he discovered the old man trying to sneak across the courtyard, how the old man tried to subdue him probably as he had done to the four soldiers that went to sleep on the guardroom floor. General Idris kept pumping Ismail for more information while the lieutenant chattered away on the laptop. At the end of the grilling interview, the general looked a little disappointed to discover that Ismail couldn't give much insight on Igo's origin or source of powers. However, he was still grateful to the private for apprehending the old man. What an embarrassment it would have caused especially after the note-worthy incident at the minister's office that brought official attention to the old man.

"Once again, I thank you for a job well done," the general said. "I want you to choose one good deed I can do for you, besides the promotion which I'll surely give you."

Immediately, Ismail remembered his former boss, Elkington. It was by a similar offer that he joined the army exactly a year ago.

"Sir, I would like to be allowed to leave."

"No problem," Idris answered. "You can take thirty days with full benefits. I'll arrange a package for you."

"I'm sorry, Sir," Ismail said apologetically. "What I mean is that I want to leave the army, to go back to my home in Birnin Bindiga to assist my father for a period before I go off on my own."

The general fell silent for a moment; creases of surprise marred his forehead. "Oh! I see, and what does your father do to need your assistance?'

"My father is Malami Suraju of Birnin Bindiga in Zamfara," Ismail answered.

"Allah be praised," General Idris chanted. He stared blankly at Ismail for a moment before he spoke. "I will arrange for your discharge, let's say ... for health reasons," the general stated.

"I am very grateful, Sir." Ismail stood up and saluted.

℘‖ Eighteen ‖℘

Soon after Igo was rearrested, Gen. Idris summoned another emergency meeting of the Life Tree team.

"I have sent for Captain Okafor to come and see us during this meeting," said the general. "He comes from the same town as the old man. Maybe he can give us a better insight on the man's origin and power source. It appears we haven't seen the full extent of his capabilities."

Professor Okediadi shook his head slightly, careful not to appear too critical of Idris' opinion in the presence of others.

"I doubt if this captain can tell you much about the Gundu. It is beyond him. The ancient cult of the Gundu were known to blend completely in culture and social life even in appearance with their host communities. However, their spiritual mode remains a highly guarded secret. The Ogwari cave seems to be their final resting place and there must be a reason for that. So, gentlemen, we have ascertained that there is a highly peculiar and probably alien and superior force that lives amongst us and the decision is whether to carve the dual carriage road through there or to reroute and let them be."

The Inspector General cleared his throat. "If there's really a formidable force in that village that has been there for centuries, then it means they are not a threat to us. Why bother them now? My opinion would be to re-route and leave them alone."

"What do you say, professor?" Idris asked.

"I kind of share the IG's view. The Gundu we know from bits and pieces of ancient history, are a powerful but peaceful people. Since I'm sure we can't really force them to impart their knowledge on us, I suggest we change the course of the road and leave them alone," the professor stated. "However, we can always send a team of scientists through your captain, Okafor, to see if we can learn certain things from them."

"Perfect idea," the IG supported.

"Gentlemen, I don't agree with you," Jibril opposed. "After all, changing the course of that road would mean extra desired activity for my ministry but the reputation and integrity of the federal government has been challenged. That old man did not mince words when he stood before me in the Federal Ministry of Works and dared us to try putting a road through his village."

"The threat of one old village man to the federal government is inconsequential," said the IG. "Odutola can send in some operatives to penetrate the village and make some findings ..."

"Sorry, Mr Odutola, not to undermine the efficiency of your operatives but your spies would be like fish out of water in Obodo Ogwari. The people don't sell land or rent rooms to visitors. Their community is highly close-knit and not visitor-friendly," said the professor.

"Then how come they came to my office with a white man who is supposed to be a naturalized member of their village?" Jibril asked. "And again I wonder why the white man wasn't arrested with them?"

"My men saw him as a foreigner," Idris answered. "You know, avoiding diplomatic mix-ups."

"The white man spoke as one of them. He was even introduced with an Igbo name which I can't remember, Ugo something." Jibril scratched his head, trying to recall Ugoabata's name.

"I think the white man should be picked up if he can still be found. A Westerner is more likely to reveal scientific discoveries than our people," the professor said.

When General Idris straightened up in the chair, his face assumed a cold sternness. It was obvious that he had a final point to make.

"Gentlemen, I wish to remind you of the strict confidentiality of this meeting. I know some of you are wondering why all this trouble for an old village man who performed some magic tricks but there's more to it. Funsho Odutola, head of our secret service, can shed a little light on the matter as he's at liberty to disclose for now. Funsho?"

"Well, this is one of those spontaneous assignments that often evolve in clandestine ops. No protocol, no red tape ..." Odutola began. "The team in such an operation is most times a motley crew that evolves spontaneously. Funding is done through a special supplementary budget. Gentlemen, this is the crew and I don't need to remind you again of the secrecy."

General Idris winked at him to get on with the main topic.

"Two years ago two of my boys investigating a band of militants operating in the Akpaka forest of Anambra State intercepted a strange coded message," Odutola continued. "We became very curious and started to investigate immediately. Well, after we had parts of the message decoded, it was clear that there are foreign spies interested in a little town east of the Niger called Obodo Ogwari. We sent in our own man to take a look around. Just like Professor Okediadi has stated, the town is socially dead. Visitors have no place there. An American spy going by the name Jake Sanders went in there posing as a miner. We succeeded in putting our own man in his so-called mining crew. The king of Obodo Ogwari accepted the American as a transient miner and even gave him an annex in his palace to reside. As the king's special guest Sanders had access to the entire town to come and go as he pleased yet he couldn't get anywhere with the villagers. My man worked as his special body guard and guide so we were positive that the American didn't succeed. The operation was dubbed 'Life Tree' for the singular fact that among the many mysteries to be discovered in that town, the major one is the secret of longevity … to discover why the villagers generally live to be well over a hundred years. Old priests like the one in the cell has been estimated by experts to be well over six hundred years old."

Odutola paused to let his last words be absorbed. He looked pointedly at them making brief eye contact with each one, assessing the appalled looks on some of their faces when he mentioned Igo's age. Only the general and Professor Okediadi looked unperturbed by the seemingly outrageous declaration. They both had prior knowledge of the fact.

"And today we have made an outstanding discovery that the man can vanish and reappear at will," the general added.

"Exactly," Odutola concurred. "Now it's up to us to prove the official opinion that it's not some kind of witchcraft or sorcery but pure science that can be taught and learned. So you can see why the express road is necessary, to carve a major inroad that would draw these primitive villagers into the open. We are in a new millennium and I think it's time for them to change. Time to let us in on some ancient secrets," Odutola concluded his lengthy speech.

"Objection," Professor Okediadi said impatiently. He had been showing signs of unease as the secret service boss spoke. "The secret of Obodo Ogwari lies not with the villagers but with the Gundu priests. In half a millennium they were known to have moved thrice. If disturbed in Obodo Ogwari they may move again to heaven knows where. I suggest we find more subtle ways to get closer to them and earn their trust and confidence."

"You contradict yourself, Mr Professor." This time Odutola spoke with a little sarcasm. "You told us that the Ogwari cave should be their last resting place?"

"Yes! I said so," replied Professor Okediadi. "But it doesn't mean that they may not run if harassed. However, I'll give you my frank and final opinion on this issue of the express road. Let us pray that these guys move away if we commence with the road. If they decide to stay and fight with the superior skills they possess, believe me, we'll have a great problem on our hands."

The silence that enveloped the room after the professor's statement echoed the quiet reflections of the newly formed administration of Operation Life Tree.

Soon afterwards, Captain Okafor was ushered in. After ten minutes of questioning by the administrators, it was obvious that he couldn't be of much help to them. He had left Obodo Ogwari as an adolescent boy and knew very little about the customs and traditional practices of the town.

When Minister Jibril asked Okafor if he knew the white man who accompanied the old man to his office. Okafor agreed. He told them that the man was an American school teacher who chose to naturalize and settle down in Obodo Ogwari, that he was presently betrothed to marry a woman of Ogwariland, and that Igwe Ajulufo would bestow a traditional title on him in the new yam festival, the Ofala. Innocently, Okafor told them that Phillip Carter, Ugoabata, had come with him and was presently waiting in a snack bar near HQ with another man of Obodo Ogwari named Ntukogu.

Immediately, General Idris dispatched some plainclothes soldiers to go to the snack bar and invite Ugoabata to the meeting. This was to Okafor's quiet chagrin. He did not know that Carter would be detained or he would not have given information on his whereabouts. Despite his loyalty to the army, the need to protect a fellow villager from Ogwari had been part of the major doctrines taught to the village youth.

Captain Okafor was dismissed and Phillip Carter brought before the administration. Before he was ushered in, the Life Tree administrators had him figured for a spy. Why else would a white man from New York City choose to teach in a small secluded village whose inhabitants deliberately reject the light of civilization?

Phillip Carter too could not provide any valuable information. After an hour of interrogation mostly by the secret service boss and the inspector general, Idris ordered that Carter be detained with Emodi and the old man.

"Isn't it obvious that this white man is a spy?" Odutola asked, more like a statement, after Carter was led away.

"Well, you no longer have to worry about a fresh lead to your foreign operatives. You now have a resident one," the general said to Odutola.

The SS boss nodded and closed his file.

*   *   *

After three days and Igo had not yet returned his fellow keepers gathered in a very large chamber. The five remaining keepers of the Ideamala did not talk to each other yet they communicated more effectively than in the use of dialogue. This gathering in a special chamber of the caves was never done except on very rare occasions of grave issues. For two days since it became certain that Igo was stranded somewhere, they had all stopped feeding and went into a joint meditative retreat. They stood in a circular formation around a tattered old straw mat that was spread on the floor of the chamber. All five wore dark-brown ankle-length robes with hoods that covered their heads and most of their faces. One who saw them from a distance could have easily mistaken them for medieval monks. Their heads were completely bowed as eye contact between them was of no importance. Jointly, they could 'see' Igo in the far-away capital where he lay on the carpeted floor of a posh office. After Igo was rearrested, Gen. Idris had relocated them to an office with hidden monitoring cameras, so that he and his aides could watch the old man.

*   *   *

Emodi and Carter were both sitting on cushioned armchairs their faces draped with anxiety. Their highly pensive mood reflected the hopelessness they felt for Igo's condition.

*   *   *

Igo had gone into a coma. Within two days his body had dehydrated and shrunken. His skin was smooth like vinyl, eyes sunken and deep-set in his skull. His breathing had become so irregular, Carter often thought that his intermittent high hanging breaths would be the last. But each time, he hung in there with new highs and lows.

Together the Gundu priests, keepers of the Ideamala, focused on Emodi where he sat at army HQ. Jointly they merged into a union of extrasensory modulations. They became one in spirit. Simultaneous with this fusion of the psyche came the instant emission of a powerful thought form that hit Emodi with a burst of spiritual reawakening.

*   *   *

Where he sat at army headquarters in the capital city, Emodi was suddenly jolted by a strong emotion. His heart glowed with joy and ecstasy as he experienced a definite feeling of alien visitation, yet the joy he felt in the face of the old man's condition seemed improper in a remote but insignificant part of his brain. Emodi was possessed. He stood up to obey instructions.

"What are you smiling for?" Carter asked Emodi when he saw the serene smile on his face.

"You will assist me," Emodi said without looking at him.

"How?" Ugoabata asked.

"Just do as I do," Emodi said moving across the room to a metal filing cabinet.

Ugoabata shrugged. "Ok," he answered co-operatively in the typical sporting attitude of the American.

Emodi pulled out two empty metal drawers and his friend did the same. All smiles had vanished from their faces.

"We are going to slam these metal drawers on the floor beside Igo's head," Emodi whispered.

"Why?" Ugoabata asked, also whispering.

"To scare him," Emodi replied.

"What for?"

"Just do as I say, Phillip, and everything will work out well."

"Ok, but are you sure he will hear us?"

"Positive," Emodi answered. "But make sure some part of your skin is touching his when the drawers hit the floor. Add some voice also."

The two men of Obodo Ogwari stood over the prostrate form of their priest as he lay dying on the floor. With the metal drawers in both hands raised above their heads, Emodi's right barefoot was rested firmly on Igo's belly while Carter's left foot was on the old man's midsection. Emodi nodded at Carter. Both men swung, the metal drawers downwards with great force and screamed at the same time. The drawers slammed simultaneously on both sides of the Igo's head in a metallic bang.

Amidst a blinding flash, Igo trans-located, taking Emodi and Carter with him. A brownish foul-smelling smoke eddied faintly over the area where Igo had lain, then faded into nothingness.

✳   ✳   ✳

As soon as the three men of Obodo Ogwari disappeared from the room, General Idris jumped up from his chair and rushed closer to the TV monitor. His two aides also bounced up from their seats and stood staring in perplexity.

"They have gone! All three of them, vanished," the general announced the obvious to his aides.

"Sir, this can't be real … an illusion," said his personal assistant, Musa. "Maybe they're still there in the room."

Hardly had Musa finished the statement than the general rushed out of his office on a trot. The secretaries in the outer office were startled when he barged through the room into the hallway. He flew down two flights of stairs and ran to the door labeled "office", his aides close behind.

"Open that door!" Idris barked at the two soldiers who stood guard in front of the office.

"Yes, Sir," the shorter one answered and saluted while nervously fumbling for the keys with his other hand.

The door was unlocked and flung wide open. The general entered with hesitant steps. The room was virtually empty, devoid of human presence. The general and his aides even looked behind the curtains. On closer observation they saw the drawers on both sides of a smelly brownish liquid on the carpet where Igo had lain. Silently, the general and his men gathered around the drawers. This was the point of departure, from where the three men had disappeared, as they had observed on the TV monitor.

Musa waved his hand in the air over the drawers to see if he could feel any tangible human substance.

The soldiers who stood guard had quietly stepped into the room fearfully wondering if they would be held responsible for the disappearance of the three men.

General Idris spun around suddenly as it dawned on him that he had a chance of catching up with the old man and his people. "Get me Ismail Suraju, the malami!" he barked.

"He's gone, Sir," Musa said apologetically. "His discharge papers were perfected yesterday just as you ordered, sir. He left this morning."

"Inna nallahi!" exclaimed the general," I shouldn't have let that malami go so soon, damn!" he punched the air to let off some tension. "Raise an alarm; get our men to spread out and look for them, now! Musa, you stay here with me"

*   *   *

Emodi and Carter appeared standing in the chamber at Ogwari cave, an unconscious Igo lying on the floor beneath them. The five robed Gundu priests who stood bowed in a wide circle around them, raised their heads almost simultenously, all attention focused on Igo. Okwulora and Ugoabata were quickly rousing from the paralyzing shock of the uncoventional transport. A metal drawer fell from Carter's hand and crashed on the ground. He had held on to it too long before their take-off.

"Where are we?" Carter whispered to Emodi.

"I'm … not sure," Emodi replied, "but I think we're in the heart of Ogwari cave."

"Wow!" Carter exclaimed.

"Gentlemen, welcome, welcome," said Ida the fifth keeper. "If you follow me, I will show you the way out."

144

⟨᠕⟩‖Nineteen‖⟨᠕⟩

Darkness was approaching. The falling sun receded to hide its golden radiance in the twilight of dusk. It cast a rusty-brown mood on the cool and somber atmosphere of Ogwari Boys High School.

Carter and Emodi sat under a row of whistling pines a path across from their bungalows. A soft westerly wind stirred a heap of pruned pine branches beside Carter's feet. A week had passed since they landed in the Ogwari caves with Igo.

"As the date of your marriage draws nearer, Phillip, you have to get to learn and accept certain things."

"Like what?" Carter asked.

"Well, like the fact that your wife is not yours alone, but also the wife of your male relations."

"What do you mean?" Carter frowned.

"Means, for instance, that your brother can give your wife a chore to perform for him and on the other hand he could assist her in time of need without getting your consent or even notifying you."

"Ok! I see," Carter replied with a nervous laugh. "I can live with that." He reflected for a moment. "Frankly speaking I thought you meant that … you know."

"That we share our wives? May God forbid abomination," Emodi replied and snapped his thumb and forefinger together and away from his body in a show of disgust. "Now let's get down to the basics of our marriage traditions. You know a lot already about the kola nut which is a basic present offered to adult male visitors in every home and also in social gatherings. You also know that the breaking of a kola is ceremonial and must be done by the rightful male person and shared in the order of rank and seniority or else it would be rejected. As a man, you have the full rights to bless and break the first kola of the day in your house, in the presense of your visitors who will give you consent freely. Thereafter, your seniors and males from your maternal kindred, your wife's kin and titled men who come into your house shall have the right to break subsequent ones."

"What if I'm at my wife's place?" Carter asked.

"Under no condition will you assume the liberty to break kola nut in the presence of any grown male from your wife's extended family or they would feel slighted and reject it," Emodi answered. "The same goes for your maternal uncles, your Ikwunne which in this case would not apply..."

"That's right, my Ikwunne are all in America," Carter said cheerfully.

"In the same token, as soon as you are joined with the Ifeadigo clan, all males and their relations who have married from Ifeadigo, your family, shall not have kola breaking rights in your presense. You will have first choice to break."

"Right on!" Carter exclaimed excitedly.

"Provided there's no Ichie, titled man or elder present to supersede you. Remember, the Ichies who are the senior chiefs in the king's cabinet have priority in breaking kola, all other conditions notwithstanding."

"Now, I see why it takes so long to decide who breaks the nut in large gatherings without an Ichie present," Carter commented.

"Exactly, the chiefs abide by their own order of seniority but the king has overall rights."

"Alright, now the head of your family, Ichie Ezeaputa, appointed a middleman for you as is customarily done. He will be your onyeaka ebe or onye ukoh who will mediate between your family, the Ifeadigo, and the family of your intended wife. Despite the fact that Ngozi is a girl from my mother's kindred, means she's my nneochie, they still had to instruct your onye aka ebe to officially make all the customary enquiries and investigations. It's called Igba nju or Iju ase."

"Meaning what?" Carter asked curiously.

"It means inquiring about Ngozi's moral character and behaviour, her ability to work hard both in the farm and at home, her level of intelligence and whether her forbears suffered hereditary diseases such as leprosy, insanity etcetera and also whether their family is jinxed with premature or tragic deaths or stricken with strange and incurable diseases."

"Isn't it like we're playing God by doing so?" Carter asked, "And again is it fair to make all these enquiries about Ngozi when her own people can't go to America to inquire about me?"

"You may be right, Phillip, but if I were you I wouldn't worry about that," Emodi replied. "He will also keep track of the basic expenditure including the dowry so if the marriage doesn't work the onye aka ebe will say how much is to be refunded. He will also help settle any dispute that ensues between you and Ngozi in future, if any."

"Ok! So what else?"

Emodi went on to tell Carter that they had appointed a time the following day to visit the oracle in the caves. Divination would reveal whether the marriage was willed by the Creator. It would also be revealed whether the union shall yield favourable prospects like male and female children, prosperity, peace in the home, cordial relations between the two in-laws and most of all, longevity. Emodi explained that after all the trouble taken to establish the marriage, the union would stand a better chance to flourish without divorce or tragedy.

"There are many other things you should know, Phillip, but I guess we'll take it gradually as they come. By the way I've heard you on many occasions call certain elderly people by their first names. They only humoured you because you were considered a foreigner. Now that you're naturalizing, you must learn that advanced men and women are not often called by their names. It is considered disrespectful. Sometimes they are called in reference to their first sons' or daughters' names, like Nne Ojiugo, meaning Ojiugo's mother or Nna Emeka, the father of Emeka. I believe that this is partially why our forefathers took expensive ozo titles like Ogbuefi, Akunne, Nnanyelugo, Ugoabata and so on, to set themselves apart from the Nna Obis and Nna Emekas and consequently enjoy the social respect and benefits that come with the title."

"Very good, Meks," Carter said. "After my title of Ugoabata, the eagle has landed, is given to me on the ofala day, I forbid you to ever call me Phillip or I would have you arrested by the last age grade."

"Dont' forget, on that day, the king is also going to daub me with the title, Okwuluora, The People's mouth piece." on that day the king is going to daub me with the title, Okwuluora, 'the people's mouthpiece'."

A week before the Yam Festival, a full-page ad. appeared in the *National Mirror.*

It called for all exiled natives of Obodo Ogwari to attend the upcoming yam festival in a special reconciliatory meeting at Ama Ogwari. The ad. offered a joyful session of feasting and merriment, assuring all exiles of their safety and warm reception.

Similar radio and TV announcements followed on the national networks. The advertisements were signed by Uzo Onicha, the palace secretary.

Igwe Ajulufo congratulated Emeka Emodi who went to the city on behalf of the king's cabinet to place the adverts.

*   *   *

Carter swept and cleaned every nook and cranny of his home. He could have asked the labour prefect to send a couple of boys to clean house for him but he preferred doing this all by himself. The personal touch was very important. He set the chairs and sitting room decorative pieces in place and even made sure the curtains were smoothened and hanging in just the right angle. Every detail had to be checked in preparation for Ngozi's first official visit to his house.

"You will have this house looking so neat and clean, she'll see you as an old bachelor so set in his ways, he doesn't even need a wife," Emodi laughed.

"I disagree, Meks, women love a man that is good and handy with household chores. Kind of helps them out," Carter reasoned.

"Believe me, Ugoabata, in these parts, women take pride in playing their roles and serving their men," Emodi said. "So, don't trespass so much into their territory."

Carter shrugged, a feather-lined duster in his hand. "I always believed that showing our women a little more respect and equality wouldn't do any harm."

"Please, Phillip, don't bring that women's liberation thing on yourself. The moment you start cleaning and mopping and babysitting for your wife, you'll end up a laughing stock, a woman wrapper."

"You mean I can't help her with dish washing or sweeping? My grandpa used to wash grandma's clothes, even her underwears at times ..."

"Abomination!" Emodi shouted, plugging his ears with his

fingers. "I've heard enough, Phillip; if you ever decide to wash undies for Ngozi, please don't let anyone see you. I'm not sure but that is enough to rob you of your title. Imagine! Ugoabata 1 of Obodo Ogwari washing his wife's pant and bra. What a disgrace!"

"It's alright, Emeka, I promise never to do it where people will see me," Carter said with a serious face.

Emodi looked hard at him and they both burst out laughing.

There was a gentle knock on the door and the two men fell silent. Carter hurriedly sought for a place to hide his feather duster.

"It must be her," Carter whispered audibly to Emodi, peeping through a part in the curtains. "Damn! It's Ngozi and two other girls." He turned to Emodi. "How come she brought two girls with her?"

"Probably her parents' idea to bring chaperones and make sure you don't try to sample the goods before marriage."

"If I don't sample the goods, how am I going to be sure she's not frigid," Carter asked.

"If she's frigid then that's your luck. Your marriage is due in a week. Open the door, Phillip."

Carter opened the door smiling and Ngozi walked in with two of her cousins, Ebele and Azuka. He set three cans of juice and a bowl of peanuts for the three girls. He had bought the goodies from a provision store in Obodo Ukwa the day he rode to the city library to research on the missionaries.

Emodi, upon eye contact with Carter, flicked his head toward the kitchen and moved. Carter followed him.

"Man, I know how you feel with Ebele and Azuka out there playing watchdog," Emodi said, seated on a stool in the kitchen.

"Hell! Meks. I can't even whisper a few tender words into my girl's ears. The two girls are watching every move I make."

"Don't worry, ol' chap, I'll bail you out."

"What are you going to do, lock them up in a room?" Carter asked, pessimistic.

"I'm their uncle, remember," Emodi said and stood up. "I'll take them away for a while so you can spin all the love talk you can muster within the time frame. You have ten minutes."

"Thanks, Meks, but could you make it at least twenty?"

"No, I don't trust you that much, Phillip," Emodi replied,

moving back out of the kitchen with a sly smile. He turned back to Carter and whispered, "Don't try anything physical. Of course you know she's most probably a virgin."

"What?" Carter shouted, shocked. "Well in that case an hour would not be enough for the job ahead."

*   *   *

"Ebele and Azuka, well this is opportunity to visit your old Uncle Emeka, since a year ago when you came during my illness. Come on," Emodi said moving towards the front door.

"Yes, Nna Ochie," the girls answered almost together. They stood up and followed Emodi obediently.

After they left, Carter sat on the couch beside Ngozi and beamed at her with what he felt was his best smile. He had often practised it before his bathroom mirror. "Welcome to your home, my love."

"Thank you," Ngozi replied shyly, inspecting her fingernails.

"Since the day I met you, I've looked forward to your being my guest, so I'll have a good chance to feast my eyes on your great beauty."

"I am not so beautiful. I am very dark."

Carter chuckled amusedly. "Your glowing darkness is the greatest essence of your beauty."

"You are very kind," Ngozi said, looking into his eyes.

"I'm not kind; I'm in love," Carter replied, their eyes locked in a moment of sweet tender romance.

He proffered his right palm and she placed hers in it.

"It was taking so long to get the consent of your people. I became worried that they didn't want me to marry you."

"I am the Ada, the first daughter of Igboneme Okechiukwu Chiukwu and they were afraid you'll one day take me to Obodo Oyibo, never to return. But now that you're taking a title and settling down, everyone is happy."

"Everyone?"

"Yes, everyone."

⊶‖ Twenty ‖⊷

General Idris made up his mind to visit the old man's village and see things for himself. Though he could have detailed a junior officer to handle the matter, he felt it needed his personal attention. He was deeply fascinated with Igo's origin and the secrets and mysteries surrounding him. Idris was a man naturally drawn to matters of the extraordinary. During the militant war he was bemused by the official reports of the giant's fetish bullet proof, the horrible death of Corporal Ekedi in connection with the dead man's dreadlocks. Idris had once, in plain-clothes, gone to investigate a stone-sculptured Virgin Mary in Benue State that was alleged to be shedding tears of human blood. Now, the general was obsessed with the disappearing act of the old village man, Igo.

This was no longer a far-fetched phenomenon but one that happened in his domain, right before his eyes. Though he had viewed the disappearance on a television monitor, the old man and his two townsmen had vanished from a locked room all the same without using the door or windows. Gen Idris remembered stories that it was a not so common belief that certain native doctors were able to prepare charms that would cause the wearer to disappear from a scene when suddenly startled or scared, ensuring instant protection from sudden accidents or attack. He also knew that other more developed, or was it spiritually digressed mystics could transport themselves from one desired place to another by supernatural means. However, Gen. Idris had a suspicion that Igo's skills were different in nature from those of the ancients.

The general had no set attitudes in mind toward the old man or the villagers he would meet on his arrival at Obodo Ogwari. He would only wait and see what would happen and deal with it. The old man had escaped from detention and that was an offense. In his mind, he did not set out to rearrest him instead the general was going to Ogwari to search and to learn.

Operation Life Tree's convoy of six vehicles came to a dead end at the boundary of Obodo Ite and Obodo Ogwari. Though

151

the road was untarred and dusty, it was a wide level road that could accommodate a couple of trucks in two-way traffic. It had suddenly come to an abrupt end at the boundary with Obodo Ogwari. A deep gorge dropped from the end of the road, a dense forest rising where the gorge ended giving an impression of being impregnable beyond the hole. The people of Obodo Ogwari intentionally left the jungle where they bordered with Obodo Ite untouched, not even for farming. This was to discourage transients from wandering into their territory. However, a clear footpath that was accessible to pedestrians and motorbikes cut into the dense vegetation. Idris felt instinctively that the large extended hole that formed the gorge was not natural but man made in the same purpose of making the village ahead less accessible.

Several soldiers were left behind to guard the vehicles while General Idris with the rest of his entourage walked into the deep crater, came up and entered the footpath.

Deep in the lowest level of the crater Idris could feel the intense heat of the sun, in contrast with the chilled condioned air of his Peugeot 607.

From the heart of Ogwari forest they could hear the rumbling of distant drumming coming from the area of an undulating set of hills that stood fence-like in the north-east side of Obodo Ogwari. These hills, coupled with a great gully that bordered the north-west, made entry into the town accessible only through Obodo Ite.

*   *   *

The giant twin drums at Ogwari Hills rolled urgently in Ogbuefi Akunne's matured hands while his son Ntupuanya sat on a rock picking his teeth, wondering why the keeper insisted that Ogbuefi sent the urgent message himself.

It was afternoon, a most unusual time for the twin drums to sound in the hills. Before the actual message was relayed, most of the villagers already knew what it would be. A town crier had gone with his gong in the morning to inform all men ranging from the Osisiego to the Ijenu age grades, able-bodied men still in their productive years, to proceed to the caves as ordered by the Igwe. When this message was resounding from the hills the young men of Obodo Ogwari were already in the caves. Only

Ntupuanya and a few recalcitrant young men were still roaming around the village. The directive had come from the third keeper through the Igwe's cabinet. It was meant to keep the belligerent young men from contact with the visiting army and also make the town seem more vulnerable-looking by leaving mostly women, children and the aged in clear view of the soldiers.

A close knot consisting of the general and members of Operation Life Tree were walking ahead while a mixed group of armed soldiers and civilian aides trooped behind them. Only the inspector general of police was absent from the team due to a religious riot that was brewing in the northern part of the country. After inquiring for directions from an old farmer in torn shorts, they went straight to Igwe Ajulufo's palace.

The Igwe received them with calm apprehensiveness. He held a kola nut and blessed them but offered very little help in questions about Igo, Carter and Emodi. He simply said that they were natives of his town whose whereabouts were unknown to him. He also owned up to having sent the three natives to the capital to oppose the express road, assuring the general and his team that it was a consensus decision by the entire people due to the town's peaceful nature.

General Idris was not one that thrived in using his position to oppress or intimidate the less privileged. In his friendly affable manner, he assured the Igwe that they were neither there to arrest anyone nor for any kind of trouble but simply on a fact-finding mission.

Igwe Ajulufo thanked him for his kind understanding but in his mind, he reserved some degree of skepticism. He had witnessed treachery and deceit from city folks before. These ones came with rifles and spoke into small radio-like gadgets with short rubbery antennas and other unseen people spoke back. They were also the same people who put Igo and the others in jail. He had to be careful with them. They were government people but they were also dangerous. At their request the Igwe gave them permission to look around the town. He knew the big soldier was only being courteous. They did not really need his permission.

As the Life Tree entourage moved through the main street of Obodo Ogwari, it was obvious to Professor Okediadi that they were being expected and villagers had been probably warned long before their arrival.

Mothers snatched their children away from their path and disappeared behind closed doors while others who stood staring in the distance quietly sneaked away and disappeared before the team got to them. Some very aged men and women who probably felt they were beyond reproach or aggression merely greeted them with icy stares. It was when a woman shouted to warn her son that those soldiers whose visit was announced in the morning have arrived, that they got concrete proof. Okediadi became sure that his speculation was correct though this information puzzled the general and others. Was there a spy among them? Some had wondered. But the professor told them that divination and predictions were simple feats for the Gundu.

"My question is, how can we find the Gundu or whatever you call them 'cause I know these villagers will never agree to show us," said the general.

"There's no harm in trying," the Minister for Works, Jibril, replied, "besides they will speak under a little duress."

"There shall be no use of force. At least not for today," the general emphasized.

Funsho Odutola, head of the secret service, walked faster and fell into pace beside the army chief. He had been silent all the while. Now he spoke subtly in a tight-lipped manner that the general understood immediately to be words for his own consumption only.

"The operative I planted in Jake Sanders' mining team is here with us. He knows his way around here."

"Then, set him loose," General Idris replied in like manner.

Funsho Odutola drew back and dropped behind to mingle with the aides and rank and file. After a few moments a dark slim man whom he identified as Uchenna took the lead and steered the entourage towards Ugwu Ogwari.

At the base of the hill, Uchenna pointed to a large boulder that marked the entrance to the triplet peaks.

*   *   *

Ogbuefi Akunne and his son, Ntupuanya, had finished relaying the coded drum message and reached the boulder at the bottom of the hill when the Life Tree team approached the other side of the rock. The old drummer and his son were startled at the sight of the crowd of armed soldiers and civilians. Though they were expecting the team, it was a shock especially for Ntupuanya whose mates were all safely quartered in a hall in the caves.

Ntupuanya broke into a run through the bushes, leaving his aged father behind. Spontaneously, three soldiers gave a hot chase after him. Instinctively for the soldiers, one who broke into such an unprovoked run must have had something vital to hide and had to be apprehended.

The general made to stop the soldiers but instantly changed his mind.

Ntupuanya ran like an antelope. One moment he was there but the next, only the bushes through which he had passed stirred and waved as if to say goodbye. He would have outrun the soldiers by far except that luck ran against him. As the soldiers made a final fruitless attempt to run around a corner after him, they heard him scream. They came around the bend and saw him hanging upside down from a long curved pole, a string around his ankle. He had stepped into an animal trap.

The general and others followed the direction of Ntupuanya's scream and found the three soldiers with the drummer who was hanging upside down.

"Who are you?" the general asked.

"I am Ntupuanya, son of Ogbuefi Akunne, a musician."

"Why were you running?"

"I was afraid."

"Of what?"

"Soldiers ... guns."

General Idris whispered to his aide. "The man is no threat. Interrogate him a bit and let him down."

"Yes, Sir," Lawali replied.

The general looked at their guide, Uchenna, and waved at him to resume the lead. Hardly had they moved thirty yards away from the scene than they heard a dull thud that told them that Ntupuanya had hit the ground.

A swift movement caught General Idris' eye about a hundred yards in the bushes. He stood still and stared at the image of an old man, the same old man who had disappeared on the TV monitors.

"What is it, General?" Funsho Odutola asked.

The whole entourage stopped and stared at the direction where the general was looking.

"That's him," Idris replied. "The old man, the one that vanished from detention. That's him standing in the bushes."

"I can't see him," Professor Okediadi complained.

"Me neither," Odutola concurred.

"Are you people going blind or what?" the general said turning to his aides and others. "Can't you see the old man standing beside that pear tree?"

The soldiers did not see the old man but out of politeness and respect for the army top brass, they kept quiet while some nodded and grinned apologetically, still peering in the direction of the tree in their own brand of sycophancy.

When General Idris turned again to look at the old man, he was no longer there.

Uchenna resumed his lead past the boulder and went up the track road that would lead them past the giant twin drums then down the slope to the cave entrance. There were many entrances to the caves but Uchenna only knew of two: the one they were headed for and the one by way of the river, where Uli the keeper of the Ita resided. It was rumoured that the cave was so vast it stretched beneath many towns to surface at Ogbunike and Aguleri, two towns many miles apart.

Halfway to the pinnacle of the hill, General Idris suddenly looked up and saw Igo standing just about fifty yards away. He held up his hand.

"What is it, General?' Professor Okediadi asked.

"Now, tell me you can't see the old man standing in front of that boulder."

"I'm sorry, General, I see the boulder but there's no one standing in front or beside it."

"Me neither," the secret service head said.

Igo beckoned on the general with his forefinger. Instantly the situation became crystal clear to Idris. The old man wanted to see him alone and he alone could see Igo.

"Wait for me," Idris addressed the team and proceeded towards the rock.

Igo turned and walked behind the rock.

The general paused then continued toward him.

"Can I come with you, Sir?" Lawali asked.

"No! Wait."

The general reached the boulder and stopped. He turned around and looked at his entourage. It was too late to retreat. He was a general. It was now do or die. He stepped behind the boulder and disappeared from view of his entourage.

General Idris stood facing Igo who was barely ten feet away. Their eyes met and locked in uncanny understanding. Idris felt suddenly relaxed in the old man's presense. All feelings of danger and caution that he felt earlier dissipated in the total sensing of Igo's innocuous nature. In a flash, Idris felt as though he was in the presence of a child but he also remembered that a child could be very dangerous with deadly weapons at his disposal.

"I am General Idris, Chief of Defence staff," he introduced himself. "And who are you?'

"I am Igo."

"I mean ... who are you, really?"

"I said, I am ..."

"I heard," Idris interrupted. "I wasn't asking of just your name ... never mind. Where did you come from?"

"I'm of the Ideamala clan, here in Obodo Ogwari."

"You have great skills," the general complimented.

"And so do you," Igo returned.

"You showed yourself to me but not to the others ... We were all looking."

"It was necessary at the time."

"You made yourself invisible at HQ and then you vanished from the detention room."

"It was also necessary ..."

"I want to learn ... from you."

Silence.

"I will pay to learn ... even the secret of longevity."

"Did you pay to learn your soldier work?" Igo asked. "I want only one thing of you."

"What is that?" the general asked eagerly.

"That you stop your government from building the express road through here."

The general's disappointment was not hidden. A deep frown formed creases on his forehead and the bridge between his brows narrowed. "I have no power over the express. It is not in my jurisdiction."

Igo edged closer toward the general. "Yes, you can. Your influence as chief of the army."

"All eyes are on you, now. Besides, this is a democratic government. I have no direct say on the matter."

"Then we have no agreement," Igo said in disappointment.

The general took two steps closer in a final frantic effort to convince the old man. "I will guarantee your safety here or give you safe passage to any place you need to relocate, but you must show me how to prepare the charms ..."

"There are no charms, no magic," Igo snapped impatiently. "It is a state of the mind, a way of life."

"Can I learn?"

"Of course," Igo replied.

"Sir, are you alright?" Lawali called from behind the rock. He came around and saw the general and Igo standing close to each other. "I'm sorry, Sir, I had to come ... we were worried."

"It's alright, Lawali, Igo and I were just rounding up our fruitless conversation."

When he turned, Igo was already moving quietly into the woods.

General Idris joined his aide. "Let's go home."

❧‖ Twenty-one ‖❧

The director of Cotrell and Abbey Construction Company received an urgent email from the Ministry of Works. He was directed to proceed with the road project through Obodo Ite to Nsukka, with utmost urgency. The message also directed him to report to the ministry immediately to receive a bank draft for this second phase of the project. For Chief Angus Okonedo, this was a very pleasing email yet strange and unexpected. Of all the road contracts he had handled for the federal government, the Anaku via Obodo Ite to Nsukka road was the most cumbersome. The project was not top priority. Payments had been tardy, retarding completion of the project eighteen months beyond the estimated deadline. Now, why was there a sudden rush? Okonedo could sense the desperate urgency from the message. Maybe a top politician whose village lay on the new road was tightening pressure screws at Aso Rock, Okonedo thought with a smile. Whatever the cause was working to his advantage. A fat bank draft was waiting for him at the capital city.

One week after he collected the cheque, work resumed in earnest on the new dual carriage road that would pass through Obodo Ite to Obodo Ogwari.

*   *   *

Chief Angus Okonedo was having breakfast in his room at the Sheraton Hotels, Abuja when he received the cellular call. It was Engineer Frank calling from the site at Obodo Ite. The network was hazy and Frank's voice was not very audible

"Sir, we need your attention down here. We have a problem," the engineer yelled frantically. "The men have refused to work."

For a man of Frank's level temperament, the desperation in his voice alarmed Okonedo. His first suspicion was that one of the workers may have died accidentally at the site; maybe in a situation that aroused the superstitious sense of the illiterate workmen. While constructing a bridge in Edo State, a fork-lift operator, apparently out of sheer carelessness, had fallen off the edge, plunged into the river and died instantly. A greater number of the workers had insisted that the goddess of the river had caused the accident in protest of the bridge. Chief Okonedo did not bother to let the state commissioner for works know about it. He had simply authorized the requested amount of money to be disbursed for the heathen ritual. The next morning work resumed without further delay. Now, the Obodo Ite road was a federal contract and there was no room for delays or superstitious tales. He had promised Jibril, the federal minister for works, utmost expediency in the job.

"Frank, tell me what happened," Okonedo yelled. "I can't come to the east right now."

"Sir! You have to come. It's the trees, the trees at the site …" Frank's voice was lost in the network.

"What trees? Hello … hello … Frank … hello."

The line was dead.

Much as he tried to get Frank or the foreman on line, Okonedo did not succeed. From the little he had learnt it was obvious that a serious matter was on hand. If the men had refused to work for a reason that had to do with trees then surely a serious problem existed. It was probably a similar fetish matter with trees Okonedo experienced on a couple of occasions. During the building of a dual carriage road some years ago, his crew had come upon a strange forest where several large trees had trunks draped in blood-stained white cloths. The villagers claimed that the forest was part of their ancestral shrine. On one instance he paid a huge sum of money for the shrine to be relocated but on the second occasion, just before payment, the villagers quarreled amongst themselves on how the money was to be shared and the plot was exposed as a scam. Work resumed without further disturbance.

Chief Okonedo called the hotel receptionist and requested to be booked on the next available flight to Enugu.

At the Enugu airport he hired a cab that drove him straight to Obodo Ite via the Nsukka by-pass. Engineer Frank rushed to the Toyota Camry that brought his boss and held the door as Chief Okonedo alighted from the car. He looked across the graded roughness of the new road where the construction had ended and saw a bunch of labourers seated on the earth.

"Where are the rest of your workers?" Chief Okonedo asked.

"They have gone, Sir," the engineer replied. "I tried to persuade them to wait till you come but ..."

"It's ok," Okonedo interrupted. "So, what's the problem?"

"Well, sir, it was yesterday while we were rounding up that I told the dozer operator to fell those trees over there first thing this morning. Anyway before we left, he asked for my permission to do it before we went home and I agreed ..."

"Frank, please get to the point before I die of anxiety. My bp is rising," Okonedo cut in again, his countenance grave and stressed.

"Sir, it's those trees over there. They were felled yesterday evening but this morning, they're all standing."

"You mean, the operator told you he felled the trees?"

"No, Sir, I was here when the trees went down. We were all here."

The foreman and the operator were standing behind Frank. Few labourers who were left at the site and other equipment operators had all clustered around Chief Okonedo.

"Well, let's get on over there and take a look." The chief started through the rough cleared terrain where the road ended in a wall of thick vegetation. Several trees stood in a loose cluster. As Okonedo moved closer he suddenly felt that he was alone. When he turned around only Engineer Frank was tagging along several arm lengths behind, a worried look on his face.

The foreman and others still stood by the car with folded arms and wary looks.

"What's wrong with them?" Okonedo asked. "Won't they come with us?"

"Sir, since the dozer operator and a few others discovered it this morning and ran back from there, no one has had the guts to get close to it," the engineer replied.

"Are you scared too?"

"No, Sir, I'm just cautious that any of those trees may fall again."

"If the trees were really felled and they somehow got up, believe me, falling down again is not in their future plan. You're a trained engineer, Frank, superstition aside, there's the scientific side. You said the trees went down before your eyes and now they're up."

"Yes, Sir."

"Don't you want to know why?"

"I do, Sir."

"Well you can't do it standing ten miles away. Come on," Okonedo ordered. Engineer Frank was responding to his boss with caution; his job security was important yet personal safety was paramount in his final consideration of the situation. Tentatively, he followed Chief Angus Okonedo who moved closer to the trees, stumbling over mounds of soil that had been piled by the dozer.

They were fairly large trees of various sizes. None was small by any standard. As he walked around them, he sought first for signs to prove that the dozer had actually done its normal work. Upon close inspection of one that stood most isolated to the right, he saw signs of digging around it for buttress roots. He saw the piling of sand on one side of the trunk which mounted pressure toward the opposite side to which the operator had planned for the tree to fall. He then inspected that opposite side and saw the long curved dent made by the full length of the tree trunk when it had apparently crashed to the earth. Okonedo swung around and stared at the other trees that had signs of digging around them. In a flash, he confirmed the same evidence he had sought for in the first tree plus one final detail he missed earlier. Chunks of earth that the trees had pulled from the ground as they were felled by the dozer were still roughly caked around the base of the trees in varied quantities. Suddenly Okonedo felt threatened standing in the midst of this cluster of trees shrouded in mystery. Nervously, he adjusted the neck of his brocade caftan and strolled out in a brisk manner that his men would not perceive as last minute cowardice. After all he had walked among the trees alone while Engineer Frank who came closest watched from a distance of over twelve feet.

"Pay off the labourers but keep them on stand-by. Secure the equipment and wait for my orders. We shall resume work, soon."

"Yes, Sir," Frank answered and started to ask his boss whether he would be back the following day but Okonedo tapped the driver's seat and the chauffeur sped off. Frank stood with arms akimbo staring at the car. It bounced over the rough terrain and disappeared around the corner as though consumed by the imposing jungle that rose on both sides of the new road. A deafening quietness prevailed at the site as none of the men uttered a word. The director's orders to suspend work indefinitely had reawakened a new awareness that something mysterious and evil was lurking around them. Some seemed to make furtive moves to leave the site, including the men who usually guarded the equipment and materials at night. Frank made a mental note to drive into the city of Onitsha to hire night-watchmen who knew nothing about the trees.

The sharp squeaking of birds in the skies caused Frank to look upwards. He noticed an unusual number of birds in flight, circling high above. What he failed to observe was that the numerous population of birds was of a wide variety of species. It was unconventional, as though something had roused them from their various nests. It also seemed obvious that something was keeping them from tree-level causing them to seek solace high up in the air.

*   *   *

The Life Tree team was almost at the end of an emergency meeting convened by the Minister of works, Hon Jibril. Chief Angus Okonedo had been invited to give evidence of the unnatural event that took place at the Obodo Ite construction site. After answering several questions concerning the tree incident, Okonedo was asked to wait in the outer office while the executives took their decision.

The general was first to speak. "I would have dismissed such a story as rubbish but after what I saw in my office, anything is possible. Gentlemen, I think we're faced with a matter that has no precedence and as such, no known solution. Your opinions and suggestions shall be highly welcomed."

"At our very first meeting, I narrated how the old man, Igo, boasted that the road would never go through Ogwari. I strongly believe that this tree thing is the beginning of resistance," Jibril spoke.

"Not just the tree, Okonedo's engineer called to report an alarming number of birds in the area, behaving aggressively," Prof. Okediadi added.

"I've had the town under surveillance for some time now," Odutola said. "The place is very quiet. Even the old man seems to be out of circulation; stays mostly in the caves."

"He's probably hiding thinking we're out to get him," the

general suggested.

"Professor, I wonder if you could shed some insight at this point."

Professor Okediadi cleared his throat and removed his gold rimmed spectacles. "I've been able to lay hands on some of the writings of one Revered Morgan, a missionary who lived in Obodo Ogwari in the early days. Referring to the Gundu priests, he calls them natural scientists who are in absolute tune with the environment and forces of nature. Telepathy and telekinesis were some of the attributes he claimed that the Gundus had, meaning that they read minds and even communicated by telepathy, also moving large heavy objects like boulders without physical contact."

"Incredible! ... if they're so advanced, why are they living such primitive lives?" Odutola asked.

"Well, what we call civilization and modernization may not be so from their own perspective," the professor replied, "and mind you, Rev. Morgan insisted in his work that these Ideamala priests, as he also referred to them, were not really fetish and diabolical heathens as his fellow reverends thought but masters in the sciences and metaphysics."

"That, I find hard to believe, Professor," Jibril opposed. "What that old man displayed in my office was purely demonic, plain black magic."

"I disagree," Professor Okediadi said. "Making your men itch all over is not necessarily black art. I have concrete facts to prove that ..."

"Gentlemen! Let us not argue over trivials. Professor, I want your professional opinion and advice on the road construction and this new problem that has arisen," the general intervened.

"I called a colleague of mine, Professor Olieh, who's a lecturer at Nnamdi Azikiwe University, Awka," Okediadi said and withdrew some glossy pictures and a stapled set of papers from his file. "Just received this report and photographs from him this morning and it's now proven that my earlier suspicion is correct."

He placed the photos before the general. General Idris inspected the photographs, kept one and passed the rest around to the others. "Professor, please expatiate."

"As you can see," the professor continued, after the photos

were distributed, "there are many trees in the picture but the ones with withered leaves are those that were felled by the bulldozer. Professor Olieh who conducted the inspection on my behalf confirmed that they were actually felled but somehow returned to their normal vertical states. Now, the withered leaves give a great insight on what transpired there and how?"

"How?" Odutola asked

"Please explain," General Idris said.

"Professor Olieh is an authority in botany and for the inspection, he went along with a don from the department of forestry. Their report states that the rate at which the trees are withering shows that they are dying. This probably shows that an external force caused the trees to return to the upright states rather than the supernatural qualities being assigned to the trees by some people."

"I knew it, I knew it," Jibril concluded. "It's that old man; he's responsible for it."

"Professor, what is your recommendation, assuming that the road must go through?" Idris asked.

"I must restate my unequivocal stance in this matter which I stressed in our first meeting that ..."

"Yes that the Gundu should be left alone and the express road re-routed through some other town," General Idris pre-empted him. "But professor, you are bound by your civic duty and patriotism to assist the federal government to achieve its aims and objectives."

"With all due respect, General, the aims of the government do not always conform with my personal moral standards. The president himself nominated me for this committee but I think I have outlived my usefulness ... I, eh .... wish to orally declare my decision to withdraw from the team. You will receive same in writing by tomorrow."

"You have not fulfilled your obligation to this team," said Idris, all friendliness gone from his attitude. The hard soldier in him appeared, making Professor Okediadi feel threatened all of a sudden.

"Well ..." the Professor hesitated. "I don't have much to contribute, but just remember that this is not a war of the conventional. You will have to adjust to any new challenge that comes up."

"I have my troops."

"Good. They may come in handy."

Soon afterwards, Chief Augus Okonedo was ushered in and instructed to resume work, that adequate security and expertise would be provided at the site to boost the morale of the workers.

Idris made a mental note to replace Professor Okediadi with Professor Olieh who had actually been to the site and was close to the area. He had sent someone to Birnin Bindiga to find Ismail Suraju but the malami could not be located.

❦‖Twenty-two‖❦

The sun had long gone down, the skies darkening rapidly to that final stage that slips surreptitiously into nightfall.

A platoon of soldiers headed by Lt. Duru pitched several green tents on a patch of land beside the new road. An area, half the size of a football field, had been cleared in the jungle. It was floored with small grey chippings of rock flattened into the leveled grounds by a big roller machine. Flood lights, fixed around the camp, were kept lit throughout the night by a powerful generator. All the trees felled by the dozer were conveyed to the other side of the road, piled and set on fire.

Engineer Frank had gone to Onitsha and hired new labourers, carpenters and other allied construction staff. The resurrected trees were knocked down again and burnt under the scrutiny of the soldiers, long before the new staff arrived. Yet they somehow got hint of the strange incident. However, the presence of soldiers gave them a strong sense of safety. Some came to work from Obodo-Ite while others shuttled on the company bus from Onitsha.

*   *   *

By 6 pm, the workers had all gone home, leaving security men and soldiers who stood around their tents chatting and smoking cigarettes. Few were resting in their tents while others, deployed on guard duty, loitered at key points of the camp's periphery.

Nightfall. Security man, Edet Etim, did not go too far into the bush to ease himself. He was afraid of snakes and scorpions. Stepping into the shrubs beyond the range of the flood lights, he flicked his flashlight on and shone it about. The dark and dangerous jungle seemed to bear down menacingly on him in dark shadows of large leafy trees and climbing clasping vegetation. Etim heard a buzzing sound in the trees. The beam of his flashlight lit up a low hanging branch to his right. An exceptionally large colony of bees was clustered in a huge ball shape, simmering with life, dark and dangerous.

He swung his light to the left from where he heard another buzzing sound and saw an even bigger cluster swarming on a fallen tree trunk. Etim forgot what he had come for and bolted out of the bushes. He found Lt. Duru resting in his tent and reported his discovery.

"Bees in the trees," Duru grunted. "Where else do you want them to be? Just don't bother them and they won't bother you," he added. "Besides, bees don't attack people at night."

"Sir, no be like dat," Etim argued, respectfully. "Back in my village at Cross River, my brother dey handle bee for honey. True talk, dem no de move for night but these ones get problem. Some don begin fly around de camp."

It was then that Etim caught Duru's full attention. The lieutenant stood up from his lying position and prepared to go with Etim who stood at the the tent's entrance. Duru was aware that there was some kind of problem at the site that required army presense. The platoon had been carefully picked to include mostly brave young soldiers from the 82nd Division, Enugu and some from the local barracks.

Outside, they heard the pounding of feet and shouts of alarm.

"Hey! Hey! Lieutenant, we're under attack," a voice called from the camp. "Wayoo! Allah."

Sergeant Shittu broke into the lieutenant's tent almost knocking down Etim who was peering into the camp grounds. Shittu quickly closed the flaps at the tent's doorway and stood panting.

"Sir, we're under attack. There are killer bees everywhere," Shittu reported.

"What's the meaning of this?" Duru asked as though talking to himself. "It is quite unusual but maybe someone or something disturbed their home." He picked up his lantern and turned it on.

Over a dozen bees were flying rapidly around the tent. They had come in with Shittu.

"Nothing disturbed their home, Sir, these things came for us," Shittu said drawing backwards to the corner of the tent, away from the bees that zipped around the room.

Edet still stood by the doorway. He wanted to run out of the tent but the shouting and pounding of feet outside discouraged him. He could hear Corporal Ngefa calling out for others to pull up their shirt collars, to cover their faces with their hands, to kneel and fold their faces onto their laps. From the helter-skelter movement, it was obvious that Ngefa's instructions were mostly disobeyed.

The bees in the lieutenant's tent attacked. They swooped down on the three occupants of the room, striking and slamming against their faces and flaying arms. Edet fought and struck out at the bees for a few minutes before he decided to take his chance and run into the yard. Moving blindly for a moment, some bees after him, he stumbled into the open ground that formed the centre of the camp. A few men were still running about the camp to escape from the thousands of bees that roamed the air. Most of the men had absconded from the vicinity of the brightly lit camp, seeking refuge down the rough, dark road.

As he ran past a flood light at the edge of the camp, Edet beheld a sight that scared him very much. The figure of a man, kneeling and curled in a fetal position, was covered by layers of bees.

Corporal Ngefa had gone into the fetal position, hiding his face and hands on his laps as the bees settled on him. Mustering a tremendous will, he kept perfectly still thinking that his stillness would make them ignore him. By the time he realized his mistake, hundreds of bees had settled on his clothes, his hair and more were landing. Ngefa became mesmerized. Terror petrified him to a statuary stillness more rigid than his initial attempt at calmness. When he felt the movement of bees creep past his raised collar, crawling onto his skin, he bit hard on the base of his palm almost drawing blood from his own skin in strife to maintain his rigid state. Suddenly the ones that had crawled down his neck and back came out and lifted into the air with the others. In just a few moments, as quickly and mysteriously as they had come, the bees were all gone.

Lieutenant Duru and Sergeant Shittu came out of the tent and saw only Ngefa standing under a flood light. With a handkerchief he dusted his hair and body, checking his entire body for bees. There was none.

"Where are the others?" Duru asked.

"I don't know, Sir. They all ran away from the camp."

Shittu moved towards the road. "Edwards! Nangibo! Taiwo!" he called out. "Come back! The bees have gone."

Few voices could be heard down the dark road.

Corporal Nangibo appeared, followed by Edet who had not

run far before the bees flew off. Lance Corporal Edwards and another young soldier came into the camp and others followed. Cautiously looking about them in readiness for another bee-attack, some of the soldiers and security men recounted their personal experiences of the incident.

"Forget the stories," Duru snapped. "Just look for dry wood and sticks to make fire around the camp. The smoke especially will discourage them from coming back."

Soldiers and the Cotrell and Abbey security staff together foraged for dry logs, sticks and dry leaves with which they set fire in heaps around the camp. Smoke swirled about bringing a new source of discomfort but gave boost to their fighting spirit. It was obvious that the lieutenant did not want open and excited discussion about the bee attack. All he tasked them to do was to remain alert and keep their morales high. Duru had his reasons for curbing their excitement. Too many negative ideas voiced could weaken the less-brave. Already he sensed a streak of panic in the air. He too, though driven by great ambition, felt a mysterious danger lurking in the dark entrails of the jungle. Strange secrets were locked in these parts. The unravelling may take pitiful tolls on people's lives. Was that why the army hand-picked men from various units just to form the platoon? Duru wondered. Though most of the soldiers were sourced locally, Sergeants Shittu and Nangibo had been flown down from Abuja. Supervising the knocking down and burning of the purportedly resurrected trees had gone without event. Now, the first encounter had just rendered their soldierly training, their guns and skills, useless. The night bee-attack was clearly a strange phenomenon to be analyzed. Now that Duru had stopped the men from unchecked excitement and discussion about the incident he felt he had to know their views or else a lack of proper communication between them may prove to be more damaging in the end. He called for the men to assemble at the centre of the camp, the company security men also. Their close encounters together had forged a camaraderie between the two groups, soldiers and civilians alike.

"Stay close to your tents, and be vigilant," Lt. Duru instructed. "If the bees return enter your tents and close the flaps and stay there until they leave. Does anyone have a question or comment?"

"Sir, I have an observation," Sergeant Nangibo said.

"Yes, Nangibo."

"Sir, we are of the opinion that those bees were not ordinary bees."

"Meaning what?" Duru inquired. The same notion had been nagging his mind but he would not dare let it show.

"For bees to attack us at night, chase us and harass us and yet not sting us ..."

"Is that your reason for saying they were not ordinary bees. Have you not heard of such a thing as stingless bees?" the lieutenant asked. "Edet, here, has a brother who handles bees maybe he knows about it."

"Yes, Sir. 'E- get bee wey no de bite, e no de sting person" Edet confirmed. "But, Oga, dis one, I no so sure say na ..."

"You see? This man's brother handles bees and he has confirmed this obvious fact," Duru interrupted the Calabar man who seemed to be countering his initial confirmation.

Sergeant Shittu looked dissatisfied with Lt. Duru's claims of stingless bees but he did not want to speak against the officer. He had been flown down on this special assignment but like the others, there was no special briefing as to any peculiar factors to expect. He was beginning to suspect that the lieutenant had something to hide about the true nature of their mission until Duru spoke.

"Attention!" the lieutenant snapped and the soldiers stamped their boots on the ground almost in unison, their feet clicking together as they all stood rigidly at attention. "Now, listen all of you and listen well. You are not ordinary soldiers and that is why you were selected for this assignment. Shittu, here, proved his bravery with the peace keeping force in Liberia. Ngefa was a notable warrior from the recent militant war and the rest of you whom I didn't know before must have good records of bravery. You've seen the trees that were uprooted but later stood up again and now this strange bee-attack. Even the general that sent us here does not know what to expect and that is why they picked us, to find out what is going on here and to protect the workers."

Duru took a few moments to look at the men. He had their full attention.

"This road shall eventually connect the one to Nsukka, but

our main concern is to see that it passes through a town called Obodo Ogwari which is just a mile ahead. Your job is to protect and encourage the workers to see that the road goes through. After Obodo Ogwari you can walk home heroes or you can abscond before and be branded a bunch of cowards." Duru paused. "Do I make myself clear?" he shouted.

"Yes, Sir!" the men replied, in high spirits.

"Are there any questions?"

"No, Sir!

"Then you're dismissed to tend the fires." Duru smiled inwardly. He knew he had them exactly where he wanted. Psychologically, they were now better prepared to face night bees or even dancing leopards.

❧ Twenty-three ❧

Monsignor Udokamma was chancellor to Bishop Obiechina. He was an elderly priest of the diocese that was supposed to oversee Obodo Ogwari. Udokamma after his routine devotional visit to the blessed sacrament chapel of adoration, met with the bishop to intimate him on a very special experience he had. While kneeling in the sanctuary he was overwhelmed by a presence he knew to be the glory of the Holy Spirit. This powerful euphoric visitation impressed upon him to suggest to the Bishop to send the radical Father Mojekwu to Obodo Ogwari and liberate the natives from spiritual backwardness and establish a new catholic church. The monsignor was not really surprised when Bishop Obiechina agreed instantly with the suggestion. Fr Mojekwu was summoned for instruction.

*   *   *

Rev. Father Mojekwu rose from a weekend of retreat and reflection at the tranquil Iselenta Monastery of Delta State. He had journeyed from his parish to this peaceful haven to meditate, in search of an answer to the nagging instinct that had been bothering him for a week. He had obtained a special permission for this retreat as a preparatory exercise before embarking on this missionary task.

Walking through the monastery's vast expanse of nature and its greenery, the songbirds, the clear blue sky and water springs, he could communicate well in the spirit. However, it was while he sat in the cafeteria having dinner that he received divine instruction to now proceed to Obodo Ogwari. He had never heard of the town and didn't know how to get there. Before he set out the following morning a kitchen staff offered directions advising him to park his jeep and rent a motorbike when he got to Obodo Ite as there was no motorable access into Ogwariland.

When Fr. Mojekwu left the monastery in search of Obodo Ogwari, he was still at a loss on how to embark on this latest task. He was a little tense and apprehensive over the journey that lay ahead. Mojekwu was a radical priest. He was not known for sinful or dubious behaviour but his peculiar approach to heathens was nothing short of unorthodox. His reputation as an unconventional catholic priest began when he was posted to a new parish at Nnago where the natives were still very hostile to Christianity.

Owing to very poor church attendance on Sundays, Fr. Mojekwu decided to express a bit of his own style of soul winning for the Lord. He had picked noon of the Oye market day when the market square was teeming with villagers. He went straight to the section where the influential and spiritually fetish and diabolic old men sat on Oye days, sampling the finest grades of palm wine, kola nut and other edibles. Rev. Fr. Mojekwu disembarked from his 4-Runner jeep wearing an immaculate white soutane and strolled into their midst. A sudden spell of silence befell them. What new holy injunction or decree had the priest come to give them, some were wondering. Was he not told that the Reverend Father before him had been stripped, whipped and his jeep vandalized for excessive spiritual aggression and open criticism of their customs and traditions?

"What's yours?" Fr. Mojekwu asked the first old man seated in the square, the priest's backhand raised in the customary greeting of titled men.

"Akukalia!" answered the dark aged man with a bushy grey beard, an apprehensive look on his wrinkled countenance.

"Mine is Ugonna," Fr. Mojekwu answered coining an ozo title for himself.

The old man quickly raised the short animal horn he used as a fetish staff to strike Fr. Mojekwu's backhand thrice in privileged greeting.

"Ugonna!" the old man hailed Fr. Mojekwu cheerfully, thrilled to identify a catholic priest with an ozo title.

Mojekwu repeated the same introduction with the second man, Nzebunachi, who didn't have to ask the Father's name. He was hailing Ugonna the white-clad priest as if they had been friends for life.

The third old man was big-boned and sporting a massive potbelly. He was not so easy. Though friendly, he gave Fr. Mojekwu only two strikes with an elephant tusk he carried like a magic wand, insisting that Mojekwu was not truly an ozo-titled man; that 'Ugonna' was only a nickname. After a rowdy but friendly argument Fr. Mojekwu won and the big man gave him a full three strikes with the short yellowed tusk. The Reverend Father had stated that the title was sponsored and bestowed upon him when he was only a boy, hence the suffix 'nna' depicting the involvement of his father by sponsorship or merely being alive when the title was taken.

After greeting the entire eight men seated in the square, Mojekwu sat with them for over an hour drinking palm wine and eating smoked antelope.

The next Oye market day, Fr. Mojekwu came back and also the Oye after that.

"I've been sitting and drinking with you, my fellow drunkards, every Oye market day yet you never bothered to ask of me," Fr. Mojekwu complained.

The men fell silent for a moment before Akukalia spoke. "Ha! People like us are not allowed in church. Does a masquerade go to church?"

They all laughed in acquiescence.

Fr. Mojekwu remained silent and serious. He spoke. "You are wrong, Akukalia, the church is for everyone, be you a robber or a murderer. God wants you to bring all your problems to him so that he will lighten your load. You can come to church whenever you want but first I want you to be my special guests at the upcoming bazzar."

The fetish old men exchanged puzzled looks but said nothing.

On the day of the bazzar at St Mary's Catholic Church, Nnago, some of the most dreaded and terrible pagans were given special seats at the church grounds, close to the high table. On the instruction of Fr. Mojekwu, the seminarians who served at the bazzar provided more than enough food and drinks for them. After the bazzar, the Rev. Father gave them sparkling cooking utensils, cutleries and other household items as gifts.

The following Sunday, most of the old men attended morning service with their families. It influenced others and within months the pews of the large mission were half-filled every Sunday. Baptisms, confessions and confirmations became more frequent over the following months.

Reverend Father Mojekwu parked his jeep behind a low-bed trailer loaded with large earth-moving equipment, all labeled Cotrell and Abbey. He met the security men who worked at the site and asked them to watch over his vehicle for a couple of hours. Scooping up the bottom of his white soutane, he mounted the rear of a battered motorbike that had followed him from Obodo Ite township. The bike rider was an elderly man named Uka who knew the terrain quite well. Fr. Mojekwu had tried to bargain with Uka, a commercial biker, to take him to Obodo Ogwari, wait for him for an hour or two then bring him back to where his jeep was parked. Uka, a devout catholic, was glad for the opportunity to serve the priest. He opted to go free of charge but pleaded with the Father for a little support in filling his tank. Mojekwu bought him a full tank of petrol in a filling station at Obodo Ite.

When they arrived at Obodo Ogwari, Fr. Mojekwu asked Uka to take him straight to the king's palace. As he alighted from the motorbike to enter Igwe Ajulufo's premises, Mojekwu was not altogether certain how he would speak to the king.

The Igwe was indisposed but his scribe, Uzo-Onicha, was there to attend to the Father.

"Why do you want to see the king?" Uzo-Onicha asked.

"Actually, I have come to see your chief priest," Fr. Mojekwu told the scribe after they had exchanged pleasantries.

"We have no chief priest," Uzo-Onicha replied.

Mojekwu hesitated. "Well, I'd like to see whoever is considered the head of your deity."

"May I ask why you wish to see him?"

"I am a priest, myself, a Reverend Father of the Holy Catholic Order ..."

"Of course I know that," Uzo-Onicha interrupted. "But it is my duty to inquire."

"I understand," Mojekwu replied. "I only want to have a word with him."

Uzo-Onicha took one long intent look at the priest weighing him, his mission. There was uncertainty in the village. The word about the express road had filtered through the entire Ogwari. Igo's trip to the capital city had certainly sparked off an increased activity in the road that was coming to change their way of life, to rapidly accelerate their social and traditional life over a century to the present, in no time. Uzo-Onicha knew that pastors and their spiritual fraud was rampant across the nation, that the era of the Dibia in Disguise (DD) was still on the rise. But, a priest of the Catholic Order would not be looking for Igo to set him up to be arrested. And that was if the man that stood before him was actually a priest. Lately he had seen too many strange people snooping around the villages, men that looked like government workers and others he could not figure out. The atmosphere smelled of tension.

"Please sit down, Father," Uzo-Onicha said to Fr. Mojekwu ushering him into the King's Hall. "I hope you're not one of those Holy Ghost Fathers who destroy other people's shrines and deities," he said joking, smiling.

"I only do that when I'm invited and authorized," the priest replied, seriously.

"Very good," the old scribe beamed. "Cause there's no deity or shrine here for you to destroy or cart away." He laughed, expecting the priest to share his humour.

"If you say so." Mojekwu did not see the joke. It made him uncomfortable that he couldn't have answered the scribe's question on what his mission really was. The Father was admiring the coloured carvings on the hard mud wall when he sensed a stirring behind him. He swung around cautiously and saw the old man, Igo, standing behind him. His body was bare except for a bone necklace and an armband. A thin white skirt flowed down from his waist to the ankles.

"Welcome," Igo said to him.

"Thank you," the reverend replied and immediately a moment of spiritual awakening flooded his psyche; his head swooned with a euphoric feeling that came with a soothing calmness that rushed through his entire body.

A strained moment of silence prevailed as the two men stared at each other. A mutual understanding that was only possible between men of their kind passed between them in a twinkle of an eye.

"You have bothered me for quite some time," Fr. Mojekwu broke the silence.

"We have not met," Igo replied.

"I am Revered Father Mojekwu. You know why I'm here."

"To correct? To change?"

"Isn't it time?"

"There's a time for everything."

"The time has come," Mojekwu said.

Igo did not answer. He seemed at a loss for words.

Father Mojekwu paused and exhaled expansively. "The Word is that the time has come. The shroud of fetishism must be lifted. The bird has to go."

Though Igo was silent, he was visibly moved by the Reverend Father's words.

He looked downwards at his feet which he tapped unconsciously in random beat. He looked very sad, crestfallen.

"We have sacrificed our kin for the welfare of these people."

"The bird must go," the Father said pointedly.

"Yes," the Gundu priest replied in a quivering voice still looking downward. "It has served its purpose." When Igo raised his face, Mojekwu noticed a greenish droplet at the corner of his left eye before he quickly wiped it off with a quick flick of his backhand.

"I must go now."

"Yes."

"May the Lord be with you."

"Thank you," Igo replied.

❧‖ Twenty-four ‖❧

When the news of Nwalie Njaka's death arrived Obodo Ogwari, it was received with mixed emotions. While the villagers felt bad for the loss of their prominent and generous kinsman, they also regretted his alien interactions which must have brought about his early death at the age of seventy-two. For an Obodo Ogwarian, it was considered an untimely death. The 'rubbish' he ate and drank in the city, in the name of food and beverages, must have contributed to his death. There were also rumours that filtered in after the sad news was brought back from the city of Onitsha. It was said that the Ajo-ofia deity of Obodo-Ite, his grandmother's people, had claimed his life for not adhering strictly to its rules. Whatever was the cause, Nwalie Njaka was dead.

Njaka had been a special man to the people of Obodo Ogwari. He had gone abroad, met success but often came home to live a lowly life with his people. Other natives who got fed up with the ancient and relatively backward life in Ogwari had moved to the city and never returned until they died. Such men were buried in Ogwari without much event. They were interred quietly by their relations and quickly forgotten. Njaka was an enigma to the Ogwarians. He left his village for the city as a young man and succeeded tremendously in trading but never forgot his roots. He came back home, got married and built a bungalow. He took an ozo title and came home on weekends to attend to village matters. He helped Ogwarians who were on exile but with all his exposure in the cities around the country, he never attempted to change the quaint and conservative nature of Obodo Ogwari. Whenever he left the city, he left everything about the township and came back a genuine village man. His kinsmen were ever proud of this desirable complexity of his character.

*   *   *

The late Njaka's extended male relations, the Umunna, met over some jars of palm wine and kolanuts to deliberate on matters concerning his funeral. A very near date had to be picked. Out of the four market days of the Igbo week, Eke, Orie, Afor and Nkwo, the Eke was carefully avoided. It was the official market day for the people of Obodo Ogwari when they brought out their goods to the Eke market square to trade. It was the only day they interacted fully with people from other towns who came not only to buy or sell but to trade by barter. At Eke-Ogwari yams were exchanged for cloth, cassava for sandals, goats for a cow and in many other variations of barter.

The Nkwo day was picked for the funeral and deliberations on division of labour began. Work, towards the burial ceremony, was assigned to each and everyone singly and in groups. Only the sick and aged were exempted from manual work but not from contributions of wisdom and advice.

Meanwhile, Umuada, women of the extended family married to other families, returned home for their own meeting while the Inyom, wives of the extended family, did the same. Njaka's burial arrangement was fully in progress.

Before dawn of the funeral day, the giant twin drums spoke from the Ogwari hills to inform villagers that the day had arrived. Soon afterwards, at the break of dawn, seven cannon shots exploded in quick succession sending the message to indigenes and across the six counterpart towns of Ebo-nasaa.

*   *   *

Phillip Carter and Emeka Emodi arrived together at the home of the late Nwalie Njaka. They parted ways and Emodi went in search of his people. Carter no longer tagged along with him as he had done in the past. Instead he scanned the outskirts of the funeral grounds, looking for his own kindred. He found the males of Ifeadigo clan where they were regrouping to enter the compound to pay condolence to the Njaka family and their extended kin. Sixty-two men of the Ifeadigo clan with Carter making sixty-three, formed a single line starting with Ichie Ezeaputa at the head. Lower chiefs and ozo-titled men followed before the younger men in order of seniority. Much further down the line, the strictness of age became less rigid. As it was with other functions and procedures in Obodo Ogwari, age and rank played important roles. It was one of their strongest tools of order and discipline. It wasn't uncommon to see a group of boys dishing out corporal punishment to their mate for insulting an elder or even his own parents.

Carter smiled contentedly when they placed him without any

special consideration. Though no one knew his age, they tactfully placed him between Okonkwo, the big burly blacksmith and Osadebe the hunter who were both in their late forties and had no special titles. Carter smiled broadly when he remembered that soon after the Igwe's Yam festival, the title, Ugoabata, would be conferred on him and his position in the town would rise instantly. It was purely on merit as Emodi assured him or he would have turned it down. It used to feel like play-acting in the beginning but now it was real to Phillip Carter that he had actually changed nationalities.

*   *   *

The dead man, Nwalie Njaka, was not lying in state. In the usual way for ozo-titled men in certain parts of ancient Igboland, he was seated on the akpako, a makeshift chair fashioned with stems and leaves. His face was made up with a chalk-white paste, his eyes open, lips parted in a deathly grimace. Three long eagle feathers on his red cap were marks of the highly valued chieftaincy titles Njaka had been conferred with in his lifetime. Altogether it had cost him a fortune in tribute fees to existing chiefs, homage to the king, purchase of cows, food items for ceremonies, kola nuts and other related expenses each time he took a title.

Carter was startled by the sitting corpse. He stopped abruptly in the middle of the long procession causing Osadebe who walked behind him to step on his heels.

"Sorry, Ugoabata," Osadebe said. "You keep moving."

Carter walked faster to catch up with the procession. He was speechless, his eyes never stirring from the old man who sat dead in a very bizarre and scary posture. Carter noted once again how important the warlike attitude was to the Ogwarians. They were a gentle and peace-loving people yet the expression of courage and valour was very much a part of their culture. It was a façade that warded off would-be aggressors. Even in death, Nwalie Njaka was made up in the offensive attitude of a sitting warrior who could rise at a moment's notice to engage in combat. Carter wondered if they had used some kind of glue to clasp his right hand to the long spear-like object Njaka held like a staff. Little did he know that the metal staff was a fishing tool called ogashi that symbolized part of his life's vocation. Njaka had started as a fisherman before he went to trade with the Igalas.

Several feet from the dead man's akpako was a fetish cluster. There was a fishing net, the wheel cover of a vehicle, a wide-mouthed pot of red palm oil, a large ram, another fishing staff–ogashi–and a jute sack filled with stones and tied at the end. There was also a long weaved rectangular basket–ukpa–which contained his charms and miniature idols. The entire cluster was the *Osha* which represented his life's vocation and substance as a man, the bag of stones called akpa okwu na uka, symbolizing the containment and removal of his life's trials and tribulations from his survivors.

The procession of the Nwajiobi kindred had just finished paying their respects to the deceased's family and were filing out when Ichie Ezeaputa led the Ifeadigos to file past the corpse.

The males of the Njaka family were seated in an uno ntu, a shed made out of fresh bamboo poles and topped with palm fronds. Many sheds were constructed around the compound for in-laws, friends, maternal kin, general guests and affiliates. Sheds were also erected in Njaka's neighbours' front yards where other visiting groups were entertained with food and drinks.

Elders of the dead man's kindred were the host. They sat in the shed with the chief mourners. The younger ones were assigned to receive guests and serve food and refreshment while others had built the sheds, cleaned and weeded the premises and dug the grave. On the funeral day, there were those who received gifts of wine, food, goats, cloths and roosters brought by visitors. Some members of the kindred who were given the tasks of notifying relations and in-laws in Ogwari and in distant lands had already completed their tasks and were now offering help generally. Among these inevitable funeral tasks, washing, dressing, adorning and setting Njaka in his sitting position, the most morbid of all, was done by old men, his ozo-titled peers.

*   *   *

Ichie Ezeaputa stood before the shed where the main mourners were seated. The gifts of wine, goat and kolanuts brought by the Ifeadigo were presented. Nwalie Njaka's two sons were seated with one of their father's surviving brothers who was there to keep his young nephews company. Other senior males of their umunna sat behind them also.

Ezeaputa addressed the Njaka family on behalf of the Ifeadigo offering them words of consolation. He told Njaka's son that it was only proper that they bury their father instead of their father burying them. He tasked them to follow their father's footsteps in industry, discipline, kindness and generosity. After his words of advice, Ichie Ezeaputa placed a currency note of small denomination in the wooden tray that was kept in front of the mourners. The Elder who followed him in the procession did the same. As they filed past, members of the Ifeadigo clan placed their small tokens in the tray, while adding short phrases of condolence, "ndo-nu, jisinu ike. Sorry, take heart." When it got to his turn, Carter fumbled in his pockets for a note. All he could find was a small wad of dollar notes which he had wanted to exchange to naira when he rode to the city in the afternoon. He withdrew a crisp one-dollar note and placed it on the heap of notes in the tray. The strange currency brought looks of puzzlement and amusement to the mourners and visitors alike.

*   *   *

It had finally become certain to Carter that the African masquerade was totally different in concept from the American halloween masks. Unlike the yearly haloween of 31st December when American children and adults dressed up in various costumes and masks, the mmanwu, as it was called in Igboland, was a cult.

The mmanwu movement was strictly a male affair. Carter learnt that adolescent boys were initiated into this esoteric spiritual sect with well-guarded secrets. Every masquerade was presumed to be a departed spirit-being, appearing in the physical form. The assumption by the uninitiated that these masquerades were actually humans in mysterious costumes did not make them any less sinister or awesome. No self-respecting male child after initiation would reveal the secret of the mmanwu to women or even to uninitiated males.

Carter could clearly remember his first few days in Obodo Ogwari when he had gone very close to an Odogwu masquerade to get a clear shot with his camera. At first, the Odogwu stood puzzled, moping at the white red-headed man. The odogwu's huge head hung in a perplexed tilt, a rusted machete in his hand. Carter had taken a clear shot before the warning shouts of the villagers spurred him into a fast retreat.

Odogwu lurched at the white man, his machete raised, before an aged man of the mmanwu cult stood in the breach.

In time, Carter learned which of the mmanwu were dangerous and the ones that were merely innocuous entertainers. The singing masquerade called Ulaga and its double rows of chorus boys who sang acapella was Carter's favourite. In the corner of its mouth the Ulaga had a short reed pipe covered on one side with a white cloth-like patch of the spider's nest. When it sang through this instrument, its voice though melodious, was raspy and rather alien. Phillip Carter thought he had seen all manner of terrible masquerades until the day of Nwalie Njaka's funeral. Before that day he had heard that the very diabolical masks of Obodo Ogwari had been phased out by the Gundu priests. Before the coming of the Gundu, Ogwarians had great medicine men who could perform all sorts of magic, sorcery and healing. After the Gundu arrived, these medicine men as they lived their lives and died, did not need replacements. A greater power had already come to be.

The Odogwu which projected their much cherished attitude of valour became the most terrible mmanwu of Ogwariland.

From the stories, Carter knew that the cult into which the young boys were initiated was different from what the aged men operated from the olden days. There had surely been more mysterious secret societies within the general one. Carter was told that there were masquerades that definitely bore the evidence of spirit-force origins. However, their function had been tied up in super-fetishism and wickedness in extremity. The British missionaries had not succeeded in wiping out these terrible cults in the six counterpart towns. But, the Gundu stopped them in Obodo Ogwari long before the missionaries arrived. Such extremely diabolical mmanwu were not seen frequently. Sometimes a decade passed, even twenty years before one was seen in the other six towns. Carter also learned that the only cause that brought out such mmanwu from its devlish lair was the death of an aged man that belonged to its cult or a close associate. Occassionally, it also appeared by special request.

Before Nwalie Njaka died, it had been reported in Obodo Ogwari that he was seen attending to the Ajo-ofia masquerade of Obodo Ite. The legendary tales that had been told about the

Ajo-ofia attracted curiosity seekers from far and wide.

It hadn't been a surprise for Njaka's kinsmen to receive a message two days before the funeral that the Ajo-ofia would attend. Nwalie Njaka had not been an average Ogwarian in his lifetime. Though he started his vocational life as a fisherman, he later joined his grandmother's people at Obodo Ite in trading with the Igalas of the middle belt and made a great fortune. He built many houses in the city and had a fleet of commercial buses yet he humbled himself in Obodo Ogwari whenever he came home. Flaunting his wealth would forge ill-will and resentment among his modest kin. Njaka's strong affiliation to his grandmother's people was well known to the Ogwarians, and also his rumoured membership in the Mmanwu Ajo-ofia of Obodo Ite. He believed that his personal god, his chi, came from Obodo Ite and that the dark powers of the Ajo-ofia provided him with greater protection and goodluck than he would ever get from the alien Gundu priests of Obodo Ogwari. His kinsmen had always regarded Njaka as one that served a strange god but he didn't care. In fact, he had been proud of it.

*   *   *

In the early hours of the day of the burial, a young acolyte of the sixth keeper approached the thick jungle between Obodo Ogwari and Obodo Ite. It was the route through which guests from neighbouring towns would cross over to Ogwariland.

The sixth keeper's apprentice, working on the instruction of his master, stood in the centre of the dusty road facing Obodo Ite and raised a short metal staff to the heavens and muttered a few words. Still muttering inaudibly, he went a few feet into the bush. The acolyte bent over and jabbed the tip of his staff on the earth. From there, he drew a continuous line from the bush across the road, into the other side. By doing so, he had lifted the force field that protected Obodo Ogwari from all natural and supernatural aggression on that side of the border.

*   *   *

The ekwe resounded with intricate rhythms of songs that were passed down from over a thousand years of Ogwari tradition. The hollowed and dried tree trunk, no bigger than a man's torso, was played with two short sticks. It chattered steadfastly in the skilled hands of Ntupuanya, son of Ogbuefi Akunne. The woody sound of the ekwe was the driving force, the heartbeat of the music. Accompanying Ntupuanya was Ukolo, the nyo man who shook a pair of conical weaved instruments with coral beads inside. Ukolo's hands on the top handle made counter up and down motions that bounced the beads in complex matching beat. Diligently, Akum the drummer pounded hard on his tightly strung antelope skins while Obunadike struck his giant twin gongs in wild and provocative progressions. Together, Ntupuanya and his village quartet played and sang songs that spurred villagers to quick sporadic dancing, rousing the bold-hearted young men to wild and aggressive behaviour. Amid dancing they would suddenly surge at the crowds of spectators as if with hostile intent, then screech to a barefooted stop raising clouds of dust. At times, children and the cowardly would draw backwards or run from their dramatic insurgence.

⊙‖ Twenty-five ‖⊙

It was late afternoon. Nwalie Njaka had been buried as a titled man, his right hand sticking out of an opening on the top of his hand-crafted coffin, Igbudu. A tender yellowish palm frond was tied on the wrist of his protruding hand.

It was time for friends and relations to pay their last respects in the usual style that would make the deceased diligent on his journey to the great beyond. In-laws, maternal relations, friends and affiliates, according to their means and closeness to the dead man, came accompanied by their own friends and relations and musicians. There were flutists, drummers, singers and various entertaining masquerades who escorted mourners to this second phase of the funeral. Nwalie Njaka had been wealthy and generous in his life so there were throngs of people who felt obligated and wished that his funeral would be a great success. Some came with masquerades that ranged from the innocuous singing ones, dancing masquerades with musicians and deathly masks who came escorted by mysterious and diabolical old men. The latter were avoided by the people as if they were plagued. Njaka's funeral attracted so many spectators who came from other towns and villages. Friends of Njaka's first son, Akubuko, came with a masquerade that sang and danced vigorously to an up-tempo drum and flute accompaniment.

Instantly, there was an increase in activity and agitation the moment Mmanwu Odogwu anya mmee rushed into the scene of the funeral. It was a huge masquerade with its body covered with a dense weaving of short, raffia palm strands that stuck out at right angles. Everything about Odogwu from its truculent drummers to its dancing style, machete in hand, reeked of aggression and violence. Its face was a big ugly mask that matched its offensive attitude. A huge man who was assigned to hold the thick restraining chain around its waist struggled to keep it from sudden surges at the spectators. A tall dark man, savage and erratic, blew mouthful blasts of kai kai gin into the mmanwu's face.

187

The odogwu anya mmee as it was called meant appropriately, the red-eyed warrior. True to its name, it charged randomly at the teeming crowds. A young handsome man stood in its way challengingly to show courage. The Odogwu struck him on the head with his machete and blood erupted. It was not out of the ordinary.

The music from so many groups came together in the arena of Njaka's compound, one blending into another, forming a potpourri of percussions, chants and singing.

Ntupuanya, son of Ogbuefi Akunne, signaled his group in a burst of his ekwe and their music ended. They were the resident group for the funeral and now it was their time to watch the numerous visiting groups and consume their own share of the food and drinks.

Many men of Obodo Ogwari wore long robes of light colourful cotton materials. The titled men wore red caps. However, some of the men wore loincloths with matching cloths hanging around their necks to their waists.

The women were dressed in beautiful prints and tye-dye wraps passed under their arms and fastened behind, leaving their backs bare. Their necks were bedecked with colourful coral beads and bangles while titled women wore ivory bands on their wrists and ankles.

*   *   *

Egodi was sixteen years old. She was the third daughter of Ichie Ezeaputa's second wife. Contrary to the customs and traditions of Obodo Ogwari, she had been meeting Azubike, the son of Ogbuefi Akunne, in the bushes where they engaged in amorous activity. By the time she found herself pregnant, the full consequence of the punishment that awaited her and Azubike grossly outweighed the love she thought she had for him. When discovered, she and her lover would be stripped naked in the market-place and subjected to serious corporal punishment. Thereafter, she would be married off to any suitor that comes along. In her pregnant and shameful state, only the disadvantaged like the very aged, physically deformed, moron or drunkard would propose. Egodi had seen it happen to her elder sister's friend and knew it was a most undesirable choice to make between the derelict and reject of society. Azubike had suggested going to a dibia at Obodo Ukwa who would give her a potion to abort the fetus but there was no money to pay for the service. Moreover, he was worried about the danger of her dying in the process which would attract a twenty-year banishment for him. Egodi was not worried about dying. Her father, Ichie Ezeaputa, was a member of the Igwe's cabinet, a titled chief of the high order. Her death would be more desirable than the shame she would bring on her respectable family. So far, Egodi had been successful in hiding her condition from her mother for two months since she missed her menstrual period.

One week before Nwalie Njaka's funeral, Egodi overheard her father and his friend, Obiokafor, discussing the upcoming burial. Ichie Ezeaputa told Obiokafor that the rumour that Nwalia Njaka was a member of the Mmanwu Ajo-ofia cult of Obodo Ite would now be proved. If the rumour was true then it meant that the evil mmanwu would attend. It was from listening to Ezeputa and his friend talk that Egodi learnt how dangerous and diabolical the Ajo-ofia was and how Ajo-ofia would help her present condition. From then, she began to look forward, meticulously counting the days to Njaka's funeral. Egodi began to yearn for the arrival of Mmanwu Ajo-ofia.

* * *

Carter was just thinking how much the funeral resembled a carnival when he noticed a surreptitious agitation among the people. In a few minutes he was certain that something was amiss. Villagers and visitors who had stood enjoying the music and the dancing now spoke excitedly among themselves. Some had suddenly become silent, while looking warily toward the wide dusty path that led to the arena of Njaka's neighbour's front yard. Suddenly, a wide path was cut across the crowd of people and masquerades. Everyone scampered out of the way to make room for the new visitor.

Carter rose on his toes and peered over the heads of the people before him. A very thin old man, black and leathery, stood in the distance shaking and vibrating all over. In his left hand was a whole branch of tender palm fronds, omu. Soon as the path was cleared for him, he broke into a run toward the uno ntu where the mourners sat. He ended his run abruptly before the mourners, glaring at them as though at arch-enemies. He suddenly swirled

189

around and ran in circles feigning motions as if he would throw the palm branch on different sheds. Finally he turned to the shed where the mourners sat and threw the branch on top of the shed. Immediately, the dark old man turned and fled in the same direction as he had come, people and masquerades still staying out of his path. A young man clothed in black loincloth was immediately sent after the old man. A ram was swung across his back, his hands grasping both pairs of the animal's legs on the sides.

Someone tapped Carter on the shoulder. He turned around to see Emeka Emodi smiling at him.

"Having fun?" Emodi asked.

"I'm not sure yet," Carter replied. "Actually, I don't understand what exactly is going on. All of a sudden everyone is looking quite apprehensive or scared or something."

"Well, I guess they have a right to be scared."

"Who was the dark old man with the palm frond?"

"He's a forerunner of the Ajo-ofia masquerade or should I call it the Ajo-ofia deity," Emodi replied. "The ram they took to him was to appease the Ajo-ofia to do less damage when it arrives. Phillip, I think you should leave now and go back to your house ..."

"Why, have I done anything wrong?"

"No, no, no ... I'm just worried about your safety."

"What's so terrible about this masquerade anyway?" Carter asked.

"Believe me, it's as evil as they come. To begin with, someone usually one of them dies mysteriously before the deity is raised for an outing. It is believed that sudden-departed spirits enforce levitation of the physical masquerade."

"If it kills its followers then why do they follow it?"

"They usually join up at a matured age and mind you, it's a cult. Some join for spiritual power and others, protection which both, sometimes, spell out the same. However, most if not all of its members are said to become substantially rich after they join. It only emerges from its devilish lair once in at least a decade or more. According to Ogbuefi Akunne whom I just spoke to, this very Ajo-ofia that's on its way here has not come out in nineteen years."

"Why here, Meks? Why has such evil come to Obodo Ogwari?

Why are the keepers allowing such dark malevolence to run on our land?"

"I thought you took the keepers to be evil also," Emodi chuckled.

"I've been changing my mind ever since I came closer to Igo the sixth keeper. It's only the killing of those two early missionaries, Patterson and Cook, that still bothers me," Carter replied warily.

Emodi reflected for a moment before he spoke. "We would never really know why they died that way and why Morgan was spared."

* * *

The young man who had taken a ram to the Ajo-ofia's forerunner came back to the arena on a trot. "All pregnant women should leave immediately. He asked me to tell you that all pregnant women must leave the area immediately before the Ajo-ofia arrives. The young man was shouting at the top of his voice. "Any expectant mother that stays shall bear the consequences."

The few pregnant women were quickly located and hustled away in the opposite direction from where the Ajo-ofia was approaching. Some other females who were not visibly pregnant left quietly without delay.

The once rowdy arena of Nwalie Njaka's funeral had suddenly grown quiet. Drummers, musicians and their escorted visitors and masquerades seemed to have disbanded, each retreating to a safe distance in the periphery of Njaka's large compound. Even the Mmanwu Odogwu with all its show of courage and aggression had tactfully left the front yard and was paying homage to some titled old men under a distant shed, knocking the side of its machete against their staffs in honourary greetings. The evil masquerade's presence was preceded by the staccato striking of a single ekwe and a very foul and offensive odour that filled the air.

* * *

Mmanwu Ajo-ofia was a circular float about twelve feet in diameter and twenty feet high. Its body seemed to have been made up of a framework of rawhide casing, on which hung all things dreadful and repulsive. Meshes of rope-like materials

191

formed a greater part of its body from top to bottom. A big live python hung from the ropes coiling apparently toward the top. A live rooster was tied upside down beside a freshly decapitated one that dripped blood on the sides. There were other motley objects of obscure coalescence that hung from the body, small rotting animals, skulls, bones from bygone sacrifices and other unidentifiable objects. At the very top of the Mmanwu Ajo-ofia stood a large clay pot that emitted a horrible stench. A scraggy old vulture stood beside the pot, watching as if with malevolent intent as the Ajo-ofia floated forward and backward. Its movement was jerky and seemed to have no constraint as to which direction was the front, rear or sideways course. From a forward movement toward the Njaka front yard, it would suddenly switch to a side motion causing the spectators in that area to melt into obscurity for fear of physical harm.

"What in the hell is this supposed to be?" Carter asked as if talking to himself.

"This is Ajo-ofia from Obodo Ite, the only masquerade I think that is partially powered by a spirit being," Emodi replied. "This is the throne of evil, the embodiment of the devil; here, a branch of satan has been given a physical body."

A shabby-looking woman came crying with a six-year-old boy in her arms. She had emerged from the rear of Njaka's neighbour's compound.

"Help me, somebody please help me," cried the woman. "Please help me beg the Ajo-ofia people before my son dies."

"Woman, what happened?" asked Okonkwo the blacksmith who stood in the cover of Njaka's barn from where he watched the bizarre scene.

"I was in the bush farming while my son was shooting lizards with his catapult," the woman began. "When I heard the ekwe of the evil mmanwu I had a bad feeling so I started shouting at my son to come. He ran across the path of the mmanwu and fell down. After the mmanwu passed I picked him up and he has not woken up since then." She started to wail loudly.

"Stop crying, woman, you better take your son to the caves for treatment," suggested Osadebe the hunter.

"Please ... please, my son will die before we reach the caves. Help me beg the followers of the Ajo-ofia," she pleaded.

"Woman!" called Osadebe. "Who do you think would have the courage to approach those deadly men in their present state? Just look at them."

The woman turned to take a look at the Ajo-ofia and its followers. There were about nine elderly men with faces made up in white-coloured nzu and red ufie. Their bodies were bare and painted with concentric circles and triangles on top. They wore short smoke-blackened skirts around their waists and on their ankles were strings of shells that rattled when they walked. Their general attitude was of distrust and apprehension. It was obvious that they were expectant of being attacked, physically or spiritually, yet there were no signs of weapons on their bodies. The magical might they depended on would suffice against any form of invasion.

Emodi volunteered to take the woman and her child to the second keeper for medical treatment. As they left, Carter was unhappy to see him go yet it gave him a little sense of freedom and adventure.

*   *   *

Egodi, sixteen years old and illegitimately pregnant, hid behind an oak tree with some boys and men. She knew that males would be too preoccupied to notice her presense, not with the baggy trousers she wore and the long printed cloth that draped her head and upper body. She had to wear men's clothes to avoid being noticed and sent away. Women were not allowed to come near such masquerades as the Ajo-ofia, pregnant or not. It was considered a challenge for any female to stand boldly watching or stand close to its path. Men usually shooed women away even before the mmanwu arrived. It was supposed to be for the women's protection. Moreover, they were usually not initiated into the mmanwu world. Only certain elderly women of notable social status were given chieftaincy titles and initiated in some towns. Egodi was well aware of all these facts which gave rise to her disguise and surreptitious movement among the men.

As the mmanwu Ajo-ofia crossed the oak tree where they stood, the stench from its smoking pot hung in the air like a mixture of rotten eggs, faeces and vomit emanating from one source. Some of the men pinched their nostrils shut while others retreated, nauseated. Egodi inhaled deeply, opening her mouth to suck in the odour.

A powerful nausea hit her like a blow in the chest, reaching down to churn and twist her intestines. She bolted from the scene struggling to keep down the vomit that was starting to erupt from her bowels. As she ran down a lonely path that led to the stream, she began to throw up.

By the time Egodi got halfway to the stream, she felt a warm wetness between her thighs. She continued to run till she got to the stream and began to wash off the blood.

*   *   *

Ducked beside a large ukwa, Carter poised his small electronic camera to snap the Mmanwu Ajo-ofia. He knew that Emodi may not have approved of it. Carter smiled at the chance of adventure the woman and her child had provided by whisking Emodi away to the caves. He had taken three shots and was posturing for the fourth when he noticed through the viewfinder that Ajo-ofia was floating rapidly toward him. At once he lowered the camera and saw that the evil structure was looking down on him. Immediately, Carter retreated and ducked behind the big tree, feeling confident that with the short rows of Ogilisi plants that formed scraggy hedges on either sides of the tree, Ajo-ofia would not get him. But, what if its followers came to attack him? Carter wondered in alarm. A few voices were already warning him to run for dear life. Carter could not move. His heart pounded so hard; he was breathless and suddenly very tired. He could feel the aura of sheer malevolence and spiritual filth upon him. Goose pimples spread all over his body.

Ajo-ofia jammed the ukwa tree with its body and the large tree shook and shivered from its roots to the top branches. It retreated and surged toward the huge ukwa a second time. More voices were shouting at Carter to run. Carter bolted as Ajo-ofia made its second contact with the tree. The huge breadfruit rose from its roots, shook vigorously and then pulling out heavy chunks of earth as it strained and heaved like a woman in birth travails, crashed to the ground.

Carter had barely cleared the prostrate length of the tree when the ukwa hit the earth. A top branch struck him on the back propelling him across the dusty soil. He rolled rapidly before his body lodged at the base of Njaka's barn. Clouds of dust rose around the whole length of the tree swirling in the already dry harmattan atmosphere.

Three old dwarfs, Ndi Akanri, in loincloths and raw hide satchels slung across their shoulders came in a single row to pay their respects to the family of the deceased. Their ancestors were considered the origin of the special universal priests of Igboland who traveled across the land when called to perform ceremonial rites such as crowning a king, handling and burial of suicide corpses. The Akanri were special dwarfs invited generally to cleanse the land of abominations committed by its indigenes, whenever the need arose. Their services in Obodo Ogwari too had been nullified by the coming of the Gundu priests. As they hobbled across the arena, they paid no special attention to the Ajo-ofia that was floating around on the side where it felled the tree.

The followers of the Ajo-ofia saw the dwarfs as they moved slowly and fearlessly across Njaka's big front yard. They formed a barrrier between the mmanwu and the Akanris till the little men came before the Njaka family. They were not received as normal visitors. Seats were provided for them immediately to sit among the mourners, a mark of respect. In other towns, their presense would have been considered a blessing against various forms of spiritual aggression.

Twenty-six

A skeletal TV production crew had come into Obodo Ogwari on motorbikes an hour before the Ajo-ofia arrived.

They went to Igwe Ajulufo's palace and paid homage to the king with a half gallon of Jack Daniel's scotch whisky, seeking his permission to take video camera shots of the town in preparation for his yam festival. They were making a documentary of the Ofala festival in Igboland. The producer, Sid Jefferson, introduced his cameraman and assistant as Tony and Kene. Three other boys that looked like locals came with them but stood outside the hall.

Igwe Ajulufo received the trio in his usual cordial and hospitable manner, offering them fresh home-made gin, kola nuts, dried fish and alligator peppers.

*   *   *

Sid Jefferson was an African-American whose nationality was once questioned in a controversial matter between Nigeria and the United States. American officials had flown him to Lagos and handed him over to their Nigerian counterparts. Jefferson had been found in a compromising situation in Washington that raised suspicion that he was a spy. Subject to interrogation without much duress he claimed to be an African and gave his origin as Ihitenansa in the Imo State of Nigeria. He gave his ancestral name as Onyekachi and spoke passable Igbo. However, his official records showed that he was an all-American born and bred 'Brother.'

Sid Jefferson was deported to Nigeria as Ralph Onyekachi, the identity in his ID card but an American passport found in his possession identified him as Jimmy Price. After his deportation he hung around tourists in the Victoria Island's Bar Beach till he was able to raise some naira and crossed over to Ghana.

Through a master forger he obtained a Ghanaian passport and a genuine American visa and traveled back to the states. In America, he destroyed his Ghanaian identity and assumed the name of Sid Jefferson, originally from Louisiana. Computer-designed latex rubber films fitted to his thumb and finger tips gave him new prints for this latest identity.

It was this new project he was working on that brought him back to Nigeria. Sid was unofficially employed by an international agency called Global Minerals Exploration Research Corporation [GMERC]. His official designation in the company was listed as researcher.

Incorporated in 1965 in New York, GMERC was actually engaged in mining for rare gems mostly in Third World countries. The founder, Brandon Givens, was a lucky prospector who in the early days made a fortune in South African diamonds before he ventured into digging for rare gems in other African countries. Upon his retirement, his son Raymond who took over the mantle of leadership in the huge conglomerate, maintained their mining interests but diversified into more clandestine areas like industrial espionage and trading in hi-tech secrets, a lucrative hobby. After he was dishonourably discharged from the US Army intelligence for subversive activity, Raymond returned to New York to take over his aged father's business. Raymond Givens, like his father, had concentrated mainly in African countries. One of Raymond's east coast operatives hooked Jefferson up with GMERC and he was hired within a short time following a rigorous physical and general aptitude test. A GMERC staff in the Cameroun who was friends with the exiled Obodo Ogwarian, Ikeadi Ntukogu, had learned of Obodo Ogwari from his exiled friend. Innocently, Ntukogu had told him about the Ideamala and the uncanny longevity of the Gundu, their great powers and magic. The adventurous Raymond Givens and his sixth sense thought that it would be a worthwhile gamble to make. Their prior mining capabilities and interests offered a good cover to the first agent, Jake Sanders, who was sent to Obodo Ogwari in search of the hidden secrets of the Gundu. When Sanders failed, Sid Jefferson was sent with the TV production ploy to gain clandestine access to the caves.

*   *   *

A high-strung squawk tore through the atmosphere, overwhelming the rowdiness of Njaka's compound. It was a terrifying sound to the Ogwarians, a sound that most villagers recognized but had never seen its source. Among the few that had ever seen it within a century, only Phillip Carter had survived the experience. The cry of the Ideamala Bird resounded over the din of Ajo-ofia's musicians and the bubbling crowds. While visitors failed to see anything unusual, Ogwarians took heed and began to search for the origin of the sound. The Ideamala Bird had never been known to appear in any social function, not even funerals. Why would it now cry so close to Nwalie Njaka's home rather than up in the caves where it resided and usually confined itself? the natives wondered. Had the bird come publicly, in broad daylight, to execute judgment on a traditional offender? What moral injunction had it come to enforce?

The huge bird swooped down from a tree and landed on an anthill at the boundry of Njaka's home with his neighbour's. Its large head flicked from side to side, wide wings flapping as it squawked angrily. It seemed to be searching for something or someone in an attitude that was very human. It focused its attention on the Ajo-ofia.

Ogwarians drew backward. Those who were nearest to the anthill broke into a run, influencing the visitors who also ran with them. This was the bird they never worshipped or made fetish sacrifice to but it represented a powerful godhead. It was the fear of the bird that kept law and order and preserved culture and tradition in Obodo Ogwari, yet they believed in the supreme God. They believed that God made the bird.

In just this singular funeral, people had run from the Ajo-ofia and now from the bird. It was unusual.

The drummers and singers of the Ajo-ofia cult continued to perform but it was obvious that on seeing the bird their morales had waned a little. Though they were not natives of Obodo Ogwari but from the neighbouring Obodo Ite, they knew about the Ideamala Bird and its legendary might. Nevertheless, they mostly believed that the powers of the Ajo-ofia was superior to whatever evil threat the ancient bird posed. The drummers began to pound fiercely on their rawhides while singers raised their voices, morales rising in parallel accent. Despite this show of bravado, their faces were streaked with wariness and uncertainty.

The bird clapped its huge wings aggressively and charged down from the anthill toward the Ajo-ofia masquerade. Ajo-ofia spun around and floated to meet the great bird. In one quick rush the

Ideamala bent its withered bald head low to the ground and raised one end of the flaps that covered the Ajo-ofia and barged into the hidden confines of the evil masquerade. The followers of the Ajo-ofia retreated to a safer distance. Even the Njaka family who sat in the mourners' shed rose from their seats and ran to the periphery of the compound. The Akanris, dwarfs, remained on their seats.

The Ajo-ofia, now inhabited by the Ideamala, spun and bucked apparently from much turbulence and agitation within. The circular structure rocked sideways, moving as though an invisible hand was preventing it from the straight course. It was jolted by a direct collision with the anthill. The large python that curled on the side of the masquerade whiplashed in the air but did not fall. The vulture flapped its wings rapidly on its way to the ground. The smoking pot rolled off and dashed to pieces on the hard earth. Its fetish contents scattered on the ground.

Sid Jefferson and his camera crew stood on an elevated ground outside the premises. Using a wide angle lens they recorded the encounter between the masquerade, the bird and the teeming crowds.

Igo and Rev. Father Mojekwu stood in the compound of Njaka's neighbour from where they could see the activity. As the Ajo-ofia rocked and spun in agitation, Fr. Mojekwu looked sideways at the Gundu priest and saw his fist clench in a gesture of deep self-control.

"Do not interfere, Igo," Mojekwu coaxed. "Let fate take its course."

Igo nodded slowly without looking at the catholic priest. His eyes were glued to the circular masquerade that now housed the bird. Rev. Father Mojekwu knew that the bird was linked to Igo, maybe like a fetish pet or something. Little did he know how closely related they were.

The smoking pot had fallen off and smashed yet smoke still oozed from the top of the Ajo-ofia. It was not apparent whether chunks of smouldering wood had fallen from the pot and ignited on the dried raffia. Tongues of fire leapt from the top, the sides and even the flaps at the bottom. It became obvious to the spectators that the smoking pot was not the source of the fire. A few minutes afterwards the circular form of the masquerade became a big ball of fire, still bucking and staggering out of control. The wailing of the Ideamala Bird sounded and reverberated in ominous timbres of deep torment. Also from within, several croaky male voices crying for help clashed with the bird's wailing to form a very eerie noise. A horrible odour oozed from the burning masquerade. Many spectators had run away completely from the vicinity of Njaka's house while others watched from what they thought to be safe distances.

The Ajo-ofia went into a spin. As the fire reached its climax the masquerade spun faster. Voices of the men could be heard screaming continuously. Squawks of the bird only came at intervals, and in patterns that gave close impressions of human speech. Bits and chunks of burning objects flew out of the structure.

When the Ajo-ofia came to a halt, the fire was waning. The turbulence within the masquerade had stopped, seeming that whatever life within had come to an end.

The crowd of visitors, even the mourners and their relations, were all watching from neighbours' compounds. Anxiously, they stared to see what the fire would reveal. The cane frame work that formed the outer part of the masquerade's body fell in a ring of flames.

The Ideamala Bird, partly charred and still burning, stood upright in the midst of the roasted bodies of three elderly looking men. The great bird squawked and looked at Igo where he still stood by Rev. Fr Mojekwu. It stepped over the corpses of the men and away from the ruins of the Ajo-ofia.

As the Ideamala Bird continued to burn, the body feathers curled and flaked off in tiny reddish sparks that fell off in black and grey ashes.

A young man who had noticed the transformation that was going on in the bird's massive head, shouted. The bird moaned and started forward in very ungainly steps. Its large beak had suddenly seemed to have melted away in what was actually an uncanny metamorphosis. Most of the wing and body feathers had burned away leaving a partly charred, goose-pimpled body. The entire parts of the body became fluid and bubbling like volcanic lava, swiveling in liquid forms yet, not dripping off; charred remains mixing with white goose flesh to form and reform weird appendages. Bare arms appeared where the bird's wing stumps had been. As the Ideamala bird approached Igo and the Reverend Father, it tripped on a little mound of earth and almost fell but its large splayed bird's feet had broadened into weird replicas of human feet. It stood an arm's length before Igo. A skeletal human head formed.

Fr. Mojekwu watched the human head mutate, the large gaping holes where the eyes would have been, narrowed down to dim human eyes. It opened its mouth as though to speak but only faint grunts came out. In a flash, Fr. Mojekwu saw the true image of the bird-man. It was a very close resemblance of Igo.

"I see you ..." Igo said in a quivering voice. "Go well, Brother Tam."

Fr. Mojekwu looked sharply at Igo.

Streams of swirling flesh, viscous and translucent, shaped and reshaped into many inexplicable forms before appearing as the Ideamala Bird. It lingered for a moment then began to disintegrate. Like a big lump of dark candle wax, exposed to high heat, it dissolved on itself melting down into a huge gelatinous mound. It squirmed and bubbled then became rigid and lifeless.

Igo turned and left as the crowds edged closer to see the remains of the legendary bird.

Fr. Mojekwu stood as if glued to a spot. What he had seen at close quarters awed him. As the crowds of people surged around, he stirred and ran after Igo.

"Your brother?" Fr. Mojekwu asked when he caught up with Igo moving between two large huts behind Njaka's house.

Igo stopped and nodded. His eyes were very green as though drops of vegetable juice had been administered into them.

"I'm sorry ..." the priest consoled.

"He gave himself for the good of these people," Igo said coldy. "Now that traditional law and order has been dismantled, this town will suffer a high level of crime and degradation it has not known before."

"Not to worry, Igo. We shall build churches, pentecostals and others shall come in with crusades and vigils."

"It will never be the same. Your people do not fear Jesus Christ, God, as much as they fear the lesser deities, the Alusi, and other spirits that are deified in shrines."

"Is that why you created the bird as a powerful god for them to fear?"

"Yes, but we never encouraged them to worship it. The Ogwarians believe in the supreme God the Creator."

"Don't you think you have kept them in the dark for too long … manipulated their destiny for centuries …?"

"This is their destiny!" Igo interrupted indignantly. "The people here have surplus food and clean water. They enjoy the greatest medical treatment in this world and live much longer than their neighbours. Now tell me, Reverend, what more do you want out of life?"

"I want the right to choose between the talking drum and the telephone, the mud hut and the hacienda, I want the chance to chose between smoked antelope in a wooden mortar and a three-course meal at the Hilton," Fr Mojekwu declared.

"The one they call Emeka Emodi left this town as a young boy to England. He came back many years later, of his own accord, and has never left since," said Igo.

"That is one man's choice," the Reverend Father defended. "What about others who want civilization?"

"I hate to hurt your feelings, Father, but this your civilization that you so much cherish is headed for nothing but destruction, if you don't start now to care."

Fr Mojekwu looked intently at the Gundu priest. "How do you know all this, Igo?"

"Your day shall come," Igo replied.

*   *   *

Sid Jefferson was furious. The images he sought for in the video recording had vanished mysteriously. From the entry of the Ajo-ofia to its encounter with the weird bird were simply not there. The followers of the evil masquerade could be seen performing but the entire structure itself did not register on film. Even the mourners and spectators were all on record but the two subjects he desired most were missing. Jefferson's ultimate mission in coming to Obodo Ogwari was not to make a documentary as he had told the king but soon as he saw the action in Njaka's funeral while nosing around town, he knew it was an exclusive shot that would fetch lots of money in the electronic media. Playing back the tape, first on the viewfinder and then on the TV monitors was to be his first major disappointment in Obodo Ogwari. After viewing the mound of rubbery substance that was the worthless remains of the bird and the circular ruins of the Ajo-ofia, he shut down his equipment and left Njaka's compound. Though disappointed, he became more convinced that there were peculiar primeval secrets to be discovered in the ancient town of Obodo Ogwari.

Twenty-seven

The day of the yam festival, the Ofala, arrived. It marked the harvest of new yam crops, fresher, softer and larger than the dehydrated old yams. From the olden days the yam was the chief crop of the Igbo farmer and the Igbo were mainly farmers. The yam was their lifeline and symbolically represented God's blessing in food crop. As it was in the culture of Igbo ancients, yam stocks kept in barns called Obaji were rationed to sustain families till the next yam harvest. It was therefore an abominable crime for one to steal yams from another's farm or barn and such a crime usually attracted outrageous penalties. The Ogwarians did not depend solely on yam crops yet the crop remained very symbolic and important in their culture.

On this day of the annual yam festival the entire town was alive with preparations. Except for centenarians, all other age grades were warming up with various types of music or dance presentations they would perform before the king, his council and visitors at the palace grounds.

Some adolescent boys who had no age grade yet, had also learned dance routines and skits they would present before the king. Even the very little boys fashioned masquerade costumes from banana leaves. They split the broad leaves along the midrib into finger-like frills and tied them around their heads as masks and on their waists in place of raffia skirts that masquerades and dancers used. Decked out in this makeshift masquerade costumes the boys used the soft midrib of the banana and plantain leaf as whips. They chased their mates around, especially the girls who dreaded them as dangerous spirit beings, all for entertainment in the yam harvest.

Unlike their Westernized neighbours, the Ogwarians did not celebrate Christmas. The Ofala, which from the ancient days was called mmemme ili-ji, celebration of yam, was their biggest and most important festival.

The people of Obodo Ogwari loved bright colours. On this special day they came out dressed in their Ofala best, resplendent in local hand-made cloths, representing most hues of the rainbow. The women tied wrappers around their chests and backs and wore colourful coral beads and bangles while the titled elderly women wore broad ivory bangles and anklets. Long wooden benches were kept in rows under makeshift sheds constructed by youths of the last age grade with bamboo posts and palm frond roofs.

Emeka Emodi had been working with the committee that organized the Ofala for three years. As he stood in the festival arena next to the king's palace inspecting the sheds, he noticed a video camera crew setting up their equipment in one of the sheds. Emodi went up to them and requested to know what media they were representing. Their leader introduced himself as Sid Jefferson. He greeted Emodi in Igbo and told him that they were freelance producers that came to make a documentary with the consent of the king. Emodi greeted them politely and offered to assist whenever they needed him.

Gradually, after noon, the benches in the sheds were filled up with guests mostly from neighbouring towns. Music from various age grades began to sound in the distance. One after the other the groups arrived, bearing gifts of goats, yams, carved and sculptured items they brought to present as homage to the king.

As they took up positions under the sheds, their musicians stopped playing and also sought for benches to sit down, where they would wait for the appropriate time to appear before the king and elders.

A high-pitched female voice rang from the doorway of the king's hall. It was the aged Nwanyieke Onwudachi, chanting ancient praises of the king in sporadic outbursts. She was very light-skinned and wrinkled. Her once-lovely face was designed with black lines of uli and red uffio. A thick hand-crafted red cloth was tied under her arms leaving her wizened shoulders bare. In a high-strung chant, Nwanyieke hailed Igwe Ajulufo calling him the king of all kings in the region; a king with a heart of gold, benefactor of the underprivileged yet a courageous warrior. As she hailed the king, Igba-eze, the special royal musicians got ready for the king's entrance into the Ofala arena. The Igba-eze of Obodo Ogwari, unlike their neighbours was a very serious and dedicated group who assembled only for the service of the king. There were seven men dressed in brown uniforms, robes of jute-like materials with red sashes tied around their waists. Most were well over ninety years of age. They had been musicians from their youth. No one under seventy years was ever admitted into Igba-eze Obodo Ogwari. Their drums were unique, big and decorated with coloured feathers, their sounds dull and blunt. An accompanying flutist played equally dull but serene tones. None of the usual fast and rhythmic beats existed in Igba-eze. Its tune was strictly meant to create a spiritual and majestic aura, as the name defined, Igba eze, meaning 'the king's drum.'

Nwanyieke kept chanting and strutting around in quick vigorous movements, yet treading softly. The heavy, padded ivory bands around her ankles which distinguished her chieftaincy title, restricted her moves only to graceful regal steps.

The Igba-eze stood in three double rows facing the doorway of the king's hall while their flutist played beside them.

The king and his queen, Mmilimma, emerged from his hall amidst cheers of the villagers. For most villagers who had no prior cause or reason to appear before him since the last ofala, this was their only opportunity to see him.

Igwe Ajulufo was followed by his council of chiefs who lined up behind him in single line procession according to seniority in title taking.

As the Igba-eze played they stepped slowly backwards while the king advanced toward them waving at the cheering crowds. In this manner, they led the king to the arena where an ebony throne was set with fine sculptured stools on either sides for the chiefs.

"I-g-w-e-e!" the crowds hailed the king continually, some also hailing the Ichies.

A short distance away from the arena, Okunna, the cannon shot man struck a match and lit a thin line of gunpowder. It ignited a fiery trail to a row of seven cylindrical canisters pegged into the earth. At short intervals, the gunpowder-stuffed cylinders resounded in deafening blasts, giving off billows of offensive smoke from the open ends of the cannons.

More applause rented the air. The surging crowds edged closer around the king and his Ichies to admire the beauty of their regalia, especially the king. Igwe Ajulufo's robe was made by a tailoring craftsman from Obosi whose ancestor had been an apprentice tailor in the service of Emenanjo Eloebo of Akataukwala. In his special vocation he had been trained to make unique regalias for royalty. Igwe Ajulufo's clothing was a green ankle-length robe embroidered with gold-like threads, his slippers were designed with the same material. A long red velvet cape fastened to his shoulders, trailed several feet behind him. It was hemmed with coloured beads and corals and, in the centre, depicted a hand-woven warrior with a spear in warring animation. An elaborate bronze crown handed down from his ancestors was firmly set on his head. It was a legendary belief by the Ogwarians that the crown must fit snugly on the head of any prospective king in the Ajulufo family to prove him a rightful heir to the throne.

There were seven Ndichies representing the various clans of Obodo Ogwari. They wore long colourful robes and high-peaked red caps with white eagle feathers stuck around them.

After the king and his chiefs had sat down, Nwanyieke returned to the shed where the umuada, women of the royal family, were seated while the Igba-eze also retired to a shed. The King's Guard, a row of able-bodied young men, had already taken up positions behind the throne, mean and taciturn.

A small shed adjacent to the king's had been specially constructed for the exiles who had returned to reunite with their kinsmen. Surprisingly there were thirty-one of them; a lot more than was expected. Out of the lot, Ntukogu was the only original exile. The rest were descendants whose parents were either dead or too old or sick to attend. Their general appearance was different from the Ogwari youths. They were clearly city folks dressed in mostly trendy Western clothes. Only Captain Okafor, Ikeadi Ntukogu and a couple of older ones were clothed in traditional caftans and tie and dye jumpers. Though she was not one of them, Nurse Okolo sat next to Okafor, a warm smile playing on her ample cheeks. She wore an ankle-length skirt.

*   *   *

Sid Jefferson and his crew had commenced recording the occasion with two video cameras and a television monitor kept in the shed.

The special seats that were usually set for the Gundu priests behind the chiefs were empty. None of the keepers attended. They had notified the king of their intended absence. As the third keeper had told the Igwe when he came to take permission for their absence: one whose house is on fire does not chase after rats.

Igwe Ajulufo took up a kola nut from the wooden platter of kolas, alligator peppers and garden eggs that was set before him. He thanked the Creator who made it possible for a New Yam harvest to return in greater success, not only in yam but in other subsistence crops. He thanked the Almighty for guiding Okafor in his army career which gave rise to the return of their long lost relations from afar.

*   *   *

Led by Ntukogu and Okafor, the exiles stood before the king. Though they were thirty-one in number, Uzo-Onicha had screened and grouped them into five extended subfamilies. Igwe Ajulufo welcomed the exiles. He reminded them that laws existing long before his time had prescribed their exile. "Today," Igwe Ajulufo stressed, "marks a great change in the history of our ancient town. Today marks not only the day of pardon and reconciliation with our long-lost kinsmen but also the crossing of the express road construction over our border with Obodo Ite into Obodo Ogwari. Both events pronounce the inevitable change that is coming our way. I know some people are murmuring that Captain Okafor's fame has brought about this long-awaited pardon but I ask you why now?" He looked around as if expecting an answer.

"Only the Creator knows why this is happening now. For hundreds of years, we have strived to keep our land free of moral and spiritual degradation and that is what has made us special among all the towns in Igboland. The Creator's plans for us is not to rob, maim, rape and murder each other. It is the evil that we create that recoils on us. In Obodo Ogwari we created a natural state in a conducive aura of purity that fostered a near-perfect social and spiritual order. All that is at stake now but I must warn that the fact that we bow to this wind of change does not mean we bow to recklessness and total bastardization of our culture. We must join hands to keep evil away."

The king looked at Okafor and then at Ntukogu, making eye contact with both. "My brothers and sisters who have come back to us, we welcome you with open arms."

A thunderous applause, cheers and catcalls rent the air as

Igwe Ajulufo shook hands and hugged the exiles one after the other. His cabinet chiefs also welcomed them in like manner. "Today, we shall eat and drink together as brothers and sisters." The king continued. "Today all your lands, your rights and privileges as Ogwarians are fully restored and you shall live and walk the grounds of Obodo Ogwari freely without challenge or discrimination ..." More applause followed. He prayed for the town asking God to be merciful in the apparent wind of change that was blowing towards Obodo Ogwari. Ajulufo pleaded with the Almighty who owned all powers to guide the keepers of the Ideamala in adjusting to the change that was to come. After praying for the lives and progress of all and sundry, he declared the yam festival open. Garden eggs were served to the crowds from large baskets accompanied by kola nuts and alligator peppers in wooden trays.

A long procession of the oldest men in Ogwariland came through the far end of the arena lined up in order of seniority. They all wore red caps fitted snugly around their heads as a mark of the honourary titles bestowed upon them by age.

They had not made much obligatory expenses in the procurement of their red caps like ozo-titled men and Ndichies, but had received the title 'Ogbuefi' connoting their God-given titles. Each and every one of them was a hundred years and over.

Uzo-Onicha the king's scribe was on hand to receive the huge ram that the Ogbuefis brought in homage to the king. He recorded it in a weather-beaten diary.

As they filed past to greet the king, Uzo-Onicha hailed them by their names. "Ogbuefi Ezelagbo, welcome, Ogbuefi Akunne, nno-nu, Ogbuefi Akalue ..."

As a mark of respect for centenarians, seats were reserved for them in rows behind the Ichies.

Meanwhile, in a patch of ground near the arena, hundreds of yams lay roasting on a rack over an open fire. Also on the wide circular rack were fish, parts of antelope, deer, beaver, goat, ram and chicken. Roasting of yams and meat was men's work. They were busy with long sticks, stoking the fire or turning over the meat and yams.

On the other side of the patch, the women folk were involved in a modernized practice of the yam festival. In huge cast-iron pots on tripods of stone they cooked jollof rice to support the yam that was to be served to the people. The rice was a new innovation, formerly alien to the ofala.

When the yams were done, the men brought several baskets of it to the king. Bowls of spiced palm oil were also kept beside the yams. Hundreds of children gathered before Igwe Ajulufo who dipped pieces of yams in palm oil and gave to them.

Yam was served to the guests under the sheds.

Phillip Carter and Emeka Okorugo, dressed in chieftaincy robes, were ushered to kneel before the king and his cabinet chiefs. In a short ceremony, he conferred the title, *Ugoabata* on Carter and *Okwuluora* on Emodi. He spoke at length, reminding the natives and guests that this was not the usual chieftaincy conferment but a special event to recognize the selfless efforts of the two teachers towards the progress of Obodo Ogwari. Ceremoniously, he placed red caps on their heads and gave them long metal staffs with which they supported themselves as the king helped them to rise. The crowds applauded. Musicians of the Ezeodu clan began to play while family members advanced to lead Okwulora and his wife, Njide, to their seats. The Ifeadigo extended family also played and danced joyfully as they escorted Ugoabata and Ngozi back to their shed.

A masquerade from Obodo Ukwa, its drummers strumming an up-tempo beat, danced before the king. In time groups began to pay homage. Various age grades regrouped at the far end of the arena and approached the king playing their brands of music and bearing gifts. Two masquerades dressed like a colonial district officer (DO) and his wife were next in line after the grades. A pot-bellied colonial warden mask accompanied the DO and wife. Their masks were Caucasian in nature to depict the features of white men that served as district officers under colonial rule. The warden played a jester with funny nuances in dance and postures.

There were huge masquerades designed with wooden frames and cloth in the images of the ostrich, elephant, buffalo and other large wild animals all accompanied by musicians and dancers in brightly coloured costumes.

A women's dance troupe appeared clad in red batik cloths, waist wrappers and frilled tops. They danced slowly and majestically, swaying their hips and waving immaculate-white handkerchiefs in unison.

The girls came next in short multi-coloured skirts and chest-wraps to match head gears with lots of coloured feathers. They danced a fast well-choreographed routine.

The Ijelle masquerade was a splendid sight to behold. A big circular float, like a big hut but decorated with bright and colourful bits of cloths, feathers, bells, mirrors and uncountable flashy objects.

Ijelle was a special masquerade. Prior to its appearance before the king, it was cordoned off outside the arena with a palm leaf and bamboo fence which hid it totally from view of the guests. Due to its size and splendour, when it emerged to perform for Igwe Ajulufo, the arena was cleared of people and masquerades. It was respect accorded to the Ijelle and its aura of beauty and grandeur across Igboland. As it moved slowly in its brand of dance, the costumed men who guided it moved on either sides, charting its movement. The musicians took up the rear. Once in a while when it rose in movement, shrouded feet of the few 'spirit men' under it were glimpsed.

*   *   *

From the town of Adazi Ani came the Atumma Oyilidie masquerade; a very beautiful mask that sang sonorous choruses and danced to the beat of the ekwe percussions.

The Okanga dance troupe of Ichida town came next with their frenzied dancing moves; Okanga, a very special art movement by virtue of its uninhibited free dancing style. There were no restrictions to the type of instruments used or mode of dancing. The beat was wild and provocative, the dancing equally wild and subject to the dancer's immediate whims. As they performed before the king they brought a lot of amusement among Ajulufo, his chiefs, the Ogbuefis and guests alike. The youth of Obodo Ogwari sensing that this was a crazy, free-for-all performance, joined with improvised percussions, striking sticks on metal buckets and plates while some danced wildly in uncontrolled frenzy.

Emissaries of neighbouring kings came with gifts of goats, carved artifacts, rams, yams and other items. They came mostly in small groups and after their homage Uzo Onicha quickly assigned ushers who took them to designated sheds where they were fed and entertained.

Finally, the people of Obosi Ukwala came with their famous Ajukwu dancing masquerades. There were six masquerades dressed in thick blue materials with long narrow wooden heads protruding at the top. Around their waists were thick coils of cloth designed to bounce rhythmically when they danced. Their dancing style was fast and vigorous, steps choreographed in strict unison. They drew a tumultuous applause from the spectators.

The Last Age Grade came last with the Izaga mask on stilts. It walked in from the far end of the arena, moving precariously on thin wooden stilts about twenty feet high, some of its followers drumming while others cleared its path of people and objects that may cause it to trip and fall.

No offensive masquerades attended.

⟨๑|| Twenty-eight ||๑⟩

On the Ofala festival day, at the border of Obodo Ite and Ogwariland, the soldiers woke up to the chirping and squawking of birds. Just before dawn, the men on guard duty had noticed an unusual number of birds in the trees around the camp. The previous night after the logs were lit to discourage another bee attack, the lieutenant deployed a few men on guard. He reasoned that despite their helplessness against the attack, it would be most unconventional for the camp to stay unguarded through the night.

There were birds on the lamp posts, on the camp grounds and even on tents. Out on the road, there was a greater concentration of birds. Most were perched on the earth-moving machines and vehicles while others just walked the grounds. There were big birds of prey, hawks, kites and eagles, and there were vultures, parrots and a host of other species of birds. They moved around nonchalantly like poultry chickens not particularly scared of humans but mindful.

The lieutenant assembled the men for a quick meeting. Standing at the edge of the camp where there were fewer birds, he sought to shore up their morales while trying to downplay the apparent superstitious aspect of it. In less than an hour, the workers would be arriving on the shuttle bus and so would other company vehicles. The attitude of his men and security staff would determine how the construction workers would react to the situation.

"It's witchcraft, pure witchcraft," declared Nangibo who hailed from the Rivers countryside. "Witches always use birds … though not quite in this manner."

"I say we open fire on them and drive them off before the workers arrive," Ngefa suggested.

"Negative!" Lieutenant Duru snapped. "That is a cave man approach, to kill off everything you don't understand. Ngefa, take a good look at these birds; they're not even bothering us. They're harmless."

"But their presence is not going to help matters when the

workers arrive," said Shittu. "We must drive them off."

"How?" Ngefa asked.

"Everyone break off a long branch and use it to chase them," the lieutenant ordered. "But don't kill them. I repeat, do not kill them."

The lieutenant's technique was partially successful. Some squawked in protest and flew into the trees while others flew up in the air and still landed in different parts of the grounds. While the men were busy chasing birds Lieutenant Duru stood aside with Shittu and Ngefa to have a private discussion.

"I don't buy your idea of witchcraft, Shittu, but I do believe that something or someone is controlling these birds," said Duru. "If not, why would these different species of birds come together and behave in this manner, contrary to their normal behaviour. Some of them probably need to be building nests, brooding their eggs or foraging for food to feed their young, yet they're here idling around."

"You are right, Sir," Shittu said. "Someone is responsible for this thing happening here even the bee attack last night and the person is probably around here somewhere."

"Why don't we comb the jungle? We might come up with a shrine or someone ... something," suggested Ngefa.

"Good idea but we have to get rid of these stubborn birds before the workers arrive," said Duru. "Shittu, get the men to spread out among the birds and get ready to fire short bursts into the air."

At the lieutenant's order, the soldiers fired bursts of semi-automatic gunfire together into the air. By the third round of fire, in unison, some of the birds had taken off from the grounds and some flew into nearby trees while most, as if jarred from an apparent trance, flew away completely. Immediately afterwards, the soldiers charged into the outskirts of the jungle, all in different directions, in search of anyone or thing that was out of the ordinary. Edet the security man had confirmed to the lieutenant that there was no village or settlement within a mile square. Therefore, Duru figured that anyone found within the outskirts of the jungle so early in the morning would be a possible culprit responsible for the strange events. Lieutenant Duru stood in the middle of the camp with his batsman, Nebo, and the security men while his soldiers combed the jungle.

Barely five minutes after he rushed into the thick vegetation, Shittu thought he saw a movement behind a huge tree ahead of him. Cautiously he moved toward the tree in quick but stealthy steps. With his rifle primed in readiness to fire, Shittu rushed around the tree. A little boy, dark skinned, his head shaven to a fine ebony gloss, stood hiding behind the tree. He wore a brown ankle-length robe with long wide-ended sleeves. Shittu was so surprised at what he saw that he almost lost his caution and alertness. As they stared at each other, Shittu noticed that the look on the boy's face was serene and relaxed. There was no sign of fear or surprise, just a plain poker face that gave no hint of his inner feelings. Shittu looked around him furtively to see if the boy had company that gave him so much confidence. There was no one in sight.

"What are you doing here?" Shittu asked.

Silence.

"What is your name and where did you come from?"

The boy still did not answer. He simply stared at Shittu with that calm, almost contemptuous attitude.

"Oya! Move!" Shittu motioned the boy towards the camp with the nozzle of his rifle.

When the boy did not respond, Shittu rushed to him and using his free left hand, grabbed his robe by the scruff and dragged him back to the camp.

When most of the soldiers had emerged from the jungle, they gathered around to inspect Shittu's catch. The taciturn little boy refused to respond to both Igbo and English languages. Shittu suggested that he might be deaf and dumb and resorted to a sign language but there was no response still. Just as Lieutenant Duru was about to order a head count to acertain that all his men had come in from the jungle comb, a sharp scream pierced the serenity of the early morning air. The screaming continued, coming from the opposite side of the camp, far from where Shittu caught the boy. The men rushed toward the voice. Reflexively, Shittu moved with the others then remembered the boy. He screeched to a halt on the dark pebbled ground and turned around. The boy was already running towards the edge of the camp to enter the jungle. With quick long strides, Shittu caught up with him and grabbed him by the shoulder. The boy whirled around and struck Shittu's hand with his elbow, tripped and fell. Shittu held his hand and pulled him to his feet. Unconsciously, it was his first contact with the boy's skin. The little boy slumped, hanging limply on Shittu's grip, his buttocks barely touching the ground. Suddenly Shittu felt an urgent itch in the middle of his palm. He scratched his palm with his other hand and switched hands, holding the boy. The itch came to the new hand and he left the boy.

*   *   *

Lieutenant Duru and his men charged through the jungle, rifles in on-guard positions, to the place where the scream came from. They found Ngefa in a deep wide ditch where he had apparently fallen accidentally as he ran. Thousands of bees hovered in and around the ditch. Duru and some of the men were stung by a few that strayed from the area of the large hole where Ngefa lay almost unconscious. Blood flowed profusely from the side of his stomach. A spike in the ditch had impaled him.

"Make fire immediately!" Duru snapped. "Gather dry wood and create fire."

The soldiers responded quickly and soon they were using fire and smoke to drive the bees backwards. Large clusters hung on trees beyond the ditch. Duru warned them to be careful not to disturb the clusters. It was clear to them that their luck of stingless bees had run out.

Sergeant Ngefa lay motionless. His face was a mask of bees even his hands and parts of his clothes were crawling with them. While a make-shift ladder was quickly constructed, one of the soldiers took off his shirt and gave it to Edet with which he wrapped his head leaving a little hole for the eyes. Edet climbed down and with a leafy branch, he brushed the insects off Ngefa's face and body and strapped a rope around his waist. After he was pulled out Ngefa was placed in a pick-up truck and rushed off to a hospital.

*   *   *

Shittu stood at the edge of the jungle scratching madly all over his body. He had taken off his shirt and trousers. The little boy was no where in sight. Duru remembered the story he was told during his briefing, about the works minister's encounter in his

216

office with a certain old man. He called for oil. Edet produced a small bottle of palm oil from the security shed. Within a few minutes, Shittu was back to his normal itchless self again.

"What a way to start the day." Duru heaved a sigh and sat on a tree stump.

"Sir, I believe it's clear to everyone that the little boy or midget, or whatever he may be, is responsible for all the crazy things that's been happening here." Shittu had wiped the oil off his body and put his clothes back on.

The lieutenant removed his hat and scratched his head wearily. "Well, it seems very likely that the boy is connected to it, but ask yourself: why was Ngefa severely attacked by bees when the boy was in captivity yet last night the bees were harmless?"

"You think it was a retaliation by the boy's people?" Nangibo asked.

"Not at all," said Duru. "I think that last night the bees were remotely controlled but while we held the boy, he lost control and the bees went berserk."

"Sir, my own guess is that while we held the boy, his people launched that serious reprisal on Ngefa and almost killed him," Nangibo replied.

"Almost?" Duru asked. "Let's just hope he survives. Ngefa was stung very badly and mind you if he dies, our stance towards this unseen enemy will change. I feel humiliated that they sent a mere little boy to deal with us."

An hour after Ngefa was whisked off for medical attention, the lieutenant received word that he died on reaching the hospital.

Twenty-nine

A few minutes past 8 am, a Cotrell and Abbey shuttle bus arrived with the first batch of workers. Chief Okonedo and Engineer Frank came soon afterwards in a white pick-up truck. Okonedo had come down to the east to stay permanently until the road went through. This was no longer a job to be left loosely in the hands of his workers. The site was calm, the army presence very reassuring. Duru had issued a strict warning to his men and security personnel not to breathe a word about the bird and bee attack and especially, Ngefa's death.

Edet took the lieutenant to a spot in the jungle where his cellular phone received better signals.

Duru placed a direct call to General Idris as he had been instructed; there was to be no middleman between them.

"We were attacked by bees, Sir, and one of my men, Sergeant Ngefa, is dead," Duru reported after salutations.

"What?" the general thundered across the line. There was a moment of silence before he responded. "What exactly is going on down there, lieutenant?" His tone was cold and listless.

"Sir, we were attacked by bees last night and this morning birds, countless birds, besieged us. There were birds all over our camp and on the road, Sir, but we've managed to drive them away."

"How did Sergeant Ngefa die?" the top brass asked sternly.

"Ngefa was chased by bees. He fell into a ditch and sustained a serious injury. He lost a lot of blood and the bees stung him very badly, Sir. His body is at a nearby hospital."

"Text me the address and I'll have men from the Onitsha barracks pick him up. You need reinforcement?"

"No, Sir, not yet. Maybe a replacement for Ngefa and some protective wears against insect attacks."

The general did not respond to the request. The line went dead.

Work resumed. The bulldozer cranked to life ushering in a grinding of heavy metals that broke the peaceful air, echoing in the proximity of the jungle walls.

One standing across the valley, on the distant Ogwari hills, would hear it as a soft purring sound yet a source of great uncertainty and even fear. The road was coming through; the road that would surely bring a devastating change, drastically altering their way of life, their culture, forever.

*   *   *

It started as a zephyr, a gentle wind that whispered from the west side of Obodo Ogwari near their border with Obodo Atulu. Gradually it built up into startling waves whipping across the great gully that ran between the two towns.

According to oral traditions of Obodo Atulu preserved in songs and fables, hundreds of years ago, the terrain between them and their Obodo Ogwari neighbour was a thick forest on very level ground not threatened by erosion. However, when the Gundu priests arrived, a strange and gradual erosion of the land began. In just two seasons a very big gully had formed between them and their cordial neighbour. It was clear to the indigenous ancients of Obodo Atulu that these new settlers were responsible for the vast devastation and alteration of the landscape to form a great canyon between the two towns. Though the Gundu were constantly seen in that area, the technique they used in achieving this great wonder remained a puzzle. It was soon obvious that the purpose of these strange newcomers was to isolate Obodo Ogwari, their host, from neighbourly interactions. They were successful. The Obodo Atulu night masquerade later sang: it is now easier to visit Oreri, many miles away than Obodo Ogwari our closest neighbour. It later became a proverb expressing the inadequacies of life that sometimes desirable things are out of reach but what comes of reach becomes undesirable. 'Odi-mma aka olu; olu aka mma odi."

Lieutenant Duru picked up the pair of binoculars that hung on his chest and observed the helicopter that had been circling the area for over ten minutes. It was an airforce issue and was definitely interested in their area of operation.

Two brand new dozers at the site had mysteriously experienced engine knocks but a third replacement was working when Duru took a few men to scout the periphery of the jungle again. Nothing new or unusual was discovered but once, they caught a glimpse of the boy hiding behind a cluster of bushes. When they rushed to the spot, he was gone.

*   *   *

The general's convoy arrived silently with beacons of the escort car flashing. In high spirits, Lieutenant Duru and his boys saluted the general in a very grand style as the top brass alighted from his green-coloured jeep. The site became suddenly boisterous with the activities of the general's entourage. It was obvious that the additional crew he brought with him were already briefed on what to do. Over two dozen soldiers jumped down from various trucks and started unloading equipment and wooden boxes. The general's aides and guards spread in a loose cluster around their boss making themselves look useful and alert.

The general led Duru aside to speak to him alone. His guards sensed his mood and kept out of earshot.

"Lieutenant, I've been severally advised to replace you with a superior officer and reinforcement but my sixth sense tells me you're the man I need for this job," the general said. "Don't let me down."

"I will not, Sir. Thank you, Sir," Duru replied and saluted again, his feet coming subtly together in unceremonious attention.

"Over there is Colonel Effiong, researcher from Army Intelligence. I call him the mad scientist."

Duru observed the middle-aged officer, gangling and unkept, who stood supervising the unloading. He did not wear that image of the typical army officer. His hair was disheveled and his cheeks bore a two-day stubble of greys.

"Don't worry, he's not staying," the general said with a grimace, as if reading Duru's mind. "He's just here to show you the toys he brought for you but first, you must show me around."

"Yes, Sir," Duru answered and led Idris toward the camp.

Idris looked up squinting and lifted his palm to shade his eyes from the midday sun while viewing the helicopter that flew over them toward Obodo Atulu.

"I detailed a helicopter crew from the Air Force base in Enugu to check the area thoroughly and get me pictures also."

"Yes, Sir," Duru replied. "They've been working before you

arrived."

"Now tell me, lieutenant, what is your nutshell assessment of the situation here?"

"Very strange, unconventional, Sir. Something or someone is clearly opposed to our presence here. We caught a boy or ... midget whom we suspect is responsible for most of the strange happenings but similar to what you told me that happened in the minister's office, this boy caused a terrible body itch on Sergeant Shittu, who held him, and escaped. Today two new dozers have mysteriously suffered engine knocks and the boy is still lurking around."

"So, what's your suggestion, Duru?"

"Sir, I truly believe that whoever is doing this does not really want to hurt us."

"But Sergeant Ngefa is dead ..."

"I think it was an accident, Sir."

"An accident?"

"Yes, Sir." Duru paused and looked searchingly at the jungle. "I believe that they're just scaring us. Sir, I believe that there's a superior force here. It's like if they really wanted, we'll all be dead by now."

The general looked sternly at Duru. He was both shocked and appalled yet admired the young officer's frankness but did not show it.

"Considering these facts, we should pack up and go home then?" the general tested Duru.

"Not at all, Sir," Duru replied calmly." I suggest we forge ahead until we're beaten or we win."

"That's the right spirit, my boy." The general smiled for the first time.

General Idris was called by his aide, Musa, to answer an urgent radio message in the green Hummer jeep that was part of his convoy. He directed Duru to see the scientist for briefing on equipment handling.

* * *

Lt Colonel Effiong emptied a stack of brown plastic strips with fasteners at the ends. There were small round button-like objects interspersed along the surface of the narrow foot-long strips.

"The buttons are sensors," Effiong lectured as he displayed a couple of the brown strips. "They will pick up any movement from the size of a rabbit upwards. The frequency could be lowered to detect even a fly. Which one do you prefer?"

"The rabbit is Ok," Duru answered. "The one of flies may cause too many false alarms."

"Exactly!" Effiong concurred. "The idea is to set it at a distance you want to be alerted when an intruder approaches. There're enough sensor strips here to link up a two-kilometre circumference or just a front between you and the enemy." He pointed at several wooden boxes atop collapsible metal tables that were set up by the general's guards. "With a shrill alarm both your personal hand-held monitor and the central one for your team will show precisely, the area of intrusion. In fact, we can hook it up to a stationery machine-gun on a tripod that would automatically fire short bursts at the intruder."

"What if there are multiple intruders from different angles?" Duru asked.

"Then it means the machine gun will go crazy," the Lieutenant Colonel joked and laughed.

Duru laughed with the soldiers who were gathered around to watch.

"I'm sorry, Sir, we haven't had need even for our own rifles so far but I'll keep it in mind."

*   *   *

General Idris was confused by the message he received from the helicopter crew. A turbulent whirlwind, cyclone or something was brewing in a deep chasm less than a kilometre west of the construction site. The pilot warned him to be on the alert.

*   *   *

Effiong ordered more boxes to be opened and shiny suits of high tensile strength issued to Duru's platoon and the company security guards.

"You're lucky to have the best," Effiong said, smiling. "These suits were used for the toxic waste clean-up at Koko beach. It would serve very well against insects or even dogs etcetera."

"No dogs yet, Sir, only birds and bees," Duru replied cheerfully, matching the superior officer's cheery attitude.

Duru and his men tried on their suits, complete with the

unitary rubber-soled footwears and headgears made of clear hard plastic. They looked like astronauts on a space mission.

Some soldiers in the general's entourage, those with soldierly instincts and thirst for action, were green with envy to see Duru and his boys decked out for this special assignment. But those who, like Musa, had become pampered and spoilt in the luxurious service of the general, desired none of this jungle mission. Secretly, Musa abhorred the adventurous spirit of the general.

Why would top brass like Idris risk coming to the front when he had every right to engage in logistics and planning from the comforts of his posh office? It was foolhardy bravado. If he died in the process no one would feel really sorry for him, Musa thought. Only crazy dare-devils like him and public speeches and funeral orations would refer to him as a brave patriot. As far as Musa was concerned, a dead hero was nothing he would like to be. Was it not on the trail of the same old man who disappeared on the TV monitors, the locked room, that the general had brought them? Why would one embark on the trail of the devil itself? Had Musa been assigned to lead the jungle mission in place of Duru, it would have been enough reason to go AWOL. He would have slipped across the Cameroonian border and found his way to Europe. Luckily, the general knew that he, Musa, was no Rambo. The top brass valued him for his smartness, administration and ability to make valuable contributions under pressure, definitely not for bravery.

The westerly wind had become suddenly gusty. At intervals, it blew across the army camp, shaking the tents, flaps clapping like birds in captivity.

A lone antelope emerged from the jungle and ran through the camp, crossed the road and entered the opposite jungle. Soon afterwards a small herd of antelopes followed also running as if they were being chased. When a mixed group of animals including porcupines, beavers, wild pigs and other species emerged, the soldiers were mostly sure that this was not a new type of siege by animals as they had experienced with birds and bees. The sky was already busy with birds when the steady stream of animals flowed from the jungle. It did not take long for the army and construction crew to realize that the animals did not come for them but were running for their lives.

General Idris was perplexed. He knew a little about animal behaviour and the fact that certain animals have early warning instincts that inform them of oncoming earthquakes, hurricanes, distant forest fires and such natural disasters. While one school of thought states that these creatures feel the remote quake rumblings from the bowels of the earth another suggests the sensing of electrical charges or gases in the air, detected by animals but not by man.

The wind was becoming more aggressive as a string of large rodents appeared from the bushes and headed down the new road. Idris buttoned the top of his shirt and squinted. He could feel sand in the air whipping his face and chest. A sound like rain and again like whistling pines filled the atmosphere. It was coming from the jungle. His cellular phone rang. It was the pilot calling to update him on his observations.

"You better be careful, Sir. There's a terrible sandstorm coming your way from the gully," the pilot reported.

"Noted," Idris replied. "What's the ETA on our location?"

"It's already coming up on you. A minute at the most. And, Sir?"

"Yes?"

"There's an old man standing at the edge of the gully. He seems to be doing something strange with the sandstorm."

"That must be Igo," the general muttered to himself.

"Sir, there's another old man that looks like him, approaching from the north."

"Another one?" Idris asked in surprise. "Just stay with them and report anything extraordinary." A pebble struck him on the forehead.

"Down! Down!" the general screamed. "Take cover."

The windstorm struck with devastating intensity. Many soldiers were knocked off their feet by the blast of the sand-filled torrents. Rocks, pebbles and other debris hit the tents, tearing and ripping them from their pegs. The soldiers and construction workers stayed pinned down by the whipping whistling wind. A terrifying sound broke out of the jungle as if some large animals were stampeding through the trees. The sandy wind hurtled through the air in high velocity, varied sizes of rocks, broken tree stems, pebbles and other varied objects raged through the jungle. Some crashed and shattered on impact while others found their way to the construction site all in a chaotic din. A rock, larger than a football, crashed into the windscreen of the general's jeep. More objects followed creating violent sounds of shattering glass, the crushing and bending of light metal.

"Fire at the old man," Idris ordered the helicopter crew. "Distract him. Fire at him now!"

"Roger, sir," the pilot replied.

*   *   *

From a hundred-yard distance, Igo observed the terrible deluge of wind and material mustered from the gully. It shocked him utterly to imagine the type of damage the rocky sandy blast would unleash on animals and humans in its path. In the eddying tufts of dust at the edge of the gully Igo caught a glimpse of Nji and confirmed his suspicion. Nji had not only defied the joint order of the Gundu but had trespassed a jurisdiction purely not his own. The defense of Obodo Ogwari, the caves, was exclusively under Igo's command and a decision had been taken by the joint order. Nji had no right whatsoever to defy it.

Moved by the intensity of his spirit, Igo leapt forth and was upon Nji in an instant. He stood behind the erring priest without touching him.

A burst of machine gunfire from the helicopter above erupted, digging up a line of red laterite along the arm's length space between Igo and Nji.

Nji swirled around.

Igo was shocked at the look of depravity he saw on his face. Nji's eyes blazed with a bright greenish tint that gave him the look of a predator. A wild wave of Nji's hand swept the helicopter backwards, its rotor blades breaking off like match sticks on a toy model. The copter crashed at the edge of the jungle and exploded in a deafening bang of pyrotechnics.

The two priests locked cold stares on each other. The cyclonic turbulence in the gully had stopped. With Nji's distraction by the copter and Igo, the circuit was broken. The cry of the wind died, the last pebble tumbled to a halt.

"You have broken the rule," Igo said to him.

"The rule has changed. The new rule says that I stay and survive," he replied. "We stay and survive."

"The decision of the council is that we leave. We created the aura of purity on this land and we shall not pollute it ourselves. Moreover, to fight is to expose the Gundu."

"You have exposed us already."

"It was not intentional. The road was coming, anyway," Igo reminded him.

"The road will never come," Nji said coldly.

"Give up this stubbornness, Nji," Igo pleaded. "Lives have been lost by the boy you sent to the site, the bees and now the men in the helicopter."

"Wars cost lives," said Nji. "War is a death sentence; we know not the condemned until they fall."

"We are not at war with anyone, Nji. The council, of which you are one, has decided that we leave before the road gets near the cave."

"To where? To roam and wander aimlessly across this universe or do you now have a solution to convey us back to our home? You can all leave but I'm staying."

"Whatever you do reflects on our good name and we cannot allow that." Igo warned. "I must run now to see what damage you have done at the site."

Nji stared silently at the sixth keeper until he disappeared beyond the forest. He considered resuming the sand blast but shelved the idea. With Igo on the other side, it would surely turn into a contest.

*   *   *

The sand blast ended abruptly. Slowly the soldiers and construction workers began to rise, one after the other. The grounds were littered with rocks and debris, the camp totally destroyed. The Hummer jeep and an army truck that had been parked at the forefront of the blast were mangled, the head lamps and windscreens shattered.

Gen. Idris made a quick assessment of the situation and saw the looks of terror on many faces including a few of his own men. If a couple of labourers bolted from the site then a stampede may follow and work would once more grind to a halt.

"Attention!" the general shouted.

His men responded accordingly and primed for his order.

"If anyone runs, shoot him! Anyone! And that is an order! Is that clear?"

"Yes, Sir!" the soldiers replied.

It was a hard decision to take but now he was sure that no civilian would abscond or soldier go on AWOL. Everyone would respect himself and behave maturedly, Idris thought, especially his valuable but cowardly aide, Musa. With his thought of Musa, he heard someone call out the name. Gen Idris looked and saw his men gathering beside the mangled truck.

"Musa is down!" Lieutenant Duru shouted. "Medics, come this way."

The two soldiers wearing Red Cross armbands hurried to the spot with their first-aid kits. "Spread out everyone and let him get some air," said one of the paramedics, a short squat guy with a dark boyish face.

Musa's condition appeared hopeless. Apparently, a huge object had struck him in the chest almost tearing off his left arm and lower jaw. Bleeding was profuse from the big open wound on his chest and lower mandible. He was barely breathing, his eyes assuming that cold distant look of death.

"He has to be moved, immediately," Lieutenant Duru said.

The general looked further down the road and saw that no vehicle could pass. The rough road beyond the parked vehicles was cluttered up with rocks, stems and chunks of laterite. He marched down the road and the men followed him, leaving the two medics who were attending to Musa.

"All hands on deck!" snapped the top officer. "We must clear the road for a vehicle to get him to a hospital, quick!"

Soldiers and civilians alike, even the ones with minor injuries, joined hands to clear the road.

They were so engulfed with the job on hand, no one saw Igo come except the two paramedics who knelt beside Musa administering first aid.

"Who are you?" asked the tall slim medic.

Igo was silent. He stooped and scooped up Musa and placed him in his arms. The two medics, still kneeling down, watched listlessly as Igo carried Musa off toward the jungle.

"Oga, look," shouted Edet.

"Stop! Igo, stop!" the general shouted. He ordered Duru and his men to go after him and bring Musa back. Duru and his men were already running after the old man before he completed his order.

Igo had just stepped into the jungle carrying Musa with the vigour and ease of a young athlete when Duru and his platoon crashed into the jungle. Igo broke into a run darting into a cluster of trees. They spread out and searched deep into the forest. There was no sign of Igo and Musa.

ᘓᴥ‖ Thirty ‖ᴥᘖ

At the end of the yam festival, Ugoabata and Okwulora brought their processions together and joined to dance home with their wives, friends and well-wishers. Their musical groups came in the rear keeping a batch of the crowd between them to avoid a clashing of rhythms. The two teachers were busy chatting while Ngozi and Njide followed them conversing excitedly about the past event.

Four soldiers sprung from behind trees, their guns poised in assault-ready attitude. In guerilla style, they hustled the two titled men into the bushes, leaving their wives and entourage shocked and confused, some darting away for safety.

Ngozi and Njide ran back to the king's palace to report the abduction of their husbands.

*   *   *

Captain Okafor and Ntukogu with other exiles sat in the king's circular hall. The yam festival had ended but a large number of friends and relatives milled about the hall familiarizing themselves with the exiles while inquiring about their welfare.

Uzo-Onicha, the king's scribe, addressed the exiles making a spirited effort to offer a sense of belonging. He reminded them of the quaint and conservative nature of Obodo Ogwari and the need to uphold the pride and dignity, the sanctity and purity that made their town a safe and peaceful haven.

More food and drinks were served in the hall. The exiles, their relations and well-wishers ate and drank to their fill.

Captain Okafor quickly set his drinking cup down when he saw two women in festive apparels run into the extreme end of the hall. Immediately he recognized the wives of Ugoabata and Okwuluora. They were talking to Uzo-Onicha in a very agitated manner. Okafor stood up and approached them as Uzo-Onicha moved away from the troubled women. As soon as he was informed of the abduction by soldiers the most sensible thing was to report to Captain Okafor.

*   *   *

Okwuluora Emodi and Ugoabata Carter were brought before

General Idris. Lawali and Lieutenant Duru stood behind their boss.

"Gentlemen, we meet again but now I have no time to lose because my assistant who was wounded in an accident was kidnapped by your priest! My man Musa needs serious medical attention and I want him back immediately. I will break all ethics and decorum to find him so you better cooperate and show me where to find Igo."

The two abducted men looked at each other but said nothing. They stared silently at the general.

"So! You don't feel like talking to me heh?" Gen Idris asked. He turned and nodded at lieutenant Duru. The four soldiers that had brought them cocked their rifles almost in unison and converged on Carter.

All four rifles pointed behind Ugoabata's head, prodding him to his knees.

The general held his right hand high above his head and began to count. "One … two!" When he made for the count of three, his hand wavering threateningly in the air, Emodi's voice rang out.

"Stop! …"

The general's hand was still up in the air.

"I will take you where you'll find Igo," Emeka volunteered. He had read of a mad general who slaughtered an entire village in cold blood. Though the man was later court-martialled, what good would a court-martial do if Phillip was killed.

"Good man," General Idris commended Emodi in mockery and winked at Duru and Lawali. His bluff had worked. "Let's go," he ordered.

It was nearing dusk when Idris and his entourage trekked through the winding jungle paths with their two hostage guides.

Emeka Emodi and Phillip Carter began to tire after walking over a mile at the fast pace the general was pushing them.

"Can we slow down or rest a while?" Carter asked, looking at Idris when they reached a clearing with scanty vegetation that stretched on to a hilly forest.

"We can't afford to lose any time," General Idris replied. "We've got to find that primitive priest before Musa dies. What does he want with a wounded bleeding man anyway?"

"I just hope they're not cannibals or ritualists," said Lawali. "Why else would he pick up such a seriously wounded man that would probably die before he gets to the village?"

"The Gundu are not cannibals," Emodi said defensively. "They are a kind and peace-loving people. Their primary cause is to serve mankind, not to maim and eat people."

"Rubbish!" Idris retorted "Your innocent and peace-loving Gundu killed Corporal Ngefa with their devilish bees, destroyed half of my convoy and inflicted a mortal wound on Musa, and where is my helicopter crew that has remained incommunicado for so long."

"Gundu, I kinda agree with Emeka, are good people," Carter cut in. "Any casualty suffered by your team must be accidental or some kind of reprisal."

"Oti-o!" exclaimed Idowu, a young corporal from Duru's platoon, who was of the Yoruba tribe.

They had stumbled to the edge of a great ravine.

"Lord have mercy!" Carter exclaimed.

"I don't understand …" General Idris muttered absently. "We passed by here few days ago and this gully wasn't here."

"We came through this point yesterday while combing the jungle and it wasn't there," Lieutenant Duru confirmed.

The soldiers and two hostages stood at the edge of the deep hole in the earth, a sharp drop about the height of a four-storey building.

"Maybe it's just an optical illusion, some sort of magic trick," Carter suggested. "Maybe it's not real."

Emeka picked up a rock and threw it down the gaping chasm. Few seconds later, a faint thud resounded as it hit bottom.

"Phillip, I'll hate to see you break your neck in this optical illusion," Emeka said in jest.

"I'm sure we can find a way around," Lieutenant Duru suggested.

Lawali was worried about the general's safety. Plodding through jungle paths at night with the rank and file was unconventional for top brass. It was also his duty to protect the general.

"Sir, I think it's getting rather late," he said discreetly to the general. "Maybe we can continue in the morning."

"What are we, soldiers or boy scouts?" the general asked aggressively. "We have sufficient flash-lights and flares. Let's go, let's go!"

Lawali's walkie- talkie crackled with life. "Ceasar One this is Bongo Two, over." At the mention of Bongo Two, General Idris and most of the soldiers paused apprehensively to hear what the radio message would reveal. The search party that went looking for the helicopter crew had been expected to make contact for hours.

"Ceasar One, here. Proceed, Bongo Two, over."

"The bird is down, repeat, the bird is down. There are no survivors. We await orders, over," reported the voice of Sergeant Nangibo who led the search team.

General Idris snatched the walkie-talkie from his aide. "Come in, Bongo Two, come in, over," he barked.

"Bongo Two, here over."

"This is General Idris. State the nature of the crash and your observations, over."

"Yes, Sir!" Nangibo responded. "The copter is down, Sir ... the rotor blades are broken off and twisted but ... it seems not from the crash. Something struck while it was still in the air or maybe after it hit the ground, over."

The general remained calm and pensive as he pondered silently on this new revelation.

"Bongo Two, convey the casualties back to base, over and out."

"Yes, Sir," Nangibo replied without consideration. Six men making stretchers out of tree stems and leaves to carry three dead helicopter crew members back to base was not going to be a bowl of pepper-soup but the general himself had spoken.

৩|| Thirty-one ||৩

Sid Jefferson's foot hit a loose stone and slipped. He grabbed a root that jutted out of the earth and steadied himself. The stone bounced down the rocky hillside and tumbled into the river far below. He had come up, winding under the cover of thick bushes that skirted the Ogwari hillside. Starting from the north side, he marveled at the water-laden nature of the hilly terrain. Halfway up, Jefferson was wet from the tiny arcs of water that sprung out of the hillside. At this vantage point, he observed that an arm of the Anambra river, from the dam upstream, was channeled like a canal into an opening barely four feet high at the base of the hill. Huge boulders lined both sides of the canal, placed in such orderly manner that made Jefferson sure that it was designed by man, not just an ordinary stream flowing into a cave mouth. By the time he got down to the opening, his clothes were snared and muddied. He stepped into the gushing currents of the waist-deep water.

Jefferson shone a powerful flashlight into the hole and saw the rocky cavity that confirmed that it was possibly an alternative entrance into the caves; one not used by the Gundu. He entered the water and swam into the cave mouth. About twenty feet into the rocky cavity he could hear a familiar sound like the splashing of a waterfall cascading down a great height. Still keeping his flashlight above water he saw a hand-chiseled crevice in the path of the water that narrowed its course, increasing the force of the current before it veered sharply down a hole about the diameter of a big well. Jefferson panicked as the fast current swept him towards the sharp drop. He scrambled to the narrow embankment on his right, clung to a ledge and climbed out of the water. The bold beam lit up the well, searching to its limits before fading into the darkness of the watery hole. Beyond the hole was dry ground. Jefferson stood shaking droplets off his aqua-proof suit. He moved to the end of the cavity and found an opening in the ceiling. Holding the flashlight in his mouth, he held onto a jagged edge in the opening and pulled himself up. Pressing his feet on the side of the hole, his back firmly placed on the opposite wall, he began to work his way up, fingers pulling on the grooves and rocky appendages on the wall. About eight feet up, the back of his coat torn, his skin chafed, he reached a landing barely enough to accommodate him in a crawling position. Bruised and breathless he crawled into the little space to see where it would lead to. Suddenly, something hit him in the face. Jefferson gasped and shielded his face with his hands. More objects struck his hands and body while squeaky sounds and flapping of wings filled the narrow chamber. What he presumed to be a steady flow of bats continued to brush over his body as he lay flat and still, waiting for their massive exodus to end. When all the bats had exited, Jefferson continued to crawl down the stuffy damp crevice. At the end of the line, he stuck his head out and looked into a small empty chamber. Entry into the room would have taken a drop about the height of a normal room ceiling. Leg first, it would have been easier for Jefferson to jump down but he had crawled through head-first and there wasn't enough room for him to turn around. He crawled forward until his head, down to the thighs were hanging inside the room. Bracing the ball of his feet on the sides of the crevice he pushed and lurched into the air. Mid-air, Jefferson flipped over and landed in the middle of the cave chamber. He had been in many caves in the United States, even in Africa but this room was nothing like he ever saw before. He pressed the button of his flashlight and it went off.

The cave wall opposite him was aglow with an unusual light that seemed to be emanating from within the wall. Slowly, he brought his finger tips close to the wall, wondering about the source of the energy that generated such shimmering fluorescence on the cave walls. Upon contact with the surface, Jefferson's fingertips and nails glowed with the same vivid lighting. Along with an uncanny coldness, the light by some form of conduction, crept up his fingers to his wrist and was moving up his arm when Jefferson quickly removed his hand from the wall. He watched his hand glow for a few minutes before it died out. Jefferson pulled out a cigarette lighter issued by GMERC'S property section and took digital photographs of the glowing walls.

He tiptoed to the mouth of what seemed like the entrance into another room and peered down a wide, chiseled corridor. As Jefferson stepped into the passage, it struck him that there was a light point at the end of the passage where the curved ceiling blended with two sturdy boulders that formed an entrance. He heard voices and ducked behind the boulder on the left where the light was dimmer. Two boys passed, conversing in a language that was totally unknown to him. Jefferson knew that it was neither Igbo nor anything close to a language he had ever heard. Dialogue was like raspy vibrating sounds as though they were clearing their throats. They wore green robes with hoods, their faces partially hidden. When the boys reached the end of the passage and turned out of sight, Jefferson moved silently after them and caught them moving down a flight of stairs. After descending the first flight of spiral steps with a mud-plastered wall he noted that this feature was also man-made within the confines of the cave. Jefferson wondered what manner of workmen were employed to attain this level of exquisite craftsmanship. There were engravings on the walls depicting odd symbols, carved pictures of capsular objects moving against the image of the sun; strange outlandish animals flying through space. As he moved further down the stairs, deeper into the recesses of the earth's bowels the pictures continued with the depiction of roundish ball-like objects set apart from each other and then he noticed the stars etched at the edges with a gleaming silvery material or paint. It was then that Jefferson realized that this was an impression of galactic bodies, planets, represented in no familiar juxtaposition, yet it was still the galaxy. Deeper and deeper, he moved stealthily behind the boys, spiraling downward until he sensed that they had gone several storeys below ground level, yet the atmosphere was cool and airy.

Sid Jefferson hid in a crack at the base of the staircase till another set of boys went past, up the stairs. He slipped out, came to a landing and entered another spacious chamber where the Gundu manufactured textile out of plantain and cocoyam leaves. He quickly inspected the stages of the small cottage industry, the apparently treated stacks of plantain leaves cut across from the vertical midriff. Large, cocoyam leaves, with stems sliced off at the base leaving the broad heart-shaped leaves stacked in neat piles beside strips of yellow palm fronds. In another section Jefferson saw three large, wooden bins, shiny with protracted use, containing gobs of different textures of tree gums. A wide, wooden carousel with three paddle-like arms turned the gum in the bins. Jefferson observed that a smooth twine that circled a groove on the carousel pulled the paddles around. He could not dectect the power source as the twine revolved from two smooth holes on the cave wall. However, having earlier seen the guarding force field in the cave entrance, the channeled water that tumbled down a dark hole in the cave, and the glowing walls, Jefferson had no doubt that some level of electrical energy was being mustered by the apparently primitive Gundu. He inspected the large receptacle which he knew was the semi-final stage where the broad leaves were soaked and washed in concoctions that converted the weak brittle leaves to a soft and tensile material. To the touch, it felt like a cross between cotton and silk. Jefferson was impatient. He did not bother to scrutinize the final stage where the pieces were bonded with the palm frond strips that had also assumed a cloth-like texture. Though he was curious, this was not part of what Jefferson was looking for. Rather it seemed like a case for textile scholars or cultural anthropologists. His quest was clearly more mundane in nature. He was looking for treasure.

From the data gathered by GMERC on the Ideamala priests, there had to be precious stones or some other valuable devices that would fetch a fortune in the open market. Specifically, Jefferson had been instructed to look for the source of the light, shaped like an egg. As he made to hurry out of the chamber, his eye caught an object at the corner of the granite ceiling. Initially he thought it was a small cluster of wasps as he had seen earlier. He pointed the powerful beam of his pen light on the object and saw that it was some sort of pouch, rather leathery in appearance, probably used to cover some other object. From the final area of textile production, he shoved some materials aside, pulled up a table and climbed up to reach the pouch. Seconds after Jefferson pulled the pouch off the egg-shaped crystal that was hung on a small wooden cradle at the corner of the ceiling, the dazzling glow of the crystal began to spread on the surface of the rock walls, gradually adding to the illumination of the entire room. He replaced the pouch on the crystal stone and immediately the glow began to recede and in a minute, returned to its source. Quickly speculating on the possible value of this puzzling light source, Jefferson thought that this might be the big break he was searching for. As he pondered on what could be the possible worth of the light source, his sixth sense impressed upon him that this could be a priceless gem in the field of science. This simple device had to be more complex and valuable than met the eye. In the least, the crystalline stone could be split into a thousand tiny pieces. A speck of it on a ring would make the wearer's finger glow like a fluorescent tube. One would not have to come too close to know who's wearing an invaluable ornament.

Jefferson crept out of the chamber and hurried back up the stairs. He sensed danger wondering as he sprinted lightly up the stairs, how everything seemed so easy in his entry and theft of the precious stone. Then he remembered that the inhabitants of the cave were very few and though sociable beings, very reclusive. They visited people but never received visitors. Jefferson's predecessor, Jake Sanders, had written in his records that he made good friends with the second keeper, the healer, to use him to enter the caves yet the priest could only bring him to a small ante-room with polished granite seats in the outskirts of the cave where they used as a visitors' room. When he tried secretly through many entrances to go into the cave Sanders met an invisible shield, a type of force field that blocked him from entering. He was still planning to make a final attempt by a neutral entrance when GMERC pulled him out. His records were handed over to Sid Jefferson to review and report. Despite Jake Sanders' apparent failure, the force field that guarded the hill top and prevented entry into the cave brought a new challenge to GMERC. It gave the boss, Ray Givens, a renewed interest beyond the quest for the so-called Tree of Life and precious stones. From close observation and surveillance, Jake Sanders discovered that even the Gundu priests were barred from entering the cave until the shield was removed. It was the simplicity of turning it off and on that sparked a renewed suspicion in Jake Sanders that there was something else there. He witnessed Obo, keeper of agriculture, draw a continuous line across the earth and over the granite ceiling of the cave entrance with a short stick-like object to activate, and a reverse movement for deactivation of the invisible shield. Truly, Jake Sanders' findings and records had provided very valuable facts for Sid Jefferson. After Sanders was removed from the Life

Tree operation, he dropped out of circulation. He could not be reached for reassignment. His cell and land phone numbers were out of service. After two weeks of surveillance, he did not show up anywhere near his apartment in Queens New York. It was assumed by the board of GMERC that Jake Sanders had either resigned or was dead.

*　　　　*　　　　*

Sid Jefferson climbed to the top of the stairs and froze in shock. He was standing face to face with Olo the keeper of Arts and Culture. Speechless they stared at each other.

"How're you doing?" Jefferson spoke.

"How did you come in here?" Olo asked.

"Through the hatch, the ceiling. I just dropped in to inquire about that cloth you're manufacturing down there ... the textile ..." Jefferson was very nervous and apprehensive but he tried to play it cool. He assessed the situation wondering what weak resistance this shriveled old man could put up to prevent him from leaving. "Well, I think I'll be on my way... You don't have to escort me. I'll see myself out." Jefferson moved past the old man and headed for the direction through which he had come.

"Have you taken something from the cloth room that isn't yours?" Olo asked in a croaky voice.

"You mean like steal something from your cloth room? Now listen, old timer, I don't steal things. I'm not a thief; I'm what you may call a collector," Jefferson replied moving away rapidly.

"Beware of the light," Olo warned.

"And I thought it was darkness that was the problem," Jefferson replied with an awkward laughter and disappeared around the corner.

*　　　　*　　　　*

Captain Okafor had searched the area where Carter and Emodi were abducted but found nothing. Too many footprints from the yam event made it difficult for him to track them. He decided to head for the caves to see the Ideamala priests. He knew it was the disappearance of the three men of Ogwari from Army HQ that brought about this recent arrest of Ugoabata and Okwuluora. He would go straight to the shrine of Uli, keeper of the Itah and make contact. Winding up the Ogwari hills, Okafor experienced an overwhelming feeling of relief from the constant nostalgia he had felt for years in exile. Just like he expected, not much had changed in all his years of absence. The rays of the evening sun shone in mild brightness setting a rusty aura on the moody hills, the dense jungle stretching around him, horizon to horizon. By the time he got halfway up the hill, Okafor felt a rush of contentment. He knew it was a special feeling that came from the serenity of Ogwariland whereas the towns and states surrounding it were rife with the ills of civilization, armed robbery, kidnapping, prostitution, drug abuse and widespread corruption. Thanks to the federal government, the express road was coming to put a change to all this backwardness, Okafor thought. When the road passes through, settlers would come in, factories and shopping malls would spring up, even a night club or two, he thought with a mild feeling of revulsion. Maybe it was not such a good idea anymore, to lose this perfect peace and order forever ... City slickers often admired the village while villagers regarded the city with intrigue. Any jungle could be made a city but the reverse is less likely.

Okafor heard voices as he neared the caves. He edged closer to see who it was. Hiding in the cover of trees, he saw a dark handsome man of African descent who wore a dirtied French suit. The other was a rugged blond-haired gaunt-faced white man. He had a gun pointed at the African.

Jefferson had swum out from the canal hole of the cave and trotted into the woods on the east side when a familiar voice ordered him to stop.

"You have gone far enough, Sid," Jake Sanders said. "Just turn around slowly and no fast moves, now."

Jefferson obeyed. A pistol was trained on him from Jake Sander's steady hand. Jefferson stared at the man whom he had succeeded at GMERC, a man who evidently bore a grudge.

"I've been tailing your black ass since they took away my prime time assignment and gave it to you." Sanders spoke in a scorn-plagued voice. "Eleven months I spent around this jungle drinking the local wine and eating all kinds of strange shit while trying to find a way into that cave that wasn't fused with that force field. Just when I started to explore the canal route, GMERC pulled me out."

"There must have been a reason," Jefferson said casually. Fully aware of the 9 mm pistol. Its bore was a black hole, a dark opening that represented abyss, destruction, death.

"The high and mighty Ray Givens thought I was becoming too ambitious and decided to give me the boot. He said I'll work the home office for a while but I ain't a kid. He was lucky I already submitted the Life Tree report which you now used to get into the cave."

"And what, may I ask, was your punishable ambition?" Jefferson inquired.

"When I stumbled on some privileged information about the Light Egg and its priceless value I demanded forty percent. To hell with salaries and allowances. I was taking top risk here. Forty percent of the Light Egg and no less."

"The Light Egg?" Jefferson asked.

"That's right, a code name that was erased from the files to make it less popular," Sanders explained patiently the pistol in his hand, steady, unwavering. "That light source that's bulging in your pocket, when adequately hooked up with the sun, can muster the equivalent of over a hundred thousand megawatts of electricity and it is thought that a greater use may be found for it in space research. Ok! Sid, end of conversation, the bushes are crawling with soldiers and extraordinary medicine men. So, just reach into your pocket, real slow, and hand me the egg."

"It's not yours to take, Sanders," said Jefferson. "There's no where you can hide from GMERC. You'll be dead in thirty days."

"Thanks for your concern, Sid. It's not yours either. So hand it over before the count of three or I'll take it from your corpse … One."

"Hold your fire, Sanders. You can have the darn thing." Jefferson slipped his hand into his bulging pocket where the light source was tucked away in its strange leathery pouch.

Captain Okafor watched and listened keenly from his hiding place. He had not fully understood the conversation but he had established some cogent facts. The black man in a dirty suit had entered the cave and stolen a valuable item from the Gundu ahead of the blond-haired man who was now out for a counter double cross.

Okafor had risen from army rank and file, even worked with military police for some years. He had worked with men, all sorts of men in their trials and tribulations, through thick and thin, men at their best and their worst, in times of stress and strain, in celebration and utter desperation. From this bank of experience, he could tell from looking at the blond bearded man that, despite his calm and chatty disposition, he was not going to leave the black-suited man alive. The armed man could cut him down immediately and still get the light source from his pocket but wanted him alive till he confirmed that the bulge in his pocket was not a decoy, a mere rock.

Jefferson spoke with his hand still in his pocket. "What guarantee do I get that you won't shoot me after I hand you the Light Egg?"

"You get nothing. I could just shoot you now anyway."

"And find out that what's in my pocket is not what you think." Jefferson was playing for more time.

"Hand it over now!" Sanders barked," or you'll lose both knee caps for starters."

Jefferson withdrew the pouch from his pocket and held it out to Sanders, his arm outstretched, hoping that Sanders would fall for his bait and come closer.

"Take it out of the pouch, now!"

Jefferson obeyed and slackened the tensile cord that tied the pouch shut. Few seconds after he balanced the light source on his palm, it gave a start, vibrating like a small dynamo that had just cranked to life. A most brilliant light, dazzling in the brightness of lightning formed in the egg. Instantly the warning of the old priest who had confronted him in the cave resounded in Jefferson's mind, *beware of the light*. But, it was rather late.

Jake Sanders' gun hand stretched taut and tight in a motion born out of his will to pull the trigger and end Jefferson's life. A fairly high speed projectile, a rock launched by Captain Okafor, hit Sanders on the side of his face. He squeezed off two wild shots that came nowhere near Jefferson. As Okafor dove behind the trees and took cover to hide from Sanders, the atmosphere was lit up with blinding white light, many folds brighter than daylight at its best.

In contact with the blazing midday sun, the Light Egg had

come alive. It shone and sparked, burning a deep lesion into Jefferson's hand. In flinging the light ball away a bar of fluorescent rays scorched through his coat fabric and burned a deep wound through the flesh above his right armpit. On its way down a light beam caught Sanders on the side of his head. It burnt right through the scalp, exposing a raw open wound on the left side of his head. Sanders lay on the ground, writhing in pain as was Jefferson whose gaping wound on the uppermost part of his arm left his arm almost dangling.

Okafor wanted to get up but noticed that the rays of the light Egg revolved around a wide diameter above the spot where it lay on the earth. It circled and beamed straight up catching the over-hanging branches and leaves of nearby trees which dissolved under its incredible heat and fell in swirling ashes.

Okafor got up on one knee. He could see the two men on the ground. They were badly hurt and needed help. They were now safe from the upward circular beam of the white light. As Okafor got to his feet, a very aged man in a white robe approached the revolving beam of light with a sheet of fabric about four feet by seven in dimension. With an alarming speed he laid the fabric on the source. Instantly, the light diminished to a firery glow that seeped out of the corners of the fabric. With the wide malleable sheet the old man wrapped the Light Egg and placed it on the earth. All traces of the uncanny light disappeared. He quickly found the pouch and transferred the light source from the wrapped fabric to the pouch without further exposure to the sun. After tying the mouth of the pouch with its string, he hung it around his neck and picked up the two injured men.

Okafor watched in awe, the speed and dexterity with which the old man cradled the two grown men. When he had them neatly tucked under his arms, he leapt out westward and disappeared from Okafor's view in a twinkle of an eye.

$\circledast$‖ Thirty-two ‖$\circledast$

General Idris and his group had walked a quarter of a mile to the end of the newly formed canyon when they realized that it ran into very dense vegetation. Idris was not one to be easily overwhelmed by obstacles. He immediately ordered his men to use machetes and axes to create a path to the other side. After a tedious trek through the thicker parts they came into a vast forest with clusters of bushes. A short distance away, a huge fire burned brightly ahead of them. It looked like a big bonfire. They could detect the image of a man on the other side of the fire. As they came closer another huge fire erupted a short distance behind them and another on both sides. They were surrounded by a wide ring of fire.

"Stand where you are," the general barked. "Don't move until I say so." Idris whirled around, searching for the weakest part of the fire to make their escape.

"Sir, I think that man behind the bonfire is causing the fires," Duru said. "Why don't we shoot him?"

"No!" General Idris replied urgently. "No shooting." He had remembered the warning of Prof. Okediadi that this would not be a war of guns and knives but adaptation to peculiar situations.

Igo appeared, seemingly from nowhere and stood behind them. "Come this way," he shouted.

On seeing Igo, some leveled their rifles on him ready to fire promptly upon the general's orders.

Idris suspected a trap. For a moment he stood petrified, staring at the sweaty old man whose body glistened in the light of the raging ring of fires.

"Let's go with Igo, General," Emodi advised.

"Why should we follow you, Igo? You have caused the death of my men and abducted my assistant, Musa," said the general.

"I'm not responsible for the death of your men. Nji is your man," Igo replied. "We're on the same side, now."

"Then, stop him," Idris replied.

"I can't, I'm not fully recovered from my detention in your cell."

Fire leaped up between Igo and the soldiers.

Igo ran. "Follow me!" he shouted without looking back.

"Let's go!" General Idris screamed circumventing the fire to run after Igo, his entire entourage behind him.

As Igo ran across the fire barrier that circled the area towards Ogwari hills, he flipped his fingers in the air as if shooing away pests. A powerful gust of wind blew through the barrier throwing flames and fiery sparks into the forest.

A narrow path was formed from Igo's effort. The old man stood on the other side of the gateway of fire while the soldiers, Carter and Okorugo crossed over on the run.

Shittu was the last one crossing when fire erupted in the path and engulfed him. His screaming made Gen. Idris and others stop in their tracks.

"Run!" Igo shouted, pointing toward the caves.

Idris stood his ground. He turned around and issued orders to Lieutenant Duru. "Hurry, take the men up the hill. I'll stay and help Shittu."

"We stay with you, Sir," Duru replied.

"It's an order, move!"

"Yes, Sir!" Duru sprinted off with the others.

When Idris turned back around, Igo had reached into the fire and pulled the screaming soldier out. Shittu's entire body was on fire as though laced with petrol.

Igo embraced Shittu. The old man's body shuddered as though caught by a cold draft before he vomited a slimy watery liquid on Shittu's head. Igo pushed him down on his back and lay on top of him. The fire on Shittu's body was reduced to little flames around his neck and waist. Igo rose to a kneeling position and using his hands, extinguished the remaining fire.

"Igo, watch out!" General Idris shouted when a naked old man leaped out of the fire and stood menacingly behind Igo.

Igo scrambled to his feet with the agility of the feline species and faced Nji. "General, take the wounded man and run after the others," he said without taking his eyes off Nji.

Idris rushed to Shittu who sat upright on the ground wiping the slimy substance from his eyes. His hair and clothes were singed. Idris pulled Shittu to his feet and started to run after Duru and the others. The resistance put up by the wounded man who stumbled awkwardly behind made Idris to look back, taking a quick critical look at the sergeant. It was then that he knew that Shittu could not see. He was totally blind.

*   *   *

Igo and Nji stood over ten feet apart, facing each other silently, waves of questions and answers, logic and counter logic passed between them on the final question of who was right.

"Let it go, Nji," Igo communicated. "We have to leave. We're a dying breed and this is not really ours to fight for."

"I will stay and fight."

"The world powers will focus here. You will never have peace."

"Rather that than risk disintegration in the trek to Og."

"We cannot stay here longer, Nji, or thousands will die."

"You have long abandoned the essence of the Gundu, bowing to their emotions and intellect, sentiments. You have become too much like them, much too weak and that is the cause of your downfall," Nji criticized.

"I did what was best for us to adapt," Igo opined.

"Now I do what is best for us to survive."

"I will stop you, Nji."

"No!" Nji's left arm suddenly shot out in the air as if he had punched an imaginary object with the base of his palm.

Igo was taken unawares as powerful vibes from Nji's blow zapped clear across the ten feet gap between them and hurled him off his feet. While he was hurtling through the air towards a line of robust trees, Igo sought to resist the powerful blast that blew him through the air. Just before he hit a tree trunk with an impact that may have caused some damage to his body, Igo broke his speed and landed softly before the trees. He was now certain that Nji had malfunctioned. His reasoning faculties had gone haywire for him to have opposed the joint decision of the council and then to attack his kin with intent to harm.

In a few quantum leaps, Nji stood before the trees where he expected Igo to be lying but there was no sign of the sixth keeper.

Igo was counting on the element of surprise to deal with Nji. Though Nji was younger and physically stronger, Igo still had that edge of smartness and superior intelligence. As Nji stepped through the first row of trees, Igo shifted around him and rushed at him from behind. Before Nji could stir for action, Igo jumped on his back wrapped his flexible legs around his mid-section, pining his arms to his sides. Simultaneously, Igo's long slender fingers, moving like tendrils, sought and found the glands he desired behind the lower parts of Nji's neck. Igo's entire body suddenly shook and spasmed releasing a mild electromotive charge just enough to stun Nji but not to harm him. As Igo unwrapped his legs from around him, Nji slumped and fell on the ground, unconscious.

Thirty-three

General Idris and the men stood huddled on the hillside waiting for the outcome of the fight between Igo and Nji. Lieutenant Duru felt a rush of goose pimples course through his skin. He remembered what the general told him about a certain professor called Okediadi who suggested that the Gundu priests were not normal beings. With all pretenses set aside, the speed with which the very aged Igo arrived where they stood waiting on the hill amazed them. Not even a cheetah could have moved with such agility and swiftness. Emodi noted this with special interest.

"Hurry! Follow me," Igo said and rushed into a winding path that went further up the hills.

Igo led Idris and his crew, Carter and Emodi through an oval-shaped entrance to the Ogwari cave; the same room where the Obodo Ogwari youth hid when the soldiers were coming. It was just a small chamber with no access to the heart of the cave where the Gundu lived. This part of the cave was a cul de sac.

After they entered, Col. Effiong with the help of some soldiers, cordoned off a wide arc with the sensor strips, covering the cave entrance. He primed the hand-held monitor as they filed into the cave.

The cave chamber was very silent, despite the two dozen panting sweaty soldiers and the two teachers.

"I cant guide you all through the jungle, it's too dangerous," Igo said. "We'll just have to hope that help comes before Nji finds us." He moved off to the farthest corner of the chamber and leaned against the rough wall.

Emodi and Carter came and stood close to him, away from the soldiers.

"After today, I finally believe," Emodi said quietly to Igo.

"Believe what?" Igo asked

"That you're not of this world."

"How and where did you get that notion?"

"The memoirs of Reverend Father Morgan, preserved in a metal trinket box, was handed over to me by the eldest of the Okechiukwu family," Emodi explained. "Morgan had been friends with Aro, the Gundu who suffered what Morgan referred to as a nervous breakdown."

"Why did the old man hand Morgan's writings over to you after a century with the Okechiukwu?"

"In the sight of our changing world, the express road coming, he said he trusted me to take it to the right authorities, maybe a museum."

"And what did Morgan write about us?"

"In a nutshell, you came from a world that had progressed or should I say regressed to a self-destructive peak in the field of science. Your little planet was gradually breaking up, disintegrating, and nothing could be done to save it. You foresaw the break-up and intensive research was promulgated and encouraged in such areas as he referred to as abstract cultural development. You excelled in telepathy and psychic projections. Science had failed you, actually you had failed science. So, in this new quest you discovered that there's no clear-cut boundary between the spiritual and physical science, all part and parcel. You had passed the age of light-speed capsules and giant creatures for transport. The new age offered telepathy, super telekinesis and phisiospiritual transport." Emodi looked intently at Igo to determine his reaction. There was none.

The old man's attitude was calm, his face hard and devoid of expression.

Emodi continued. "In your bid to find a suitable new home, the mode of transport posed another grave problem. Had it been before the disarmament and destruction of super-scientific modes and structures, space travel would have been a cinch by capsules you had used in the ancient past. In fact, it was the fall-out of this scientific revolution that led to the decay of your world and consequently to the elimination of destructive technology, including vehicular space travel and its attendant adverse effects on your delicate environment. The decay had reached its peak, therefore, your movement was inevitable. Your galactic search yielded two possibilities. Your first choice had been to find an uninhabited planet where you would settle and survive in your true physical form, free from the initial stress of adapting to a new outward appearance. The two choices found to be atmospherically adequate were earth and a tiny unihabited planet

248

you named Og. Of all the Gundu tested, only thirteen were found fit and capable for transport. Unfortunately, no Gundu of the female gender passed the test which created another grave problem of extinction even if the males succeeded in reaching earth and Og."

Again, Emodi searched for a reaction from Igo and found none so he asked, "Shall I continue?"

Igo simply shrugged so he continued. "From your home, after profoundly studying the culture of man, eight were appointed for earth and the rest for Og. One of you did not survive the transport and in the process you lost your navigational instrument which caused that very lengthy delay in finding Obodo Ogwari, your actual destination. The same conditions you needed here were obtainable in Iowa, USA. You had predicted the mass exodus of Europeans into what we know today as North America and so preferred the African continent where you could hide unnoticed, disguised like some backward dibias yet very advanced and civilized."

Igo looked sharply at him and smiled.

"When you arrived here," Emodi started again, "your benevolent brother, Tam, volunteered to assume the ardous persona of the Ideamala Bird, the godhead that upheld faith and discipline in Obodo Ogwari."

"Sorry to interrupt, but it appears the bird went a little overboard when it murdered the two missionaries, Patterson and Cook," Carter said.

"It wasn't murder," Igo answered defensively. "The established force of justice paid them their due worth … Like the force of nature it was set up without partiality, no mercy; just a program that must go on. Does a hurricane cease when it sees a child? A flood will sweep your St. Peter's Basillica away when all necessary conditions are primed.

"The missionaries came here with their 'judgment day' brand of Christianity and unleashed it on these naïve natives who had been used to instant judgment for ages. It surely threatened everything we had worked for to maintain peace and order in Ogwariland. The Ideamala deity which was initiated ages before the white man came was meant to fight fire with fire. Preservation and enhancement of life was our ultimate goal for the Ogwarians yet the elimination of life was a special tool for purity to prevail."

"Capital punishment! So the bird became judge and executioner?" Emodi asked in sarcasm. "Why kill the Priests?" he added.

"We set the laws by your own standards except we increased the penalties. Reverend Cook, in all his righteousness, fathered a child in another man's home, hence the light-skinned descendants of the Ezelagboh kindred you see today," Igo explained.

"And Patterson?" Carter asked.

"That one was worse. He was a medical doctor and a priest and helped induce the termination of a three-month old foetus from the womb of one of his young converts. Morgan was a good priest and lived a decent life. He was our friend."

Emodi and Carter turned to each other. A look of understanding passed between them. They had shared the same views and feelings on the killing of the missionaries. Now that the truth had surfaced they both felt that death by execution was too high a price for them to have paid for a crime that would have attracted banishment for a layman. But, Patterson and Cook were priests ... It was also a great relief for the teachers to finally have an answer why servants of the Most High God were so easily annihilated by the ancient bird. On spiritual war paths, 'right or wrong' formed or deformed shields and swords. The two executed priests' protective armour had been corroded by their sins of the flesh.

Igo stood rigidly at the corner, a rubbery look on his face. He had slipped into a mode, trancelike, almost comatose. Idris tried to speak to him but seeing his countenace from the streaks of light that beamed in through cracks in the ceiling, he cut his speech midway.

After they entered the cave, Igo had rolled a large boulder easily as if it was made of light plastic and blocked the entrance. Before he went into the trancelike state, he told the general that they were to hide in the cave chamber hoping that help would come before Nji wakes up and finds them.

"How do you expect help to come when no one knows we're here?" Idris asked but Igo was already preoccupied.

"Enough is enough," the general continued speaking, glancing furtively from Lieutenant Duru to Emodi and Carter. "I've been trying for a peaceful approach to this situation but we can't just stand around and watch that old man, Nji, throw fire bombs at us. It's time we did what we were trained for. Cock your weapons, men."

Immediately in quick succession, the metallic claps of rifles being primed resounded in the cold musty chamber.

"I plead for caution, General," Okwuluora Emodi said in a polite but imploring manner. "Shooting Nji may only compound the problem."

"That's right, General, I suggest we wait for Igo to snap out of his sleep or trance or whatever," Ugoabata Carter supported. "He has brought us this far. I believe he'll lead us out."

Three electronic beeps sounded in quick succession on Effiong's monitor.

"Sir, someone is coming," he announced to the general.

A streak of uncertainty creased Idris' forehead but he quickly rejected it with a shake of the head. "We have run far enough. This is now war and we're soldiers."

There were subtle nods and grunts of approval especially from his aides and Lieutenant Duru.

Suddenly, a cold draft blew into the chamber as the large rock that Igo had used to cover the entrance flew away like a dry leaf in the wind.

"Prepare to fire upon my order," Idris announced to his men who were already alert, rifles pointed to the cave mouth.

Tension mounted as they waited for Nji or whatever foe to appear in the entrance. For over two minutes, nothing happened or they did not feel anything until they heard the scratching sound. The sharp-sensed ones could feel a crawling creeping feeling that came with the slithering evil sound. The sensing of posturing doom, that uncanny presence in the air that one can perceive but cannot see. Such prevailed with them in the dark sun-spotted cave chamber, damp and deathly quiet. Hissing sounds came at very short intervals.

Lights!" the general ordered.

A soldier began to scream on Duru's side, and then another as flashlights were flipped on to bring better illumination to the very dull enclosure. Hundreds of thousands of insects, predominantly soldier ants, had crawled into the room. The men in the forefront began to hop and dance around in attempts to crush the insects and also to keep them from climbing up their bodies. The three screaming soldiers were already infested with the biting insects. They cried out writhing painfully in a macabre cave dance, conceived by sheer hurt. Some soldiers in the second row started to run out of the cave.

"Snakes!" an elderly sergeant with the general's entourage shouted.

The cave mouth was crawling with dozens of slithering hissing reptiles, snakes of many species rolling over each other, cobra heads raised on the offensive war path.

Ugoabata Carter and Okwuluora Emodi rushed to Igo where he was hunched over, his countenance rubbery, static, moribund. The two teachers shouted his name repeatedly to rouse him. None dared to touch him.

Igo was silent. He did not stir at all from his suspended state.

"Do something, Igo, please," Emodi yelled frantically.

"Fire!" the general screamed, pointing at the snakes that blocked their escape route.

Bursts of machine gunfire erupted, cracking with metallic violence in the already hyped-up atmosphere. Numerous bullets hit home decimating the snake population, causing a majority of them to twist and flip in the terminal dance of death. The soldiers now felt relieved that their reptile adversaries were flesh and blood, not some phantoms, aliens, indestructible. Their second round of fire wiped the reptiles virtually out.

Meanwhile, the men who had been screaming quietened down. Those who hopped around halted. The insects had left them quite suddenly as they had come and headed, as though with urgent intent, for Igo. In a few minutes, the insects had formed a small mound at Igo's feet and mounting.

"Reload your weapons and prepare to move out," General Idris told his men.

The image of the old man, Nji, appeared in the cave entrance. He stood like an apparition, grainy and smoky, wavering like a thin lace material hung before a soft breeze, flowing, undulating. The look on his face bore a mark of malevolence, evil intent, wickedness. Though Gen. Idris saw this ghostly image as having no substance or tangible mass, similar to a three-dimensional picture issued by a modern film projector, he ordered his men to shoot. The steady flow of bullets passed through the image as though it was not there at all. High speed metals found granite at the cave mouth and ricocheted in sharp pings. A soldier was struck on the foot, probably by his own shot.

Suddenly the image appeared in the midst of the soldiers, smiling causing the men to jump out of its way. The mound of insects before Igo had grown into a big dark crawling orb, a huge ball simmering with bugs.

The wicked grin on the face of Nji's image became suddenly frozen. Nji was turned, sideways and suspended in mid-air as his image fizzled and faded and died.

"Help is here at last. Let us go!" Igo spoke for the first time since he went into a trance. In both hands, he balanced the ball of insects and moved to the cave mouth, trampling on dead snakes.

Emodi and Carter followed him closely as though their lives depended wholly on his ingenuity. The waning sunlight paving way for a somber evening was quite welcoming to the two teachers when they emerged from the damp danger-bugged cave.

General Idris emerged, his entire entourage behind him. They moved towards Igo and the teachers.

"You should know better than to disturb me when I'm ... eh meditating or should I say, praying," Igo said looking at Emodi.

"I'm sorry, Igo. We were desperate. Things were beginning to happen," Emodi apologized.

"I had to try and keep Nji out, physically, while managing the ants, Igo explained. "I'm glad the general took the bold step to kill the snakes." He hurled the ball of ants away like a shot-put. It flew into the jungle out of sight.

"Thank you, Igo. I had to do something than just sit there waiting to die of snake venom," the general joined them. "Where's the help you spoke of and how did they find us anyway?" he asked.

From the hillside, Igo looked fixedly at a clear patch beyond the base of the hill. Four Gundu priests stood at the centre of the patch. Two of them carried one long bundle tucked under their left arms, sharing the load. From that distance only Igo could recognize the bundle as Nji. True to the last image of him they saw in the cave, he was stiff as a board, in suspended animation, comatose and hanging sideways.

"Gentlemen, you're out of harm's way now," Igo said, addressing the entire group, before he turned to speak to the teachers. "Okwuluora, Ugoabata. It's time for me to say goodbye." His eyes took on a moist turquoise tinge.

"You mean goodbye, as in adios, forever?" Carter asked excited but rather appalled.

Igo nodded slowly. He had seen some tell-tale signs amongst his kin that told him that while he was busy protecting the people from Nji, a suitable course for their movement had been established.

Before General Idris opened his mouth to speak, Igo pre-empted him.

"You will find the wounded men at the infirmary. Emodi and Ugoabata will take you there."

"This isn't fair, Igo," Emodi said in protest. "How could you have been planning to leave all this while without telling Phillip and I? What are friends for?"

"I'm sorry, my brothers," Igo pleaded.

"You don't have to go. We can fight on … we … you have the skills," Emodi urged.

"Lives would be lost," Igo replied.

"Death is a by-product of war, of freedom," Carter cut in. "Even mine can be sacrificed."

"It's of no use. In time we would still have to leave," said Igo. "The nature cloud is being destroyed … The earth is aging fast."

"The ozone …" Carter began.

"Whatever … Goodbye, my brothers."

General Idris came round and stood before Igo. "I make no promise but I'll do all that is in my power to divert the express road from here if you change your mind to stay."

"Thank you, General. You're a brave man. The nation is lucky to have a man like you," Igo commended him.

"I'm honoured," Idris replied.

Emodi and Carter stood close to each other sharing a countenance that cut across disbelief and disappointment.

Igo turned to leave then turned again to the teachers. Two green droplets seeped out of his eyes.

"Won't you even go to the cave to pack a bag or something?

Have brunch ... or dinner?" Carter asked in a futile attempt to make Igo's stay a little longer.

Igo shook his head slightly. "All I need is my robe and my brothers have it down there." He shook hands with his two friends and the general before he turned finally to depart.

Igo did not disappear. One moment he was standing with his back to them, looking down on the clear patch. There his brothers stood staring anxiously at him. In this final showof his unusual skills Igo zipped off like a dragonfly kid-chased from a puddle. General Idris and the rest could barely keep up with his flight. They now saw him standing among his fellow Gundu, accepting a bundle from one of the hooded priests.

Emodi kept his eye on Igo until he donned his robe and appeared in uniform with the other keepers' shiny robes. Even after the priests had mingled, Emodi was almost sure that it was the one he identified as Igo that accepted another huge bundle from one of them. The bundle was covered by the same dark but shining material that their robes were made of. When it was unveiled, a large, glassy globe twice the size of a human head appeared, similar in appearance but much larger than the light egg.

Like a small procession of blind men led by the proverbial one-eyed man, the Gundu priests linked themselves up in a short queue each one placing a hand on the shoulder of the one before him. First came Igo with the globe held high up above his head, followed by the two who had the stiff Nji under their arms; others came afterwards. As they moved out of the clear patch of land, Igo's hand shook and bucked as the globe came to life. A magnificent brightness issued from the globe that Igo held with both hands stretched taut above his head. As the procession moved deeper into the jungle, strange colours seemingly tangible like shrouds of super-light chiffon flared and billowed, taking on a tubular structure, forming a casing of shimmering glitter. Unusual purples twinkled within the framework of an outlandish orange and alloys of colours that hemmed the light tube.

From the hillside, soldiers and the two teachers squinted to adjust to the brightness. It was like looking directly at the shining sun.

A jagged streak of white light, like lightning, sparked to and from the light tube and vanished. All alien lights and colours disappeared in a blink leaving the vegetation unscathed.

*   *   *

Gazing at the now lackluster jungle where the fusion of lights had taken place, General Idris marveled. "Incredible! I came to this jungle expecting darkness but what I've seen is light, advancement like I've never seen before."

"Yeah!" Carter commented. "So bright a darkness."

Emodi looked sideways at the rolling triplet hills of Obodo Ogwari and saw the apprentices of the Gundu priests. They were standing close together on the pinnacle of the centre hill. There were seven boys in all, the oldest not more than fourteen. Emodi was silently pondering what would be the future of the boys when Carter spoke.

"I suppose they're going to need rehabilitation and maybe some kind of deprogramming."

Emodi laughed. "Can't you see, Phillip, the Gundu must have known they were going to leave soon. These boys are to rehabilitate and programme the villagers for the oncoming civilization, the new life."

Ugoabata nodded slowly as it dawned on him that Emodi's statement was pure logic.

Thirty-four

The slime from Igo's vomit had crusted and peeled off Shittu's left eye and he began to move about on his own. His right eye was still shut.

*   *   *

The infirmary of the Gundu lay in a sprawling compound a quarter of a kilometre east of the caves. There were two long halls that served as the male and female wards, and three other bungalows, all brick walls and rubber-glazed thatch roofs. It was obvious that the coppice of umbrella trees that formed a cozy sanctuary in the vast table valley was the reason for the clinic to be sited there. Even in the peak of the hottest day of the year it stayed cool and gradually dropped to chilly at dusk, when the sun fell in search of the west.

The smallest of the three houses which they first met on the way into the infirmary grounds was the consultation office. Here, non-emergency cases first came for physical and abstract diagnosis before treatment commenced. They went past it to the dispensary. A tall man in shorts and singlet emerged and smiled when he saw the two teachers among the small crowd of mostly soldiers.

"Okwuluora. Ugoabata, nnoo-nu," greeted Nwora Okechiukwu, sole agent of the Gundu whose ancestors also served before him.

"Ogoh," Ugoabata addressed Okechiukwu as in-law. The ageless gaunt-faced elder was his wife's great-grandfather.

The little boy who had lost consciousness on the path of the Ajo-ofia masquerade stood by the doorway of the main ward looking curiously at the general's entourage. His mother rushed from under a tree shade where she had been washing clothes and picked him up protectively. When she recognized Okwuluora among the group, she smiled and waved.

"Are you the man in charge?" the general asked Nwora Okechiukwu.

"Before the Gundu's departure, I was placed to supervise the apprentices, the boys."

"I'm looking for my wounded aide."

"Musa? He's here with us," Nwora said, cheerfully. "I'll show you the male recovery hall, Sir."

Musa sat on a bed in the long dormitory, a far away look on his face. When he saw the general, Lawali and Duru, he simply stared. There was no sign that he recognized them.

"Musa!" the general called loudly to jar him out of his stupor. They saw a faint smile cross his lips but the strange detachment did not change.

Lawali called Musa's name several times but there was still no response.

Musa was bare-bodied, clad only in a pair of brown boxers. A pinkish-red scar tissue was visible under a covering of gauze material that seemed like a network of cobwebs. The length of raw scar traced the wound from his chest below his armpit and around his jaw line.

"Did it affect his brain?" General Idris asked.

"No-o! Not at all, Sir," Nwora Okechiukwu laughed, amused by the general's notion. "Musa is fine. He whispers well in conversation when he's not under medication. Right now he cannot communicate but he knows you're here."

When the general turned to him again, Musa had a definite smile frozen on his face but his eyes showed that he was very far.

"He has to be this way to bear the accelerated repairs to his wounds," Okechiukwu educated them.

"There are very tiny ants on his wounds, under the gauze," Lawali said, peering down on the healing wounds.

"I've been wondering," said Duru who had been pondering on the movement he saw under the light mesh of cobwebs like shifting lines of brownish powder.

"He's in the final stage of repairs," Okechiukwu explained. "The opening is being sealed." He turned away from Musa's bed and walked past three other beds where two young men were lying down in recuperation. Okechiukwu stood in the aisle between two opposite beds. Both occupants of the beds seemed unconscious.

"I'm wondering if you can help us identify these two men. They suffered very severe burns and were brought here by Olo.

"The black one is Sid Jefferson," Okwuluora Emodi

volunteered. "He's a journalist that came to make a documentary on the yam festival."

Funsho Odutola chuckled. "More like a spy who came to steal the Gundu technology. The white man is Jake Sanders, also a man of many clandestine talents, a rogue of sorts."

"Then I'll call Interpol to pick them up."

"Please allow them to recover first. They will surely die if you move them from here," Okechiukwu pleaded on the patients' behalf. "I will personally notify you as soon as they're fit to be collected by the law."

"Musa will stay, too," the general concluded. "I had already given him up for dead. I must confess that you people have done an incredible miracle here."

"Thank you, Sir, we do our best."

Epilogue

The Gundu priests, keepers of the Ideamala, departed taking with them light years of knowledge, wisdom and development. Legend proclaims that they had borne a tunnel into the bowels of the earth. Till today, Omegwalonye, the mysterious night masquerade of Obodo Ogwari still laments in song that the Gundu have gone up to the skies to live with God, by virtue of their selflessness and benevolence. It sings that they have come and gone, leaving behind tracks of love and discipline morality and superior medicine for those whom it would reach and aid.

*   *   *

Six months after the express road came through, Reverend Father Mojekwu in company of Ichie Ezeaputa and two other chiefs of Igwe Ajulufo's cabinet came to a vast table land on the east end of Obodo Ogwari, beyond the plains of the Ifeadigo. They were accompanied by a team of surveyors and officials dispatched by the bishop's office. After the dimensions of the land were pointed out by the king's men, the surveyors set to work, to beacon the portion where St Raphael's Catholic Church, Obodo Ogwari would be built. Full support had been granted by the Vatican for a magnificent edifice to commence.

The initial rush of curiosity seekers, city folks attracted by rumours of the wonders in Ogwariland, had come and gone. They had quickly lost interest in the 'drab boring town.'

A couple of recalcitrant construction labourers who had worked with Cotrell and Abbey stayed on to build shacks where they sold palm wine and smoked bush meat served with a thick sauce of seasoned ground peppers and oil bean seeds in palm oil.

Motorists often stopped by to enjoy the coolness of the bamboo shacks nestled under broad-leafed trees. The influx of settlers into Obodo Ogwari had begun.

THE END

Kraftgriots

Also in the series (FICTION) (*continued*)

Onyekachi Peter Onuoha: *Idara* (2012)
Akeem Adebiyi: *The Negative Courage* (2012)
Onyekachi Peter Onuoha: *Moonlight Lady* (2012)
Onyekachi Peter Onuoha: *Idara* (2012)
Akeem Adebiyi: *The Negative Courage* (2012)
Onyekachi Peter Onuoha: *Moonlight Lady* (2012)
Temitope Obasa: *Strokes of Life* (2012)
Chigbo Nnoli: *Save the Dream* (2012)
Florence Attamah-Abenemi: *A Bouquet of Regrets* (2013)
Ikechukwu Emmanuel Asika: *Tamara* (2013)
Aire Oboh: *Branded Fugitives* (2013)
Emmanuel Esemedafe: *The Schooldays of Edore* (2013)
Abubakar Gimba: *Footprints* (2013)
Emmanuel C.S. Ojukwu: *Sunset for Mr Dobromir* (2013)
Million John: *Amongst the Survivors* (2013)
Onyekachi Peter Onuoha: *My Father Lied* (2013)
Razinat T. Mohammed: *Habiba* (2013)
Onyekachi Peter Onuoha: *The Scream of Ola* (2013)
Oluwakemi Omowaire: *Dead Roses* (2014)
Asabe K. Usman: *Destinies of Life* (2014)
Stan-Collins Ubaka: *A Cry of Innocence* (2014)
Data Osa Don-Pedro: *Behind the Mask* (2014)
Stanley Ekwugha: *Your Heart My Home* (2014)

Printed in the United States
By Bookmasters